WIELDERS OF WOE

INFERNO

JEFFERY A. ROARKE JR.

CONTENTS

ACT I

CHAPTER I

"Bless Empyrea onto thee," Hal said under his breath.

Hundreds of starships sailed through the skies of the capital planet of Athos and toward the Gate of Athos. Hal stood on the bridge of his flagship and scanned the armada assembled for the Empire. Like a blanket of metal war machines, the ships darkened the land below, and the force of their engines sent the trees into a shaking frenzy that only a violent storm could bring. But that was what this fleet would soon become: a storm of metal and energy sent to deliver the final blow of the war.

The shine of the twin suns glared on the metal hulls of the ships, only to be dimmed by the observation window of Hal's flagship starcarrier. Smaller scout corvettes sailed in front of the main fleet and patrolled the skies. Dozens of energy cannons and weapons were trained forward in anticipation of the battle to come. He stared at his reflection in the window where his diamond-shaped pupils marked him and his ancestry for all to be known.

Battleships each with their own set of twenty hypersonic energy cannons flanked Hal's carrier while other cruisers and frigates patrolled the edges of the fleet. Hal looked ahead to see a few of the smaller ships, destroyers, leading the fleet to the awaiting corvettes in anticipation of what was to come. He ran a hand through his brown hair as the bridge crew attended their stations.

Today was important, not just for the soldiers, but for Hal. He was, after all, responsible for beating the Polarians so far back. Their encroachment on sovereign Imperial worlds in the Yasu System would not be tolerated. Hal had been trusted by his father and the Imperial Council to lead this mission in the name of the Empire. He had to do this if he was to prove himself worthy of ascending the Imperial Throne, and the burden of the last two years would be worth it.

As he caught his reflection in the large windows of his starcarrier, he saw himself as a proud twenty-two-year-old son of Athos donned in battle-tested armor, and he knew he was ready.

The Imperial Council of Athos needed a reason to ascend him, as dictated in the Imperial Code of Athos one thousand years ago. Having royal blood made him a prince by birth, but that meant nothing if he couldn't act in the name of the Empire and ensure he was the future heir. Being bestowed the title of Crown Prince of Athos would show he had more than just fancy blood in him. He would make sure they wouldn't have any reason to deny him after today.

In the distance, the Gate stretched nearly to the stratosphere, its large pylons rooted deep into the earth. It had withstood millenniums of battle and weather, strengthened by the seeds of time. Thought of as relics of an age gone by, nobody knew if they could ever work again.

Hal took that as a challenge.

An interconnected Realmverse where planets could access one another and where space travel wasn't the only way to transport goods and services stood to ease life for everyone, and the Gates of the Gateway system provided the answer.

If they were able to pass through the Gate, there would be no turning back. He had to do this if the Empire were to survive, to be respected, and to usher in a new age of science. All those days spent on bloodied battlefields would mean nothing if he failed today.

"Prince Halcion," the captain of the starcarrier said. "We're nearing the Gate."

Without turning to look at the captain, Hal fixed his ice-white eyes on the Gate and said, "Prepare the ships for the jump."

The captain nodded and turned to carry out the order.

Everyone in Hal's fleet worked in unison. They'd made it this far with loyalty and duty, and their days of bloodied combat had strengthened the kinship amongst those who'd served. The want for revenge only sweetened the reward. Those responsible for the assassination of the Empress of the Empire of Athos—Hal's mother—would pay.

Hal cast a glance to the portside of the ship, where the twin suns began to fade under the horizon as his late mother and the rest of his family drifted into his thoughts. He had not set foot on his own home-world in two years, and as he flew in Athos's sky, it only strengthened the desire to end this war. He longed to see his home again, to smell the sweet scent of wildberry trees that were in bloom at this time of year and filled the streets of Imperius with a sense of calm. As he closed his eyes, he could almost smell their aroma, and his soul ached.

He pulled a small golden locket from his left breast pocket. Though it was outdated by the standards of today, he cherished something tangible and real instead of a digitalized projection.

As he opened it, a photo was revealed. In it, he stood in the middle flanked by two girls. One was his younger sister and the other his love. They had smiles as wide as any and were locked in one another's arms, dressed in elegant clothes. The picture had been taken only days before he was sent to war, just after he and his love, Kristilin, had graduated from the Imperial Academy.

On the other side of the locket was a photo of Hal and Kristilin, their faces close and smiles as wide as the oceans. There was a lot of lost time he had to make up for, and he wanted this cursed war over with. He just hoped that their love outlasted her time alone on Velra and his time at war.

As the captain commanded the crew, a young woman strutted into the bridge. The click of her heels made it impossible to not recognize who it was. Her presence could be felt throughout the entire command bridge, and everyone paused to recognize her. Even the pilot took a moment to salute her before he continued his duty.

Miri took her place beside Hal and looked at him with the same white eyes. "How many do you think are waiting for us on the other side?"

She brushed a stray strand of blonde hair from her eyes, and though she wore the same armor, hers was free of the scars of battle. Even her silver circlet was polished to shine as bright as the night stars. Hal couldn't have cared less in a war zone. Appearances did not last long, and his sister would learn that.

Hal returned his gaze to the massive gate before them. "The terms of surrender were returned. You and I both know what that means." He surveyed the land below, hills and forests passing underneath as his armada roared overhead. His people looked up to him in cheer, ready to end the war that had cost so much. He was ready to deliver on that promise. "I expect every soldier in the Polarian Kingdom to be on the other side of that portal."

The itch to repay the pain to the Polarians had never been stronger than it was now. This was about showing intimidation and power. He would let them know that whatever they did, his family would come back ten times greater.

He was in charge here. He was the general in command, and he'd make those royals in the palace at Rahallo bend the knee. To take a powerful kingdom and make them surrender would be the ultimate peak of his young list of accomplishments.

The Gate dwarfed them now as the ships sailed closer. Shadows crept along their hulls—first the bow and then the bridge—and soon the fleet flew in darkness.

Nobody knew exactly when they were built, but everyone believed them to have been built by the Primordials, the beings that had created the star systems of the Realmverse. Hal knew them as mystical gods from the stories the elders used to tell. The power they had to make this construct amazed him. It amazed everyone.

"Hal," Miri said, her voice quiet but stern.

Hal looked at her, and she raised a brow. He glanced at the other officers in the bridge, and a wave of embarrassment washed over him for his distraction. He composed himself and said, "Activate the Gate."

As the technicians started to transfer the keycodes to bring the Gate to life, his sister nudged him.

"Don't ruin this for our father," she said with a coy smirk. "The only assassination of a royal in the history of the Empire happened under our name, and now the council worries if the Skyborns are able to lead in a new age."

"There's a reason I'm in command here. Let them wonder. There won't be a reason to after this," Hal snapped before he took a deep breath. "You follow my orders in battle, Miri. I've spent two years chasing this, and I won't be stopped now. This is for every Imperial citizen, not just the emperor or the council."

Miri's smile faded into a fixed stare as the Gate roared to life. "Of course, dear brother."

The Gate flashed, and electrical arcs collected at the center, sparking and growing larger. The arcs of electricity began to pull back from the center, shrinking to the edges of the Gate as if pulling something with them.

It looks unreal, Hal thought.

For the first time in over a thousand years, a Gate had been activated, and Hal was thankful he and his sister were together to witness history.

"We'll all be remembered today," Hal said to spur confidence in the soldiers. "Take the fleet in."

Miri leaned in and said, "I can't wait to grab the Treths by their throats and make them bow. I can finally put that annoying Zahra in her place. It will be a glorious sight."

Hal did not pay any attention to his sister, though he understood her disposition. Revenge would be served, but it would be his way in accordance with the Imperial Code of Athos, and he intended on making a statement not only to the Polarian royal family but to the entire Realmverse. They would be looking at the next Emperor of the Empire, and he would earn their respect.

Hal reached into a pouch along his belt and pulled out a rolled-up scroll. He flashed it for his sister to see and said, "They need to sign this list of demands if the war is to be truly over and assure us that this will never happen again."

"Oh, they'll sign. They have no choice but to," Miri said.

"There's always a choice," Hal said. "Whether they make the right one is up to them."

The fleet of warships moved closer to the portal. As the blue glow grew brighter, Hal felt his heart jump at the spectacle before him. He grounded himself and braced for whatever would happen as his flagship ventured into the abyss first. The blue energy absorbed them, and flashes of white danced across the walls of the portal before everything went dark. Hal was weightless for a moment, suspended in idle awe. The cool energy touched him and washed over the entirety of the ship and crew. Miri grabbed him by the arm and squeezed just enough to remind him of the scared younger girl he'd left at home nearly two years ago.

They'd been reunited when she'd returned the deciphered keycodes he had sent, and though it had only been a couple of days, he could tell there was a lot going on at home by the stress in her voice. It had been some time since he'd spoken with his father and even longer since the injury that had led the emperor to be homebound. He wanted to ask a hundred questions, but this was neither the time nor the place to catch up.

Just like that, he and the rest of the ships emerged into the Polarian sky. Hal snapped out of his daze, expecting warships to swarm them in an instant, but the skies were empty. He looked toward the desert surface and saw nothing but an ocean of red sand.

Something did not feel right. The Polarians would not let them walk into their homeland uncontested. Suspicion began to creep through his body.

Hal turned to the captain. "I want every ship on high alert. Scan the skies. They're here. Find them."

They have to be here somewhere, he thought as his armada scoured the skies. He appreciated their eagerness to engage in a battle that would be remembered for centuries.

The ships sailed closer to the Polarian royal capital of Rahallo, and the edge was almost unbearable. The empty skies cut through his stoic presence as his eyes strained to find any hint of the enemy. It felt like they were being stalked.

"What's the matter, brother?" Miri said from beside him. "The Polarians knew we were too much for them. They just accepted their defeat. I wouldn't be surprised if they offered us King Treth's head and bowed before us as we claim their royal palace."

"Your overconfidence is misguided, Meer," Hal said, knowing the childhood nickname would annoy her. "Last I checked, one of us was leading the war while the other sat at home."

Miri scoffed. "We wouldn't be here if my Codebreakers hadn't cracked the encryption."

"The encryption I found," Hal shot back.

When the ships crossed over the mountain range that encircled the city, streaks of purple lasers flew through the air, and the Polarians finally revealed themselves. Their ships uncloaked one by one, and the remnants of the Polarian armada bared their teeth, prepared to defend the city of Rahallo.

Cowards, Hal thought at the sight of cloaking technology.

"Return fire!" Hal ordered as the lasers ripped through one of the escort ships off the starboard side of the carrier. It was engulfed in a ball of fire as the hull fractured in two and fell toward the sea of sand below. Streaks of blue and purple filled the evening sky with a laser show for the residents of the royal city.

"Launch the corsairs!" Hal ordered when a laser skimmed the hull of his ship, tearing off a line of protective outer armor.

The corsairs, smaller and more nimble fighter aircraft, raced from the hangars at the belly of the carrier and swarmed the airspace like angry wasps. They harassed the Polarian warships and buzzed by their bridges, some managing to drop their photon bombs directly on the bridges. The explosions reverberated through Hal's ship as the enemy warships dropped out of the sky one by one. The Imperial fighters were too much for the larger warships to handle by themselves.

A satisfied smile crept onto Hal's face as his plan began to take effect and the pride of the Polarian navy fell ineffective to his massive fleet.

Hal ordered his flagship to align with a nearby Polarian cruiser. The fighters peppered its hull with laser bursts while Hal's ship maneuvered into position, and then Hal ordered the broadside attack. The force of the cannons rocked the entire ship, and waves of energy crashed into the Polarian vessel with such impact that it was ripped to pieces. Debris from the now-fractured ship fell from the sky as it took the nosedive of doom in a ball of fire.

Hal gave his sister a small smirk, and Miri returned a disgruntled look before turning away. He knew she was disappointed there was not a catastrophic failure somewhere in his plan where her quick wit could've come to their aid, but the battle was not over yet.

"Captain, order all warships to focus fire on the city's defenses. Destroy all the batteries," Hal said, then turned to his sister. "Let's make ourselves known."

Miri smiled. "Finally."

They made their way to the ship's hangar, where a few battle-damaged corsairs sat next to their personal transport shuttle. Much smaller than a frigate, the personal shuttle resembled a common cargo freighter modified to the needs of Hal and his family. But most importantly, it carried the diamond crest of House Skyborn, and the insignia for the Empire. A pilot and engineer saluted them as they got on board and moved only after Hal and Miri had acknowledged them.

As they entered through the rear cargo hold and moved into the main hall of the ship, an explosion rocked the carrier. The battle raged on, exemplifying the need to end this war now.

When they came to the bridge, Hal sat in the copilot's seat while Miri sat in the row behind him, watching the explosions outside the shielded hangar wall. The pilot performed a quick preflight check, and Hal brought up an image of the layout of the city. Ground forces already skirmished in the streets, and it would only be a matter of time before the full might of the Imperial army knocked on the palace's door. Miri leaned in behind Hal and scrutinized the map before she spoke.

"Our forces will tear them down before we get there," she said. "Where's the fun in that?"

"Take us down," Hal told the pilot with a smirk.

The pilot started the engines and took the transport ship out of the carrier hangar with the two corsairs on their flanks. All around them, warships dropped out of the sky as corsairs let their ballistic bombs fly free. The powerful laser cannons of the Polarian ships could not keep up with the nimble corsairs.

Smoke rose from the city's battery emplacements, and another explosion shot up through the air. It was a slaughter, and one orchestrated by Hal. When a few Polarian ships engaged their cloaking technology and disappeared from the sky, he knew the air battle had all but just been won. Now they had to make it to the palace.

A loud blast rocked the ship, and the weightless feeling returned, only this time it was not from the Gate. Alarms went off, and Hal looked at the screens on the command console to find the fire alarms had been activated.

He turned to his sister. "Miri, deal with that fire."

As she left and ran down the main hallway to handle the fire, Hal tried to help the pilot regain control of the ship. He took the control stick and pulled as hard as he could while the pilot furiously worked the other controls. Another blast exploded nearby and blew a hole in the cockpit that sucked the pilot out, and smoke clouded Hal's eyes. Hal's stomach rose to his chest as the ship nosedived through the air and when he looked out the window, the desert ground grew larger with every second, and all he could do was brace.

CHAPTER II

The transport ship struck the ground and skidded along the sand before coming to rest near one of the rock formations. Smoke rose from the crash site as Hal dragged himself out of the mangled mess of metal, blood running down the side of his face. Intense pain came from his right leg as he turned over and examined where the fabric was torn. Blood trickled down his leg, but the gash had missed his artery. He ripped some of his torn clothing and wrapped it tightly around the wound to slow the blood loss.

Grimacing, he channeled the pain and pumped up his adrenaline as he set his eyes on the fight over the royal city. His own discomfort would have to wait. Nothing would stop him from making those responsible kneel before him. But one thing did cross his mind: *Where's Miri?*

Hal spun back toward the wreckage and searched through the pieces of hot metal that popped from the heat. He pried open the rear doors using a stick of sheared-off metal for leverage. Smoke billowed out as he ducked down to see fires raging inside. He stepped in, and the sting of smoke blinded him, but he had to find his sister.

"Miri," he called out. "Miri, where are you?"

Metal clanged near the back of the cargo hold, and Miri crawled out from under it. Hal rushed over and pulled her up, both coughing in the heat and smoke. He led her out and away from the smoke, gasping for clear air.

"Breathe, Meer. Deep breaths," Hal said between fits of coughing.

Hal searched her for injuries, and to his fortune, she only had a few cuts and bruises and a couple minor burns. None were life-threatening, thank the gods, but now they had another dilemma: being stuck in the desert.

"Are you all right to travel?" Hal asked as he stood up and offered Miri a hand.

"Are you?" she replied, taking his hand and helping herself up.

There was the unmistakable hiss of a fuel leak, and Hal looked back at the wreckage. His eyes quickly widened before he took his sister and dove away, using his body to shield her. The right engine exploded, sending a fireball high into the sky and raining pieces of metal down all around them.

When they stood back up, the ship was completely destroyed and engulfed in flames. They could not stay here. The ship was a giant signal fire now, and the thunderous vibrations would certainly alert the native sandworm population. They had to get out of the desert and to the city fast.

"We need to get moving," Hal said as he helped Miri back up. "I doubt the radios survived, but it can't hurt to look."

"You're crazy. The ship just exploded, Hal."

"It's our only option, Meer. Or do you want to walk the ten miles to the city and risk becoming worm food?"

When she went to speak but no words came out, Hal placed a hand on her shoulder and said, "I'll be quick. Just stay on the rocks."

Hal crossed the sand to the cockpit, where flames roared out like a fiery pillar. The heat radiated off his face, and only sparks gave any sign that there were any electrical components left. There was no way anything electrical had survived that heat.

He balled his hands into fists and turned back to join his sister on the rocks, but she was nowhere to be found. "Miri?" he called, but there was no sign of her.

A group of Polarian special forces uncloaked their armor suits. Two held Miri down on her knees as a couple more joined them and hopped off their duster bikes. They wore their signature dark brown armor with a red cloth around their waists. Hal got into his defensive fighting stance, ready to strike, as another Polarian uncloaked next to his sister.

The Polarian removed his helmet and said, "Well, if it isn't the illustrious Fire Wielders themselves. We have you surrounded, Prince Halcion Skyborn. Your invasion is over, and you are now our prisoners. Surrender in the name of the High King, and we shall be merciful. Act out, and we will be forced to execute you both."

Miri had a determined look on her face. She was up to something.

Hal suppressed the urge to smirk and looked at the Polarian in charge. In a tone fit for a commander, he said, "Brave words from a dead man. Try me."

The Polarian smiled and drew an energy sword. It glowed purple as the Polarian got into an attack stance. The others did as well.

Warmth brewed within Hal's body, and he charged himself with the mystical energy known as charna. Energy flames emitted from his hands and had engulfed his elbows by the time the Polarian attacked.

Hal easily avoided it and sent a ball of fire at the two seekers guarding Miri. The flames crashed into the seekers and sent them flying into the dunes behind them. Miri jumped up and instantly pushed streams of flames from the palm of her hand at the closest Polarians while Hal dueled with the leader.

The Polarian swung his sword, but Hal raised a wall of fire to deflect it. The sword crashed into the firewall and seemed to lock into place before Hal swept the Polarian's feet out from under him. As the Polarian fell to the sand, Hal shot streams of fire at him. The Polarian used his sword to absorb the intense heat of the flames before sending it back toward Hal. Hal jumped to the side, which gave the Polarian time to regain his footing. A couple other Polarians attacked Hal, but he easily dealt with them by evading and sending flames their way.

As he focused on the Polarian leader again, the pain in his leg returned. He fed off that pain and remembered his training, absorbing the power and channeling it through his body. In one swift motion, Hal avoided the Polarian leader's strike and grabbed his hands. Fire engulfed them, and the Polarian dropped the sword in a cry of pain. Hal grabbed the warrior's throat and looked him dead in the eye before unleashing a stream of flames right into the helmet.

The Polarian dropped to the ground, smoke rising from his body.

Hal turned to find his sister defeating the last Polarian soldier. She held him by the throat and unleashed a short but powerful ring of fire around it before she kicked him over. The look on her face was one of pure satisfaction.

"If this is the best King Treth can send, then I'm afraid they've already lost," Miri said confidently. "What do you say, Hal?"

"I don't speculate," Hal said as he boarded one of the Polarian duster bikes. "We still have a battle to finish."

They sped across the desert landscape to the great city of Rahallo in under fifteen minutes. Smoke rose from the city's walls as hundreds of Imperial soldiers descended to the streets. Hal burst through the gate with his sister close behind him and sped down the main boulevard as fighting ensued around him. Shops burned, and government buildings began to crumble under the bombardment from the warships. Hal came to stop behind a company of soldiers dug in before the royal palace. Streaks of purple crashed into the rubble they used for cover while explosions from plasma grenades sent shock waves through the air and threw sand in every direction.

"Captain, what's the status?" Hal said as another shot ricocheted off the debris.

The captain tossed a radio to another soldier and said, "Sir, we can't breach the palace defenses. I have two squads in a flanking position, but they're pinned down by Polarian rotary gun emplacements."

Hal looked to where the captain pointed. The palace had to fall as swiftly as possible; any delays would allow Polarian reinforcements to swarm the city. That could not happen.

Hal glanced to his sister, who wore the shocked face of a baptism by fire. He knew this was her first foray into official combat, but she was a fighter. The shock would wear off.

"Hold your ground here," Hal said to the captain. "This does not fall. We'll handle the rotary guns."

"Roger, sir."

As Hal and Miri backed off, Hal turned to his sister. "I go one way, you go the other. Got it?"

"Race you to the palace doors."

"This isn't a game, Meer. Just clear out that rotary gun."

Rolling her eyes, she bolted behind cover and down the alleyway to where one of the squads was. Hal watched her disappear until another bolt threw concrete dust at him, and then he turned and went the opposite way.

As he ducked under fallen walls, he spotted the squad behind wrecked vehicles and shattered buildings. Purple bolts of energy fired at a deafening pace from atop the palace walls and rained down on the soldiers. Any time a soldier tried to return fire, the rotary gun spun up its five barrels and locked onto them, spitting out more superheated pain. Another soldier tried to lob a grenade, but it was zapped out of the air by an ordnance disposal unit hidden somewhere behind the Polarians.

Hal slid in behind cover with the soldiers, and the sergeant's eyes widened at the realization of who he was. Hal only nodded.

"Prince Halcion, we thought you were still on the carrier," the sergeant said.

"I heard you all needed some help."

After stumbling for words, the sergeant said, "Yes, Prince Hal. The rotary emplacement has already stricken some of my men, including our explosives technician." He pointed to where a soldier lay lifeless in a heap of rubble on the edge of the street. "We're too close for a barrage, and I don't know how much longer we can hold this flank."

"Leave that to me," Hal said. "I'll get you your opportunity. Just be ready when I do."

Hal left the confused sergeant and hurdled over their cover. The rotary gun trained its aim on Hal, and purple bolts flashed through the air and raced toward him, ready to cut him down. But the bolts of energy crashed into a ward of flames and dissipated upon impact. Hal stood tall as the flames flowed from his hands and cast a wall of superheated fire that provided protective cover for the soldiers. Nothing came through. The sergeant looked at his soldiers and ordered the attack.

With no shield or protection, the Polarians atop the wall fell victim to the onslaught of Imperial firepower. Energy bolts ripped through their armor and scorched the wall. Hal held the ward up until every Polarian fell. Only when the shooting stopped did Hal drop his ward and launch a fireball at the gun. It exploded with a fiery gust as the munitions in storage ignited, bringing down that part of the wall in a heap of rubble. Dust blew by Hal, and he stayed still until there was nothing more than the scattered shots heard in the distance.

He looked back to the soldiers and said, "Alert your captain that the flank is secured. Hold the line."

Without another word, he hurried up the steps spared from the collapse and toward the palace doors.

As he crossed the small stone courtyard at the top of the steps, Hal easily dealt with the few guards who tried to defend the outer doors. Miri arrived with a frown on her face, for she was not the first to the finish line. Hal ignored it. They still had much to do before they could claim victory.

Hal looked at the great palace behind them, virtually pristine and untouched by the battle as respect for the history it had. That did not matter, though, because as Hal marched toward the palace doors, he had one thing on his mind: revenge. It would be an honorable revenge and a statement heard across the Realmverse.

He turned around with a final order to the soldiers below. "Secure the perimeter."

Hal threw the large stone doors open with the force ignited by the fire spewing from his hands and entered the palace walls, where massive columns of marble stretched high toward the dome ceiling. Banners with the jayhawk insignia of House Treth hung from them, and a lavender carpet stretched the entire length of the royal throne room. At the other end, the High King stood with the royal family, surrounded by knights in purple armor.

As Hal and his sister got closer, some of the knights pushed forward and attacked them with energy shields and swords. The siblings dealt with each of them, showcasing their power in front of the High King himself. Fire blazed inside the palace and singed the banners and carpet, leaving the mark of the Fire Wielders: destruction. They fought and defeated every wave of knights until they were only feet away from the Polarian royal family. Nothing would stop them.

For a moment, it seemed like time stood still. Hal stared right at the High King, whose eyes revealed everything: regret, fear, concern.

Hal wanted the High King to feel as he had the day their spy had murdered his mother. He wanted the royal family to know that crossing him or his family would result in retaliation. This was the price to pay.

The High Queen shielded young Prince Tiron behind the king, and Princess Zahra furrowed her brow at them in a defiant stance as he stood in front of her mother and brother. No older than Miri, she would now learn what happened when someone attacked the Skyborns.

Hal was the first to speak. "High King Torsai Treth, you have caused the Empire of Athos great pain and sorrow."

King Treth stepped forward dressed in his pristine white robes and said in a confident tone, "We have done nothing to anger the Empire of Athos. Imperius continues to encroach on our claimed realm on Yasu, yet we have done nothing to instigate."

"Oh, please," Miri said. "Most of the Yasu System has been under the control of the Empire for the last couple hundred years. We discovered it. You have no right to speak on this." Flames emerged from her fingertips, and she charged her hand with fire. The flames danced on her hand, ready for the command to act. "Be content that we allowed that petty demilitarized zone for the sake of your religion on Yasu itself until you broke the treaty."

The king gulped as the fire sizzled with intent.

"This war has caused much sorrow to everyone involved," King Treth said. "Why do you see the need to cause more?"

Hal did not respond. The king was trying to talk his way out of this like he had tried to do at the Roundtable gathering before this whole ordeal had started. Hal nodded to his sister. She tossed a data chip to the floor at the king's feet and smirked.

The king's face betrayed him.

"You know what that is, don't you?" Hal said. "Allow me to erase any thoughts of doubt. That small data chip was the switch your technicians used to make that android fulfill your needs. You took one of the empress's most trusted confidants, created an android in her image, and waited for the time to strike." Hal took a step closer, heat burning within his chest. "I would say clever, but that would require you to actually formulate a plan to see it through. Instead, you left a trail of breadcrumbs that led right back here. This war is on your hands, and for what? Ego?"

The High King stayed silent for a moment as he looked at the data chip on the floor. When he looked back at Hal, he said through gritted teeth, "What do you want?"

"Retribution," Hal said. "For your actions, the Empire has outlined a core set of tenets for you to follow and sign: demilitarization, subjugation of the Kingdom as a nonaggressive planet to Athos, war reparations, and removal of you as High King to stand trial for war crimes, just to name a few." Hal handed the High King the list of demands. "And you will sign."

After a few moments of silent reading, the High King said, "We can follow the reparations."

"No. Everything," Miri corrected. "Don't test us. Be grateful we don't execute you right here."

"How are we supposed to protect ourselves if we cannot have an army and you tax everything we own?" High King Treth said. "The desert is home to dangerous creatures. What protection will we have?"

"You should have thought about that before the war," Hal said. "An offensive force of warships and soldiers is forbidden. The Empire of Athos will govern your actions now. As for you." Hal eyed the king. There was so much he wanted to do to him. Not even the most prominent of war criminals deserved a trial, but Hal respected the Code enough, lived by it.

"High King Torsai Treth, you are hereby under arrest for acts of terrorism and war crimes against the people of the Empire of Athos." He looked behind the king at the confused and frightened faces of the royal prince and princess. "I assure no harm will come to your family so long as you obey these orders."

The king looked back to his family. Hal waited for a response while Miri paced back and forth beside him. She clearly wanted to fight as she eyed Princess Zahra, but Hal knew that would upset his father and ruin the chances of his ascension. It took a lot to restrain his sister, but his father's word was law. Hal simply crossed his arms.

Imperial soldiers stormed the throne room, making their way up to where they stood. Hal smirked as the Treths witnessed the might of the Imperial army in their palace. If anything, it served as intimidation to the next rulers of the Polarian Kingdom.

When the king turned back around, he nodded to Hal and bowed before him. The rest of the family did the same, even Zahra, and Hal could not help but smile in his triumph. The Polarian royal family submitted to the Empire right before him, and now he was one step closer to ascending the throne.

CHAPTER III

Hal stood in the throne room of Athos a day after the battle of Polaris. His sister stood beside him as they awaited the entrance of their father. A dozen council members from across the Empire took their seats at the large holotable in the center of the throne room. The dim blue glow of the hardlight tabletop, where photons of refined and structured light reflected a soft glow against Hal's face, held lines of data that rushed from one end of the table to the other before starting anew. The columns of data broke the deafening silence with a soft beep before the next line began its run across the table. Though the table stood no higher than his hip, it contained enough information to rival the Imperial Archives.

The wait made Hal squirm and threatened to knot his stomach up. He shifted his weight from one foot to the other. He hated waiting. In his right hand, he held the document signed by King Treth, and sheathed on his left hip was the ceremonial Polarian sword gifted to the royal court as a sign of submission.

All around the throne room, past emperors and empresses immortalized in stone stared with soulless eyes. They made him feel scolded, not in anger or resentment, but in the knowledge that he still had to obtain. Each one of them was there because of their feats and mastery of Wielding. They'd served their terms gracefully and for longer than most past rulers only to be removed by the abdication, when emperors reached the highest age cap dictated by the Imperial

Code of Athos. It was necessary, though, to ensure the leader of the Empire still had enough cognitive function to perform.

Hal felt he'd followed the Code as well as any of the Empire's heroes, if not better. He looked at the council members, representatives from various districts of the Empire, until his eyes met one, the high minister. If there was one person who needed to believe in him, it was Varim.

Had the royal family not existed, High Minister Varim would've been the most powerful man in the Empire. He was the face of the elected representatives and made sure of that. Varim had the ears of the people and enacted the council's views and policies. Second only to the emperor in terms of the political sphere, Varim worked with the emperor to move issues along, including war.

He sat in the middle of the other council members, and Hal tried to guess what thoughts were running through his head. One way or the other, Varim would try to discredit him, perhaps even throw out a veto. But this was not something they could put on pause unless of an emergency.

Beside the throne, the High Justice sat in his seat and awaited what came next to make an official ruling. An indifferent face greeted Hal, custom for the High Justice as to not let any emotion sway his thought.

If there were no council, the Empire would've felt more authoritative, like the kingdom they had fought. But that was the whole point of including a council during the inception of the Empire over ten millenniums ago. The first emperor knew one person could not oversee the needs of a people stretched across the realm. A council of representatives alleviated that burden. But that did not mean Hal had to like the people who served on it.

Excitement, nervousness, and even some fear twisted within his body like a knot. It was an important moment for him, his family, and the future of the Empire. He hadn't seen his father in over a year, and that meeting had been via a simple holocall from a holotable. But light projections of someone didn't feel the same as seeing them in the flesh. Whatever the outcome of this meeting, he would have to give his father a massive hug—in private, of course.

If the council accepted Hal as heir to the Empire, he would become the Crown Prince and heir to the throne. His life would change.

Butterflies fluttered within his stomach as the curtains next to the throne parted, and the first Imperial honor guard, a Praetorian, emerged.

In unison, Hal and Miri knelt before the throne and bowed their heads as the elite guard entered the room. They stayed in that position, frozen, as the thunderous march of the Praetorians filled the chamber.

When the march stopped and silence fell upon them, Hal stood and saw not the man he called his father but an empty throne. He looked at his sister for an explanation, but not even she seemed to understand the absence of the emperor.

Shuffling came from behind him, and as Hal looked back, Minister Varim walked past him and up the stairs to where the throne stood. Hal eyed him like a hawk but waited for the minister to explain himself. High Minister Varim looked around the room and met Hal's eyes before he spoke.

"Children of the royal court and members of the Imperial Council, I regret to inform you that the emperor could not make it to this important congregation today due to the injuries sustained in the attacks on our city one month ago."

Hal stood frozen. Nobody had told him about his father being ill. He'd assumed it was because of the war that he had not heard from him. Anger stirred in his chest at the notion of his father's well-being having been kept from him.

Hal broke his silence and said, "Why weren't we informed?"

"We did not want to compromise your chances at victory."

"Royal and court dealings are important for us to know, and your refusal to even mention our father's injury status is reprehensible," Miri said. "I was on-world a month ago."

"And you had valuable information that you were trying to decipher for the prince. We could not jeopardize the outcome," High Minister Varim said.

"What is the nature of his injuries? Is he receiving medical attention?" Hal asked.

"That is not the subject of today's—"

"Answer the question, Minister," Hal said as he charged a hand full of flames.

The room filled with gasps. Hal knew better than to display such incorrect political methods during the congregation, but keeping important information such as the well-being of the emperor from the royal family was uncustomary and blatant disregard toward the Imperial Code.

Varim stood rigid and cleared his throat.

"Emperor Tiberius Skyborn was subjected to the fumes of an unidentified gas in a recent attack. He is stable but unconscious and is recovering as we speak," Varim explained. "More information will be available once the doctors permitted to enter have determined what exactly the gas was and has done to him."

Hal exchanged a look with Miri. She'd spent most of the war touring the Empire, but even she seemed to know nothing of the attack. Her duties as a princess would carry her across the entire Empire, but someone should have at least told her.

They'd intentionally hidden it from Hal and Miri.

It didn't matter, though. If Hal became the Crown Prince, he would order an investigation into the mishandlings of this instance the second he sat on the throne. Disregard for the Code had no place in his eyes. For now, he had to convince the council, which made this even more important. And as he glanced at the High Justice, he swallowed whatever anger he had. The flames in his hand fizzled out, and he stood tall once more.

Varim took a deep breath and said, "Now, I assume with you standing before the council that our message was delivered?"

"It was," Hal said. "The Treths have submitted. King Torsai sits in the bowels of Fort Bracca."

"Their city burns as we speak, and the flag of the Empire flies atop the royal palace," Miri added.

"Words mean nothing. What is your proof?"

Hal approached the throne and handed the signed document and the ceremonial Polarian sword of peace to the steward. They brought it up to the throne for the high minister as Hal returned to his spot next to his sister.

It seemed like forever as the high minister examined the sword, admiring the fine craftsmanship of the blade used centuries before. When he swapped to the signed parchment, however, a wave of nervousness washed over Hal, and the silence gnawed at him. He tried not to let emotions get the better of him, but he knew how important this was for the Empire of Athos. As he glanced over, Miri gave him a stern, almost frightened look.

If the council failed to grant him the title of Crown Prince in accordance with the Code, all of this would be for naught. He knew his father was nearing his Abdication Day, and the chances to prove himself to the council were becoming limited as the years went on.

Every emperor before his father had had an heir in place to carry on the Empire. Without one, the council would have to assume duties until a new emperor or empress was deemed fit for the throne, and that would take years. The tradition of having an heir prove themselves had withstood all the tests the last millennia had thrown at it. Yet here he stood now, unsure of what the council thought and unsure of his future.

The high minister glanced at one of the other council members. Hal knew better than to move, but out of the corner of his eye, he saw several council members nod. The whole scene smelled of political theater. There wasn't even a discussion. How could people decide the fate of the Empire without even talking about it? Hal looked around as more council members nodded in agreement.

He glared at Varim, who didn't even bat an eye as he silently watched. Hal balled his hands into fists again as pressure built inside his body. He could give them another reason to grant him the title of Crown Prince.

Little flames flickered through the crevices of his fists. Miri looked down as the flames pulsed with anger. She caught his glare and shook her head. Hal took a deep breath, and the pressure began to subside. As much as he would like to right now, he would not go against the Code.

"A signed document is valuable, and the sword is a nice touch of appeasement, but what you failed to gain was their total submission. A peace treaty only lasts until one of the parties breaks the vow. Total submission ensures they don't," Varim said.

Hal narrowed his eyes, baffled by what he had just heard.

"I followed the orders of the emperor. I did what you asked, what the council asked, what Imperius asked. I liberated our lost worlds, found keycodes to ancient Primordial technology, defeated the Polarian fleet, claimed Yasu for the Empire, conquered the Polarian System, sieged the royal city, and brought justice to the Empire, and you say I didn't ensure their submission?"

He looked at Miri for help, but she only bowed her head. Hal continued.

"How would I gain total submission unless the city was wiped from existence and I brought you the head of the king? That would be murder and go against the Imperial Code." Hal composed himself. "I followed the Code with honor. As we stand here in the emperor's court, the eyes of those before us smile at my feats."

"It wasn't enough," High Minister Varim said.

"Perhaps the young prince wasn't ready," another council member added from the round table. It cut through Hal's ears like a hot dagger through ice. "A change in leadership would have offered a different outcome, I believe. A civil minister, for instance, with the goals of the council in mind."

Hal took a deep breath and exhaled, steam exiting his nostrils, as the other council members began to murmur amongst themselves. It was unfair. He'd set out to do an impossible task and had returned with the Polarian Kingdom without a head of state and their submission, and that still was not enough. They had the dust hole of a city under their control, a puppet state just like his father wanted for their treachery. The entire realm was theirs to do with for payment of the war. Resources were everywhere, and yet the narrow-minded view of this court and his aging father could not see that.

Frustration built up inside him, beginning to boil. He felt cheated. And in line with his feelings, the crystal around his neck began to glow a faint orange. The crystal marked him as a royal, but it served a greater purpose. It focused his fire energy, his charna, and allowed him to wield the Primordials' gift to mortals.

"This was your chance to invoke change, young prince. To show absolutely no mercy. You followed orders but did not make your own. You allowed fear and normalcy to guide you and chose not to take risks. Now the council will have to clean up your wreckage. How can we let someone so structured have more command in our social and ever-changing society?"

"The Code forbids it, high minister," Hal said through gritted teeth.

Varim shook his head and looked toward the council. "Let's ask the High Justice, then, shall we?"

"As decreed by the Code and the customs of our world, Prince Halcion Sky-born has shown every measure to keep the Empire in graceful hands and continue the Empyrean Dynasty," the High Justice said. "However, with Emperor Tiberius still with breath in his lungs, the vote of succession cannot continue. He must bear witness."

"I've studied the Code. I've never heard of that," Hal shot back.

"Hal," Miri whispered beside him.

"Section thirty-five, chapter eight, page five hundred states: '*A vote of succession must have the current sovereign and heir bear witness,*'" the High Justice read.

"The Code of Athos only has four hundred and ninety-seven pages," Hal said as he looked around the room of council members before he glared back at the High Justice. "What Code are you reading?"

"Enough," the High Justice said as a gavel echoed throughout the court. "The Court has spoken."

Varim smiled and nodded to the other council members.

"All in favor of postponing the vote of succession, raise a hand." When seven of the nine council members raised their hands, the high minister nodded. "Let it be known that on this day, the Imperial Council voted to postpone the ceremonial Crowing of the Heir to the Throne until the emperor is able to bear witness."

The high minister walked down the steps and stood right in front of Hal. "Best we wait until cooler heads prevail. Hopefully before Emperor Tiberius's Abdication Day." He cast a sideways glance to Miri. "Or maybe the young princess can rise to the occasion since you already had a chance. Exciting times, no? Would that be in accordance with the Code, Prince Halcion? Oh, apologies, I forgot about her condition."

"Walk away," Hal said as he glared at where the throne stood.

Varim smiled before he strutted out of the room. Hal wanted no more than to deck the high minister right there for insulting his sister.

Miri hung her head, staring at the polished floor. She was, unfortunately, an illegitimate heir for being sterile. Nothing of her own fault, but it was what the Code dictated, which made this decision even more dangerous. And now it seemed the council wanted to play games with who earned the title of Heir to the Throne. None of this would have mattered if the council just got their heads out of their rears.

He wanted to prove the high minister wrong, but there was nothing he could do right now. His father was ill, and the council was disbanded for the time being. But now he felt confused and lost. His father had given him this test to prove himself, and he felt he had, but the council thought otherwise. They played political games, and now the fate of the Empire's future lay in limbo because he'd failed in their eyes.

Council members began to file out. Their murmurs filled the emptiness of the room as they shuffled for the door. No doubt they spoke of how unruly the prince was and how he'd spoken defiantly to the high minister. Even the high minister's remarks felt dull in comparison to what had just happened.

"Hal," Miri said.

"What games are they playing?" he said under his breath.

His sister wrapped a hand around his arm, and a look of concern crossed her face. It was not often he saw her look this way, but this was a strange time, and it brought about different emotions. Hal felt betrayed, but he knew his sister would have felt the same way.

"Come on," Miri said as she lightly tugged on her brother's arm. "We've had a long couple of days. Time to relax."

He followed his sister out of the throne room, still fuming with frustration, and barely saw who waited outside. An older man in fine robes saw them and walked over. Hal stopped beside Miri and waited for the old man to get closer before he remembered who it was. The old man saluted Hal and Miri with a single fist to the heart before he spoke.

"Prince Hal, Princess Miri, I am sorry for the way the council handled matters today."

"It goes against the Code, Minister Nakami," Miri said.

"What kind of circus is Varim running here?" Hal asked. "Since when does the Code contain five hundred pages? It ends with '*Should the Empire not have a rightful Empyrean ruler, then the transition of power goes to the elected representatives to decide whether or not the Empire can continue as is.*' This is not a time for games, Minister. If I don't get chosen by the council to replace my father, then who knows what happens to the Empire."

The politician nodded in agreement before he continued. "High Minister Varim let the power get to his head in the closing days of the war. With no head of state, he assumed emergency control."

"Why didn't he contact Miri? She was still in Imperius and the next in line behind me. She should be acting empress if the Code was followed," Hal said, placing his hands on his hips. "The high minister violated the Code and the chain of command."

"Have no fear, young prince. I will talk to Varim and ensure he follows the guidelines in the Code. A proper ordainment must be done, but we need to wait until Emperor Tiberius is able to participate," the minister said. "I believe that is part of the hesitation from Varim to go on with customs."

Hal shook his head as the frustration of political life resurfaced. Two years was a long time away from the headaches of politics, and now he almost missed the chaos of war. At least then he'd been free to make decisions. Here he felt like a repressed soul fighting to leave an invisible cage.

"I'm sorry, minister. This is just not what I was expecting. Dozens of past Crown Princes and Princesses have served honorably in conflicts. This is no different. The judgment should be left to representatives of the people and not some career politicians who have sat on this council for four decades."

"I understand your concerns, milord. I wish there were a way around this, but until Varim gives up emergency powers or the emperor improves, there isn't much we can do." Minister Nakami smiled. "If you become the next emperor, you can introduce those term limit measures."

"If . . ." Hal said as his gaze shifted toward the ground.

"I'm sure we can convince Varim somehow," Miri said.

"I will try to reason with him, but you know how the younger ones are. All filled with bravado and ego," Minister Nakami joked. "You have my full support, Prince Halcion."

"Thank you, Minister."

"I have to return to Nihon. Farewell, Prince Halcion, Princess Miriam."

As the minister bowed and left the courtyard, Hal took another look at the throne room with a burning desire in his eyes. One day he would claim it as promised by his destiny. A new emperor would rise as one fell, and it would be he who shaped the Empire's future. For now, though, he had to pick the times of his battles, and this was not it.

CHAPTER IV

The airspeeder flew above the forests as they traveled to Fort Bracca, where High King Torsai Treth awaited his tribunal. Massive trees of lush green blotted out the ground below as the dual suns rose high into the sky. Birds with black-tipped wings soared just over the treetops, soaking up the warmth of the suns.

Hal had missed the simplicity of nature during the war where bombs weren't exploding left and right. It was a welcome change from the destroyed battlefields of the Yasu System, though he wished he could enjoy it more.

His thoughts traveled back to the day before. He couldn't fathom how the council had denied him his birthright. Prince Atkis had become Crown Prince for taming warring clans on one of Athos's earliest colonies centuries ago. If that feat was good enough for heirship, then besting the Empire's greatest foe in combat should've been no question.

He knew it bothered him too much, but it felt like time was running thin and the council was stalling. With his father's sixty-fifth birthday nearing, so too was his abdication from the throne. If Hal could not pass the Code's sole tenet of raising the Empire to new heights, he feared what could come.

He had done what the Code asked; he'd fought for Athos and brought the Empire out of the slump it had been in after the death of his mother. He'd broken the Polarians' backs and ushered in a wave of patriotism the Empire hadn't seen in years. But the final say was that of the council, elected by the people of Athos, though it was more a courtesy custom than anything else. Now the fate of his home world hung in limbo because of one man.

His eyes focused on Varim, who sat a couple rows ahead of Hal and Miri, and he tried to think of what the man had planned. Phony rules from a fake excerpt of the Code had gotten him this far, but Hal would not let that stand for long. After the trial, he would start a new one solely based on the foundation of the Imperial Code of Athos and not whatever Varim—or anyone else—wished it to be. What frightened him, though, was how nonchalant the High Justice had been about what had happened in the Court. It only beckoned him to ask what else had happened in his absence.

"How do you feel?" Miri asked, pulling him from his thoughts.

His glare softened when he looked into her eyes. They warned him of her worry. He took a deep breath and forced a small smirk to cross his face.

"I'm fine. It's just stress."

"It'll fade in time." She placed a hand on top of his and smiled. "Things will be okay."

Hal nodded. "Enough about me. How are you? How's my little sister?"

"Must you say 'little' still? I am twenty now, you know," she said, rolling her eyes.

"Yes, but you'll always be my little sister no matter how old you get," Hal said as he threw an arm around her. "But I guess I can lay off on saying it in public."

"Mm-hmm. And 'Meer'?"

"Oh no, you're stuck with that one," Hal said.

Miri rolled her eyes again, with a smile this time. "I'll take what I can get."

The two laughed for a moment as the airspeeder continued toward its destination, and then Hal's thoughts wandered again. Though it was good to be back home and with his sister once more, it still felt like a part of him was missing. He thought of Kristilin and yearned to hear her sweet voice. Though word of his arrival had traveled quickly through the Empire's communication lines, inter-system and inter-world communication was another story. The void of space and its many cosmic forces made it hard to get news elsewhere quickly.

He looked down to where his datacard sat on his lap; the last message he'd sent a couple days ago was still unread. He should've expected that, though, after the way he'd left her for the war without a single goodbye. It had pained him then, and it pained him now, but he had to live with the consequences of his inaction. He couldn't make her forgive him, but he hoped in time she would. All he could do was wait.

The airspeeder sailed over the mountains, where snow-covered trees turned the valley white. In the center of the valley was a massive complex of concrete towers and guarded walls: Fort Bracca, where those who'd committed crimes against the Empire faced their judgment. Buildings covered the area inside the walls, but they were dwarfed by one. Situated in the center of the complex was a large building that stretched nearly to the top of the walls. The Imperial sigil, the diamond, was etched into the front of the building, marking the place where judgment was passed: the Hall of Judgement.

The airspeeder turned as the landing gear touched the landing platform, the momentary jolt of force enough to wake any dozed-off official.

As Hal and Miri rose from their seats, the exit hatch split open and exposed the walking ramp. Hal followed his sister and Varim to where a detachment of Imperial soldiers and two Praetorians awaited them, saluting as they walked by.

The twin suns shined bright, and Hal squinted through their light. Despite being in the mountains of the north, the burn from the twin suns heated the back of his neck. At the end of the platform awaited an Imperial officer in a silver-and-gold uniform.

"Greetings, Prince Halcion, Princess Miriam, High Minister Varim. It is an honor to welcome you to Bracca."

"Yes, Director, it is," Varim said. "Excuse the pleasantries, but I must meet the High Justice."

Varim moved past the director, and Hal took a deep breath as Varim disappeared through the sliding doors and into the Hall.

"Excuse the high minister's rudeness," Miri said as her golden gown blew in the cool breeze

The director smiled. "He has a lot on his plate."

"Doesn't mean respect should go to the wayside," Hal replied, noticing the soldiers behind him were still in a salute. "At ease," he said, then turned back to the director. "What do you think about getting these men back inside?"

The director nodded in agreement. "All right, men. You heard the prince. Back inside."

The officer in charge of the detachment barked an order. In unison, the soldiers spun on their heels and marched back into the Hall of Judgement. Hal and Miri followed the director and entered the Hall flanked by the two Praetorians.

Inside the Hall, Hal sat beside his sister and the high minister in the atrium seating that overlooked the courtroom below. One pedestal stood in the center while a large chair surrounded by a polished wooden judge's bench sat across from it. Behind that hung a massive royal banner of gold with silver tapestries. On the field of gold rested the diamond insignia with script that read '*Bless Empyrea*' above one point and '*Long Live the Empire*' below.

Soldiers in golden armor, special to this installation, guarded the few entrances and exits around the chamber. Hal wondered how these soldiers could stay in this routine every day: wake up, stand and guard trials, patrol the grounds, repeat. It sounded mundane, but then he remembered he'd lived a similar routine for two years. Every day that he woke up during the war was a race to see who could kill the other side best, and one slipup could mean death. Though this prison was more relaxed compared to the Yasu System, the routine he'd faced had been similar: wake up, coordinate strategies, patrol, kill. It was a routine he was glad was over with now.

Hours went by as he sat in the balcony and watched judicial proceedings take place. The boom of the High Justice's gavel rang in his ears, and he thought he was back on the battlefield every time it came down to strike. He watched those in violation of the Code be handed their sentences, but they did little to garner his attention.

He looked at the clock on the side wall; the time was near.

Two doors slid open, and two soldiers escorted a bound disheveled man. His hair was thrown in every direction, and his beard looked just the same. Holes in his cloth tabard and pants told of an uneasy time. In just a few days, the High King of the Polarian Kingdom had been reduced to nothing more than a common civilian.

He staggered up to the pedestal, thanks to the soldiers who escorted him up. Though he was a former king, he still needed to answer for what he'd done to the Empire. There would be no exceptions.

"Now we will see what enemies of the Empire receive. Thanks to you, Prince Hal," Varim said.

A compliment from a snake meant nothing, and Hal stayed silent. With the strike of a gavel that echoed through the chamber, the High Justice spoke.

"High King Torsai Treth of the Polarian Kingdom, you are in this court of law to answer for your crimes and the crimes of your star nation."

Hal leaned forward eagerly as the High Justice delivered the opening remarks.

There should be no qualms about how this trial should go. It was simple, in his mind. The High King had committed acts of terrorism against the Empire itself. As decreed by the Code, a terroristic attack required a death sentence. It would serve as closure to the people who'd lost their empress and a warning to those who'd dare try to attack the Empire again. All that was needed now was the High Justice's ruling.

"How do you plead?"

The High King stayed silent. One of the guards thrust the butt of his lightrifle into his back. A pained grunt echoed through the mic, and High King Torsai grabbed the railings of the pedestal.

"How do you plead?"

"G-guilty."

The High Justice looked up to where Hal sat. As he stared back, he could tell the High Justice wasn't looking at him or his sister. As he followed the path of his eyes, Hal looked at Varim, who gave the slightest nod.

Hal's blood boiled; he smelled something brewing.

"Then as decreed by the Code: Voluntary surrender of a sovereign of a star nation will result in life imprisonment."

"Objection," Hal shouted as he stood from his seat.

"You can't object to judicial matters," Varim said in retaliation, but the bang of the gavel hushed the high minister and brought focus back to the High Justice.

"He is in accordance with the Code, High Minister Varim. Let the prince speak."

Hal shot Varim a glare before he continued. "The Code states that a sovereign of a star nation can voluntarily surrender themselves or their sovereignty only in times not of war. We have been at war with the Polarian Kingdom for nearly three years. High King Torsai Treth ordered the murder of Empress Irina Skyborn. He deserves the same fate as dictated by the Code."

"I second his motion, High Justice," Miri said as she rose beside him.

The High Justice's voice boomed through the chamber as he spoke.

"While you are both correct, section 3, chapter 4 of the Code states: Upon defeat of a star nation with a sovereign intact, and not destroyed through the conflict of war, the sovereign may give up both their sovereignty and the sovereignty of the star nation."

"That doesn't even make sense," Hal said.

"Then you should have fulfilled the Code."

"He was unarmed. Section 3, chapter 2 states that a sovereign or royal shall not strike down an unarmed adversary or face exile," Hal said.

The boom of the gavel silenced him, and he felt the guards behind him shift closer. He knew if he spoke any more, they would escort him out and back to the landing platform, so he stood tall, eyes fixed on the High Justice.

"The Court of the High Justice has spoken," the High Justice said. "High King Torsai Treth, you will serve your life in prison."

With the boom of the gavel, the guards escorted the High King out of the chamber.

If Hal could breathe fire, smoke would've been billowing from his nostrils. The ineptitude of those in charge and their defilement of the meaning of the Code made him want to yell in fury. What was it in place for if people were going to ignore it? It was not there as courtesy; it was the law of the Empire. But this was not the Code he remembered.

Varim stood from his seat, and his cape of gold fluttered as he slipped through the door behind them.

Hal turned to his sister. "Wait here."

As the guards parted and the door slid open, Hal emerged into the hallway. Large windows lined it from floor to ceiling. Outside, soldiers patrolled as the twin suns twinkled high in the clear blue sky. But he was not here for the scenery.

"High Minister Varim," Hal called out down the hall.

Varim stopped and slowly turned around. A wide grin crossed his face.

"Prince Hal, a fine showing today, huh?"

"Don't play coy with me. What was that in there?" Hal asked as he closed the distance between them.

Varim furrowed his brow and brought a hand to his lips as he cupped one elbow. "I don't understand what you mean."

"Where did all this new verbiage in the Code come from? I've studied it since I was a child. I know it like the back of my hand," Hal said.

"Then you should know that new amendments can be passed," Varim said.

"With the presence of a royal," Hal quickly shot back. "And I thought my father was gravely ill. Your emergency powers don't make you immune to the law."

"Young Hal—"

Hal narrowed his eyes and crossed his arms.

"Prince Halcion, I am only trying to do what is right. The Empire was in disarray when noble Emperor Tiberius was stricken ill. Someone needed to quell the panic."

"Why didn't you alert my sister?"

"She was busy researching and deciphering the Primordial keycodes you sent her. It was a monumental task, and I couldn't allow the two young Empyrean descendants to be distracted while a war threatened the Empire." Varim shrugged. "You are free to protest this with the High Justice, but until Emperor Tiberius is well, I'm afraid my hands are tied."

"Don't worry. I plan to. You know this is against the Code. Not one but two royals are able to stand in until the rightful heir takes the Throne, yet you deny custom and pervert the Throne with your ass. You have emergency powers, yes, but that is for government and not palace matters."

"I'm sorry you feel that way, Prince Halcion. But like I said, my hands are tied in accordance with the Code."

"I can smell the bullshit coming from you," Hal said through gritted teeth. "What Code are you following?"

Varim flashed a small smile and cast his gaze downward. Hal tried to study the man's face, but the high minister showed little to no emotion other than a coy smile.

"The Code states our course of action. I have no more to say."

As he started to leave, Hal called out, "You will stop and answer my questions, High Minister Varim."

"No, I will not." The high minister turned to face him. "I am the overseer of the transition of power and the committee who will vote on what is to come next. I am the civilian leader in charge of what the people wish, and I will execute that duty as told by the Code, Prince Hal."

The high minister turned on his heel for a second time and exited the hall. Hal stood alone, ready to lob a fireball after him.

But the last words struck a nerve within Hal, and he didn't know if it could be true or not. The possibility that this wasn't entirely Varim's fault and that perhaps the people had voted for this crossed his mind. If that was true, there was nothing he could do in official matters. The people voted to postpone the coronation ceremony. But he wanted to know why and when these new amendments to the Code had happened. It could've also been a political stunt meant to gain favor with the council or even Emperor Tiberius, but that was too grand for the high minister. Varim was up to something, and Hal needed to know what that was.

As he looked around the gilded hall, he felt lost and confused, out of touch. He knew the Code, but now he had to prove to the people, to the Imperial Council, and to himself that he was worthy. Brewing on it helped no one, though, and he needed to relieve the pressure that had built up inside him before it blew.

CHAPTER V

"Again."

Hal assumed the fighting stance he had learned and modified to his style and focused on the three Imperial training droids in front of him. Fire energy charged up his arms as he analyzed their fluid movements. They mimicked humans with precision and grace, unlike previous droids. They were practically human.

When one attacked, Hal easily countered the blow and redirected the droid before he raised a protective ward of energy to block another strike. A metal training blade smashed across the ward and sent energy ripples out to the edges. Hal shoved the second droid and launched a ball of fire before the third could strike. The force of the fireball sent the poor droid across the room. He ducked as one of the other droids returned and kicked its feet out from under it before he spun and raised another ward of fire to block the last droid's strike.

Hal dropped the fire ward and began his own attack, striking fast with fists of fire energy, pushing the droid back. With one last punch, he sent a short stream of flames at the droid and knocked it back with sheer force. He took a deep breath, but out of the corner of his eye he saw the tip of a hardlite sword, a xiphir. The blade of photons shimmered and reflected off his face a golden glow.

He looked over to find his mentor holding the xiphir. A sigh escaped his mouth as he looked into the eyes of Lord Carnn. The older man tilted his head so his one working eye could stare through Hal, and he braced for the corrections Lord Carnn was about to give.

"Good, but you allowed yourself to become clouded with desire, distracted by what you wanted and not by what presented itself," he said as he walked in front of Hal and deactivated the sword. He slipped it back into the sleeves of his robes. "Always be prepared for what is not seen. Your desire for victory left you vulnerable, and had this been a real battle, you would've lost your head. Allow yourself to not only see your opponents but feel them as well. Take what they give and use it against them." Lord Carnn returned to his previous position behind the droids. "Again."

Like before, Hal assumed his stance and sized up his competition. Their light feet and loose postures told him they were about to attack, but Hal had another plan.

He lunged and grabbed the first droid's arm, twisting it behind its back and nearly snapping it before he sprayed flames toward the second. Hal landed a strong kick to the chest of the droid and sent it reeling backward before it caught a ball of fire in its chest. Hal brought two waves of flames crashing against the final droid, leaving it stunned in spasms of electroshocks on the ground.

Instinct became second nature. Hal whipped a ball of fire toward the opposite side of the training arena and turned around, his hands still charged with flames up to his elbows.

Lord Carnn stood with the xiphir extended toward Hal's chest, a small frown across his face. "You've been compromised."

The few watching, including his sister, likely thought it was out of frustration for another failed attempt that the ball of fire was thrown, but Hal understood the message his mentor was trying to instill in him.

Lord Carnn spoke.

"What did I just tell you?"

Hal remained silent. He met Lord Carnn's disappointed gaze. He knew the power he had within himself and the amount of control he had when it came to the art of Wielding. Only a Wielder could understand it, though scholars tried to mimic the understanding. It was in his blood, not theirs. What his mentor was trying to teach him was how to be calculated, which he agreed with.

As he shifted ever so slightly, his fireball ricocheted off one of the pillars in the arena and headed toward them. It screamed between them before exploding along the wall at the back of the arena, leaving scorch marks in its wrath. Lord Carnn's sleeves smoked, and he looked on in surprise. Hal only stared back at him.

"Training is complete for today," Lord Carnn said as he looked toward the droids.

As the droids returned to their power docks and the spectators left, Lord Carnn walked back to the training rack behind him and hung the sword's hilt on its stand and said, "You are powerful, Halcion. You have the power of the Empyreans, gifted from the Primordials themselves, yet you don't know how to use it."

"I just bested you in combat, Lord Carnn," Hal said when Miri joined him.

"Unconventionality is our way, Lord Carnn," Miri said.

They had the skillset to use Wielding, and they'd practiced and studied since Hal could remember. They meditated together in the Chamber of Wielders, basking in Primordial knowledge that had spanned hundreds of years. Besides their father, they were the only other Wielders in the Realmverse, which made Hal wonder why Lord Carnn had any reservations about their knowledge and skill. They could generate heat and illuminate darkened rooms like it was a part of them—because it was.

Combat was new to him even after two years of war, though, and especially to his sister, but that was why they came here to train, and the experience he'd received from the war only strengthened his fighting ability. Unless the lord thought they lacked knowledge of combat partnered with Wielding. But battling another Wielder was something not in their time. They were the only Wielders.

Lord Carnn shook his head as he stepped in front of Hal. "Victory in combat means nothing if you don't understand the nature of your tools." He looked at Hal. "Why do you come here every day?"

Hal looked at the statues and murals of famous past Wielders and legends that lined the halls outside the arena. His eyes stopped on one that stood taller than the others: Emperor Atis Skyborn, the first of the line, and his wife, Empress Sarin Skyborn. The story he'd heard time and time again was how a mortal rose to become an Empyrean and forged an empire out of ashes.

He said, "To be like them, Atis and Sarin. If I can show the council that I have the strength they once did, then I'll prove myself as a worthy heir to the throne. They wouldn't be able to say no."

"Do you believe the Empyrean strength came from their physical mastery of Wielding or their fundamental understanding of it?"

Hal looked back at him and said, "What difference does it make?"

"Quite a bit." Lord Carnn exhaled a deep breath. "The intricacy of this power is something not even your father understands fully and is what your late mother set out to discover. When the Primordials were vanquished—"

"Their teachings vanished, and so did their secrets," Hal said. "I'm not interested in knowing their history, Lord Carnn. I've studied it for nearly two decades now."

Lord Carnn placed an arm around his shoulders. "Young prince, have you ever been inside the ruins of one of their temples? Laid eyes on one of their story murals? Solved one of their puzzles?"

Hal remained quiet for the moment. He had never really thought of that before. Usually when he was out of the city it was to tour the various towns and villages that called the rest of Athos home. Sometimes it entailed the occasional strolls on the forest floor, but even then he'd had a detachment of guards with him for protection from hostile wildlife. He knew of Empyrean ruins in distant caves and shrines dotted throughout Athos, but they lay beyond his freedom to explore, almost like a cruel joke to hide information from him.

When he'd finally come of age to explore the surrounding lands himself, he'd been shipped off to war, and before then, straying from the safe zones his father and the council set down had been forbidden. He could not dare go against his father's orders if he wanted to be the Crown Prince of Athos. He had to impress everyone, and violating the emperor's word would be seen as disrespectful and rebellious, traits of an heir unsuitable for the throne. But he trusted Lord Carnn enough to hear him out and listen to his wisdom.

"The Empyreans, Atis and Sarin, are much more than the deities you and the entire Empire claim to worship. You should care greatly about their history if you are to understand their power and wisdom." With a sigh of frustration, Lord Carnn said, "Meet me at the sky port tomorrow morning. Both of you need to know the full story of Atis and Sarin."

Before they could say anything, Lord Carnn waved a hand and left the training arena.

Miri stepped in front of Hal, still looking at the weaponmaster, then turned around and said, "Don't listen to his nonsense, Hal. You are the future Crown Prince even if no one knows it. At least I do."

"I suppose that's a compliment?"

Miri smirked. "The entirety of the Empire will reward you on Inception Day, my dear brother. And their voice will pressure Varim and the council to make a formal decision. Think about it. What's a better way to start recognizing their new Crown Prince than a return parade to mark you the hero you are on the day the Empire was founded ten thousand years ago?"

Hal looked at her in confusion. "A parade? I wasn't aware of any parades."

"A war-weary veteran such as yourself needs to be appreciated," Miri said. "I organized it . . . like a few weeks ago."

"And if I'd died in battle before then?"

His sister punched him in the arm with a quick glare. "Don't say things like that."

Though Miri had some outlandish tendencies, she was still his sister, and a sudden wave of comfort washed over Hal as he looked at her. Her smile seemed filled with want, revenge. For what, Hal did not know. It could've been for what had transpired a few days ago in the throne room or for the information that had been kept from them. The glare in her eyes seemed to be fighting something or wanting something. Either way, Hal smiled and shook his head.

"Why do I have a hard time believing this?"

Miri rolled her eyes. "I can be cold, or I can be warm. Depends on my mood." She shrugged. "Besides, it's not for a few days. A hero needs to be properly welcomed, and you need to come with me to prepare."

Without another word, she grabbed him by the arm and pulled him out of the training arena. She led him through the palace and out past the courtyard where politicians from various lands under the Empire came and went for official duties. Though they stopped to congratulate them on a victory, Hal could only return their salute before Miri dragged him off.

"Meer, where are we going?"

"Hush. Trust me. You will appreciate this," she said.

Hal knew better than to argue with her when her mind was set on something.

She led him to the steps of the palace and blew by the guards without a word, who didn't even try to stop the Princess of the Empire of Athos.

Hal stopped when she jumped into the driver's seat of a vehicle just outside.

It was an ordinary currus fit for two people. Repulsers glowed silently underneath the floorboards, waiting for activation of the engine. Hal shook his head and raised an eyebrow as he pointed at the vehicle.

"You? Driving?" he said. "You hate driving."

"I can make exceptions, you know," she fired back. "Now get in."

As soon as Hal closed the door, the currus came to life. The top of this particular currus lowered so the full warmth of the twin suns could touch them. Repulsers warmed up and raised them off the ground as Hal sunk back into the soft seats. They sped off through the narrow streets before coming to a roundabout that led to the downtown district, where skyscrapers reached for the sky over a central lake.

Wind blew his hair back, and more buildings and other vehicles whizzed by in a blur as they entered the downtown district. Gold and silver trees lined the boulevards. Citizens stopped on their toes before they crossed to avoid the oncoming royals. The heat of the currus's repulsers sprayed puddles on the unsuspecting ones who sat on nearby benches.

Hal sank as far back in his seat as he could when Miri took a corner and nearly gave him whiplash.

"Watch out!" Hal said, but Miri blew through the stoplight. Horns were blared by drivers who didn't recognize the driver of the vehicle, not that they could be blamed. Hal and Miri typically had an escort, but this was all unplanned.

Hal gripped the door handle as he looked over to his sister, her long light blonde hair flying in the wind behind her like a head cape.

"I can see you got better at driving, at least," Hal said, bracing himself as they approached the teleportation travel center.

The massive building had every sort of warning for vehicles along the side where the glass windows stood. One or two might have been the result of Miri.

Citizens glanced at them from the lounge inside, the large glass windows giving them a clear view of who was in control of the vehicle. They met Hal's eyes before they scattered as the currus bared down on them. No amount of air-braking would slow the vehicle down to take the turn, and their reflection in the glass grew larger by the second. He imagined them being scolded by their father when he got word of this joyride. He would have to call it another driving lesson.

Miri swerved hard, nearly rolling the currus, and threw Hal to the side to miss the glass entryway before she said, "I did, actually. Thank you for noticing. I still prefer flying, though."

As the traffic began to thin out and Hal remembered to breathe, he took in the sight of the city. Grand buildings angled in symmetrical structure to appear twisted all around towered over smaller buildings, while sunlight shined toward the west where various office buildings stood. The roar of a starship moaned in the distance, and Hal looked up to see a long, blocky cargo ship sailing toward the spaceports with a gentle whine as it descended through the atmosphere, ready to offload valuable trade, or perhaps more soldiers returning home to greet their families. Another smaller starship rose from its platform at the spaceport and engaged its double engines, sailing toward the twin suns with a purple glow.

As his eyes drifted back down to the city skyline, he followed a five-car tram that left the spaceport and traveled deeper into the city, chugging rhythmically every time it went over a new section of rail line. It disappeared behind high-rises and apartment buildings in the east, where the residential and private homes were. It had been a while since Hal had heard the familiar sounds of the city.

The currus left the stone roads of the palace district and came to the start of the forest. Green overtook everything, and the shrubs turned to trees that towered over the artificially cultivated forest. The currus flew down the dirt path, kicking up leaves with its twin fan engines, and came to a stop near a suspended waterfall. The water flowed over the crest of the fall with a crystal blue shine. It traveled down the small river and cascaded over an opening in the ground to rain on the land below before the river carried on through the forest. The sound was nothing more than utter peace and silence when Miri turned the currus off.

She looked at him with a smile and said, "We're going to be here in a couple days."

"So we came early to get the best seats?"

She smirked and punched him in the arm. "No. I just thought we could stay here for a bit. Catch up. It's been nothing but nonstop chaos for two years, and I missed my brother. I just want to be with you before everyone else swoops in."

Hal looked at his sister with a smile. While she was headstrong, bold, and sometimes a little on edge, she always made him feel cared about when things got rough. This small act of kindness reminded him of their younger years when they would venture here together and explore what they could. They become more daring in their later years and would descend to the land below and explore the frontier.

"You know I always have time for you," Hal said. "You're my sister."

"I know," Miri said, staring at the wheel for a second.

Hal caught it and stayed silent for a moment. Something was troubling her. He knew she would tell him in her own time. When she didn't move, he spoke up.

"So, how are you? It's been so long since we just talked."

Miri reached for a strand of blonde hair and looked down.

"Something bothering you, Meer?"

"No. No." Miri's eyes turned steely and fixated on the floor of the currus. "It's just . . . Why did they send you to war?"

"Miri, you know it's the duty of the firstborn. I didn't ask for it. But I am grateful that you didn't have to see what I saw: the carnage, the destruction, the loss of life." Hal looked through the forest, where shadows danced in the low light.

Birds flew from the canopy of tall trees, sending leaves drifting to the ground. Peace was plentiful here, unlike in the Yasu System.

"I only saw two years of it, and I saw a lot in those two years. Father, when it started, fought in it a year before me. I was nervous when he came back home and I saw his wounds. Now he's hurt again."

"But we could have gone together," Miri said. "Fought together. Shared the glory of victory together. Father would have been proud of us. We could've shown the Realmverse who we, as children of the Empire, are and avenged our mother." She leaned back in her seat and took a deep breath. "You get everything: First say in court dealings. Glory. Recognition. I'm just Miri, sister to Hal."

Hal turned in his seat to face her and went to speak but caught himself. What she'd said was true, but that was how the Empire functioned. The firstborn was the first choice in almost every aspect and had greater sway than the younger siblings. But that didn't mean it had to remain the same as before. Like him, Miri was a child of Empyrean blood. Maybe a little less rigidness would be good for the Empire.

He looked at her furrowed brow, and it hurt him to see her feel neglected. It certainly hadn't gotten better over the last two years, and that was his fault for not being there for her. Changing something so core to the Empire's function would be met with stiff competition, and he knew his father would be too traditional for that, but she was his sister. He had to become the heir if he wanted to even bring it up in court proceedings.

He reached for his sister's hand and cupped it in his.

"Miri, you deserve more recognition. Second born or not, you are Princess Miriam Skyborn, descendent of the Empyreans, daughter of Emperor Tiberius

Skyborn and Empress Irina Skyborn. You, me, we have the blood of gods in us. We can either make the Realmverse better or cast it into darkness like the firsts of our ancestors. They had a choice. So do we. But we, you and I," he said as he pointed between them, "need to do it together."

Miri smiled and leaned in, wrapping her arms around him. Hal embraced her and held her close. They stayed like that for a moment, comforted by each other. It was one of the safest places Hal knew of, and it was reassuring to know his sister had his back. And he would always have hers.

Miri pulled back. "I love you, Hal."

"I love you too, Meer. Always. Never forget that."

She played with the end of a long lock of hair before saying, "Shall we meditate together? Like before?

Hal smiled as he nodded. "I'd love that."

Hal opened the door and followed his sister over the small wooden bridge across the river. Birdsong caught his attention as he thought about the future. If everything stayed as it was, then he had no need to fret. Family was on his side, and that was all that mattered.

In the clearing on the other side of the bridge was a circular stone grown over with grass. Light from the suns shined down and brightened the clearing with its warmth.

They sat back-to-back on the stone and leaned against each other for support. Without a word, they held out their hands, and flames engulfed them. The flames grew in their palms before they reached out and formed a link with each other's fire. Hal took a deep breath and closed his eyes as the warmth of his sister's fire massaged the ailments of his thoughts away.

CHAPTER VI

Deep in the woods below the capital, Hal found himself sitting in the back seat of a small airspeeder. Its wings were short, and given it had only one engine in the back, he was surprised the little aircraft could carry the weight of four people. As air beat against its hull, it only reinforced his thoughts. He would've felt safer if it were he who piloted the vehicle and not the good Lord Carnn himself.

It wasn't that he didn't trust the lord; it was that he had spent so much time in command and doing things himself that it felt strange to be chauffeured around like the days before the war.

As he shifted in his seat, strapped down by the safety belts, the gnawing apprehension of not being in control wore against his resolve. He had to relearn that he didn't always need to be the one who dictated orders. Such ways were not compatible with the Code.

As he looked down, he felt as though he could reach out and touch the bushy green treetops. Though the man-made forest in the capital was impressive, the natural untamed beauty of the forests on the planet's surface compared to nothing. It served to soothe the apprehension that had wrapped around his shoulders. Those who lived across the planet in cities not suspended above the surface were luckier than most. Imperius was beautiful in its own right, but he had to admit architects and engineers could only do so much to rival nature.

Miri sat beside him, and next to her sat Neeux. Encased in golden full body armor, he wore the fire hawk emblem of the planetary guard's thrusterpack troopers on his chest piece and shoulder guards. Hal looked at the young man, who was no older than himself. Hazel eyes scanned the terrain below, while a metal arm replaced the previous one and rested on top of his helmet beside him. Hal knew the battle Neeux lost it in, for he was the one to pull the soldier out of the collapsed building. The sight made him realize how lucky he was to have only a few scars. He was happy to see that his brother-in-arms, and friend, was doing well after the injury.

Hal leaned forward in his seat and said, "So, Neeux, have you been keeping my sister out of trouble?"

Neeux turned to Hal, revealing the scar that ran from the top of his head down to the bottom of his left cheek, and said, "I have. Although, she's good at finding it."

Hal looked at his sister with a raised brow.

"Oh, come on. He counts every time I cut my finger as trouble," Miri said in defense.

"Vixera told me that this would be an easy job," Neeux said as he rubbed his short brown hair.

Miri only rolled her eyes with a small smile.

Neeux looked back to Hal and said, "Why do you ask, Prince Halcion?"

"Because he is Prince of the Empire and wishes to know more about what has happened in his absence," said Lord Carnn from the pilot's seat. "Knowledge is power."

"Or he's just being a good brother," Miri replied.

Hal smiled as the two bickered and Neeux scanned the treetops below. He loved the fact that his sister always had his back. She had a fire in her, lit by the torch of Empyrea, and was destined to do great things with it. With someone as loyal and skilled as Neeux by her side, there wasn't anything she couldn't do.

A sense of pride washed over him as his sister finished her last point, and Lord Carnn winked at him in the rearview mirror.

The airspeeder banked to the right, approaching a clearing in the forest. A circular building of concrete and stone with a golden spire on the roof took up the space in the clearing. Despite the location being off any Imperial map or chart, Lord Carnn seemed to know exactly where they needed to go, which brought more questions to Hal's mind than he wanted right now.

The engines blew dirt and pine needles into the air as the airspeeder descended. A circular path ran around the perimeter of the clearing, and more stone paths—five he counted—connected it to the building in the center.

The doors to the airspeeder opened, and the ramp formed. Hal followed the others out but fixed his eyes on the building in the middle, where the Imperial diamond of the Empyreans was carved.

What is this structure doing out here? He rarely traveled this far north, and the curiosity of finding something new on his own home-world excited him.

"Do you know what this is?" Lord Carnn asked. When nobody answered, he nodded. "Come with me."

They followed Lord Carnn to the double doors that led into the structure. Beside the doors stood a small pedestal with a palm reader that Lord Carnn rested his hand on. After a few seconds, the pedestal chimed, and the locks on the doors opened.

Inside, dim light lined the hallway that ran down to a central chamber. Stale air entered Hal's nose, telling him not many people came here or knew about it. Even Miri, who was in the Imperial Investigative Bureau, had eyes wide with curiosity.

As they followed the hallway and came to the inner chamber, light defeated darkness, revealing story etchings along the curved walls. One showed a hooded man cupping something in a hand while a sword of flames emerged from the other and was held outstretched. Another figure ten times his size with massive bat-like wings slumped to its knees in front of him.

He pointed to it. "Is that Xirna?"

Lord Carnn smiled in the way only a happy teacher could. "The Primordial Queen herself, fallen to the likes of the first Empyrean, Atis."

Hal looked around the room, trying to take in as much detail as possible, from the cracks in the ceiling to the dust and cobwebs in the darkest corners. He couldn't shake the wonderment he felt in this isolated place. Something in him yearned to understand something, but what it was alluded him. For now, he basked in curiosity.

"Why are we here?" Miri asked as she followed his gaze.

"To hear the true story of how Atis and Sarin, Empyreans, and the Primordials came to be," Lord Carnn said.

"I thought we knew that already," Hal said. "Atis bested Xirna in Wielding and banished her to the Kaleidosphere."

"Yes, but not in its entirety," Lord Carnn said as he stood in the center of the room. "Join me here."

The three of them moved toward him, and Lord Carnn raised a hand.

"I am sorry, Neeux, but this is only for those of the royal bloodline to witness."

"That's hardly fair," Miri said.

"This is sensitive information the Empire keeps highly guarded," Lord Carnn said.

Before Miri could interject, Neeux spoke. "It's okay, Princess Miriam. I'll stand guard outside."

Miri frowned as Neeux walked back down the dark hallway, the light from the entrance silhouetting his figure.

Hal placed an arm around his sister's neck and smiled when the ground below them began to shake. Lord Carnn stepped onto a part of the floor that sank into itself. The entire floor sank below the hallway and into a chasm.

As the floor descended further and touched the ground, Hal looked to where they now found themselves. Translucent trees formed their own forest along the bank of a lake, while blue and green light reminiscent of the bioluminescent jungles of Eroura shined along the rocky walls and ceiling. Rivers ran into the lake before it cascaded down a waterfall into an underground chasm. Hal could only stare at the beauty as Lord Carnn proceeded down a path.

He led them to the bank of the lake, where a hardlight generator activated and cool beams of blue hardlight formed. The beams met with another receiver in the middle of the lake that connected to a large hexagonal-shaped platform.

"What is this place?" Hal asked, but Lord Carnn kept his lips sealed.

As they walked across the lightbridge, blue light shined through the clear water like it did above. It was like looking through glass. Seeing no fish or foliage, Hal had more questions about the lake.

Lord Carnn stood in the center of the platform, where three swirls joined in the middle. As Hal and Miri followed, five pedestals rose around them in the water but offered nothing on their surfaces.

"Sit, young Empyreans, and brace for the story of your ancestors."

Hal and Miri sat like children in a schoolroom and waited for the information Lord Carnn contained. Hal only wondered what the Lord offered that the Imperial Archives did not. The older man dropped to his knees and gazed around the underground area before he spoke.

"Emperor Atis was here before. So too was Empress Sarin. How does it feel to walk where they once did?"

"It feels stagnant," Hal replied.

"Do you recall how the Empyrean bloodline came to be?"

"Once Atis and Sarin learned the Primordial magic, the Primordials granted them divine status, and so began the reign of the Empyreans," Miri said.

"Intelligent is the young princess," Lord Carnn said. "Though mere Mortals at first, created by the fundamentals of the Primordial beings entrenched in the laws of nature, Atis and Sarin learned the hidden art of Wielding."

"They were the first Fire Wielders. The first Wielders," Hal said.

"That they were." Lord Carnn looked upward before he continued. "They even caught the attention of the cunning Primordial queen, Xirna. Given their prowess and aptitude at honing and mastering Fire Wielding until it was a part of them, Xirna thought they would make good mediums between Primordials of the cosmos and Mortals of the Realmverse. She even helped the two leaders create a new plane of existence where those worthy mortals would go after death, Empyrea. Hence, they became the first Empyreans."

A splash in the lake caught Hal's attention, the sudden sound of life conflicting with his earlier observations. The water rippled as Lord Carnn continued.

"Do you know what happened after?"

Hal looked back to the older man. "Xirna betrayed them."

"But how?"

"Xirna used Madness on Sarin," Hal said.

"You know the ending. But do you know what led to that point?"

Hal went to answer, but nothing came out. He looked at Miri for a hint, but she too was at a loss for words.

Time after time he'd been told the Primordial Queen betrayed the first emperor and empress, but never had he asked how or why. The lore of the Empire said that Atis and Sarin freed it from the grips of the Primordials, but that was all, no detail or explanation. Perhaps he'd been young and naive, but that realization angered him. He'd always questioned orders during the war because he needed to know why his soldiers were being sent into harm's way. But now, with a simple history lesson, he failed to answer the Lord's question.

Lord Carnn nodded. "The Empire spread across Athos and united it under one flag for the first time in the planet's history. The moons followed soon after, and the young Empire of Athos became interplanetary. Atis became entrenched with Primordial knowledge and sought to learn everything he could while Sarin played a more motherly role to the Empire." He took a deep breath. "Xirna was impressed by her new mediums and offered them an accord: Pledge allegiance to the cosmos and receive rule of the Realmverse for eternity. Deny it and face subjugation."

"They rejected it?" Miri asked.

"After, Xirna called on her guardians to invade, but Atis, the ever knowing, had a trick up his sleeve. Through his studies of Wielding and the magic he harnessed, he created another realm through the very same Primordial cosmic knowledge Xirna used to aid in the creation of Empyrea and formed the Kaleidosphere."

"A void in the cosmos where life stagnates and is forgotten," Hal said. "The Kalidosphere was meant to be a place of punishment for cosmic entities."

Lord Carnn smiled and nodded. "With each guardian force sent there, Xirna and her Primordial brethren brought the fists of the cosmos down upon the budding Empire."

"Seems rather harsh," Miri said.

"What would you do if a new power rivaled your throne?" Lord Carnn asked. She didn't answer.

The lord had made his point: a threat was a threat and shouldn't be taken lightly. The question struck something deep within that made Hal question what he would do if something like that ever occurred. Before his thoughts could wander too far, Lord Carnn continued.

"At first, the Primordials seemed too great for our beloved Empyreans. Fire rained down on the Empire for years, burning all the way to Imperius. People went mad from the chaos, the never-ending fear and pain. The people begged Atis and Sarin to accept the offer, but the leaders would not have their people live as servants to cosmic gods or force their will upon the many other denizens of the Realmverse.

Another splash echoed through the cave, but Hal remained focused on Lord Carnn.

"The first true Primordial that stepped foot in the capital was banished into the Kaleidosphere by Atis and Sarin. And then the second. The third followed, and Xirna watched as her brothers and sisters disappeared from the void of space."

"So, what did she do?" Miri asked.

Lord Carnn raised his arms and looked around the chamber. "With knowledge accumulated from years of conflict, Atis and Sarin led the queen here. I'm sure you can still find the scorch marks from their battle along the walls. Xirna was cunning, but so was Atis. As the trio did battle, Atis opened a portal to the Kaleidosphere and sent the queen into the stagnant realm, but not before she inflicted her deadliest trick onto poor Sarin. As the queen vanished through the portal, Sarin's stone necklace glowed a dark purple, and she turned on Atis. Within a moment, Atis had to strike down the love of his life."

"Madness," Hal said, and Lord Carnn nodded. "How did she do it?"

Lord Carnn smiled. "I can't tell you everything, Prince Hal. That is for you to find out."

The light of the chasm brightened almost on cue and revealed five pillars in the lake with lights illuminating them for all to see. Etchings wrapped around them, depicting scenes that almost matched what Lord Carnn had explained. The pillars slowly rotated, revealing more of their stories, and Hal couldn't help but notice the similarities between what they depicted and what Lord Carnn had said. But despite the correlation, a wave of skepticism fell over him, and he wondered once more why this place was off the maps.

Hal focused on the closest pillar; it depicted Atis holding a pendant on a chain with swirl marks inside it while a creature with wicked spikes coming out of its head reached for it before being sucked into a portal.

This place wouldn't be here if it wasn't important to the Empire, Hal thought. He needed to know the full story of what this place was, but Lord Carnn's sigh broke him from his thoughts.

As he stood up, he said, "It is up to you to believe in what you want to believe in, though history has a way of repeating it whether we want it to or not." As Lord Carnn walked by them, he said, "Come now, before night falls on us."

CHAPTER VII

Early the next morning, Hal opened the rear door of the royal currus. Stretched longer than the others, it offered more room than a conventional passenger currus and provided a safer mode of transportation than his sister could with her driving.

As he stepped out, the spire of the Imperial Investigative Bureau towered above him just before the city wall. Clouds flirted with the tip of the spire while the twisted framework radiated the twin suns' rays in every direction. Near the entranceway stood a stone sign that read 'IIB Station Athos.' Patrol craft sirens blared from the hangars as a couple shot out and sped off.

Some agents were dressed in common tattered shirts and pants and looked more like laborers than special agents as they came and went from the tower. Others wore sleek silver jackets with soft padded armor under. The agents who passed Hal saluted and carried on.

Miri stepped out beside him, the silver sheen from her circlet blinding in the sunlight.

"So, what do you think?"

"Impressive, Meer. Never thought you would become an agent," Hal said as he turned to look at her. "I thought you were in the Academy to be a nurse like Kristilin?"

"Well, things change. I thought I could do better for Imperius by taking down criminals who violated the Code. Besides, one nurse is enough between the three of us. And enough noble children from Athos and Velra go into nursing."

"Are you saying she's unoriginal?" Hal teased.

Miri rolled her eyes. "No. I'm saying that while she is medically qualified and you're battle hardened, I can be the investigative one of the bunch. That way we all cover something different."

"Like a team."

"Exactly," she said. "Besides, I practically get free reign from the IIB Director so long as I stay within the bureau's parameters."

Hal smiled at her response, though now his thoughts wandered to his love. It had been days since he'd returned home, and though he knew lives were busy and people had things to do, he thought he would have seen her by now. He couldn't remember the last time he had heard her voice, let alone feel her touch. He felt a little guilty for that. War left little time for personal communication, but he could have tried a bit harder. He was a prince after all. But all he wanted to do now was hear her voice again.

Miri led the way to the front door of the IIB, but Hal stayed planted where he was. When he didn't follow her, Miri stopped and turned around, brow furrowed in concern.

"Hal? What's wrong?"

He looked up at her and realized he hadn't moved. "Nothing."

"No. Something is wrong. What is it?"

Being his younger sibling, Miri had a way to coerce information from him. Such a skill would be useful in her new line of work.

Hal took a deep breath and finally said, "Kristilin. Do you know where she is? It's odd for her to not show up."

Miri averted her eyes and looked at the concrete walkway at her feet. "Weird things happened after you left. Velra shut off communication with everyone. They went silent. Nothing in or out, and nobody knows why."

"Has anybody tried to make contact? Use the teleporters?" Hal asked. It felt like his heart sunk to the depths of his body and he couldn't pull it back up.

"Coordinates are blocked by something out of our reach with the teleportals," Miri said. "And agents tried to enter the hyperplane junction to Velra, but they were attacked."

"By whom?"

Miri shrugged. "Nobody knows because the teams never made it back. More attempts were made, but they met the same fate, and we've yet to figure out what's causing it. We've been too concentrated on the war and domestic issues."

"Well, the war is over now. Velra has been our longest standing ally. If something happened there, we need to figure it out."

"Hal, I know, but there are other things out of our control."

"Nothing is out of our control. There's always an option, a way. If Kristi is in danger . . ."

His voice grew hoarse as he thought about the worst possible outcomes, and he started to pace back and forth. He stifled the prickly feeling in the back of his throat. The thought of something happening to Kristilin was just as painful as something happening to his sister or father. She was practically family. If he could, he would blow open a channel in the hyperspace lane and sail toward Velra. But his sister had more knowledge on this matter, and he couldn't go in blind.

Miri walked over and placed an arm around him. "Kristilin is my friend too, Hal. I want to find her as much as you do, but resources are spread thin right now."

Hal managed to nod in agreement, though it stung his heart to know there was an uncertainty about Velra and Kristilin.

"Come on," Miri said as she tugged his arm. "I want to show you what I've been up to while you were away. Hopefully it can take our minds off this for a while."

She led him through the lobby of the IIB, where guards saluted them. Most agents had to at least flash their identification cards before they entered, but being children of the emperor had its perks. They stepped onto one of the swiftlift elevators, and the doors closed behind them as Miri hit the button for their floor.

She turned to face Hal and said, "This building was instrumental to the war effort, you know."

"How so?"

"Besides decrypting the Primordial Gate codes, we also repelled domestic attacks."

The floors sped by with a beep to signal. Hal looked at his reflection in the polished silver of the walls as the soft hum of the swiftlift eased his worried mind for only a second before he spoke.

"Who would dare attack Imperius?"

"Not so much the city itself, but villages and towns across the world. At first, we thought they were nothing more than bandits preying on civilians," Miri said as the doors to the swiftlift opened.

They stepped out to continue down a hallway decorated with various pictures of notable IIB agents from the last thousand years. Before then, the IIB had only been a branch of the military, but the empress at the time had deemed it necessary to make the bureau its own entity.

As Hal followed his sister down the hall and saw the bureau's achievements and how many cases had been closed, it brought him great satisfaction to know Miri wanted to be a part of this group.

The door at the end of the hallway slid open for them, and Hal followed his sister in. Miri plopped down on a chair behind a bluewood desk that encased a smaller version of a holotable in the center. To one side of the room was one-way glass that looked into a vacant interrogation room. On the other side of the room stood an investigation panel with various handwritten notes and images of people of different races: Human, Polarian, Zeran, and Digard. Miri sat with a proud expression on her face as Hal looked through the large windows that overlooked the forests below.

"My little sister went off to become an IIB agent," Hal said with pride. "Imagine that."

"Someone had to take care of the planet while you were off fighting," she said with a smirk.

Hal nodded in agreement. He pointed to the investigation board. "Who are they?"

"Remember the domestic issues? Well, they call themselves Codebreakers. Radicals who want to overthrow the throne and establish their own form of government. We've identified some of their leaders. Most of them aren't even Human; they're planetary nationals from surrounding star nations."

"So, what are we doing about them?"

Miri sighed, and Hal tilted his head at her response.

"We have rumors that they're planning an attack on Imperius. The scale can't be that big because they're a small group of disgruntled off-worlders who don't like us. But we can't get the resources we need to put in place because of—"

"Varim?" Hal asked.

Miri nodded. "He froze all IIB activities outside of the planet. Of course, he didn't tell the team working on decrypting the Gate codes. By that time we were all preparing for the finale of the war. And now we know the rest of the story."

"So, these Codebreakers could be terrorizing other worlds in the Empire right now," Hal said, his voice laced with frustration.

"Yup. I only found out after our first meeting with Varim when we returned home. We've been limited to Athos activities only to, and I'll quote him, 'Strengthen the defensive and investigative resources of the home world.'" Miri shook her head and spun around to face the glass windows that overlooked the forest. "Because we need all one thousand agents to investigate a group of barely a hundred terrorists. Seems like overkill to me."

"This is why we need Father back," Hal said as he crossed his arms. "He carries more weight with the people than Varim."

Miri spun back around and typed on her holographic keyboard, and an image of the Athonian star system appeared. Athos was fifth in line of orbit around the twin suns. Several other celestial bodies under the Empire orbited peacefully, like nothing was going on in their worlds.

With a sigh, Miri brought up holographic images from various worlds showing ruined buildings and destroyed vehicles. They looked more like warzones than worlds within the Empire. Fires raged in one of the images, and corpses lay scattered around—dead Imperial civilians. The sight angered him, and his muscles tensed.

"This is from the moon Jurrium. Two weeks ago, apparently. The local guard tried to repel the attack. Unfortunately, the Codebreakers used an unmanned drone to cause this."

"They need to be stopped. Bloodshed within the Empire should not happen," Hal said as he leaned over the chair his sister sat on.

"Which is why I could use a favor from you," Miri said as she turned to look at him. "I know you and Varim don't really like each other—I don't like him either—but he will listen to you. You are the eldest, and if you push him to—"

"Consider it done, Meer."

Miri smiled in agreement. "They need to be stopped."

Before they could say anything else, an explosion rocked the IIB. Alarms sounded throughout the halls, and another explosion followed. The windows shattered, and Hal shielded his sister from the airborne glass. A voice barked orders over the intercom, alerting of an attack, while agents swarmed the hallways.

A small gunship only big enough to fit a few people passed by the blown-out windows. One of the doors opened upward, and a flurry of energy bolts let loose. Hal and Miri charged themselves with energy, their necklaces glowing a hot orange, before they raised a ward barrier of flames. The bolts slammed into the protective wall of flames as the gunship ascended out of view.

Hal hurried to where the windows were and looked up to see a couple assailants jump the gap left by vacant window frames and into the building.

He looked back to his sister. "Any ideas? Codebreakers?"

Miri frantically brought up a map of the building. Various sectors were now covered in red while others were blue. The ground level, mid-levels, and top spire were all in red. Smoke began to cloud the hallways as more agents coordinated efforts to figure out what was going on and to help those injured by the blasts.

"Damn it. They are Codebreakers. Level 623," she said as she pointed to the map. "There was an interrogation going on with a suspected Codebreaker picked up a few weeks ago. They're trying to break them out."

"Any ideas on how to get up there? We're below the mid-level explosion. Stairwells are probably collapsed, and the swiftlifts most likely aren't operating."

"I can call a patrol craft to us," Miri said as she worked on the holotable.

After a few seconds, sirens from a patrol craft rang through the air, and one came to a stop just outside the windows. Its door separated to open, and Hal and Miri jumped in. Displays faced them on the dashboard, and a terminal with a slew of information separated their seats. Miri went to work typing on the console while Hal took the controls in both hands and went to meet the assailants.

Chatter came through the radio. "Shots fired. Shots fired," the voice on the other end said before another explosion cut the communication.

A moment later, the assailants boarded their gunship and sped off. Hal punched the throttle and gave chase with lights and sirens blaring. The gunship darted toward the surface only to pull up in time to skim the treetops of the forest below. Hal stuck close behind them, not willing to give up an inch of distance. If they dared attack an IIB facility, they had courage to do something even greater.

"Get me close," Miri said as she brought the gun turrets on either side of the patrol craft to life.

It felt personal. These derelicts had attacked his home and sister and had made his people suffer. Unlike Varim, Hal would not sit idly by and watch it happen. Something would get done under the watch of the royal siblings. The only thing that awaited these Codebreakers was a tribunal and a cell to rot in.

The gunship rolled and dipped below a mountain, following the contour of the surface. Hal followed and pushed the throttle as far as it could go. Both ships' engines sprayed water as they went over a lush river delta lined with trees as green as emeralds. The gunship turned and followed the river upstream before it cut left into a valley, but Hal knew better than to fall for such a simple diversion. He pushed the airbrake and tailed the gunship into the valley before punching the throttle again. A sonic boom shook the treetops as the patrol craft raced toward the gunship.

They gained on the gunship through the valley, and Hal could taste the satisfaction of catching the criminals. By the look on Miri's face, she wanted nothing more than to catch them too.

The gunship was only a couple hundred yards in front of them now, and Miri let loose the autocannons.

Heavy bursts of ballistic rounds raced through the sky as the gunship's tail guns fired a laser volley. Hal swerved to avoid the attack while Miri aimed and fired another burst. Dozens of heavy rounds pierced the gunship's unshielded hull and ignited a fuel cell. The explosion rocked the Codebreaker ship, and it crashed to the forested ground below.

Hal brought the patrol craft to a hover near it as another explosion shook the area. Off in the distance from the direction of the city, half a dozen blue and red lights were heading toward them.

Lowering the ship a safe distance away, Hal breathed a sigh of relief. He looked over to his sister and said, "Good job, Agent Miri."

She glared at the ship with pure anger. If anyone had survived the wreckage, he felt bad for them, because they would have to deal with her. Hal looked back to the city, where black smoke billowed from the IIB tower. The sight made him want to watch the gunship explode into a million pieces.

Sirens from the other patrol crafts echoed as they approached. Hal and Miri disembarked their patrol craft and shielded their eyes as the patrol crafts descended, sending debris flying in every direction. Someone crawled from the wreckage, and officers rushed the ship and slapped energy binds onto the survivor before throwing them into the back of the patrol craft. More officers swarmed the scene in a cacophony of deafening sirens and blinding lights.

Miri turned to Hal and said, "Well, ready for your parade now?"

CHAPTER VIII

Not much could beat the view of Imperius from the air at dusk. Marked with the diamond crest of the Empire, the small royal airspeeder Hal found himself in sailed above the megascape, where soft lights from the city illuminated the grounds during the twilight hours. The running lights flashed off the tips of the wings as Hal looked down to the streets. Currus limited by gravity filled the busy roads and highways that connected the different city districts. The hum of traffic echoed off the high-rises and made its way up to the royal transport ship.

Airspeeders raced through the air channels between the buildings while citizens enjoyed themselves in the various parks or admired the scenic views from the tops of towers. A city in the sky built by the hands of mortals—nobody had fathomed such a creation could come to fruition.

Centuries ago, architects from across the star systems had laughed at Athonians for even suggesting such a thing. Like his people usually did, they'd turned the laughs into a dare. But now time looked at who'd laughed last.

The city stretched for as far as he could see in every direction, a sea of skyscrapers separated by terraformed forests and lakes able to withstand the frigid temperatures.

More lights from buildings began to replace the waning light of the twin suns, and some even displayed 'welcome home' signs for weary soldiers on their sides, flashing the royal colors of gold and silver with the returning units' names. The sight made Hal smile. Imperius was a marvel of Athonian engineering, and no one would allow it to be tampered with.

"We're nearing the start of the parade," Miri said from beside him as she shifted in her seat. "Pilot, hurry up."

Beside her, Neeux sat and looked out of the windows of the airspeeder. Hal knew he was stoic in nature. Even during the war, he could always count on Neeux to keep a level head no matter what. When he pulled him out of that building, Hal saw the mangled arm and knew because of his orders that his friend would lose it. It was an unpalatable part of war. To send men and women—brothers and sisters—to what could be their last minutes alive always weighed on him and he saw the effects first now with Neeux's arm.

Hal adjusted the belt of his silver robes as the ship crossed the boundaries of a district where streets and buildings turned to lakes and forests. Replicated from the infancy of concept, everything found in the scenic areas had been handpicked and sculpted to live amongst the citizens in the city, and some decided to live with them. The lack of street noise provided a quiet place to rest, and the woods sang with the chirps of crickets.

Large pillars with display screens dotted the land and towered over the treetops. The display screens kept those out here in the loop regarding city affairs. No one went without access to some sort of information.

The trees looked just like those down on the surface minus the dangers that came with them. Animals native to the forest below had found a home in the sky city. Deer pranced through the wooded areas while birds squawked at them from overhead. A flight of graceful valor eagles soared next to the airspeeder like a fighter squadron, their golden feathers reflecting light back onto the ground like roaming spotlights. Hal smiled at the symbol of the Empire. It was a moment to reflect on everything that had happened over the last two years.

He gazed out toward the city. Everything felt different from before, like a nation trying to learn how to live properly again. Time had been taken from him, and now he had to earn it back. Hal cleared his throat.

"I didn't even get to see you walk the stage at the Academies of Imperius."

Miri stopped scrolling on her datacard and lowered it to her lap.

"It was different not having you there," she said. "Empty like. It wasn't easy." Miri covered her exposed leg with her golden robes and sighed. "When you left, I felt lost. You'd just graduated from the Naval School of the Academy and taught me so much in the two years we had together, especially in our leadership classes. Kristilin graduated from the Medical School, and I was so proud of you both. Seeing you and her walk the stage was amazing, and it made me eager to follow you. Then you were sworn in as a junior officer in the navy and . . ." Her voice trailed off as she looked out the window of the airspeeder. She straightened the parts of her hair that weren't braided to perfection as the soft orange glow of the sunset turned the interior of the vehicle the same color. "The last two years of the Academy weren't easy. The war came, and I saw things I didn't like. Some even made me angry at you. So much political arrogance from everyone."

"Is that why you ignored my calls and messages?" Hal asked as he pointed to his sister's datacard, a wave of guilt washing over him as Miri's lip trembled. The war seemed to have affected the Empire more than he'd thought, and it was his father and sister who'd had to bear the weight of it back home. It pained him, but it was true.

"You know it wasn't my idea to leave. Not like that anyway. Everything was a rush."

"I know, and I wanted to see you off, but I couldn't," Miri said. "Father thought I was weak for that. He said the Imperial Council wouldn't stand for a weak leader. Even wounded and disfigured early in the war, he managed to see you go, but . . . I was too angry and sad to see you off. Things weren't the same after that. I had to fight for everything." She looked back at him, tears glistening in her stoic eyes. "I didn't take anything from anyone anymore, and it pushed a lot of people away. So I changed my area of study and joined the Law Enforcement School of the Academy. I guess I changed a little."

"We all changed, Meer. This war wasn't what any of us wanted, but it was something we had to do for our home world," Hal said. "You've become a strong young woman, and I've always been proud of you."

She nodded with a smile, the sunlight reflecting off the silver of her circlet. "Just wait until you see what happens," Miri said as the aircraft began its descent, her eyes stern and fixed.

Hal looked out the window, and the tops of the trees disappeared as the ship lowered into a clearing. All around, hundreds of Imperial soldiers guarded and waited near vehicles and equipment. No doubt all of this was to show the might of the Imperial military in conjunction with Hal's return.

As the doors opened, Miri said, "Right . . . Okay. Yes, we're in position now . . . Just make it worth it."

"Business?" Hal asked as Miri put her data receiver away.

"Just a little surprise at the end," she said with a smirk as she stood from her seat. "Come now. We need you in position."

As Hal followed her across the clearing, hundreds of people prepared escort ships and special barges for the parade. The setup stretched deep into the woods, and workers snaked through the trees, rushing to finish up the last bits of work before the parade started. The array of people—from the common shipbuilder and maintenance crews to the highest of military brass and ace pilots—caught him by surprise. He'd thought the parade would consist of a few open-platform barges and some fireworks, but this was far more elaborate.

Anytime a soldier or citizen aiding the parade came near, they stopped and saluted him. When he saluted back, the smile on their face was enough to make him think the last two years had somehow been worth the pain. His people were safe.

As he continued to follow his sister, he felt the strange presence of someone lurking nearby. When he turned to look, he was instantly knocked to the ground. The person pinning him down was dressed in armor, and Hal was ready to order them to a firing squad when they spoke.

"Gotcha now."

He recognized the voice. "Tavis?"

"Right on," the soldier said as he removed his helmet and smiled at Hal. The two exchanged a laugh as Tavis helped Hal up and said, "Been too long since I saw your mug."

"I know. You ran off and joined the city guard," Hal said with a chuckle.

"I couldn't let you play the hero by yourself. I mean, from a high-altitude shock trooper to commander of the invasion force is an accomplishment to be reckoned with," Tavis replied with a slap on the shoulder.

"You know what they say," Hal began.

"From H.A.S.T to Brass," the two said together with a laugh.

"I've been assigned to your personal detail for the parade," Tavis said.

"Yes, and that can be changed rather quickly," Miri said as she came stomping back. "I need my brother to be in one piece and clean for the parade." She brushed the dirt off Hal with a glare toward Tavis.

"Relax, Meer. This is the most work these robes have seen," Hal joked as he threw an arm around Tavis's neck. "I just wish Kristi were here to see this."

Miri froze and looked at him like a deer in headlights. Her eyes darted to the ground. Kristilin's absence pained them both, and he'd brought it back up at a horrible time. His own eyes drifted to the dirt, but before he could say anything else, the grumble of engines from more aerial vehicles landing drowned out any conversation. Without another word, Miri turned around and walked toward the curruscraft before them. Hal looked at Tavis, who only shrugged before they followed.

Larger than a normal currus, the curruscraft version had two large engines on the back with an open square shaped design. A pilot's tower sat at the center with railings and plenty of seating all around the vehicle. Already onboard were a young man and woman, the remaining members of the Ragnivrok clan.

Dressed in a silky silver shirt and fine golden pants, the dark-haired man greeted Hal with a firm handshake.

"It's been a while, Haywell. Glad to see you."

Haywell smiled with a simple nod. "It has, and what a time to reacquaint with a dear cousin. I apologize that my brute of a brother smudged your robes."

"Nothing a quick wash can't take out," Hal said with a smirk.

"Hopefully my sister—"

The redheaded woman beside Haywell threw her arms around Hal and brought him in for a hug that could've made the toughest soldiers gasp for air. She pulled back and looked at Hal with deep green eyes.

"Nevermind," Haywell said as he shook his head.

"Look how my little cousin grew up," the woman said.

"I'm younger than you by, like, a few days." Hal smirked. "It's good to see you again, Vixera. How's the Marshal Service? Any big hunts going on in the Realmverse?"

"More than you can imagine, Hal," Vixera said as she showed off her dark blue-and-black dress uniform. "But we'll have more time to catch up later. Maybe race dusters again like old times."

"Sounds like a plan. I always have time for family," Hal said.

Miri stood beside Hal and looked him over, making sure he was in tip-top shape. "Cousins or not, get in your positions, you two. This needs to be perfect for my brother, and I won't let anyone ruin it." Miri turned back to Hal with a smile. "Whatever anyone else thinks, I'm happy for you. You sacrificed a lot, and I didn't know it at the time, but I am proud to be your sister, Hal."

"Are you trying to get me to cry? Because it's working."

"Please don't. That'll ruin the pictures," she said with a playful smile as the engines of the curruscraft roared to life.

The first part of the parade through the forest district proved to be a little boring. Only a few farmers paid them any mind. As he glanced back at the others, Neeux, Vixera, and Tavis exchanged weapon knowledge and Haywell sat with his nose buried in a datacard. It was safe to say that the parade was a bore so far. But once they entered the industrial district, the caravan was met with thunderous applause as they sailed in between the buildings. Hundreds of citizens waved as Hal marked his return for all to see.

It felt nice, but as Hal scanned the audience, he noticed patrol crafts hovering at the tops of the buildings all along the parade route.

Hal leaned over to Miri. "Security?"

Miri nodded. "Can't have enough, especially with what happened earlier."

Hal looked back at the patrol crafts flanking the parade and spotted stagnant officers on the tops of buildings while flashing lights from other patrol crafts monitored the crowd below. The sight of so many officers brought some ease to his crowded mind. He knew they would keep those in attendance safe from any hostilities.

Confetti rained down on them as the parade left the industrial district and moved into the capital. Even more patrol craft hovered close by while some of the most trained soldiers lay perched on rooftops with sniper rifles at the ready.

The crowds thickened along the streets below, and sirens and horns blared over the normal noise of city life. Beautiful orchestral music played, amplified through the speakers around the parade line, as the Imperial Palace of Athos glowed silver and gold. When their curruscraft crossed over the royal courtyard, the first of the fireworks exploded into the air. Hal looked up and smiled when he read the message in the sky: 'Welcome Home.' It felt like Inception Day, and if this was anything to go by, that would be an even greater event.

Tavis leaned in and said, "Welcome home, buddy."

"Hal, when you do eventually become the most popular emperor the Empire has ever seen, do please remember us commoners," Haywell said with a friendly pat on the shoulder.

"Let's not get ahead of ourselves," Hal said with a smirk.

"It's only a matter of time," Neeux said from behind him.

Lights of gold and silver roamed all over the courtyard as people danced below them, laughing and shouting Hal's name. Flags with the diamond insignia in front of a silver sash that stretched from one end to the other, and on a blanket of gold, waved in the breeze. The sight triggered a slight burn in his nose, and he stifled the effects of becoming teary-eyed. Nothing made him feel more patriotic

than to see the Empire's banner fly high and proud. It showed that after everything, they were resilient and would never back down.

Hal almost worried if all the attention would upset the high minister, but right
now, he didn't care. To see the people care for him and chant his name meant more
than anything. If this was not reason enough for the council to grant him the title
of Crown Prince, then he didn't know what was. He threw an arm around his
sister and smiled.

"Thanks, Meer."

She responded with a smile.

The parade inched closer to the palace at the acropolis, and people nearly hung
out of their windows to catch a wave from the prince. Hal indulged them and
waved back, making sure to get as many as he could.

A flash of light from a far-off building blinded Hal for a moment, like something reflecting off a window, and when he looked down, a red dot of a laser was
dead center on him.

He charged his hands with fire energy and raised a wall to catch the energy bolt.
An audible gasp came from the hundreds of people who witnessed the event,
and everyone onboard their curruscraft ducked for cover behind the pilot's tower
while other patrol crafts hurried in the direction of the energy bolt with lights and
sirens blaring.

Tavis activated a hardlight shield, the photons of refined light connecting to the
outer framework. It produced a sturdy shield made out of pure light. He stood in
front of Haywell and scanned the other buildings for another attack while Vixera
and Neeux drew their weapons. Miri turned to the pilot of the curruscraft and
ordered them to make an emergency landing when the patrol crafts opened fire
on the suspected building and put the firework show to shame.

"What in the hell?" Miri exclaimed. "Are you all right?"

Hal kept an arm around her with one hand still charged. "I'm fine. Are they
Codebreakers?"

"Almost certainly, and I hope those patrol crafts didn't kill whoever that was
just yet," Miri said as her piercing eyes looked at Hal. "I have questions."

CHAPTER IX

Hal opened his eyes and grimaced at the headache throbbing at his temples. He lay there for a moment, his heartbeat pounding in his head. Last night had certainly been a fun one. It had consisted of a few too many beers amongst a small private group.

Praetorian royal guards had locked down the event hall with a heavy presence to deter anything else from escalating. It was their sworn duty to protect the royal family, and they'd done their job last night. Hal would have to put in a word of high praise about them when his father improved. It was a shame he was under such tight lock and key, but Hal assumed it was for the best considering all that had occurred since his return.

When he found the strength, Hal pushed himself up and threw the silk sheets off. He hung his legs over the side of the bed and rested his head in his hands as he took a deep breath to relieve the discomfort.

Beside his bed stood an end table where the liquid of life sat patiently for him. As he downed the glass of water, his body thanked him, and the drums in his head dissipated for a moment.

He looked at the table again, where a holoframe scrolled through a few pictures. As he took it in his hands, the pictures brought a smile to his face, but one in particular stood out to him.

Kristilin was dressed in white and purple silk clothes and held his arm, her white hair flowing over her slender blue shoulders, striking lavender eyes looking back at him. Her long, pointed ears poked through her straight hair, which he'd always found cute. Hanging around her neck was the double lily necklace he'd gifted her for her birthday prior. He recalled the location where his sister had taken the photo: a secluded island on the moon of Jurrium, where their families vacationed. They had been about sixteen at the time, but now, at twenty-two, he remembered it like it was only a few days ago. Times had been much simpler without the fear of war.

As he stared at the photo, he realized the war had taken a toll on everyone involved. He wanted to find Kristi for a chance to explain what had happened and to know she was safe. If what Miri had said was true and Velra had shut all communication down, he had to find a way to get word to her or about her. There was no telling what her reaction would be, but if there was a chance their love had outlasted two turmoil-filled years of violence and separation, he needed to take the chance.

He reached across the bed where his silver jacket lay and slipped his hand into the top pocket. Out came the locket he always kept with him, and inside were the two photos he cherished: one of him, Miri, and Kristilin, and the other of him and Kristilin. She always wore that necklace just like Miri always wore her circlet.

For two years it had kept him going to be able to see them again. He felt halfway complete having been reunited with his sister, but there was still a large void in his heart. He had to find Kristilin.

Hal placed the holoframe back down before walking across his room to where a mirror stood. Tired white eyes stared back at him, and his dark brown hair was a mess. His reflection reminded him of the cost of war. Scars from plasma burns and shrapnel wounds were scattered across his body. One scar from a Polarian energy sword stretched from the top of his left shoulder down across his chest. He'd been naive to what battle could become, and his inexperience had cost him that day. Maybe Lord Carnn was right in that he didn't understand how to use the art of Wielding fully. Perhaps there was more for him to learn.

A loud knock came from his bedroom door, making Hal wince.

Miri strutted in, her gold and silver robes pressed to perfection with the diamond crest embroidered above her left breast. Stopping before him, her gaze shifted to the holoframe before she spoke. "Simpler times. We'll find her. How are you?"

"Fine," Hal said with a groan as the drumbeats returned and he took a seat back on his bed.

"That wasn't exactly the welcome home party I'd had in mind for you," she said as she sat on the edge of the bed with him. "If there's one good thing that came from last night, it's that we caught the shooter."

"That's what we need now. More issues," Hal said before he took another swig of water and ran a hand through his hair in an effort to tame it. "Codebreaker for sure?"

Miri nodded. "A lone wolf operative it seems. Not affiliated with the larger cell, judging by preliminary reports."

"Sounds more like a malcontent."

"Either way, they're off the streets, and it gives us another one to interrogate."

Hal nodded and stood up. He walked to the large windows that overlooked the city. The light battled his eyes for a moment until the glare was gone. It looked quieter with not as many ships roaming the skies.

"So, why are you here so early?"

"Varim. He wants us to explain what happened last night," Miri said as she met him at the balcony windows. "I've worked too hard to get where I am, and with his emergency powers still in effect, I'm afraid he'll take me off the terrorist investigation unit."

"Meer, we'll handle it."

She looked at him and took a deep breath. When she exhaled, she reached for his hand and nodded. "It's good to have you back."

The two of them stood in front of High Minister Varim with their hands behind their backs. Minister Nakami stayed silent beside the throne, wincing at the sheer volume of the angry words that echoed through the hall. Varim lashed out between breaths, pointing out in fine detail how idiotic and unsafe the children of the royal court had been to expose themselves while a threat to Imperius still wandered about.

Verbal abuse was nothing new; Hal had years of experience standing up to the council and pompous elected officials who thought they were the next best thing since the invention of the HoloNet so long ago. His father was never aggressive like them, just stern and clear in his guidance. Varim had the clarity of a blind goat searching for grass. Hal only hoped the tense meetings would fade away once their father awoke from his sickness.

Hal found it ironic, though, considering this entire issue had been made relevant by Varim's legislative actions. Surely the high minister knew the reduction of IIB agents across the system would only encourage such extreme behavior.

High Minister Varim smacked the end of his elaborate cane on the marbled floor. "I demand an explanation for this! Why are terrorists running around in the city?"

"It was a mistake," Miri answered. "More preparations should have been made to ensure nothing would jeopardize the people. I should have been clearer to the guards."

"You should have been clearer in your head," Varim said. "I will not stand for this insolence. It is your duty as Princess of the Empire and an agent of the Imperial Investigative Bureau to weed out these stains in our society. Had you done your job, the emperor would not be in a critical condition."

Miri's eyes widened.

Hal bit his tongue for as long as he could, but to pin the attacks on his sister's supposed lack of results was too much.

The emergency powers have gone to Varim's head, he thought, and the look from Minister Nakami backed up his claim.

Hal took a step forward. "High Minister Varim, Miri has alerted the palace guard and police forces to potential terror attacks and assassination attempts before. This is nothing new. Our forces are spread thin between the Empire and now Polaris. This was bound to happen, and proper measures need to be taken before we have a crisis on our hands. Had the council acted on her investigations in time, this whole ordeal would have been avoided. Trust in my sister, because I do." Hal looked at his sister with a wink. "But I'm sure this newfound threat will gain the attention of our *temporary* sovereign."

The high minister stared at them with cold and calculating eyes, a certain smugness on his face. Hal had never liked him, but this was not the time to act out of order. Varim shared a look with Minister Nakami before they both nodded.

"It has," Varim said. "To combat this stain on our history, I will grant the bureau permission to extend its investigative efforts back to where they once were. And you, Princess Miriam, will have any means necessary to weed out these traitors. Do not disappoint, and make sure whoever leads this faction is dealt with. Succeed, and this might be a worthy effort the Imperial Council will consider for heirship."

"Heirship?" Hal said. "On what authority?"

"Section 7. Chapter 5. *In case of immediate problematic events that would hinder the furtherance of the Empyrean legacy from ruling the Empire, all requirements regarding an heir will be null and void,*" Varim said.

Hal tensed up. This was nothing more than a slimy political game, but this one hit differently. He was happy for his sister to have her chance to prove she cared enough about the Empire to serve as an empress, but he felt betrayed by the council for not deeming his two-year sacrifice in fighting the Polarians as worthy enough. He stayed from any outbursts that would further jeopardize his own chances to prove himself. When his father recovered, there would be an investigation into the following of the Code.

"We will discuss this in an emergency meeting once Emperor Tiberius is well," Hal said.

Varim shot a quick glance at Hal. Hal only stood tall and proud. He knew what kind of reaction the high minister was trying to evoke, but he refused to allow it to take hold.

Miri looked on in shock, glancing at Hal before going back to the high minister.

"Thank you. I won't," Miri said.

The high minister nodded and turned back to Hal. "As for you. This was all done in your name. Lives were threatened with senseless festivities."

"Hardly my fault," Hal said under his breath. He cocked his head to the side, his voice stern. "We just won a war, a war the people across Athos and the Empire suffered through. Done in my name, yes, but it was the result of years of blood, sweat, pain, and loss."

"Also in your name," High Minister Varim added.

"The war? In my name? I can point out the reason the council wanted to wage war, but allow me to reacquaint you with what war means. I have held people—brothers and sisters of the Empire—in my arms as they took their last breath, high minister. When were you on the plasma-scorched battlefield where the smell of burnt corpses filled your nostrils? Have you seen the blood of innocents spilled? I have. I've seen people burned alive and heard their screams. I've seen bodies riddled unrecognizable by explosions and arms and legs separated from their torso. Tell me, High Minister Varim, what have you done as the highest representative on this council besides spit poisonous lies and treat the Code as nothing but wasted words?"

"It was started in the Skyborn name, was it not?" Varim added.

Hal nearly lunged at the man.

"Bite your tongue," Minister Nakami said. "You would be so disingenuous, High Minister Varim, to see the late empress as nothing more than a commoner. I won't stand for disrespect in this sacred hall built by our Empyreans. You are a representative of the Third District of Athos and speaker for the council. Act like one."

Varim glared at Hal as the minister finished lashing out. Hal stood there with a gaze that would make any soul tremble before him. The high minister was nothing more than a politician who'd long outstayed his elected welcome. So many things would change in accordance with the Code if Hal took the throne, but he had to do it the right way. That was the only way he wanted to do it.

"I have a simple task for you, one that you have done numerous times," Varim finally said as he removed a small datacard from his pocket. "Our Inception Day is near, and we will hold a grand celebration to mark our victory in battle and the anniversary of our empire. We hope Emperor Tiberius will be well enough to attend." High Minister Varim leaned forward on the throne and held the datacard out to Hal. "Go to the vault within the Imperial archives and extract the files marked for Inception Day. Try not to read them, young prince. These plans are meant to be seen by everyone at the same time, including you." Varim smiled. "This simple task could amount enough evidence to the Imperial Council to reopen talks about your future."

Hal narrowed his eyes. "You can't be serious. After everything? You're playing games with the Code, high minister."

"I am dead serious, Prince Halcion."

High Minister Varim stared Hal down, and the sternness of his words sent a shiver up Hal's spine that hit every nerve ending. Something in the high minster's voice concerned him. He worried if he was being played again or if he was too blinded by frustration to see that Varim was being truthful. His chest knotted up, and he shifted his stance before giving the man a nod of acknowledgement. Hal approached Varim and snatched the datacard from his hands, avoiding the crooked smile Varim showed.

"Good. Now go. We have much to prepare for."

When they turned to leave, the high minister called out, "Except you, Princess Miriam. We have things to discuss about the security of our people within these walls."

Miri looked at Hal with confusion, but he placed a hand on her shoulder and smiled. He didn't trust Varim as far as he could throw him. Miri's confusion turned to a stern gaze as she side-eyed the high minister. Hal knew she could handle herself, and this was a chance for her to stand out without his help. As much as he disliked the man, Varim was only a politician, a human.

As he glanced back at Varim on the throne, the sight almost made Hal engulf it in flames. Such a sight would have angered the past rulers of the Empire.

"Something wrong?" Varim asked.

Hal squeezed his sister's shoulder and smiled. "Just making sure my sister is okay. It's been a rocky few days."

"Well, leave your idle chitchat for later. I am sure she is more than ready for these talks."

Miri nodded and gave Hal a small smile before she joined Varim. After they disappeared behind one of the side chambers in the throne room, Hal turned toward the massive oak doors carved with the diamond insignia and left the throne room.

CHAPTER X

As Hal crossed the courtyard toward the Imperial Archives, he looked at the building the assassin had perched himself on. Smoke rose from where the patrol crafts had laid into the structure with energy weapons, skeletal frames and hanging glass broken into a hole. He could not understand why someone in the capital would result to terroristic attempts. Things would change for the better if he became Crown Prince; all he had to do was get it.

Footsteps approached from behind him. He pulled out his kyr and aimed it at the throat of whoever had tried to sneak up on him. When he saw who it was, though, he sighed and sheathed the golden hardlight energy knife.

Tavis stood in front of him with a stunned but amused look. Leather buckles and straps held his energy-dampening cuirass in place, while boots, leg guards, and leather arm guards were strapped around the compression suit under the armor.

Hal looked his cousin up and down and shook off the worry he'd had just seconds before.

"A little on edge? You can't walk the streets alone, Hal," Tavis said. "General's orders."

"I've done it before," Hal replied as he continued toward the archives. Rumbles of thunder echoed in the distance as a thunderstorm began to form over the plains beyond the mountains. "I've had more than a few shots try to take me out."

"May be true, but I'm not going against the general's orders. Plus, my commander would skin my hide if I went against orders."

"Fine," Hal said. He looked at Tavis, who kept pace with him. "Maybe you have some more information. Kristilin?"

"The hyperspace junction is cut off and no interplanetary transmissions are coming in or out."

Hal stopped in his tracks and looked at his friend. He took a deep breath before exhaling his frustration. "I know all of that. What I need to know is when someone last made contact with her or with Velra, who she was with, and what caused Velra to virtually disappear from the star charts and go into isolation. Our longest standing and oldest ally is gone. And that doesn't worry anyone? I need straight answers, Tavis."

Those walking the plaza grounds turned to Hal, who stood with his fists balled and nails digging into his palms, almost shaking with anger and frustration. He glared at Tavis before his eyes shifted to those who'd glanced at him. When their eyes met the prince's, they quickly looked away and moved out of sight. Hal looked up to the sky, closed his eyes, and took another deep breath.

Tavis crossed his arms. "I'm sorry, Hal. We just don't know."

Hal began to walk again, the tall, cylindrical shaped building of the archives with a large stained-glass window that ran down the length of the front was in sight. "We were all so close."

His heart sank to the deepest part of his body at the news. He and Miri had grown up with Kristilin. Every time they took a teleporter to Velra, all three of them would visit the snowfields or mountains together. They'd grown close, and he'd become even closer with Kristilin. He knew her better than anyone, and she knew him even better than Miri did. Friendship had turned into courtship as easy as night turned to day. Before the war had started, he remembered sitting around a fire in the forest and just talking. To think those days would possibly be no more hurt.

Hal stood straighter as his mind raced to different possibilities. He didn't distrust what Tavis had said, they very well could not know what happened, but there had to be more, and he would spend many more sleepless nights trying to uncover the truth.

There had to be some sort of explanation for the silence from Velra, and he thought of the Codebreakers. If they were somehow behind the actions, they needed to be stopped. He could use the Praetorian guards. It was their sworn duty to protect the royal family and carry out their will, enshrined in the Code. He would have them hunt down those vile traitors with whatever it took. But the only way he could order Praetorians was to be the Crown Prince, and he needed Miri to be successful in finding them and their leader.

To become the Crown Prince, he needed to seek out the secrets of his ancestors. It was the only way: to be a scholar and a warrior and wield not only the sword but the book of knowledge too. Then he could not be denied, and only then could he rebuild an exhausted empire.

As they entered the archives, Hal passed through the public access room, dodging compliments and inquisitive journalists, and headed to the back where the secure databases were. He did not have to show any identification to the guards, but they stopped Tavis.

"He's my guard," Hal said.

"Sorry, Your Highness, but he is not cleared to enter the secure rooms. He'll have to wait out here with us."

"It's fine, Hal, erm . . . Prince Halcion. Sorry, official titles right now. These are secure rooms anyway. I doubt any Codebreakers are lurking in there."

Hal nodded at the two guards before he turned and entered the database room. Inside, servers along the walls flashed all different colors while columns of terminals stood ready to access any and all information within the Imperial database.

As Hal entered his credentials, a small power fluctuation dimmed the lights before the servers ran at full strength again. He searched through thousands of entries for the information Varim wanted, only to narrow it down by a keyword. When he found the files, he stuck the datacard Varim had given him into the port and pressed the download button.

Nothing happened.

The files came up red and said, *Locked Under Vault Security Terminal 03. Download From Parent Server.*

Hal sighed in frustration. *Nothing is ever easy*, he thought as he pulled the datacard out.

He searched the room for any indicators of a vault and noticed a red light bar near the ceiling above the servers. As he looked down, a green light flickered above a scanner.

That has to be a door, he thought. But he had never ventured into that part of the server room and had no idea what to expect. Hal took a deep breath and bent down so his eye was level with the scanner, and a single beam of green light shot out. It traced his retina before it withdrew the laser. The light bar above turned green, and the server in front of him swung open to a room of darkness.

Stepping inside, he looked all around the dark room. It felt like being in the forest on a cloudy night. He could not even see his own hand in front of him. The only saving graces were the ten consoles in the back of the room. His footsteps echoed as he walked along the polished silver-tiled floor.

Standing in front of the terminal marked 03, he was overcome by a wave of nervousness. These were obviously highly restricted files even he should not have been able to access. Secrets of the Empire, military information, and sensitive plans all called these servers home, but curiosity caught him, and he wondered as to why the unrestricted files Varim requested were locked in the restricted servers. These were meant only for the emperor's eyes and a few top generals. But what would the head of the council think if the supposed heir to the Empire could not even retrieve a few files? Hal would not stand for incompetence from his own men and definitely not from himself.

Hal placed the datacard in the port and entered his credentials again. Restricted. At first he thought he'd entered his codes wrong, but when he tried again it read the same message.

How can this be? he thought as he looked at the screen. Too many incorrect entries would notify the Praetorians outside that he was accessing servers not meant for his eyes, but he needed to retrieve the files. He would not be made a failure for something so simple. Hal entered credentials again, but this time they were his father's. When the screen flashed blue, he knew it had worked, but now he had to work fast.

After he wrestled with the fact that he used his father's codes, Hal pushed the button, and the files downloaded onto the datacard Varim had given him. He watched the stream of information transfer to the small device as he tapped his foot on the ground. This was borderline breaking the Code; to seek information not meant for oneself, but no one else could. His thoughts overcrowded his rationality. He was Prince of the Empire downloading simple files. Everyone knew he would never betray the Empire. But when he was about to disconnect after they'd finished, an error message popped up, and the files began to open without control. He tried to stop it, searching for the right buttons to press, but the dim light made it almost impossible to find the disconnect.

A hologram projected itself on the floor, and Hal jumped back, wide-eyed, as the figure spoke. It sounded like a voice modulator, raspy and robotic. The figure's face was covered by a mask as they looked back behind them. Elegant robes covered their body while a thick cloak of furs provided much needed warmth as Hal noticed the small piles of snow in the background. He tried to see who it was, but the hologram fizzled in and out like a bad signal.

"To whoever hears this . . . beware of the . . . The Polarian war is just the start. They . . . plans I cannot say here. It has already begun with the High King and Queen . . ." The figure took another look back. "It's too late for me. They're here. Travel to Starlite Temple. There you will find everything you need to know . . ."

The figure drew a xiphir and slashed at another figure. Energy bolts ripped through the room as the figure navigated them, screams of pain echoing. Then the recording stopped.

Hal looked at the empty space where the hologram had just been in disbelief. Just before him, someone had stood pleading for help. He hadn't the slightest idea of who it was thanks to the poor quality and muffled voice, but whoever it was had to be someone of importance. It could also be a trap meant to lure him in and ruin any chance he had to claim the throne. But the hologram, whoever it was, seemed sincere and had asked for help.

"Who are you?" he asked the space where the hologram had been. "Where are you?"

Only terrorists would be so bold as to attack Imperial officials, and it seemed like this was nothing new. It violated everything he stood for. It violated the Code that had stood as the guiding principle since the time of the first Empire. Information was key to weeding these pests out, and instead it sat here in darkness. But the file was marked restricted unlike the ones he was sent to obtain.

Hal thought for a moment, and it was one of the toughest decisions he had to make. This was not information to be taken without prior knowledge, and he would go against everything he held close. Knowledge sought in ill fate was akin to black magic and witchcraft. To him it wasn't that, but he knew how the optics would look. He would've broken into a secure archive vault and taken Imperial secrets. Couple that with the ongoing Codebreakers, and someone could easily paint him as a sympathizer for not being granted Crown Prince.

They would ostracize him and send him to the place where people never returned from: the Ashlands. Hal glanced to the dark door behind him, which looked like a void directly into those tarnished lands. He remembered the tales told to him when he was young, and the thought sent shivers up his spine.

As he turned back around, he fixed his gaze on all the computer consoles before him. It was a political game. It would go against what the high minister had said. And he would have to do it alone. He couldn't bring his sister into this and risk her status as well, but this had to be done.

He inserted his own personal datacard into the terminal and downloaded the hologram file. *Another chance*, he thought as the download bar completed.

After Hal closed everything up, he slipped the datacard Varim gave him into his pocket and his own into the top pocket of his jacket before he exited the server room and rejoined Tavis.

CHAPTER XI

Days went by, and the stress only mounted. It felt like Varim's eyes were always on him. Guards seemed more abundant than before. He didn't know who he could trust and who would turn on him. The optics looked horrible. Hal Skyborn, Prince of the Empire, had not only accessed files he wasn't supposed to see but now held them in his possession. The Code forbade knowledge sought in revenge. Dirty knowledge had no place in the Empire. It only served to destabilize and divide. The council would surely paint him in this light even though this information could prove vital to understanding the rise of the Codebreaker traitors.

Hal watched from the shadows as Imperial guards moved through the streets. They were not in the normal shift rotations he remembered from before the war. Stricter security measures had been implemented since the attempted assassination, but Hal had no desire to be escorted around his own city. Whoever wanted him gone had to settle it face-to-face, and he would be waiting.

He turned to Tavis, who lay slouched in a hammock with a leg over one side. Haywell sat in a hardlite chair to his right, no doubt thumbing through the latest online market data. The soft blue light particles of the chair glowed around him and illuminated the immediate area.

They were tucked away under the cover of dense trees in the terrestrial forest. Vixera lay on the ground the amount of starship traffic leaving the spaceports during the evening rush hour.

The aching feeling to tell someone what he'd seen gnawed at Hal, but he couldn't wrap them up in whatever was going on.

Tavis scrolled through his datacard; it seemed the current situation did not faze him even though he was the one in charge of providing security for Hal. Hal just shook his head with a smirk and reached for the juito resting beside him. He took the long-necked instrument in his hands and ran his fingers across the strings before he spoke.

"Any news?" Hal asked.

Tavis looked up for a moment. "About what?"

"This." Hal pointed to the guards roaming the streets like a horde of animals.

Tavis shrugged. "Security threats."

"No shit," Hal said as he plucked a couple juito strings. "Why is there a curfew?"

"Varim's orders."

"You don't take orders from the high minister. City Guard abides by the Code, and the High Justice when the sovereign is ill."

"When Varim claims emergency powers, we have to listen," Tavis said. "Relax, Hal. Things will be fine."

Hal should have known he would be given the same answers his sister and others had given him. He plucked a few more strings from the juito. No one wanted to speak plainly to him. It all revolved around mental gymnastics that got no further than a kind greeting or change of subject. Things had changed, and he didn't know whether he liked it or not. Everything felt tighter, like one misplaced word or action would result in some public humiliation. It didn't make any sense. This was supposed to be a new age, but it felt like a dark age with a blanket of shadow looming over everything.

As he looked up, the twin suns began to dip below the horizon and give way to the stars. How he would've loved to look upon them for wonderment instead of stress relief. He could only hope for one day.

"Oh no," Haywell said from beside Hal.

"What's wrong? Miscalculated your share of EviTec solar panels again?" Tavis asked.

"Ever so sarcastic, Tavis. I don't miscalculate. The markets shift, and I reassess, but I wouldn't expect someone with your monetary aptitude to understand," Haywell retorted. "Unfortunately, that's not the issue." Haywell handed his datacard to Hal.

Hal took it and read the headline of the news article on the screen. His eyes narrowed at the literature under it, and he cocked his head to the side. In bold letters, the screen read: Crown Prince or Empyrean Liability? The words that followed detailed his shortcomings, from lost battles early in the war to not achieving the Imperial Council's and High Justice's favors. The bullet points under each subheading seemed to stretch for pages, and as Hal scrolled through the article, his blood began to seethe.

"They blame me for the terror attacks across Athos?" Hal asked.

He'd lost battles; that was something he wouldn't and couldn't deny. Fellow Imperials had died under his command, had been blown to bits by artillery and shredded by plasma rounds. Hal stared at the screen as he recounted holding a soldier in his arms as they took their last breath. Oricus was the young soldier's name, and there were many others he would never forget because of that damned war. And now to see his own people ask if he was a liability seemed improbable just weeks before when he was about to end the war.

"Whoever wrote this said you should've reinforced the city guard instead of inviting more, and I quote, 'shit-filled nonsense' into the Empire by waging a war," Haywell said.

"How in Empyrea could I have done that if I was learning how to dodge enemy plasma bolts and shrapnel?" Hal shot back. "For well over a year I was on the ground serving side by side with the common soldier, leading squads, platoons, and drop shock troopers. I formed plans and tactics to ensure we found victory and my soldiers found safety. Only within the last few months did I earn command of the entire operation." Hal exhaled deeply, steam trailing from his breath. "Only when I found the keycodes."

"Sounds more like a hit piece," Vixera said. "I wouldn't sweat over it."

The four of them were silent for a moment. Hal stared aimlessly at the ground, scenes of the war flashing into his mind. He could taste the dirt and smell the smoke of the battlefield like he was there right now. The Yasu system was supposed to have become a new regional sector, finally incorporated into the Empire. Now it was nothing more than a system of broken souls waiting for what was to come next.

"Who wrote it?" Tavis asked, breaking the silence.

"The who doesn't matter. It's written," Hal said as he handed the device back to Haywell. "They think I failed the Empire."

"Actually, it might," Haywell said. "The author of this inarticulate article is a journalist at ImperiNow. Apparently, the person they interviewed was once an aide to Varim." Haywell scrolled down and sucked air through his teeth in disgust.

"How do you know that?" Tavis asked.

"Because, my simple-minded brother, I have ways and contacts you could only dream of," Haywell stated. "I will not for the life of me give up those secrets."

"Yeah, well, there's more than one way to skin a cat," Tavis replied.

Haywell sighed. "That doesn't even make sense."

"Look, this is the two-time Junior Duster Racing Series champion here. Who can hate on that?" Tavis said as he pointed at Hal.

Haywell only shook his head.

Hal took the device again and looked through the article once more. He saw the interviewer name and the interviewee, but it was a stretch to assume this former aide to Varim would connect the high minister to anything.

"Political theater," Hal said under his breath as he handed it back to Haywell again. "That's too much of a stretch. I don't trust Varim, though."

Hal quickly bit his tongue, afraid to divulge too much of what he knew. His eyes met Haywell's, and he could see the ponderance in them. He wanted to tell someone what he'd found in the archives, but even he did not fully know what it all meant. Once he did, he could tell everyone and make a case against the high minister.

"Anyway, your popularity seems to be stable on the HoloNet for the time being."

Haywell laid the datacard down flat, and a small projection of a holographic world emerged. Users in avatars ran around the virtual city. Several avatars of Hal's likeness formed an Imperial tower to retrieve a golden egg at the top of a tower.

"I don't even know what to say to that," Hal said.

"Those social media things are nothing but trouble anyway. Just a bunch of loudmouths beating their chests in an echo chamber," Tavis said as he placed his arms behind his head and leaned back into the hammock.

"Insightful knowledge from the cave dweller," Haywell said, earning an amused grunt from Tavis. He closed the HoloNet and turned back to Hal. "The article could be damaging if it festers, but we have to see if the people read the headlines or do their own research. If they pick the latter, they will know this is all political disinformation."

"And if they don't, it could mean a complete political revolution like what happened to Zeramor. It could mean a rewrite of the Code, something that has lasted thousands of years," Hal replied. "Or a complete dissolution of it."

"I'll see what more I can find. Don't fret, Hal. Remember, I have my ways."

"He means that," Vixera echoed from where she lay in the grass.

As Hal pushed himself up, he said, "I think I'll head back to the palace."

"I'll escort you," Tavis asked.

"No," Hal said. "I think I can find my way."

"Are you sure?"

"Leave him be, Tavis. I'm sure we'll see streams of flames erupting in the distance if anyone tries something on Hal," Haywell said. "I would feel bad for them."

Hal smiled. "I'll see you three later."

Streets where guards and citizens had been minutes before were now vacant and empty. Devoid of life, the shops and buildings stood dark. A star cruiser sailed through the sky, ferrying its passengers to one of the Empire's moons. The cruiser's moan was the only sound that filled the desolate street.

As Hal walked along, he remembered how vibrant this street had been a few days ago. Hundreds of people had gathered to welcome him back home, a war hero, but now it stood empty, and he stood alone. He stopped and looked around for any sign of life, but all he saw were the scurrying tails of rats.

Continuing along the street, he came to a shop stand where he'd grabbed milkshakes in celebration after graduating the Academy. Miri was a couple years behind him at the time, but he'd still brought her along. She was his sister after all. He remembered sharing one with Kristilin while Haywell and Tavis bickered about who could down theirs the quickest. Those had been simpler times, and everything had been so clear. He recalled the call of battle looming over him at the time. It had been inevitable. He only wished he could have told Kristilin in time.

Back then, graduates had filled the entertainment district square in celebration of their accomplishments, but that seemed to be something of a distant memory. Now the stand he and his friends had frequented left much to be desired. Stains ran down its wooden sides, and the spokes in the wheels were cracked and splintered. Guards were too busy to deal with something so minuscule, and he had not seen the owner in some time. Whether it had been damaged by storms or was just uncared for, the stand looked like a haunted memory of what it had once been, and it wasn't alone.

Shop buildings were empty across the square. Trash blew in the night breeze and frightened a nest of rats. They scurried into the holes and entryways of the vacant buildings they now claimed refuge in. Past the fountain in the center was the holocade; once filled with adolescents and people his age enjoying the games and events, it now stood dark and devoid of life.

He knew the war had taken a toll on the people and Athos, but the suffering of Imperius, the crown jewel of the Empire, showed how far the war had reached. Regional capitals and towns, frontier settlements, all felt impacts stronger than the capital city. They had to. A simple entertainment square wasn't only a place where rambunctious youths ventured to; it was a place where Athonians worked. Lives depended on the simple operation of a holocade to get food and necessities for a family, or two, or three. The war had taken it all away.

Hal stood there for a moment more as the emptiness and darkness of the square reminded him of others who'd suffered. He was only one. There were many more.

He felt the chill of someone watching him from behind, but Hal knew they were no threat. Vixera stood beside him, their eyes nearly the same level when Hal looked at her. She had normal pupils without a diamond, and that seemed to be more desirable now if that article was anything to go by.

She put a hand on his shoulder. "Are you sure you're all right? What's on your mind?"

Hal hesitated. Everything he knew and had seen sat on the tip of his tongue, but he still didn't fully understand it. Someone in interplanetary system law would be the perfect person to tell, yet he took a deep breath and swallowed the urge.

"I'm fine, Vixy," Hal said. "I'm just getting used to all of this again."

"You know we have your back, right? Whatever it is. Tavis, Hay, your sister, and I all are here whenever you need us."

Hal placed a hand on hers and smiled. "I appreciate that, truly. You all are more like siblings to me than cousins. I know Meer feels the same way."

Vixera smiled. "Just without the fancy diamond pupils."

"They have artificial lenses for that now," Hal said, which earned a laugh from Vixera.

"Is Neeux adjusting well? I know the war took a lot from him."

"From what I've seen, yeah. Stoic as always," Hal said.

"Good." Vixera smiled. "I'll catch you later, Hal."

As Vixera turned and walked back to where the others sat, Hal faced the palace that sat on top of the acropolis.

Hal made it to the palace grounds. Praetorians patrolled the courtyard and saluted him as he walked by. Hal could only return an unenthused salute before continuing through the gardens.

Deeper inside stood a fountain with a statue of the late Empress Irina Skyborn. He smiled at the sight of his mother eternalized in stone. The Skyborn coat of arms, an eagle holding arrows in one foot and a scroll of paper in the other, overlooked her, backed by a diamond-shaped border. The statue had been erected in remembrance of her after the assassination. Hal could still remember laying rose petals around the statue with Miri the day before he'd left. It was honorable and the right thing to do according to the Code. She was the empress and had been slain in cold blood.

It pained him to remember that day. He'd spent many tears here, and it never got any easier. As he looked up to the stars that now dominated the sky, one shot across the darkness, and it brought a short-lived smile to his face.

The memory of the archive incident flooded back into his mind. He desperately wanted to forget what he'd seen, but it was impossible. Something had happened there, and it was important enough for that person in the recording to risk their life. There had to be more to it, and by the gods, Hal would discover it. All he wanted was closure. He wanted the truth, an answer. And as he looked up through the palace windows, he eyed where he wanted to go.

The halls of the palace lay quiet under the starry sky. A routine patrol of Praetorians marched along their route as Hal strode along. Portraits of past emperors and empresses hung on the walls, displaying over a thousand years of unity. Each one was remembered for something great, and he stopped at the portrait of his father. He looked as strong and wise as any others, with a look of ferocity but also compassion. To think this painting had been done only a few years ago made Hal realize how unpredictable life was. He had not seen his father since the war had started, except for a quick holocall, and now he lay in a bed riddled with sickness.

So much had been taken from his family. Some toyed with the thought that this was a curse on the royal family for besting the Primordials thousands of years ago, but Hal did not entertain such fairy tales.

Hal moved to the portrait of the first emperor, which was dated and on the verge of needing some extra care. Hal stared into the still eyes of Atis Skyborn, first of the Skyborn line.

Hal wished to someday be remembered like him, to know he had done something that had bettered the Empire, but he needed the chance to even start. He turned to face the swiftlift at the end of the hall. He needed to see the man everyone else called emperor.

The doors opened, and as Hal stepped out, he was greeted by two Praetorians who guarded the hall. Two more of the elite guard stood on either side of a door near the center of the hallway. Before he took another step, one of the Praetorians stopped him. He spoke in a heavy accent of ancient Athonian and reached his hardlight war ax out. It sizzled with refined energy as the golden glow bounced off his face.

"I am sorry, Prince Halcion, but this floor is off-limits to everyone except medical personnel."

The guard's gold-and-silver armor twinkled in the dim light of the hall, and his golden eyes stared back at Hal from behind his full helmet. The size of the guards would intimidate many who crossed paths with them, but Hal knew they were doing their job in defending the royal family.

Hal took a deep breath. "How did the city fare during the war, guardsman?"

"Many tried to harm the palace. The people worry. But overall, Imperius has been safe. The moons and wildlands of Athos have other tales to tell though."

"And my father? Before he was injured?"

"As good as he always was. Rests now. Wanted to see you after the war."

"Well, here I am," Hal said. "I haven't seen him in a long time. What would you do if you hadn't seen your family in two years?"

"The Praetorian Guard is my family, Prince Halcion."

Hal nodded; he'd expected the answer from the dedicated warrior.

"And you would do anything for them? Care for your brothers and sisters when they were injured? Or ill?" When the guard didn't say anything and shifted his weight, Hal knew he'd made progress. "I just want to see my father and let him know that it wasn't done in vain."

The guard's glowing eyes stared back at him for what seemed like an hour. Hal didn't look away. Much could be deciphered by the sight of someone's eyes, and Hal had found that out through blood, sweat, and pain. Any flinch of his body or diversion of his gaze would ruin the sincerity in his eyes.

The Praetorian finally spoke. "Ten minutes, Prince Halcion."

Hal nodded. "Thank you, guardsman."

"Make way for the prince," the Praetorian instructed the other two guardsmen down the hall.

Hal gave the guardsmen a respectful nod as they parted from the door. The door slid open to his presence, and Hal stepped inside.

The coolness of the room made him shiver. His teeth chattered, and his heart beat rapidly.

Everything was how he remembered it, and as he scanned the large elaborate bedchamber, his father laid in the large bed with translucent golden curtains pulled shut. Under the glow of moonlight, Emperor Tiberius looked as pale as the moons themselves under perfectly laid silver sheets. His graying hair and goatee were well-kept, and there wasn't a thing out of place, which wasn't unusual given what a perfectionist his father was. Even the tray of medical utensils sat organized: a silver syringe, bandages, and a simple thermometer were evenly spaced.

It made Hal relax a bit to know his father still had the bark to keep his room in order. But as he took a few more steps into the room, he noticed there were no medical machines monitoring the emperor. Nothing was hooked up, and he didn't see a medical droid anywhere. Hal wondered why the emperor, of all people, didn't even have a simple intravenous tube set up. But perhaps this was a sign of better things to come. Maybe his father was well enough to return to his duties. He could only hope.

Hal slowly stepped closer to the bed, careful to not make any noises that might awaken the emperor. If something was still wrong, the last thing he wanted to do was startle his father.

As he neared the bed, the emperor opened his white eyes, and Hal froze. *He was awake*, he thought. Joy and anger flooded his mind. Not only was he lied to, but Varim toyed with the Code at the cost of his family. But he was also glad to see his father coherent.

"Who dares come to the emperor's bed at night?"

"Your son," Hal said. "Apologies. I didn't expect you to be awake."

The older man looked across the dark room and met Hal's eyes. The emperor reached over and touched the light on his bed stand, and light engulfed the room, revealing his frailness. Weeks bedridden, his father had lost muscle mass, and his cheeks were sunken.

Hal would've been lying if he said he wasn't a little alarmed, especially at his father's advanced age. The emperor took a breath before he spoke again.

"It's been some time, Hal. The last thing I wanted . . ." Emperor Tiberius paused to catch his breath. "Was to greet you in my sickbed."

"Even Atis and Sarin needed time to regenerate their health, Father," Hal said. "I just wanted to check on you."

"I'm surprised the guards let you in."

"Well, you know me. I have a way with words."

The emperor stifled a chuckle before wincing in pain. Hal knelt by the bed and listened to his father's bated breaths for a moment before he spoke again.

"What happened, Father?"

"Some sort of poison gas." The emperor paused to catch his breath. "They got me when I was doing my rehabilitation exercises for the arm I lost in the war."

The weight on the bed shifted as the emperor lifted his right arm. The metal shined in the moonlight streaming through the grand window and served as another reminder of the war.

"Took the lives of my nurse and doctor," the emperor said. "They died because they were helping me."

"They died serving the Empire, and they will be remembered for that," Hal said. He looked back out the grand window as nighthawks darted across the night sky, chasing bugs. "I have an uneasy feeling about the high minister, Father."

"Varim has declared emergency powers to ensure the Empire functions. Regardless of my health, the powers he claims must stay for a minimum of a month. Only then can the High Justice transfer the ruling powers back," Emperor Tiberius said, wheezing faintly. "But you are worried Varim will not relinquish them as told by the Code. It could be true simply because they have pumped me full of drugs. I can't say that I am all the way coherent. Some days are good . . ." Tiberius coughed from deep in his throat before sighing. "Some are bad. Either way, when the time comes to transfer, the High Justice can declare you the new emperor. My Abdication Day is near anyway."

Hal froze as his father stated a path outlined by the Code. It would have been an easy route if he'd already been declared Crown Prince, but the facts remained the same. He inhaled deeply before speaking.

"They denied me," Hal said. Emperor Tiberius turned to look at him, stern eyes piercing through his resolve as if he didn't believe him. "All this political banter is not what the Empire needs. I've done everything imaginable to be worthy of the title, and yet Varim refuses to make me Crown Prince. Your Abdication Day is growing closer, and I am the only one able to ascend the throne, yet I've been denied. But Varim, or the council, keeps changing the Code. I don't understand what is happening." Silence filled the room. Hal looked out the window. "I'm sorry. I should not have brought my issues here while you are ill."

The emperor reached for his hand, and Hal placed it in his. The cold metal of the prosthesis sent a cooling sensation through Hal's arm, but the gentle squeeze made him feel like a boy again, walking through the city with his father.

"My son, I raised you to be a respectful leader, but I also raised you to fight. If they denied you again, then you must rise and meet their challenge. You need not gain Varim's favor but that of the High Justice. The Code favors you in this no matter what Varim may claim to change."

Hal sighed and closed his eyes. He would not play their games, but he would stand by the Code and its guiding principle.

"They said Varim is holding out until you get better."

"Or die."

"Yes."

"Luckily for you, I don't plan on dying."

Hal smiled and knew his father could sense the relief it granted.

"I need to let you rest. The guards are probably counting the seconds before they come barging in."

As Hal stood to leave, the call of his father stopped him.

"Hal, I wanted to tell you I am proud of everything you have accomplished in such a short time. No one has done what you have at such a young age. I am proud to call you my son and Miri my daughter. You two are children every father wishes they could have. You deserve the title."

Hal closed his eyes. Praise was nothing he clamored for, but when it came from his father, it always meant a little more than usual. He couldn't help but feel uplifted.

"Thank you, Father. Now get some rest. I expect to see you at the Inception Day festivities."

Emperor Tiberius chuckled before shooing Hal out.

In the hall, Hal kept his head down. To know his father was safe and out of any immediate danger comforted him. But to hear his voice again and speak with the man who controlled the Empire gave him the most comfort of all. He wanted things to go as planned so his father could retire in peace after everything he'd been through. If Varim wanted to get in the way of that, he had a lot more to worry about than playing political games.

Two can play at that, Hal thought as he marched down the hall.

CHAPTER XII

The stars gave way to the first rays of light as Hal sat at his desk in front of the terminal. The hours dragged on; he was too stressed to sleep. Ever since he'd returned home, nothing felt the same.

After two years at war, he'd thought a hero's welcome would set him up for his future. That was why he'd felt the need to win—not only for his home world, but for himself. Those years away had made him grow though. He'd dealt with stress and chaos, suffering and frustration, but none of that could measure up to what he felt right now.

Betrayal was something he'd never thought he would experience, but nothing he had seen so far repressed his feeling of it. After everything that had occurred in the last couple of years, he couldn't fathom it. Either way, he held treasonous information as he looked at the computer console in front of him. The weight of the world pressed its full might against him, and he felt it.

Hal watched the hologram on repeat, hoping to find something that would identify the figure. In his haste to download the file, it had corrupted, and what he now had was little more than a staticky mess. He remembered what he could from earlier: a mask, a fur cloak, the xiphir. That did little to help further a hypothesis though.

As he leaned forward, Hal decided to try something different, though risky. If it worked, it could change everything. What he had now was not enough to make any moves, and he did not like to speculate. He needed the facts, the truth. Only then would he have enough to make a case. He had to know who that person in the hologram was and what they were doing there.

"Computer, sync file with original. Passkey . . ." He paused. He knew there was no going back after this. But his mother's passkey was the only one he could use. If everything worked, he didn't have to worry, but if something went awry, it could be blamed on the terrorists. Or he could stop. He shook his head at the thought. That would just be more weight on his conscience. He had to do this for himself, his family, and the Empire.

"Enter passkey: /IE-T:E/I/S/."

The computer screen flashed and brought up the original next to the file he had. Hal adjusted the resolution on the monitor to get a decent picture. When he was done, he uploaded the file and merged it with the original. Normally he would've had a tech do this for him, but he did not have that luxury.

"Computer, modulate the audio file and refine. Sync with the video source when complete."

As the computer worked to put the new files together, Hal leaned back in his seat and stared out over the awakening city. The city lights faded off one by one as the twin suns rose to bathe the land in golden rays. Hal rubbed his eyes, yearning for sleep, but he needed to know what was in that video. Either way, he had Varim on withholding information from the throne, and that alone went against the Code.

The computer chimed, and Hal snapped back to the monitor. The video resolution greatly improved, and he saw the person in the video clearer. They had a more feminine body type, but the face was still concealed by a cloth mask. "Playback speed: low." Hal watched as the form slowly turned back and forth, and something caught his eye. "Stop! Enhance that frame." Hal's eyes widened in disbelief. The figure was wearing his mother's golden crystal necklace. He reached up to where his dangled around his neck. "Mother?"

The video continued, revealing more of the scene that was not shown in the archives, and Hal watched in shock as he leaned over his desk. He followed every movement his mother made, trying to decipher who or what she fought when the first assailants appeared in the frame. They were covered from head to toe in simple garments, and Hal couldn't decipher any notable markings about them as he watched his mother do battle somewhere in the depths of the Realmverse.

As the synced video continued to reveal more information, Empress Irina raised her other arm and deployed a hardlight shield. A flurry of energy bolts slammed into it, and the empress braced against the shock. When the flurry stopped, she slashed her hardlite xiphir at one of the cloaked assailants before an energy bolt crashed into her, knocking her to the ground. Then the room once wrought with chaos became still, with only the leftover burns of energy bolt scars. As smoke rose, a muffled voice spoke off screen. A figure in a dark cloak surrounded by armored men walked in front of the recording, and when they turned to face the camera, High Minister Varim's devilish eyes looked directly at him.

The video stopped, and Hal sat back with barely any breath in his lungs. Anger raged inside him. Shallow, rapid breaths sent his adrenaline through the roof as he plotted a way to bring this traitor to justice. Plain as day, the high minister, trusted ear to the throne and speaker for the council, had slain a royal. Hal wanted to rip Varim's heart out and send it deep into the Ashlands. The assassin had not been a Polarian android or a terrorist; it was his own countryman and one who lied about it. If Hal fought that war for nothing when he could've thrown Varim in the dungeons, he would never be able to live it down.

This was high treason against the Empire, and it violated every aspect of the Code he held near. *Who is to be executed next?* he thought. If anyone touched a hair on his sister or father, there was going to be hell to pay.

As he stared at the image, another thought came to mind. Why his mother? Surely his father carried more weight, and if Varim wanted to throw the Empire into turmoil, the elimination of its leader with no clear heir apparent would've achieved that. His mother was just a scholar of the Empyreans and Primordials. She was no Wielder.

Why her?

The only thing he had to do now was get this information to the council safely and put an end to Varim before he committed any further treachery.

But as he pulled out the datacard, the door to his chambers flew open. A squad of Praetorian guards stormed in with hardlite xiphirs drawn. Behind them, wearing a royal gold-and-silver dress, stood Miri.

She strutted toward him without a word, heels clicking on the marble floor, and glared at him before bringing her hand down against Hal's face. The slap echoed through the room, and he looked back into his sister's angry eyes.

"Arrest him."

"What?" Hal said. "Under what premise?"

"How dare you play dumb. You know what you did."

"Miri, what in the hell are you talking about?"

"Father is dead, and you were the last one seen entering his chambers. Do I need to put the pieces together for you?"

Hal froze and stared at his sister. That couldn't be true. He'd spoken with his father last night, and he'd seemed well for his condition.

Hal looked into the golden eyes of the Praetorians who now filled his chambers. This couldn't be right.

"Miri, listen to me—"

The Praetorians slapped energy binds onto his wrists. This had to be a cruel joke, but the buzz from the energy cuffs felt all too real.

His father had been murdered, and they blamed him.

Miri stood right in front of him, her fists balled and nose wrinkled in anger, and her glare said everything her voice failed to. Something had changed.

The Praetorians ushered him out of his room. All he could do now was beg for an audience.

"Listen, Miri . . . Miri . . ."

But his calls went unanswered as he was led away.

CHAPTER XIII

S ilence. That was all he heard.

Days blended with nights, and Hal found himself locked in an isolation chamber with nothing to do and no one to talk to. The walls had no windows, no vision to the outside world where he used to freely walk. The pipes leaked in a maddening pitter-patter that used to drive prisoners insane. Now it was he who fell victim to the noise. When it stopped, though, all he had was the silence of this box and the beat of his own heart.

Looking at his hands as he sat on the ground, he tried to sever the energy links with his flames, but nothing happened. Conventional chains wouldn't have stood a chance against him, but the hardlight prevented his flames from doing anything. If he could, he would've melted right through those by now and stormed the palace with an immeasurable fury and taken that slimy politician under his boot.

It seemed Varim was smarter than he'd thought. He knew Hal was powerful, more powerful than his sister.

He yanked on the energy link weakly. The only food he'd been given was a loaf of bread, and he had one bite left. Despite the hunger and silence, his thoughts drifted, and he came to the reality of his father now gone. He'd only seen him for a few moments, and now he would never see him again. It was just like his mother, ripped away from him. His muscles tensed, and his fists balled up. The veins in his arms popped through his skin as his blood pumped through them.

Anger. That was all he felt for those who'd caused his family harm, and he knew exactly who to blame.

There had to be another reason why Varim had sent him to the archives. The high minister lacked access to the Archives. Only the royal family could access it with their codes. If it was another trick to get rid of him, it might have worked. He could've refused, but Inception Day loomed, and it marked another year of success for the Empire—or so he'd thought.

Hal shook his head at his failure to recognize a ploy against him, blinded by the chance to gain the title he wanted. He flinched as the hardlight cuffs burned his wrists and shifted them to an area that wouldn't burn him. He wanted to strangle the life out of Varim for his treachery, but to do so would go against the Code. That man had to stand trial no matter how much Hal wanted to handle it one-on-one. The court would judge him soon enough.

But the pain stung far more now that he knew Miri thought he was the murderer. Where they were united after the death of their mother, now they stood against each other. If he couldn't convince her, his only other chance would be to convince the people he wasn't what Varim said he was. At least he stood by his morals. But he needed his sister to help, and he feared by the look he'd seen on her face that it was too late.

His eyes drifted to the darkness of his confines. He'd been told he was a failure since the war had started. Superiors and those who disliked him for standing true to common sense had wanted him to pick a side and lambasted him if he didn't. Their words always fell on deaf ears, but now it seemed they'd gotten what they wanted.

He'd had enough of the political games after two blood-filled years. He'd had enough pain, enough regret. Soldiers had died under him, for him, for the Empire. They'd all sacrificed blood and lives for the Empire, and for the first time, he felt scared—not for himself, but for those soldiers' sacrifices to go in vain.

He'd thought he and his sister would rule the Empire together, change it, but it seemed Varim had gotten to her. Something changed after she met with Varim the day he'd summoned them, and he could not help but feel regret. All of this was his fault. He should've stayed with her then, but he'd had no idea Varim would stray this far from the Code. If he'd acted sooner and brought the evidence against the high minister to the council, or even Miri, maybe there would have been a chance to rectify it, but that mattered not as he sat like a common criminal in a dungeon.

The door creaked open, and Hal fixed his eyes on the entrance. Miri strode in, her white-and-gold dress fluttering as she walked while a small silver jacket covered the top part of her torso. She stopped in front of him, and Hal held her unfeeling gaze. Her eyes felt cold, unlike the warmth he was used to, and now they seemed even more distant, unrecognizable by the emptiness they held.

"So, does the Code mean nothing to you now?" Hal asked, his throat dry from lack of water.

"I'm not the one who killed Father," Miri said before kneeling in front of him.

"What happened from just a few days ago?" Hal said through gritted teeth, eyes narrowed.

"It doesn't matter, Hal. Not with what I have seen. Varim showed me everything I needed to see, and everything boils down to you. You're more harmful for the Empire. Haven't we suffered enough? A war, the death of our mother, but that couldn't satisfy your hunger for power." She looked up to him, and for a moment, Hal thought he saw the sister he knew inside. But then her eyes returned to that iced-over gaze he barely recognized. "You killed our father to expedite your coronation, Hal. How am I supposed to trust you?"

"Miri, I didn't kill Father. How does me killing him help anything? I saw him for a few moments to check on him. When was the last time you saw him? I just wanted to see him. The Praetorians were right outside the room."

"It doesn't help, but with our father dead, the council will be forced to make a decision. And one of those possible outcomes could be a dual throne where we could rule together. But you never wanted that. You wanted it for yourself. You never cared about Father or Mother . . . or me."

"Miri, all I care about is the Code being followed in these political games." Hal softened his tone and searched his sister's eyes. "I would never do anything to hurt you, Meer."

"Explain this, then." Miri pulled a small silver syringe from a pocket in her jacket, and Hal's eyes went wide. He recognized the object, which had sat on the nightstand beside his father's bed. "Why does this have your fingerprints on it?"

"Miri—"

But it was too late. Without another word, she ushered in the Praetorians, and they deenergized Hal's binds. They grabbed him by the arms and forced him out. Hal didn't bother to give his sister another look.

They took the swiftlift from the dungeons and toward the central courtyard of the palace. Miri led them through the halls, where lines of soldiers stood at attention, and then to the balcony that overlooked the city.

They forced him down to his knees, and Hal shrugged the guards off, feeling betrayed by them too, but he knew it was the weight of the Code that forced them to do what they did.

"He's lying to you!" Hal shouted at them. "He's trying to pick us off one-by-one."

Not one of them paid him any attention. A couple of Praetorians fastened a cloth gag around to stop him from shouting anything else and slapped the energy binds back on his wrists. If only he could make them see. But this time something felt different. As Hal turned to face the overlook of the city, he felt out of place, like an object lumped into the wrong pile.

A horde of his fellow countrymen jeered as they saw him on his knees. And then Varim strode in. Grinning from ear to ear, Varim waved to the crowd as he made his way to where Hal sat, Praetorians flanking him on either side. The high minister made a show of everything. A roar of applause and cheers washed over the main square as citizens dressed in Imperial colors fought for the attention of the de facto leader. They'd never done that before, and it made Hal tremble with anger. With another wave, the crowd was silenced.

Varim looked back at Hal. "You see? Discipline. Something you drastically lack." Varim took to the balcony and spoke, his voice amplified across the square. "Today is Inception Day, my fellow Athonians and Imperials alike."

Again, the crowd cheered before being silenced by a single hand wave.

"Years ago, our forefathers built this Empire in the vision of the Primordials. Every year we recognize that day as our inception."

The crowd cheered in agreement as Hal watched with disgust.

"It has become synonymous with rebirth and strength through a unified world. But as the age of war ends, so does our outdated system. A new dawn is upon us where we are all equals, not separated by dangerous magic."

The crowd rejoiced with a deafening roar of acceptance, their applause vibrating through the stone balcony. It seemed like the entire planet had shown up for this.

"The throne has always brought destruction and sorrow to these lands, and this past war of selfishness was no different. Selfishness is contagious; our prince showed that with the heartbreaking murder of Emperor Tiberius Skyborn." Varim looked back to Hal and continued. "If not for our valiant princess, his murder would have been unsolved for who knows how long. She will be a fine addition to our utopian society. Emperor Tiberius will not be forgotten, but he will be the last emperor."

The crowd cheered with fury. It made Hal sick to hear them cheer in blind appreciation. Like sheep, they followed their shepherd into an unknown slaughter ground where the life that was known ceased to exist.

Despite the energy cuffs, he jumped up and fired a ball of fire behind him, knocking out a guard before he was subdued by a stun gun from another. As he lay there, aftershocks of electricity jolting through his nerves, the crowd cheered. Just days ago they'd cheered his name and offered him gifts, but now it was like a public hanging.

Hal tried to stand up again, but Miri held him down. He looked over to her and hoped this was all an act, but as he looked into her white eyes, he saw nothing but desire and contempt. He knew what she wanted, and there was nothing he could do about it now.

"So, my fellow Athonians, citizens of the Empire, I ask you, what should the punishment of this treachery be?" Varim asked as he held up a xiphir in one hand and a feather in the other. "Choose carefully."

Like a chorus of singers, the crowd shouted out one word: "*Exile*." Hal's heart sank. He knew what treason was. It did not matter what he thought or did, because at the end of it all, Varim had the upper hand.

"No one is spared the consequences of defying our Code—not even our beloved prince." The crowd booed in unison as the high minister turned back to Hal and smiled. "This is what happens when you betray the Empire."

Hal would spit venom at Varim if he could but he had to settle for a glare.

Miri forced Hal up with a twist of his arm that made him clench his teeth through the gag. She didn't even flinch at his discomfort.

Now he knew he was alone. He tried to shrug her off, but the other guards joined in the restraint. He was bound and outnumbered as he looked Varim in the eyes. Inside, his fire burned and smoldered. He wanted to do so many things, but he could not. Nobody would listen.

"Prince Halcion Skyborn, for your treason against the citizens of the Empire of Athos and the Imperial Code, you are a Wielder no more."

The high minister placed his fingers over Hal's face and took a deep breath. As Hal tried to fight off Varim's touch, a jolt of pain ripped through his body. His muscles tightened and locked up before a wave of white light flashed over his vision and sucked what felt like his soul out of his body. Hal fell to the ground, paralyzed as Varim stood over him. The roar of the crowd filled his ears as cannons shot to mark the beginning of Inception Day, and everything faded to black.

ACT II

CHAPTER XIV

When Hal awoke, he didn't know where he was. Groaning, he managed to push himself up from the ashy ground. His body ached with pain that shot across his chest and down his legs. He felt empty inside, like something was missing, stolen. A sudden chill slapped his exposed skin and made him shiver. When his vision finally came to, he looked out and gazed at the landscape he found himself in.

Mountains dominated either side of him, and gray-white flakes covered the ground. Withered trees stood around him like demoralized soldiers on a lost battlefield, coated in gray and left behind. A hazy sky peered down through a blanket of thick, puffy clouds. A single mountain farther away stretched above the clouds, looming over the rest.

He could not believe it. After years of hearing about it from stories and elders, he was actually here, in the Ashlands of Asha, the proverbial purgatory in Imperial and all the other realms' lore. Everyone who had been sentenced here either went missing or never returned—even Imperial patrols, though no one cared enough to check.

The Forgotten Lands, Land of Exiles, the Ash—all were names he had heard throughout his childhood. The fate of any who set foot where he now stood was the same: to never return to Athos.

He fell to his knees as a breeze blew from behind him. All around him was a depressed land covered in ash and minimal sunlight. He reached down and took a handful of ash in his hands. It felt like nothing, empty, discarded. Useless. The wind blew it from his hands, his skin now stained gray.

As he stood and overlooked the land, the gravity of his situation settled over him. They'd cast him out like a common outlaw. They just wanted to get rid of him. Varim wanted to get rid of him. To begin their new plan, they had to. He'd been the final obstacle, and they'd made sure to handle him.

At first, Hal had been hesitant to believe, but as he stood before the ash-covered land of the forgotten, he could see the high minister's true thoughts of him. He was a threat to the throne, and eventually, he would have taken it. Familial bonds and years of proven trust did not mean anything, it seemed, and he saw that now.

Sadness and despair filled his heart. Everything he had worked for, suffered for, had been ripped away from him. And as he stood in the open fields of ash, he felt how he looked: a lost soul in a barren land.

He fought back his tears, but no one would hear him cry in these lands. The tears rolled from his eyes as he stared at the massive mountain in the distance. His brow furrowed, and he unleashed a shattering roar that could wake the heavens. But when he finished, the Ashlands gave him no audience, only silence.

Along the ground lay broken armor pieces and bones not yet covered by the ash. He knelt and brushed some ash away to reveal what hid underneath. Sheathed in a leather holster tattered and torn from its stay was a lightvolver. Hal removed it from its holster, and the barrel of the weapon was almost as long as his forearm. He gave it a onceover and spun the light-cyclers. Everything seemed to be operational, and he took a shot. When it didn't explode back in his face, he knew the weapon was still usable. Then his gaze shifted down to the scraps of belongings on the ground, the remains of those who'd violated the Code, stripped of flesh and meat. He did not want to end up like them.

He knew wolves roamed the ash to devour the bodies of those sent here, though he did not want to see one up close. If he wanted to live to see his plan through, he had to find water and shelter. Never had he heard of any survivors coming back from the Ashlands, but he was not going to die here.

A few feet away from where he found the lightvolver was a tattered cloak blowing in the breeze. It wasn't much but it would keep the ash from building up and sticking to him. As he placed it on, he looked back to the ground where a hand frozen still gripped a small handle. Hal knelt down and pried it from the hand as fingers broke off and released their grip. He activated the button on the side when a golden hardlite dagger sprang up, a kyr. Hal sighed as he stuffed it away along his belt. Stealing from the dead was a dishonorable deed but he had to scavenge for everything he could use.

Hal stood and began his trek through the twisting paths and untamed dead brush that lay under a veil of ash. He had to be careful. One wrong step and he could end up injured and easy prey for whatever lived out here. Predators loomed in the back of his mind, and the wolves weren't all he was worried about.

Elders spoke of a dragon-like snake creature that wormed its way through the ash. The thought made him think of the Polarians' sandworms. No one ever saw these dragonsnakes with their own eyes though. The thought made him shiver. He was used to being the hunter, the one who attacked and fought for what he needed, but in this alien land, he was nowhere close to becoming a predator. Not yet.

As he moved through the unforgiving ash, he kept an eye out. He stood out like a giant target. Misplaced. He knew he did not belong here, in a realm for the forgotten, the exiled. He pushed through a mound of ash and slid down the hill before he came to the openness of the valley. He had to find a spot to gather his thoughts and take a breath before the sun gave way to the moon.

Like cacti in the desert, translucent treelike silhouettes stood out in the middle of the ash. Cool blues and greens moved across their trunks and branches in a chevron pattern, only to change colors when the wind shifted direction. Hal stared at the strange trees. They found a way to live out here, constantly berated by the wind. He was reassured by the sight; it was a small glimmer of hope in the Ashlands.

Hal took one step, and the ground gave way. Time slowed as he fell through a hidden crevasse encased by rocky walls. Ash and rocks tumbled down as Hal used his legs and arms to wedge himself between the walls of the crevasse. He waited for the dirt and rocks to stop before he looked up at the faint glow of light above. Below him, darkness shrouded a void he'd rather not explore. Shrieks of creatures from the darkness only told him further that it was not a place he wanted to go. Upward was his only solution.

When he tried to push himself up, the wall gave way, and Hal used all his strength to grip a small handhold. The rocks fell and shattered as they hit the distant ground with an echo. Hal pulled himself up to a ledge that could barely fit his body and took a deep breath. This land held danger at every corner, and it was his distracted thoughts that had almost led him to his death. He had to get out of here. Handholds lined the way up. All he had to do was climb and not slip.

The first was easy. Hal positioned himself and reached for the next handhold, pushing himself up. Slow and steady, he reached behind him for the next. Just out of reach. He'd cursed this land so many times, he could've filled a swear jar twice. The light above started to fade, and he knew night approached.

A gargled hiss came from the darkness below. Hal readied himself and leapt to the handhold across the gap, grabbing the rock as tight as he could. The handhold did not collapse, and Hal sighed in relief. The rest of the climb was much easier, and he soon pulled himself up and over the ledge and back into the cold embrace of the ash.

Hours went by as he wandered through the ash. The only sense of direction he had was that great mountain in the distance, though at this rate, he didn't know how much farther it was. To make matters worse, the dim sunlight began to fade from the gray ground. If he wanted to last the night, he would have to find shelter.

The mundane gray offered a little reprieve as Hal walked through a dead forest of twisted trees. The cold seeped through his clothes and sunk to his bones. As he emerged from a dead forest of broken trees, Hal came to a small river that ran downhill. Turned gray like the ashy sky above, it wasn't suitable to drink. He needed to purify it. Farther along the bank was a cave nestled into the ash covered rocks and he headed for it. It left much to be desired, but anything that got him out of the ash worked. The only thing he needed now was a fire.

As he approached the cave entrance, Hal poked his head in, and the rocky cave appeared vacant, a sign he welcomed. Hal stepped in and was met by damp, musty air. Though most would have been turned off by the sensation, to him it meant there was water somewhere deeper inside. It could've also harbored some animal he wasn't aware of. Despite his better judgment, he pressed on.

As he shimmied through the narrow rocks, the air got thicker and wetter. Small collections of algae built up on the walls and produced a soft blue light that led the way. He squeezed through a series of more gaps before coming to an open chamber. His eyes widened.

A pool sat in the middle, bubbling up from the ground. Warmth kissed his skin, and he rushed to it. Sliding to the edge, Hal knelt and brought the warm water to his face and sipped. It was bitter, but it gave him life.

After he finished his drink, he looked up, and on the far wall of the cave was an etching of some sort. Intrigued by its ornate style, Hal moved closer. Age had eroded most of what had been there, but he saw what appeared to be two people looking upward to a circle. Hal studied it for a few more moments.

"What are you?"

An echo of rocks fell from where he had come from, followed by the sound of paws running on the stone ground, and he snapped to the sound of it. Creatures lurked everywhere but stayed hidden. If he was to survive out here, he would need a fire to keep them away.

It did not take long to gather rocks and firewood. Dead trees were scattered everywhere, and all he had to do was brush away the ash. The trees snapped with barely any force, showing how brittle life was here. After placing everything in the pit, sheltered by the cave, he held up his hand to send a quick burst of flames out. But something felt off. The warmth he used to feel within was gone, replaced by a sense of emptiness he'd never felt before. When he tried to charge his hand with flames, nothing happened. Hal looked at his hand for a moment before trying again. Nothing, not even a spark.

Then the realization hit him.

"You are a Wielder no more."

The words struck him like a brick wall as the emptiness grew colder inside.

He couldn't believe it. To have his Wielding powers stripped away made him feel alone, vulnerable. Everything he knew was gone. A void filled him. No feeling. Numb. He'd been born with these gifts from the Primordials, learned by his Empyrean forefathers, and to have them taken away felt like nothing short of having a limb ripped from his body.

This had to be the greatest failure of an Empyrean, a Skyborn, there had ever been. He'd failed his family, the throne, and the people he cared about. Hal sat back against the cave wall and sighed. His family had been torn apart, and his sister now aided that snake of a minister. And he still never got to see his love. There were so many people he'd failed.

Darkness crept into the cave. He needed light to be able to see and keep the predators away. He needed it but could not create it—not like he used to. As he stared at the empty pit, he thought of the fire and how easily he could have generated it. They'd sent him here to die.

The firepit became everything he was and everything he was not. They would not stop him. Hal pushed himself up and gathered a few pieces of wood, collecting tufts of thatch that banded together with the aid of the ash. He threw some thatch and fibers on the larger piece of wood and positioned the other over it with the point downward. As he took a deep breath, he began to spin it back and forth. He remembered Imperial scouts using this technique when he went with them in the forests. It had been archaic to him then, but now he saw why they practiced it. They'd shown him how to make fire without Wielding. Now all he had to do was remember.

Hal used his weight to provide pressure as he spun the wood in his hands. Despite the cold, heat built up in his palms, and sweat dripped from his nose. He tried to avoid the small amount of tinder he had, but the darkness made it almost impossible to see. The air felt still, silent, almost as if he was being watched. The hair on the back of his neck rose.

He kept rolling, gritting his teeth as his shoulders and biceps began to burn. Blisters formed on his hands, but he had to get this fire started or die. Those were his only options, and he did not feel like dying yet. Soon, a small stream of smoke formed, and Hal kept rolling. He'd had no idea how tiresome this could be.

As the smoke grew larger and more potent, Hal saw the first signs of an ember. He quickly removed the piece of wood and blew gently on the small ember. More smoke rose from the tinder, and he kept blowing. The first flames sparked to life, and Hal quickly added the twigs. As they popped and crackled, he added larger pieces of wood. The warmth bounced off the cave walls and grew into a fire fit to live upon.

Grunts and growls filled the cave. They could smell his fear.

With one motion, Hal grabbed one of the larger pieces of flaming wood and pointed it at the cave entrance, where three large figures stood. Nine glowing eyes stared at him. Long arms with four massive claws tensed in anticipation. The beasts snarled and bared their long teeth, drool pouring from the sides of their lips, while one beat its muscular chest. Scraggly gray hair covered most of their bodies.

Hal yelled and thrust his wooden torch at them in hopes to make them leave. He gripped the lightvolver, ready to blast holes if he needed to.

Two of the ghostly figures left, but the third stayed for a moment. It growled at him before it too left down the rocky path. Hal let out a deep breath as the fire danced, its flames reaching out to touch him with their warmth.

This was his world now. Varim had placed him here. Back home, he was probably filling the city with lies about his betrayal and how the Empire was strongest when together and using Miri as a pawn. Though she was the victim of circumstance, one thing stayed true: Varim was the traitor, not his sister.

When Hal thought of Miri, his gaze became soft and sad. The pain he'd felt when he realized she betrayed him was more emotionally jarring than he could have imagined. Something had to have happened for her to change that quickly, but he had no idea what. That wasn't her.

A tickle came into his nose as his eyes began to cloud with unwanted water. He tried so hard to hold it back and fight it, but the tears came regardless. He sat there as the life he once knew ended with the sound of his own cries.

CHAPTER XV

Hal held a branch against his leg and sheared off slivers of wood with a sharpened stone. Food was as essential to survival as practice was to honing skills. The rumbles of his stomach had kept him up most of the night, but he'd been too afraid to go out in the dark after the encounter with those beasts. The days spent locked in a cell did not fare well for his nutrition either. He could only stand the taste of stale bread for so long, and now he needed protein.

He remembered seeing a bend in the river later the night before. It was a little farther on where the water calmed to a steady flow and knew animals would venture there to get a morning drink. Risky to say the least, Hal wanted to know what his surroundings contained and the only way to do that was to venture out. But to reward his bravery, he had found a small and scratched metal canteen nearly buried under the ash along the bank near the bend. It was a small victory but that proved the river bend to be fruitful, and in more ways than one, he hoped.

Whatever creatures came by there he had to get. This place so far had been barren to the core, and it seemed only predators called this place home. He shook the thought of becoming food for one of them from his mind. It would take time, but he would conquer this land like he had done others.

He held up his wooden spear and narrowed his eyes in determination. Nothing would stand in his way of revenge.

The sun had just started to crest over the mountains in the distance, turning the sky into the hazy fire it had been before. Hal hid in dead shrubs, letting the ash cover him. It did not matter how long it took; he would eat today.

The Ashlands held so many mysteries that he would've loved to explore under normal circumstances. But these were no ordinary circumstances. He had no army, no ships, and no sense of direction. All he had was the primal instinct to survive and not fall victim to the horrors this land contained.

A snap broke the stillness. He turned as a small furry creature dipped its head to drink. His eyes grew wide with anticipation as he readied his spear. Everything went still as he focused on the creature. His blood pulsed with every beat of his heart as he took aim. A breeze blew toward the bank as he slowly stood, and the creature turned its head toward him.

Three large eyes and long twin teeth stared back at him. It only took a second for the beast to scurry off, and the spear crashed into the dirt where it had once stood. Hal kicked the ground and cursed into the breeze.

As he collected the spear, he peered into the river. It didn't flow like the rivers back home, with white waters and rapids, but instead flowed so slowly it could've passed for stagnant.

Something has to live in there. As if his thoughts had somehow called them, a fish thrashed and rippled the water. He would not waste another opportunity to fill his stomach.

Perched on a nearby rock, Hal leaned over and stared into the ashy water. He could barely see the bottom and the fish that swam there. Like one of the majestic herons he watched back home, he waited patiently. Only his eyes moved. Anything else would spook the fish. His body soon felt the effects of stillness, but he suppressed the calls of discomfort. A cold breeze made his eyes water, but he only cared about proving himself. Failure after failure had withered his resolve, but one fish would change all of that. If anything else, it would prove he was not a failure.

Not here.

A sizable fish swam by, its dorsal fin breaching the surface of the water. Hal waited for the right moment. He noted the direction of the breeze, then followed the fish, his eyes trained just in front of it, analyzing the right place to launch his spear to account for the water's refraction. The fish swam under the rock he stood on, and he thought he'd missed his chance. His shoulders and arms began to burn as he held the position. He'd almost decided to take a break when the head of the fish peeked out from under the rock. Hal made his move.

The spear sliced through the water, and Hal pulled out the fish, which was the size of his forearm. He laid it on the rock he stood on and smiled as it flopped by his feet before lying still. Months of training in Imperial encampments and fortresses allowed him to do what most city folk could not do. Life in the outdoors, away from the bustle of the city, proved to challenge him. Even his sister did not know how to make a fire, because there was no reason to. But oftentimes he and his fellow soldiers had had to forage for food in the Yasu System.

On nights when plasma artillery bursts weren't lobbed onto their position, he'd searched for viable food sources should supply lines ever be cut off. Berries, small game, palm hearts, and even the fleshy bulbs of knife-grass bushes had all been essential. He recalled an earlier part of the war when he was still the commander of a platoon when they were caught behind Polarian lines. With no food besides their rations and little water, they'd had to survive until reinforcements could reach them.

Like then, he now scavenged. He had not received special treatment then and certainly wouldn't receive it now. Mother Nature cared not for who he was. Survival mattered only if he was able to put his training to use, and this catch reminded him of that. He was nothing out here, just a body.

"Bless thee upon Empyrea," he said as he picked his catch up.

As he looked out past the pond where the ash had built into hills before the mountains, he realized he was still at war.

The fire crackled in the cave, and Hal sat back and smiled, inhaling the alluring scent of roasting fish. Some said something caught and cooked by oneself tasted better than anything else, and Hal had to agree as he took the first bite. It was flaky and sweet, and his mouth watered for more as he finished his piece. For the first time since awakening here, he felt a sense of comfort. Warmth from the fire reinforced that as he took a swig of water from the canteen he found. He had everything he needed, and now he could focus on the task at hand.

His thoughts drifted back to the days just before his exile when he saw his mother on the video. For as long as he could remember, she had been a staunch Primordial researcher and Empyrean scholar. She'd been murdered in cold blood by that rat of a high minister while trying to warn him, his family, the Empire. The secrets of what she knew lay in the temple she'd mentioned. If he was going to take back the throne, he had to start with the only clue he had: Starlite Temple.

A distant hum from outside the cave caught his attention. It sounded through the darkness like a haunted banshee in search of a poor soul. The hum grew louder, then stopped. After grabbing his lightvolver, he took a few steps outside and gazed around. Ashfall grayed everything out, even the forest of dead trees. Then he heard it again, louder this time, almost too close.

When he turned around, an android leapt from the top of the cave. Its thunderous fall knocked him off-balance. The android charged Hal and threw its shoulder into him. The blow sent Hal tumbling down the hill, and it felt like he hit every rock along the way.

Lost in the blanket of ash, Hal pushed himself up with a groan and quickly scanned the area. The red eyes of the bot emerged from the veil of ash like a ghost. Half of its face was gone, ripped apart, and the mechanical innerworkings coupled with synthetic flesh flapped in the wind.

Hal raised his lightvolver and fired a shot right between the android's eyes. The red faded until empty sockets remained, and the android fell to the ground.

As Hal caught his breath, another hum came from within the ash. He glanced around to see where it had come from, then ducked when a rusty metal arm swung at him. The android's fist crashed into the tree and splintered wood like a bomb had gone off. Hal jumped back and shielded himself as the wood splinters flew through the air, and when he turned to face the android, it had vanished.

Hal gripped his lightvolver and listened closely, blocking out every noise except for that hum. When it stopped for a moment, Hal fired a shot of energy from his lightvolver, and sparks danced within the veil of ash. The android fell face-first at his feet, and Hal breathed a sigh of relief.

He knelt beside it, sparks still flicking into the air, and turned the android over. Rusty metal and pitted carbon alloy greeted him with a lifeless face. As he looked toward the chest, he noted the Imperial serial code, make, and model. They were outdated models, last-generation androids discarded by their owners.

But before he could inspect anything else, the hum returned. As Hal turned around, another android gripped him by the throat and raised him into the air. Its grip tightened, and Hal gasped for air, staring into the android's soulless red eyes. It felt like a constrictor around his neck, and with every breath he took, the hand of the android tightened. His vision began to blur as oxygen struggled to reach his brain. Hal raised his lightvolver slowly, which caught the android's attention. With a single motion, the android threw Hal against a tree like he was made of paper. Splinters and wood shattered upon impact, and Hal fell into the ash.

Pain coursed through his head, and he clutched his leg as the android closed in on him. His vision blurred, and he struggled to keep his eyes open. Blood oozed from around a piece of wooden shrapnel lodged in his thigh, coating the ash red.

The android stood right in front of him. A red light emitted from its eyes and ran up and down Hal's body. When it finished, the android transformed its arm into a barrel and aimed it at Hal.

Hal glared at it and vowed not to let this creation take his life. There had to be something he could do.

His lightvolver lay in the ash just a few feet away. He reached for it, grabbing the ash and feeling the ground in an attempt to pull himself closer, but the android stepped on his wounded leg. The pain overloaded any sense of thought, and Hal yelled as the weight of the android pressed down on him.

There was a crack, and a violet flash of light crashed into the android's chassis. The machine dropped to the ash in a flash of sparks. Oil leaked from it just as blood leaked from him.

He could not fight the pain any longer. As his vision began to dim and consciousness faded, a masked figure emerged from the ash.

CHAPTER XVI

Hal's eyes slowly opened. An intense pain throbbed in his head, and he raised a hand to rub it away, but the soothing feeling only lasted a moment. As his eyes adjusted, Hal stared at a fire, and the smell of smoke filled his nose. Supplies lay about, neatly separated from one another: a couple pots on one side, wooden utensils on the other. Even a bag hung in one of the trees as shadows danced in the dim firelight. The light was fading from the sky as thick ashclouds brewed in the distance, and darkness loomed.

He tried to push himself up, but the pain in his head and leg made his vision blur. He could only push his back against the tree behind him. He glanced down to where his wound was, and somebody had tied a bandage around it, though the bandage was already bloodstained. It felt like he'd been run over by a duster bike and thrown off a mountain.

He sat and looked around his surroundings. This wasn't the same place where he had first entered the Ashlands. There were no ghost trees that changed color; instead, trees with dark, sickly gray leaves stood high for as far as he could see. Their solid wooden trunks were peeled and bored into, and their canopy of intertwined dry branches caught ash from above. It reminded him of the aftermath of a forest fire, but then the cold breeze blew through and bit down on his flesh. A shiver overtook him, and he scooted closer to the small fire.

A crack of wood out in the woods caught his attention. Hal snapped his gaze over to where he'd heard it and reached for a rock that lay nearby. Everything else faded as the rustling of the foliage grew louder. If he was going to go down, he was going to bring one of those androids with him.

From the cover of twisted branches emerged a young woman in a white suit that hugged her body. She moved quietly, almost stealthily toward him, a karver sword folded into the hilt and hanging at her waist.

Hal gazed into the woman's lavender eyes, and a wave of surprise washed over him. His heart sank with concern and erupted into joy at the same time.

"Kristilin?"

Tears almost welled in his eyes. Her eyes were unforgettable. They were a color palette of beautiful purples, and they always calmed him.

The young woman moved closer, ice-blue skin peeking out above her face mask. She looked him straight in the eyes without saying a word.

She slid her face mask down from her nose and slowly removed her hood to show her snow-white hair and icy-blue skin, then took a seat across from him and stirred the fire.

Hal searched her eyes, but her expression was unreadable.

She leaned back, hands braced behind her, and canted her head. A smile formed on her lips as she shook her head.

"Halcion Skyborn," she said in an accent that made Hal melt. It wasn't like the common accents that spanned Athos and the Empire. Her voice was like music, foreign and soothing as it danced around his ears. "I was beginning to think you were never going to wake up, but I should have remembered the Skyborns' resilience is stronger than most."

Hal was at a loss for words. He shook off the confusion and said, "What are you doing here? I thought you were . . . Well, I don't know."

She glanced away. "That is what happens when you fall victim to the Ashlands. People forget about you—your name, who you were." She turned back to him with a glare. "Out here, you are nobody. People disappear for better or for worse."

Hal scooted closer to the fire and held out his hands. The bitter cold had finally gotten the better of him, and he welcomed the warmth.

Kristilin got up and went for the bag that hung in the tree. She retrieved a thermos and two cups before returning to the fire. She filled the cups with a dark liquid that steamed in the cool air, then offered it to him.

Hal took it. A whiff of the cinnamon filled his mind with memories of the days when he'd stayed at Kristilin's chateau, where her mother used to make fresh cinnamon buns that filled the entire palace with that same smell. Two years had gone by since he had smelled anything like it.

"It will help with the pain in your head," she said.

As Hal drank the liquid, the warmth of it traveled down his throat and instantly began to relieve some of the pain in his joints and head. He looked at Kristilin. "You're the one who killed that android?"

Kristilin ran a hand through her white hair. "I did."

"Thank you."

She nodded and smiled as she wrapped her arms around herself. He wanted to hug her so much, but he knew the time wasn't right. But he had to say something.

"Kristi, I'm sorry."

"Not now, Hal. Not here," she said. "There is too much danger."

Almost on cue, thunder rumbled in the distance, and massive clouds rolled across the sky.

"I have tracked you since your arrival in the Ashlands," Kristilin said. "I saw the Imperial enforcers step through the transporter and thought it was just another poor soul. But when I saw you with my own eyes . . ." She looked down to where ash had collected on her boots. "At first I thought it was a mistake. Hal Skyborn in the Ashlands? That could not be. I prayed it was not true. But as the days went on, I saw you struggle and fight, and you did not Wield. But I wanted to make sure it was my Hal. I have more questions than answers, Hal. Why are you here?"

Hal hesitated for a moment. She'd referred to him as *hers*. There was still a connection after so long. There was so much he could say, but also so much she would not believe. Even if she did believe, he had no idea how she would react.

On the other hand, lies sent men to graves, and there was already enough of that going around. What past they shared did not necessarily mean she would believe, but he needed to tell someone.

The ideals of the council and high minister could not be allowed to come to fruition. It would be crazy talk to her. But if he was to stop them, he had to start now, and he would be nowhere without allies, friends. Trust had to be the foundation he built upon. And he knew he could trust her with everything.

Hal looked at Kristilin and said, "The Imperial Council betrayed the Code, and the high minister plans to restructure the Empire how he sees fit."

She narrowed her eyes, brow furrowed.

Hal shook his head. "I was supposed to become the Crown Prince when the Polarians surrendered. I could have built a new Empire of Athos, one founded on determination, loyalty, and respect."

"You were denied again?"

"I've always been denied," Hal said as he stared into her lavender eyes. "Everything I did, *tried*, all came to a crashing end with the council's disapproval." He looked away and sighed. "It wasn't supposed to be like this."

"So, how did you end up here?" Kristilin asked as she warmed her hands by the fire.

Hal looked into the orange flames, which reminded him of the ones he'd had. "They said I killed my father. And Miri believed it."

Kristilin jerked her hands away from the fire and stared at him with soft eyes. "Hal, I am—"

"That's not all. I found a hidden video." He looked back at Kristilin. "I saw a recording of my mother in the moments before she died. She said something about a temple—Starlite Temple—and that I would find answers there. And I know who her killer is: Varim."

Kristilin mumbled something in her native tongue before she spoke. "Did you tell the court before you were exiled?"

"No, but I tried to tell Miri. Her ears were deaf to my words. Varim did something to her, to the people in Imperius."

Kristilin leaned back with her arms to brace herself and said, "Any idea where this temple is?"

Hal sighed. "I had no time to research. She—" Hal looked at her and stopped. "I don't know."

Kristilin tilted her head in response. "I am sorry, Hal. But everyone should know that you had no part in it. That is common sense."

"Common sense isn't common anymore," he replied. "I don't know who I can trust now."

"Well, I know one thing: we need shelter before night falls." She nodded to the north. "There is a group of Ashborn I trade with, exiles who formed a community. If we move quickly, we can be there by tomorrow evening. Maybe someone knows something about this temple. You never know. I have a friend there who may know something." She stood up and stretched out her hand. "The past is the past. The Ashlands have a way of reinventing you, Hal. I was alone when I first arrived here, but you will not be."

"Why were you sent here? Last I heard, Velra closed all communications with everyone."

"A new matriarch took control of the government. She rescinded all noble titles on the planet. Took the land that had been in our family for generations." She took a deep breath. "Some protested the changes. I did, even though my parents thought it was—how do you say—fruitless. We were all imprisoned. Most executed. My parents negotiated for exile instead. I still do not know what became of them."

"By Empyrea, what is going on?" Hal stood up with her, a whole head taller. "I won't leave you again. We need to figure out what's happening to the worlds we know."

She smiled. For the first time in a while, he felt honesty and kindness. Hal extended his arm and grasped Kristilin's gloved hand. It felt good to have her by his side again. It felt like a piece of him had been put back into place, but that piece still needed to be polished.

All in time, he thought.

"Good," she said.

Thunder cracked overhead, and the clouds now had a green hue. The wind began to pick up and throw ash everywhere. Kristilin looked at Hal with wide eyes. "We need to go now."

Without another word, she grabbed Hal by the hand and led him down a narrow path to a duster bike. The handholds and footholds on either side of the slender frame glowed a dim blue. The vehicle sat in perfect suspension over the ground, the underside glowing a dim purple.

Kristilin quickly pulled a blanket from one of the saddlebags on the side of the duster and tossed it to Hal.

"Cover yourself with it, and hop on," she said as she raised her face mask and hood.

Hal wrapped the blanket around his shoulders as rain began to fall. He thought he saw steam rise from a tree branch, but Kristilin's call made him hurry up and hop onto the back of the vehicle. The rain pattered across the blanket, a sturdy yet malleable fabric. Kristilin flipped a switch, and the vehicle roared to life with a distinct whine as she accelerated.

She was a brilliant racer. Oftentimes they would compete in aerial races, despite protests from their parents, with the victor always in alternation. This vehicle, though, was not aerial, and his heart skipped a few beats when some trees got a little too close.

Minutes felt like hours as they rode across the ash to the rumble of thunder. The wind dried out Hal's eyes, and he used the blanket to mimic the hood and face mask Kristilin had, though to no avail. Ash still found its way in.

Large hills of accumulated ash stretched for as far as he could see, which was only about a mile or so as the ashstorm stirred up more ash. Still, the duster glided over and down the hills and skirted along the valleys between them, and Kristilin drove the duster right into a cave just as the sky opened up in force.

As they disembarked, Hal looked back out at the haze of greenish rain, which disintegrated the ash like a recycler made by nature.

"What is that?" Hal asked as he turned to face Kristilin.

"Acid rain," she said as she fiddled through a container nearby.

A few other containers and loose items lay scattered about: a shovel against a cave wall, a few scraps of metal piled near the back, some more containers stacked neatly together. A tanning rack with some sort of gray-blue hide stretched across it stood on the other side of the cave, and a bedroll was unrolled near the back wall. It seemed Kristilin had kept herself busy.

"It comes every now and then when the weather moves over the volcanoes."

Hal looked on in disbelief. This place was a literal hell. The fire within him began to burn once again as he cursed Varim for betraying him and sending him here.

"Here. You'll need this." Kristilin held out a full two-part black bodysuit. Like hers, a zipper attached the hood and face mask to the rest of the suit for ease of removal. "It's an evosuit, an enhanced environmental protection suit. If you're going to live here, you're going to need one."

"Thanks. Where did you get this?"

"I traded with a roaming Ashborn merchant. It was included with the leathers I traded." She pointed to the tanning rack. "It doesn't fit me, obviously, but an evosuit is valuable out here. The fabric can regulate your temperature and forms a barrier against the wind and acid rain. It is as strong as padded leather armor but more durable. Take it."

Hal took it, and the fabric was sturdy. It felt almost like leather armor but was much more pliable. Inside, however, the suit was incredibly soft and smooth.

"Behind the tanning rack is a cutout in the cave. You can change there if you want."

Hal nodded. He found the cutout and tossed his tattered clothes aside. Though the cutout was there, it hardly provided enough space to not show himself. As he slipped his legs through the evosuit, he looked out and caught Kristilin's gaze before she quickly turned away. Normally he wouldn't be so shy, and neither would she, but it was like they were relearning each other, and scars now marked his body.

They were the same people as before the war, but different, and they would have to figure that out. Still, he couldn't help but feel like it was his fault she had ended up here. If he hadn't left, she wouldn't be suffering in this hellhole.

He finished changing into the suit before returning to Kristilin. The fabric hugged his body, and the coolness he'd felt had been replaced by warmth and comfort. He held his hands outstretched by his sides and said, "It feels nice."

"Comfort is a necessity out in the ash," she replied. "Here. Take one of these too."

She handed him a small earpiece that reminded him of the communicators he'd used during the war. If the weather they'd traveled through was any indicator, this would make it much easier to talk despite the wind's howl.

As he took it, Hal looked out behind him. Darkness consumed the land. The wind whipped by the cave opening, and ash fluttered into the cave. The ashstorm was almost overtop of them. Green lightning painted ominous pictures in the backdrop of the dark clouds. Hal turned back to Kristilin, and there was a glint in her eyes. He was happy to be here with her. It was awful they were here in the first place, but being together made it all right. Hal stepped up to the cave entrance, and the harsh scent of sulfur entered his nose. It stung and made him gag.

Kristilin came up beside him with her face mask and hood up. "You will get used to it. It took me a while to adjust."

Hal threw his hood and face mask up. The air felt much crisper and purer than before as he took a breath. He wondered how many new things he had to learn and adapt to.

Varim had thought he would easily get rid of him by throwing him here, but he'd made a grave mistake.

He wasn't alone now.

CHAPTER XVII

The hours went on into the early morning and so did the howl of the wind. Hal had never experienced something so dangerous yet beautiful at the same time. As dawn turned to high morning, the ashstorm swirled over them, the winds growing to hurricane force and throwing ash in every direction. Kristilin said this was a weaker storm, but it made little difference. The sheer power and awe-inspiring scene captured Hal's interest. Blue flashes pulsed within the storm clouds while the ash created a wall of pure gray. It came over them and darkened what light poked through the veil in the sky.

As Hal raised his face mask, ash rained in, and the winds blew. He stood at the edge of the cave and smiled behind the mask. It reminded him of the sandstorms of Polaris and the hurricanes that slammed across Athos.

When the first bolt of lightning struck the ground, the explosion from the impact rocked the land, generating a burst of heat. Hal's hood fluttered behind him in the wind, and the absence of sulfur in the air made him realize this storm had one intention. Another flash and another explosion rocked the land. A flash of blue struck a dead tree, and wood splintered in every direction. Destruction for a destroyed land.

As fast as the storm came, it vanished, and in its wake were broken trees that smoldered on the ashy ground. Kristilin approached and stood beside him. Only the rumbles of the ashstorm's thunder carried over the ashlands. Thin rays of sickly sunlight poked through the thinnest of the storm's clouds as it continued its path of destruction elsewhere.

As much as they tried to fight it, nature always reigned supreme. It reminded him just how small he was in a world so big. Again, Hal smiled when Kristilin broke the silence.

"We should go before the next one comes," she said as she looked at him. "The town is a few miles north, and we have a mountain range to cross." She moved to her duster and placed a canteen and some dried food in one of the saddlebags before hopping on. "If we hurry, we can be there before evening comes."

"Are you sure your friend will want to help me?" Hal asked.

"I am positive. She is a student of the arcane. If anyone here knows something about the Empyreans or Primordials, it's her," Kristilin replied.

Hal took a seat behind her as the engine fired. He would never tire of the jetdrive coming to life. It was like music to his ears and one of the best things he'd heard out here, besides Kristilin's voice, of course. They both covered their heads and faces before Kristilin grabbed the handlebars and punched the throttle.

❧⟫⟫⟩ ⟨⟨⟨⟨❧

Hal looked back at the high plume of ash the duster turbulence had stirred up. Ash-covered rock replaced the soft dunes as they came to an outcrop. They had made it to the mountains, and it was just before noon. Kristilin checked her watch every now and then to make sure they were on time. Hal assumed time was precious here. The ashstorm from last night and their brisk pace to the rocks only reinforced that.

The sky was unlike any other. Hazy gray coated it and blocked the sun from view. The engine of the duster whined at its deepest pitch as it ascended the steep rocky slope of the mountain pass. Hal had his hands around Kristilin as he peered down at the steep fall they would take if something happened. It wasn't the first time the land had tried to intimidate him, but the comfort he felt with Kristilin put his mind at ease, at least until the repulsers hit a bump that felt like it would launch them over the side. The land was definitely not as smooth as the forests back home.

When the duster stopped, Hal looked around the flat spot of land where the rocks formed a natural clearing.

Kristilin looked back at him. "I have to stretch my legs."

Hal quickly released his grip from around Kristilin and disembarked with her. He walked to the ledge and looked out over the vastness of the Ashlands. Valleys, craters, mountains, and ridges stretched for miles. Ash coated the sparse trees and shrubbery, leaving those exposed to stand out with sickly leaves. Down below, some sort of deerlike animal grazed on the shortest grass he had seen while a flock of gray birds merged into the horizon. He wondered how something so hideous and unwelcoming could be so beautiful. It matched every description of purgatory he'd heard, but something about this land spurred the primal instincts those on the other worlds seemed to have forgotten.

"It takes a while to get used to," Kristilin said as she sat on a rock, dried meat in her hand.

Hal took the piece she offered and sat across from her. He shook his head. "I never thought I would be here. Not like this."

"Neither did I," Kristilin replied.

Hal looked up at her. "The last thing I expected was to find you here, Kristi. What happened to the worlds we knew? By Empyrea . . ." Hal said under his breath. "I had no clue where you were or . . . I tried to call when I had the chance, but every time we came under fire, and . . ."

"It is not your fault, Hal," Kristilin said as she stood up and walked to the ledge. "Politics have no remorse. Either you conform or you are silenced. Those with individual thoughts are weeded out and disposed of."

"But it wasn't supposed to happen to you," Hal said. "You were my . . . We were . . ."

"Not now. We will talk about that later," she said, her voice trembling slightly. She turned back to him. "Come now. The temperature is dropping, and we still have a ways to go."

Hal had no words. He wanted to say everything right then and there, but Kristilin was right. He couldn't pour his heart and mind out in the middle of a wasteland. They had to get to wherever they were headed first.

>>>>> <<<<<

They made it just before the first real ash rained down as the sun set. It came just like snow did and turned even the closest structure gray. Kristilin parked the duster along a dirt road while people stared, confusion on their faces. Hal pulled his hood over his head and looked away. His eyes told too much. People didn't have his pupils here. No one did. It was a dead giveaway, but he couldn't hide it. Who knew how these people would react when they saw someone associated with those responsible for their sentence here. He had to be cautious.

"Welcome to Hellas, the only real city I know of here," Kristilin said.

"Are all these people from the Empire?"

"Most are. I haven't seen too many of the other races here," she said.

Hal looked at the people, who glanced at them. It was hard not to look and see who his parents and perhaps Varim had sent here over the years. His body tensed. They all looked like they felt the same: uneasy.

Kristilin touched his arm. "Hey, you'll be fine. Don't worry."

The main road was lined with dozens of different shops, doors swinging as patrons came and went. Some buildings had furniture outside and looked more like residential dwellings with solid doors. Hal focused on the massive building in the back. Two stone towers sat connected on either side of a two-story building. Steps led up to the massive wooden archway and double doors. No doubt it belonged to someone important—a warlord or whoever owned this town.

Kristilin led him to a wooden building with large windows smudged by ash and threw open the swinging doors like some ranch hand from one of the frontier worlds. Those inside only glanced at them before returning to whatever they were doing. An awful smell filled Hal's nose as small plastic perko chips bounced on the wooden tables, followed by disgruntled sighs and snickering laughter.

At the table beside Hal, a man dressed in a similar evosuit took a puff from a cigar and blew it at him with a smirk. The smoke stung his nostrils. Such an act would have had the man's hands burned back in Imperius. But he had to remind himself that this was not Imperius. These people had no clue who he was and did not care in the slightest. But if they caught a glimpse of his eyes that could change quickly. He had to keep his head low.

They took a seat at the bar, and Hal looked around. He was surprised, in a way, to see something other than a withering husk of a human. No one survived the Ashlands but these people seemed to be doing just that, though they looked as hardy and weathered as any warrior he had seen.

Hal turned back around when something metal hit the wooden countertop and was surprised to see a few copper pieces. It had been a few hundred years since any form of tangible currency had been used across the Realmverse. The barkeep took his time and wiped the ash from the counter before taking the copper.

"What is it this time?"

"We need a room for the night," Kristilin said.

The barkeep pushed the coins back to her. "Afraid not."

"Why?"

"Disappearances out in the ash. Our people are going missing." He pointed behind him with a crooked thumb. "Asher doesn't want any outsiders in here until it's taken care of."

"You cannot be serious," Kristilin said. "I have traded with Hellas before—"

"You're not a clanmate. Roamers have no place."

The barkeep poured himself a drink and downed it. The sound of perko chips scattering across the floor caught Hal's attention, and he turned to face the table. One of the men stood up and waved an angry finger at the one across from him. Words were exchanged before a blaster bolt ripped through the air, and the man dropped into his seat. Hal's eyebrows shot up as blood pooled where the shot man sat slouched over. He was unaccustomed to such desperado-type behavior.

"Excuse me," the barkeep said before he left his place.

Two more men took a seat at the bar. The stench of outdated smoke and sweat curled the hairs in Hal's nose as the one beside him plopped an elbow onto the counter.

He looked at Hal and said, "You givin' the barkeep a hard time, *Outsider*?"

The tone in that last word made it clear they were not here to give him a tour of the town. After all, this was the place of exiles.

Hal shook his head. "Nope."

The man shifted in his seat. "Name's Dash, and 'round here we got a sense of hospitality for those who deserve it. I don't much like your tone, which means our hospitality ain't for you."

"And I don't appreciate your breath," Hal said as he fought the onslaught of stale hot air berating his nose.

Dash grabbed Hal by the collar and threw him back. He crashed into the table behind him, knocking beer and glass all over the floor. Hal jumped back up just in time to avoid one of Dash's fists. He threw the man back, but not before he felt the blow of a fist to his side. A bottle came down over his head, and Hal fell to the ground. Kristilin used her smaller frame and hit the pressure points of the second goon. The momentary stun was all she needed before she landed a swift punch that knocked his lights out. As Hal regained his footing, Dash returned and tackled him to the ground. A few good blows from Dash crashed against Hal's ribs before Kristilin pushed him off and helped Hal back up.

With blood trickling from his nose, Dash said, "Oy, what's the problem, Outsider? Gonna let your girlfriend do all the work?"

With all the force he could muster, Hal brought his fist down and across Dash's face and sent him crashing headfirst into the bar with a force so great it sent the whole saloon into a hush. The haymaker hurt his wrist for a moment, and he shook out his hand with a wince.

The twin doors flew open, and two figures stood silhouetted in a veil of gray ash. Hal turned to look, noting their weapons and the armor over their suits. As they approached, he could make out an insignia on their shoulders. All of his strategic plans and warrior training told him these were no ordinary townsfolk.

"Outsiders," one said. "Come with us."

Hal turned to Kristilin, who had a confused look on her face.

"Now," the other said as they placed a hand on the grip of a plasma pistol.

With a faint nod, Kristilin and Hal followed the guards out of the saloon. The guards led them down the street where townsfolk tended to their shop fronts. A drill whined through the open door of a garage where two men repaired a rusty duster. Beyond the row of shops, the guards brought them to a grand wooden hall with two large wooden doors. Guarded by a couple of others, they opened the doors and led Hal and Kristilin inside.

They found themselves in a somewhat humble keep for a leader. A mixture of stone, wood, and metal made up the walls, which were lined with torches. A giant chandelier of horns and bone hung above to give light all around and illuminated a wooden platform at the rear of the room. A large chair stood atop the platform, wrapped in gray leather, the armrests made of the curved bone of some animal. It looked completely handmade, simple but beautiful.

The doors behind them flew open, and in walked a tall man with shaggy brown hair. He looked no older than thirty but had the gaze of an experienced politician. Hal could smell it on him. His neat clothes were creased to perfection, and his long blue cloak reminded Hal of the one who'd betrayed him.

A frantic older man followed him, dragging a staff of polished wood with a crystal on the top. The dark circles under his eyes told Hal that the old man had been frazzled for a while, but he didn't look incompetent for his age. He must've been hardy to have survived the ash for so many years.

"We don't get many Outsiders in these parts," the younger man said as he looked at Hal. "It's like that for a reason. Your partner here is one of the few we allow in."

"So, now you kick us out?" Kristilin said. "Why? You have not left your hall for over a month."

"You don't have permanent status here. We take care of our own people first. Trading leathers here doesn't make you part of the clan."

"You know that is ridiculous, Asher."

Now Hal had a name to the face. Asher dismissed the comment with a wave of his hand. Hal cocked his head at the disrespect to Kristilin, a fist balling up, but he couldn't do anything outlandish yet. Asher walked in front of them and turned around, his arms folded across his chest.

"What's Prince Halcion Skyborn doing here?"

Hal froze. "How do you know me?"

"The eyes tell all," Asher said. "Your name travels far and wide here in the ash."

He looked at Kristilin, his eyes meeting hers, and she nodded. As he looked back at the man, he straightened up.

"Same as anyone caught here," he said as confidently as he could.

"I don't much like the sound of that. Something had to happen for you to be exiled here. Royals don't get exiled. So tell me. Trade some information from the outside systems, and you might be able to stay."

Hal bit his tongue, weighing the pros and cons of divulging information he wasn't too sure of himself yet. But Asher's eyes were honest and concerned. Judgment served him best, and it made the decision easier.

"The royal family has been purged from Imperius. My mother and father are dead, and my sister is left confused and in danger. And I am now where you see me."

"So, Imperius is in strife and so too will the rest of the Empire be," Asher said after a moment. "Who stomped on the Code?"

"High Minister Varim."

"Why are you here in my hall? You're more dangerous to us here than in Imperius. They left you alive for a reason."

Kristilin stepped forward. "Shall you tell us? Your guards dragged us in here and said we were not welcome."

Asher shook his head and shrugged. "Fear. It's what drives us all here. Stricter rules had to be implemented in the wake of the recent disappearances."

"People vanish all the time here," Kristilin said. "Why are you only now concerned about it?"

"Because it's gone on long enough," Asher said. "I won't have my people sold to other clans like slaves or let those Ashen heathens use them as ransom any longer."

Hal listened intently. What Asher had said made sense, and they were outsiders in the eyes of the people who called Hellas home. No doubt in this land there had to be rules. Asher had a right to be wary of his people and that earned respect from Hal.

The old man beside him paced back and forth, mumbling something, not at all concerned with what was being said. Whatever it was sounded important, but Hal had other things to worry about.

Asher looked back up and said, "My apologies. I am Asher Zyte, mayor of this town of exiles. Everyone here was exiled for one reason or another. As much as I would like to help you, I need to ensure the safety of my people first."

There was sarcasm in the last sentence. The mayor of this so-called town didn't really care what happened to them, but if Hal could do something to at least get Kristilin back inside to trade, then he had to try.

"What if we helped you?" Hal said. "We take care of something for you, and you give us free roam of the town." He looked at Kristilin, who had a questioning look on her face, but he knew how to handle these situations.

The mayor studied him for a moment, as if trying to weed out any sense of dishonesty. With a glance to the old man, Asher sighed.

"Okay. Travel to the enclave located in the mountains over the northern hills. Misselie, Mister Stravis's assistant"—Asher nodded to the old man pacing back and forth—"was reportedly going there."

"Misselie? She's missing?" Kristilin asked, her lavender eyes going wide.

"I fear something happened to her," Stravis said as he leaned over the staff, almost out of breath from pacing, his eyes pleading.

If this would give them a base of operations to collect their thoughts, then so be. He looked over to Kristilin, and her eyes were full of concern.

"How long has she been gone?" Hal asked.

"Five days. She was certain there was something of Empyrean design at that old enclave, but I have been there a hundred times before and found nothing. I thought it would be a good chance for her to explore by herself for once, but I should've been smarter than that," the old man said.

Asher placed a hand on the old man's shoulder and looked at the two of them. "If you do that, clear out whatever is there and find Misselie, then I'll grant you access to the town."

Before Hal could say anything in return, Kristilin spoke up.

"Deal."

CHAPTER XVIII

It was the first decent night's sleep Hal had gotten in the last few days. Though hay for bedding and a blanket with strands of wispy gray animal hair were far from what he was accustomed to, it was better than the dark cold confines of a cave.

As he rolled over and pushed himself up, hot breath blew in his face. He looked up, and a horse-like creature stared back at him as if to ask why he was there. The gentle creature had a thick coat of dark fur and grunted when Hal raised an arm and touched it.

"Easy there. Sorry I had to sleep in your house," Hal said as he rubbed the fluffy fur along the creature's muzzle. "Seems like you have a nice place here though. It's warm, out of the weather, out of danger. Hopefully we can find something like that. Permanently."

The creature snorted and flashed its teeth at Hal before shooting a thick ball of slime from its mouth. Hal closed his eyes as the goo ball covered his face with sticky wetness. Never in a thousand years had he expected to get spat at, let alone by a horse creature.

The animal flapped its lips and made a series of snickering huffs as if laughing at him.

"Thanks," he said.

As he wiped the spit from his face, the scent of fresh bread drifted into the stable and lifted his spirits. When he turned to look, Kristilin stood in the open doorway with raised eyebrows and a smile.

"He spat at me," Hal said as he pointed to the horse creature.

"He likes you," she said as she stepped in and sat beside him. "He is a bernaton, much like the horses you have on Athos. They are gentle but can be mischievous."

"Sounds like my sister . . . or, well, the one I knew," Hal said.

"We will understand what happened after we find Misselie. But first you need to eat," Kristilin said as she handed him two bread rolls. "It's not much, but it's what I could trade for."

Hal took the soft, flaky rolls, then tried to hand one back to Kristilin, but she refused.

"I may need to eat, but so do you, Kristi. We need to count on each other out here, and whatever we get, we're sharing evenly."

She gazed into his eyes, and Hal almost melted away again. He could've gazed into her eyes forever. They were like a portal to calmness and unaltered beauty.

Kristilin smiled and took the second bread roll, her fingers touching his for a second. It felt like they were in school again; every little touch seemed larger than it was, and the nerves he felt worked to the depths of his stomach. A small blush rose on Kristilin's cheeks, turning her blue cheeks purple, and heat steamed from the collar of Hal's evosuit. There was so much to say, but it still wasn't the right time. Not yet. Not until they got situated.

After they finished their bread rolls, the taste still sweet on Hal's tongue, Kristilin led him outside the stable, where two dusters sat waiting. The second one, rusted and with torn fabric, looked like it had been through several storms and was not nearly as well-kept as Kristilin's.

"Where did this come from?" Hal asked as he ran a hand across the pitted metal of the rear fins.

"It was included in the trade. The shop owner had no use for it, and it sat for a long time, as you can see. I figured you will need one too if we are going to travel these lands."

"You didn't have to do that," Hal said.

"Of course I did, unless you like riding behind me."

"I mean, I'm not against it," he said, earning an eye roll from Kristilin. "Thank you. Empyrea bless thee, you've been providing for me, and I haven't done anything to return the favor."

"You being here is enough, Hal," Kristilin said as she gripped his forearm.

Again, they locked eyes, and hers were full of want. His heart fluttered, the hair on the back of his neck jumped up, and her warm touch made him think of the times they'd shared before the war. But as he thought of what to say to her and how to say it, the bernaton spat at the inside wall with a thud and followed it up with a series of grunts.

"Okay, we are leaving," Kristilin said with a smile.

She gave his arm a squeeze before turning to her duster. Hal looked back, and the bernaton flapped its lips at him again. Hal shook his head and sighed, then boarded his new duster.

They left just as the sun peeked over the mountains. Kristilin had said it wouldn't take more than a couple hours to reach the enclave, and Hal followed her as they sped through the open valley between the two mountain ranges. Hellan guards had said the enclave was nestled in the mountain somewhere near the town. Hal had tried to dig for more information, but they'd kept their lips sealed. Good soldiers followed orders, Hal knew, but the thought of it being used against him made him uneasy. They had no reason to care about him; after all, they'd been sent here by the Imperial Council for one reason or another.

The ash lay in sheets across the mountains, distorting the view. As Hal scoured the terrain, something poked up through the ash on a rock outcropping in the middle of the sea of dunes. It looked like an antenna or a relay tower, but to what, he didn't know. Ash dunes and rock formations dominated the land. He pulled up beside Kristilin and pointed to it. Nodding, she pointed her duster in its direction and sped toward the path.

They disembarked just before it, unsure of what to expect. After all, anything that could cause people to disappear had to be approached with utmost caution.

Even more so now, Hal thought, since he did not have the security of Wielding he was used to. That emptiness inside him made his skin crawl with weakness.

He unholstered his lightvolver as they crept slowly up the path and hid behind an ash-covered boulder. A few wardroids roamed around, yellow lights for eyes scanning the area while a couple dug through containers. Rust covered their metal chassis, and each carried a short blaster rifle, enough to down anything without armor. Their strides were rigid, their joints having not been properly maintained for a while. Still, they were nothing to be taken lightly. He couldn't have a repeat of the android situation from earlier.

More boxes of old supplies lay scattered near a door under the rocky overhang; old clothing, food, and miscellaneous supplies had been thrown across the area, deemed useless by the wardroids. As Hal looked closer, he noticed diamond markings on them.

"Those are Imperial wardroids," Hal said. "What are they doing here?"

"Left behind like everything else," Kristilin replied. "Stay here."

Before Hal could say anything, she leapt from their hiding spot and charged the droids. She drew her karver, and a purple blade of focused hardlight unfurled along an articulating metal rod from the hilt of the sword and pierced the first droid. The photons of her karver coalesced together to form a strong bond along the metal rod and melted through the droid's old metal. She ripped it out and slashed at the next droid before drawing her pistol and firing a single shot at the last droid.

As sparks flew from their chassis, Hal emerged and looked at the mangled mess of droid parts. Kristilin closed her karver and approached Hal.

"Seems you had practice with that," Hal said.

Kristilin clipped it back onto her belt. "Many hours."

"How did Misselie get by without alerting these droids? They're older models, but Imperial developers know how to create smart droids." He knelt beside one. The wires still sparked with energy, though not enough to revive the droid. "Or maybe she didn't?"

"Shh. Do not say such things, Hal," Kristilin said. "You have to be resilient and adaptive to survive out here. Misselie learned."

"I didn't mean it that way," Hal said. "What if they captured her?"

"Many things seem strange in the ash, but Misselie knows everything about it. A few outdated droids would not be enough to stand between her and the knowledge she sought."

Hal stared at the steel wall in front of them, wondering how to get in. These droids had barely put up a fight and could not be the reason behind the disappearances. Whatever lay inside had to be. Or this was a ploy to send them to their deaths and out of Asher's way.

Wouldn't be the first time that's happened, Hal thought.

Hal strode along the wall and searched for any sign of an opening. Nestled off to the side was a small room with a window, likely a security station for whoever had operated this place before. The door was sealed, but as he looked to the ashy ground, he saw one set of small footprints. Undisturbed thanks to the overhang, they matched that of a young woman. Misselie, or someone, had been here at some point, but now they had to find the way in.

Hal looked back to the door and eyed the console. It was open, wires exposed. He grabbed the two wires and touched them together, and the door opened. But as he entered the room, the door closed behind him. Kristilin quickly ran to the window beside it and tried to open it back up.

"Damn," she said under her breath. She fired a shot at the glass and even tried to stab it with her karver to no avail. She looked at the console, where smoke rose from the wires. "The circuit is inoperable."

Hal looked around. Dust and ash fluttered in the air as he searched for something to release the door. A chill ran along his face as loose papers blew in the breeze. He stopped and watched them for a moment before turning around. A lone bookcase stood upright against a gray wall and stretched high to the ceiling. As he placed an open palm to the edge of the bookcase, the pressure changed against his hand. It took little effort to move the ornate piece of wood, revealing a hole in the wall and a narrow crevice that led deeper within.

As he forced himself in, he realized how uncalculated this risk was. If he got stuck, there was no way to get out, at least for a while, and time meant everything to him. But the secrets that lay within called to him, and the possibility of a door control on the other side beckoned.

After he pulled himself out, dim lights glowed above. A lever sat right next to him, and as he pulled it, the steel wall began to rise. He stood there as Kristilin stood on the other side, a none-too-pleased look on her face.

"You need to be more careful, Halcion Skyborn," she said as she walked in, eyes like daggers.

"You know how I am," Hal said, trying to shrug off her glare, though her use of his full name sent a shiver up his spine.

She stopped and turned to face him. "And that's what I'm afraid of. Hal, this isn't the Polarian desert or forests of Athos or mountains of Velra. Your maverick lifestyle can get you killed here if you're not careful."

"I've already been stripped of my abilities, Kristi. Whatever happens now doesn't matter."

"It does to me."

She furrowed her brow and looked into his eyes before walking farther into the enclave. Hal inhaled deeply. After all this time, he still meant the same to her as he had two years ago. They were going to have a lot to talk about, but that weight removed would relieve them both. She was right though. He couldn't tell her what she meant to him if the ash claimed him. He had to be smarter.

Flashes of light illuminated the walls as they tread deeper into the abandoned sanctuary. It felt good to be out of the elements, but where comfort was found, Hal had a renewed sense of danger and curiosity. Different rooms stood vacant with their doors open, tables and furniture scattered over the floors.

They walked down the hall and opened a circular room, where a large table sat in the middle. Smaller side rooms had their doors sealed shut while consoles sat dormant along the walls. Hallways in between the side rooms crissed crossed into the room they were in. It seemed this had been the main chamber of sorts for whoever had used it.

Out of the corner of his eye, Hal saw something under the ash. He approached the corner of stacked boxes and wiped the ash away to reveal the diamond emblem of the Empire. He pulled on the fabric and shook it loose of the clingy ash, and a small sense of comfort came over him as he held the flag of the Empire. Though tattered and weathered, it had survived, and if it had, then so could he. The flag deserved better than to die in a forgotten hole. He folded it best he could and placed it into his bag before he turned and faced the holotable behind him.

Hal wiped the dust from the touchscreen of a console. Its lights still responded to his touch, which meant there had to be a generator of sorts that powered this place. As he pressed a button, the table flashed to life and glowed a cool blue.

It was a holomap.

After a few short seconds, the map homed in on its location and generated the terrain of the area.

"Interesting," Hal said as he admired the durability of the device.

Sitting on the edge of the table was a small square device. As he picked it up and analyzed it, it appeared to be a remote signal opener, one for the main door he presumed.

"Hal . . ."

He stuffed the small device into his pockets and turned toward Kristilin as a small droid appeared around the corner. Its hum echoed through the halls but had been absent to his ears until he'd heard his name called. The droid slowly hovered toward him and Kristilin. A beam of blue nearly blinded him as it ran up and down his body. But just as he placed his hand around the grip of his lightvolver, the scan stopped, and a robotic voice spoke to them.

"Empyrean . . ."

The droid rotated its spherical body and its eye oscillated. Hal stared back. He didn't know what to do or what the droid would do. This land was so unpredictable, he had to be ready for anything.

"Empyrean . . ." the droid repeated before speaking in a language Hal had never heard. The droid continued to repeat itself like it wanted Hal to reply, but he had no idea how. After the droid stopped its phrase, Hal spoke.

"I am Prince Halcion of House Skyborn, heir to the Imperial Throne of Athos."

The droid oscillated again, and Hal prepared himself. Kristilin placed her hand on the hilt of her karver. But then something stirred in Hal, and the dark void in his soul churned. Where emptiness lay, warmth returned, but only for a second. It sent a small shock wave through his body, over each nerve ending and into every muscle. He felt awakened until the feeling subsided and withdrew back into the deepest part of his soul, and darkness returned.

The droid oscillated once more as if it was trying to communicate with him. But he didn't understand. It spoke in its robotic tone and hovered over to the back of the room, where one of the sealed doors stood, and inserted something into the keyway. The door slid open, and the droid hovered inside.

Hal took a step, but Kristilin stopped him. "Wait. Can we trust it?"

Something beckoned him to follow. He didn't know what or who, but that emptiness he felt without his Wielding sparked for a second. It was like the fire inside had tried to reignite itself, and the answer lay somewhere here. Hal took a step toward the sealed room.

Inside, light cast shadows, which danced against the walls. As he walked, his hand ran against the smoothness of glass, and more light graced the room. It revealed what he had touched, and he had no clue what it was. Large glass containers, almost like tanks used for aquariums, stood in each corner of the room, drained of their liquid.

"What are these?" Kristilin asked as she stared at the one across from Hal.

"Tanks for something . . . to hold something," Hal said, though he was just as confused as she was. "Experiments, research."

Near the back of the room, the droid hovered over to a console that rose from the ground. Hal stepped up to it, admiring how the craftsmanship had survived the harsh conditions of this place. Its cylindrical form drew his interest; it was like nothing he had seen, though that was fast becoming a theme. Still, it impressed him. The droid spoke again and seemed to urge Hal to touch the console. With a skeptical look from Kristilin, he took a deep breath. An echo from where the warmth of his fire once was told him to listen to the droid. After a moment, he placed a hand on the console.

The console lit up with a blue glow. The contrast from the darkness made it especially bright, and Hal had to shield his eyes. But then something formed in the center. It took a few seconds, rebooting, and then the form appeared, and Hal could not believe what he saw.

A humanlike form stood up and looked at them. The image of his mother caught him off guard for a second, but he knew it was a recording left by her like breadcrumbs for a curious beast.

"My children, welcome to the enclave." The hologram flashed before she continued speaking. "I've used this place many times during my research. If you are seeing this, the droid remembered to lead you to this recording. If you are here, then my suspicions were correct, and something is amiss in the Empire. Travel to Starlite Temple. Join me at the holomap."

With a flash, the hologram disappeared, and the droid buzzed before it too floated out of the room. They moved back to the holotable, where Empress Irina's hologram stood. The map zoomed out, with a few points of reference scattered around.

"Here it is," Empress Irina said as the map zoomed in. "Starlite Temple. Much about it is unknown, and only those who were close enough to the Archkell had access to it."

"Archkell?" Hal said.

"The master of all forms of charna Wielding. The charna level within such a being far surpasses that of even the greatest Wielders. Only one has ever existed," the hologram answered, as if it had expected the question.

"I need to get there," Hal said as he looked at Kristilin. "My mother led me here for a reason, and this has to be it."

"Maybe Hellas will help us after we help them," Kristilin said.

"Then let's find Misselie."

Empress Irina turned to them. "Be wary of the guardians that lurk in the ash and serve the mad queen. I hope to see you soon. In the meantime, feel free to use this enclave. It serves no purpose to me now."

The hologram disappeared, and Hal turned to face Kristilin, who gave him a questioning look. It all felt strange; none of this information was in the Imperial archives, and they were supposed to contain all Primordial and Empyrean history. Unless they didn't.

"There might be some leftover supplies we could use," Kristilin said.

Hal nodded. "Let's scour the place and find anything useful."

Just as they were about to do so, a clang came from deeper within the enclave. In tandem, they drew their weapons and faced where the noise had come from. The bang echoed through the halls again as Hal approached a door. Something thudded against the door, and Hal aimed his weapon to eye level before tapping the keypad. Kristilin stayed back with her karver ready to absorb any blast that came their way. The universal code worked, and the door hissed open.

A massive droid fell forward through the doorway and almost caught Hal as he jumped back. Smoke rose from the back of the machine, and someone sighed from deeper within.

"I guess you're my rescue party?"

"Misselie?" Kristilin said. A young woman with raven-black hair sat on a metal bench inside. "Misselie, you had us all worried."

"I was only supposed to be gone for a few hours . . . days, but I got locked in. I brought supplies though." She pointed to a satchel that sat at the back of the room. "But then this droid woke up, and it didn't want me to run tests on it. I just wanted to know what its model number and processing units were. And then it went haywire and started to bang on the door so I shot it," she said. "Looks like Stravis sent you at the right time. I don't think I could stomach the smell of burning oil."

She stepped out and holstered her weapon before taking a deep breath. When she looked at Hal, she smiled. "I know those eyes. Hello, Hal Skyborn. Oh, I mean Prince Hal Skyborn. Am I supposed to bow now or kiss your finger or something?"

"No, nothing like that," Hal said with a small smirk at the young woman's unfamiliarity with royal customs. "How did you get here?"

"I walked."

Hal shot Kristilin a glance in disbelief. It had taken them a couple hours to get here on dusters. To walk would have taken many more hours, perhaps a day at least.

"Don't look so surprised. If you know where to go and the routes to take, then everything is fine. Shortcuts. Stay off the main roads."

"You should still be more careful," Kristilin said as she elbowed Hal in the side to gain reinforcement like a mother trying to discipline her child.

"Right. Uh. Dangerous. There's a lot of . . . Wait, why am I doing this?" Hal said as he turned to look at Kristilin.

"You guys are cute," Misselie said as she crossed her arms and shook her head with a smirk. "Kristilin has told me so much about you."

Hal glanced between them. "Good things I hope."

Blushing, Kristilin looked away before she said, "Yes. Good. Okay, we, um, need to . . ."

"Right. Don't worry," Misselie said with a wink. "I'll meet you back in Hellas. I'll be sure to put in a good word."

After a quick hug, Misselie departed from the room, and the door closed behind her. Kristilin ran fingers through her hair and said, "So, what now?"

Hal focused on the map and the location of Starlite Temple. "Same as before. Then we go."

CHAPTER XIX

After they gathered a few supplies from the enclave, they wasted no time setting out for Starlite Temple. Plumes of ash rose behind them as they sped across the ash flats on their dusters. The whine of the jetdrive accelerating to its top speeds drove the adrenaline in Hal to its peak. He gripped the handholds firmly, his knuckles turning white. The power and elegance of this machine coupled well with its primal thrill and made Hal feel alive as he leaned forward in the seat. Offset with each other, Hal turned in tandem with Kristilin, and ash sprayed out from under the repulsers. He loved it.

As they weaved around ash dunes and pit falls, the wind stung the exposed area around Hal's eyes, but it did not faze him. As he leaned forward on the duster, the explosive force of the wind blew over him like a slipstream but the protection of his evosuit negated the effects. All that remained behind him was a large plume of ash.

He felt free, freer than he'd ever felt in the walls of Imperius. For years his fellow city dwellers had lived high above the wilds of his homeland and rarely set foot on its surface. All that time above left little use for vehicles like these, but every time he sat in the driver's seat, he felt the same thrill.

As they sped through the ash together, they came across a pillar sticking up from the ground. They slowed and approached it as the wind blew ashen waves around them. Weathered marble stood broken from the earth, cracks and chips torn from its smooth surface. In the distance, more pillars poked up through the ash. Hal nodded, and they followed the trail.

Sunken into the ash was an octagonal gazebo that had stood the test of time. Rust stained its marbled walls, and the golden domed roof had chipped and discolored under the harshness of the ash. A swiftlift sat in the center but it had its metal floor stripped away by the ash to reveal the mechanical structure underneath.

Hal stepped off his duster and approached the structure.

"Hidden temple?" he asked.

"It looks horrible," Kristilin said as she swung a leg over her seat.

As far as he was concerned, the lift was the only way in. Anything else was already buried in years of ashfall or weathered beyond recognition.

Something pulled at his soul again. A pulse of heat shot through his left side and tugged at him. But as he turned to look, he saw nothing but mounds of ash. He shook his head and thought he was going crazy until he felt it again in the center of his chest, and his suspicion began to mount. Hal looked in the direction where the pulse of warmth directed him and scoured the ash for something.

Droids emerged from the ash like archaic machines that had spent years devoid of power. Their eyes flashed to life, chassis hissing as they turned to face them. Ash fell from their frames, staining their chipped paint a sickly gray. The droids aimed their twin blaster-infused arms at them, ready to fire.

Hal acted fast and fired a few shots from his lightvolver, the blasts ripping through the armor of the first few bots. The sound of energy piercing metal echoed in the stillness, and the droids dropped to the ground like scrap metal. The lightvolver echoed with a loud *peer* noise as the cycling chamber absorbed new light to fire. Kristilin cut through another two with her karver, slicing them like they were made of paper.

More and more emerged like they'd been reawakened by some master switch. More targets meant more practice, and Hal fired blue bolt after blue bolt of energy into the rusted chassis of the droids. Kristilin made quick work of the others. Her light feet and decisive swings highlighted how elegant and deadly she was with a blade. It was like an extension of herself.

Sparks and metal flew before the last bot fell to the ashy ground.

Satisfied, Hal let out a sigh of relief as he looked over the carnage, but then something rumbled under his feet. It grew louder and more violent, almost knocking them off their feet, before the ash exploded in the distance. A massive snakelike creature with fur that could warm hundreds of people slithered into the air and turned to face them. With an ear-piercing screech that wreaked havoc on Hal's ears, the beast slammed its two arms down to the ground and ash exploded high into the air. At least eight emerald eyes stared back at them. The creature bared its jagged teeth, which looked like they could tear through any bone or structure. Hal and Kristilin took a step back as the ground shook, and the creature hissed before diving back under the ash.

"By what god was that thing?" Hal said as he took another step back.

A tsunami of ash bore down on them. It dwarfed the ash dunes and only grew bigger. Hal had seen nothing like it, and he didn't want to see it up close.

"I have no idea," Kristilin said. "Get in the lift. Let us go."

They hurried to the lift, and the doors closed. Darkness consumed them, and Hal's heartbeat was audible in the silence, coupled with Kristilin's heavy breathing. He stood ready for whatever lay beyond the doors.

Just as the lift lowered, a massive snap rocked the cell they were in. Kristilin fell onto him, and the weightlessness of the freefall lifted them up before they smashed into the ground with a final jolt of pain.

Hal groaned as Kristilin helped him up. "What happened?" he said as he steadied himself.

"A warning," Kristilin said as she used her karver to pry open the doors. "Whatever that thing was, I have never seen one before."

Kristilin finally forced the doors open, and they stepped out of their confines and into a spectacular sight to behold. An underground chasm spanned for as far as Hal could see and as deep as the light allowed. Waterfalls of ash rained down from the surface while fungi of light illuminated the paths and chambers. It all looked strangely beautiful, and the thought of life in somewhere so remote and barren fascinated Hal.

As they walked, the fungi brightened the darkened paths like it sensed where they were about to go. Hal ran a finger across a few spores, and they danced at his touch. He had heard stories, even seen the beauty of the Erouran rainforests and their bioluminescent foliage, but this defied everything he knew about life, all the basics of survivability.

Emerging from the path, they came to a large structure. Something stood on a pedestal in the center, and as they neared, Hal noted the intricate designs on the archways and ceiling of the structure. Spirals and abstract shapes lined the walls, as if they all pointed to what sat in the middle.

Hal stepped up to it, keeping a wary eye out for defenders of this place. A cube sat in suspension over the pedestal, canted to one side. A slot for it to go into was just below it.

Kristilin looked at Hal for a second before she reached for it and was greeted by a shock that sent her hand reeling back.

"Are you all right?" Hal asked, placing a hand on her shoulder.

"I am fine," Kristilin replied as she reached for her karver. She ignited it and used the tip to move the cube, but no matter what she did, it bounced back into perfect suspension. She let out a frustrated sigh and stepped back. "What is this place?"

Hal studied the cube. There had to be a way to move it, but no switch or lever to lower the cube stood anywhere. He clenched his jaw at how close the cube was to where it had to go, like it was meant to toy with them. Then a thought came to mind. He reached for it despite protest from Kristilin and grabbed the cube. A jolt of electricity raced up his arm, but it did not hurt him like it had Kristilin. It tingled against his nerves in what felt almost like the pins and needles sensation. Then it stopped, and the cube moved to his command.

He lowered it and placed it in its slot, then smiled and stepped back. A staircase emerged from the floor they stood on and descended even farther down.

"What?" Kristilin said, her brow furrowing in confusion. "How?"

Hal looked at the pedestal before returning his gaze to hers. "Empyrean ruins only allow Empyreans access through a blood seal. That much I know. A safeguard Atis made to ensure Primordials couldn't gain access."

"And you have Empyrean blood," Kristilin said. "How handy."

Hal nodded. "I wasn't expecting it to work though. These seals are ancient."

Hal drew his lightvolver and descended the steps with Kristilin right behind him. It felt like walking up a lighthouse, only in reverse. Strange etchings glowed softly along the walls of the stairwell, and they brought interesting thoughts to Hal. He had no clue what they meant, but that did not stop the curiosity.

When they finally emerged, orbs of light lined the rocky ceiling above and converged at the center structure. Swirling towers intertwined like lovers to the top while a single door stood at the end of a bridge made of rock. As they looked over the edge, a river of ever-changing colored liquid bubbled and flowed harmlessly, pulsing blue and purple before its final lasting orange. They crossed the bridge, careful about their step, and the hiss of the snakelike monster echoed through the chamber. It caused them to freeze, but when nothing happened, Hal pressed forward.

Two ancient marbled warriors stood on either side of the door. A smaller pedestal sat off to the side, but the grandness and beauty of the structure caught Hal's interest. To be so smooth and elegant, perfect even, made Hal question what had to be done to achieve such immense design. Nothing in Imperius could compare. Imperfection was the way of craftsmanship, yet here he stood in front of perfection.

He looked at Kristilin. "How do we get in?"

She shook her head. "No idea."

A single beam of blue light traced up the pedestal and disappeared, only to repeat again. Hal approached it with Kristilin over his shoulder and reached a finger out. He had not yet touched it when the same form of his mother appeared.

"Welcome, children. You have made it this far and found Starlite Temple."

Dust fell as the doors rumbled open. Inside, orbs of blue light illuminated a central table like the one at the enclave. Hal entered first with a hand on his weapon and looked around. Steps around the whole room led down to the table as they walked toward the glow.

When they neared, a hologram of Empress Irina Skyborn appeared.

"Greetings, my child," she said. "I hoped you would find this."

Kristilin moved next to Hal. "She was here?"

Hal stepped up to the table, brimming with questions. He studied the holographic form of his mother. It was different from the one he'd seen in Imperius. She looked younger and less tired.

"After a year of researching and archeology, I've finally found what was left here thousands of years ago. Buried somewhere in this hellhole is a Lumnis Stone, the same stone that granted the first Wielders the knowledge of Wielding. The Imperial Council will be thrilled to know of this discovery and the possibility of developing more Wielders," Empress Irina said with a hint of sarcasm in her voice. "For years it was just the Skyborns, but with this stone, the vast knowledge of Wielding could be anyone's."

Data files of the Lumnis Stone appeared. The glowing red crystal looked as beautiful as any ruby Hal had ever seen. But the sight made him curious. He had never heard of such a stone and had never seen it referenced in any of the Imperial Archives. As he looked down to where his necklace had once sat around his neck, he wondered if any mention of a Lumnis Stone had been purposefully omitted. If that was the case, then this only further implicated the council.

"I think I've found where this one was hidden. Grace of Empyrea guide me, it was worth the pain, but I can go no further. Not now. Not with the council eyeing my every move, for they fear the unknown." The hologram turned and looked at them with pleading eyes and Hal fought back the sting of tears behind his eyes. "The knowledge tucked into that stone could change the Realmverse as we know it. It contains a set of tools that anyone passionate enough—like you, my children—could use. Find it and let the teachings flourish." Empress Irina's hologram stopped for a second before she turned back around. "But if it fell into the wrong hands, the consequences could be catastrophic. This cannot be allowed to happen, which is why I was silent on my expeditions in the presence of the council. So, my children, will you find the Lumnis Stone to bask in its knowledge or use it to fuel more wars?"

The form disappeared, and Hal stood with his jaw clenched. He let out a frustrated growl and kicked a pile of ash as he looked out to the chasm of colorful liquid.

"What?" Kristilin asked, standing behind him.

"Damn puzzles. I don't have time to waste while an empire burns," Hal said as he turned around. "We're playing games here." He shook his head with a sarcastic chuckle. "My mother died because of a lousy stone."

"There has to be something else," Kristilin said. "She spoke highly of this Lumnis Stone."

"Even if there was, Kristi, where do we start? This was my only lead, that something lay here to stop Varim and help me regain what I lost, but it's locked behind a Wielding puzzle I can't solve because I can't Wield anymore."

Kristilin placed a hand on his shoulder and looked into his eyes. "We still have Hellas and the enclave. Maybe there is something there."

Hal let out a breath. "Maybe." A moment of clarity was disrupted by the ghastly hiss they'd heard before. Hal looked at Kristilin. "Let's get out of here."

As they ascended the stairs and came to the top, they had another problem. The lift had been destroyed, and they had no way out. The stairwell closed behind them, and the cube rose to its place above the pedestal.

The ground began to quake, and Hal and Kristilin braced themselves as dust fell from the ceiling. The monstrous snakelike creature rose from the cavern below and towered over them, its gray fur dropping ash everywhere. Its many emerald eyes stared down at them as its head lowered to their height. With a huff from its nostrils, ash blew all around them, clearing the floor.

Hal raised his hands to it, his stomach up to his throat as he tried to settle down. "Beast, I have no quarrel with you. I only sought the knowledge that lay inside."

The beast coiled up above them, saliva dripping off its many jagged teeth, arms prodding the air in a pattern as it searched them with its eyes. An energy field formed right next to them, blue lights running up and down from a hole in the ceiling, and the beast stopped its air prodding. The beast gave one last look at them before it lowered back down with a hiss. As the ash settled, it stared at them. Hal stayed frozen in place, unsure what the giant beast had in mind. Then, just as it had appeared, it dipped below the platform and vanished into the darkness of the underground, the rumbles of it traveling echoing throughout the chamber and then fading as it got farther away.

Hal and Kristilin stepped into the energy lift and floated upward toward the light. When they popped out, they landed in piles of ash near their dusters. Hal watched in shock as the hole closed. He had to know more, and there was only one way to do that.

CHAPTER XX

Hal had lost count of how many days he'd been here. The hours had melted together until day and night became indivisible. The beauty he had seen here had faded from the forefront of his mind and had been replaced by a fitting gray cloud. Rain started to come down and cast its blanket of darkness on the horizon.

For days they'd found nothing to go off of. The enclave only housed bits and pieces of technology that served no purpose in helping them understand what had to be done next. It was a place of refuge, nothing more, though it was still a brighter welcome than the town.

Hellas offered little in aid and comfort. Whenever they walked into town, storefronts locked their doors and people dispersed around them. No one wanted to make eye contact. He understood why, but that didn't make it any easier to deal with. A vouch from Misselie only went so far. He should have known not to trust the word of Asher. After all, he'd only met the man for a few minutes. It should've been obvious, but at least they could still roam the streets like a pair of homeless wanderers.

Even the weather played tricks. Three days straight of acid rain and thick ashfall kept them from venturing out to the town. He felt stuck and wondered for the first time if this would be his final resting place. Kristilin had to drag him back to Hellas for one final search.

Their dusters came to a stop along the wooden boardwalks, and they hopped off, their boots stirring up puffs of ash. As they walked, the lights in the shops turned off in front of them and eyes peered through the dark windows to watch them. The message was clear: Hal wasn't welcome here.

He began to worry—not for himself, but for Kristilin. It was no secret the Hellans detested him, but their hostility didn't need to be pushed onto her. If he just disappeared, she would at least have a place to rest. She was as much an exile as anyone here.

As they walked, she glared daggers at those who glanced through the windows. They pulled their curtains shut so as to not catch the ferocity of her bite, which he knew all too well.

One shop had a door open with an old man sitting in a rocker outside. Hal recognized Stravis, but he doubted the old man's advanced memory would remember him. If Misselie was around, maybe they could find something, but that was wishful thinking. She was an adventurous woman, much like Kristilin, but to find something that would help gain his abilities back out in the ash was the equivalent of taking his own life into his own hands. There had to be something within these walls.

The old man did not wear the same protective suit Hal wore, just old dark robes tattered by years of use, and a pipe hung from his mouth as smoke gently rose. They stopped before him and looked at the weathered sign in the window. *Eyes of the Old*, it read. They looked at each other with a shrug.

"Excuse me, Mister Stravis," Kristilin said softly. "May we enter your shop?"

Startled from slumber, the old man woke with a snort and turned to them. "Oh dear. Of course. Of course." He pushed himself up with his staff and smiled as he ushered them in. "Please go ahead."

Inside, Hal took a deep breath. A hint of cinnamon spice wafted through the air and made the whole shop smell like a freshly baked cinnamon bun. It reminded him of simpler times and why he was here. The nasty thoughts he'd had earlier parted for some clarity to come through.

Staffs and swords hung along the walls. Rows of bookshelves sat in the center, and display cases lined the walls. It looked like something out of a different world, a different time, and it was fascinating.

A crash came from the rows of books, and someone cursed before they poked their head out.

"Misselie," Kristilin said. "I'm surprised you're here and not in some ghastly ruin."

Misselie threw the books back on the shelves before stepping up to them with a smile. Her dark skirt hovered above the floor and hid her legs, and she wore the top half of an evosuit, which mirrored the likes of a corset with a long cloak to match. Her bright blue eyes reminded him of the oceans back home, and her long dark hair was pulled back into a ponytail, a stark contrast to her pale skin.

"I have to help this oldie," Misselie said with a smile. "A neat shop attracts more people, doesn't it, Stravis?"

"Bah," the old man grunted. "These relics have been here since before you were born, young one."

"What is all this?" Hal asked as he looked around.

Stravis smiled. "You like it? Years and years of archaeological findings and adventure." He sighed. "Though those were my younger days. I can't delve into ruins at my age anymore. This is my collection."

Hal's eyes went wide. "You studied Empyreans?"

"Ah, a student of your ancestors?" the old man asked with a smirk.

"My ancestors? How did you know?"

"The eyes tell all. Gifted by the Primordial makers to the first two Empyreans who mastered their art."

Stravis motioned for them to follow him to a large counter along the side of the shop. He reached under the counter and pulled out a hefty book. Dust and ash flew as he plopped it onto the counter.

Hal raised an eyebrow at the old piece of history, so foreign and dated compared to the realm of technology he came from.

Stravis opened to a random page. "These are all the notes I've ever recorded. As you can see, there are a lot."

"This must've taken a long time to collect," Hal said as he looked at the thickness of the relic.

"Since before my exile. I had to rewrite what I could from memory after being sent here. But this world offers so much more information."

A lump formed in Hal's throat, and he met the man eye to eye and said, "You're Imperial, aren't you?"

Stravis nodded. "A long time ago."

"What happened?"

He thumbed a few pages. "I was a young explorer then and made a mistake chasing Primordial knowledge I shouldn't have. Locked behind some Empyrean vault. My apprentice was a stickler for the Code. You know how it goes." He closed the book and smiled. "But you're not here for an old man's life story. You're looking for something, yes?"

Hal looked at Kristilin. "Actually, now that we've found you, yes." His eyes returned to the old man's. "I have no Wielding abilities, and my mother left something behind in a sealed temple that needs Wielding to pass through."

"Ah, the beautiful conundrum of charna." Stravis shook his head and looked down with a smile.

The gesture stung Hal. It felt like he wasn't being taken seriously, and heat rose inside him. When the old man looked up, the smile remained.

"My dear boy, you are a Wielder not by birth or lineage, but by ability. The Empyreans before you were not born with charna mastery. They tamed it, learned it, and impressed with it. Whatever happened that caused you to lose your wielding abilities, you severed your connection to your charna."

"My charna?" Hal questioned. "What does it have to do with anything?"

Again, Stravis nodded. "I have it. You have it. We all have it. It's in all of us. It's a part of our biological makeup, our DNA. To say that you have lost it is untrue. What you lost was your connection, severed by sadistic means, and that you have to rebuild. Reconnect."

"I've never heard of this," Hal said. "I was taught that we used crystals to project our power and that only we, the Skyborns, could do so masterfully."

"You were taught wrong," the old man said. "You are Empyrean, and you have a special connection with charna and the Wielding arts. That is true. But anyone can harness the power of charna if they are determined enough. The crystal was an amplifier. It helped project your power, but without it, you need to learn the way the first Empyrean Wielder did."

Misselie joined Stravis behind the counter. "Think of charna as stored power," she said. "When you unlock your connection to it and open your mind, the limitless possibilities of various elemental controls are at your very fingertips. That act is Wielding."

Hal leaned on the counter, taking in everything they said. After a few seconds, he looked back up to Stravis. "How?"

The old man reached for another book and slid it to Hal. The symbols on the cover and words inside looked exactly like the runes he had seen, but he couldn't understand any of them. He pushed it back.

"I can't read any of this."

Stravis sighed. "As I thought. We'll start simple then." He pointed at Kristilin. "You can learn this too."

The hours felt like minutes. Hal soaked up Stravis's teachings like a sponge devoid of the water it so desperately needed. It all fascinated him, from the runic language the Primordials had spoken to how they'd cultivated the next generation of languages. Everything flowed from Primordial origin, and everything was connected. It reminded him of his lessons back in the Imperial Academy, though less rigid and formal.

"And that's the basis of the Primordial language," Stravis said as he slid the book toward Hal. "You still have much to learn, but that will come with time."

Hal looked at the images and runes and smiled, as he could identify each one like it was his own language. In more ways than one, it was. "I can't thank you enough for this, sir."

Stravis waved a hand. "If you find any trinkets during your excursions into Primordial ruins or crypts, you know where to bring them."

"I think you have enough 'trinkets' for now," Misselie said.

"Well, that is three languages for me," Kristilin said, nudging Hal with her elbow. "You need to catch up and work on your Velran."

Hal rolled his eyes with a smirk, but a thought crossed his mind. "I really do thank you for this, but this isn't going to get my abilities back."

"No, it won't," Stravis said. "Like I said, you need to learn the natural way to rekindle your connection. The first step is to find the Watcher Stones and commune with them. They will only guide an Empyrean. That's you, kid."

"Where can I find them?"

Stravis turned to the wall behind him where a satchel hung and dug out an old torn map. He pointed to a mark. "Few days journey north from here, even on those dusters of yours. Look for a spring, and you'll know you're close."

"Thank you," Hal said. "I will repay you."

"You know how. Stay safe."

"And if you need any help exploring ancient temples, please let me know," Misselie said.

With a nod, Hal tucked the book in a bag, and they left the shop, the door closing behind them.

A cool breeze swept through the streets, blowing dust everywhere. Hal turned around to shield Kristilin from the gusts of wind and brought the hood of her evosuit up over her head, making her smile. He hadn't thought about it; it just felt natural. Hal pulled his hood up, and they walked a bit farther before taking a seat at a table outside the overhang of the walkways. Hal pulled the book from his bag and set it on the table.

A few moments later, the rubes from the saloon approached with Dash in the lead. Hal didn't bother to give them the time of day, but that didn't halt their pestering. Dash took a seat right beside him and looked over his shoulder.

"What we got here?" Dash asked.

Hal didn't answer. Instead, he silently read while his blood boiled with annoyance. Anywhere else this would never happen. To approach someone of royal blood like this would end in incarceration at least. Though he knew this wasn't Imperius, he still wanted to reach over and deck the prick.

"What's the matter?" Dash asked, looking to Kristilin. "You bit his tongue?"

"I would watch yours if I were you," Kristilin said, casting a glare at the goon behind her.

"I suggest you leave," Hal said, his gaze burning into the book.

Dash shifted in his seat while his two goons stood squarely behind him like some failed traveling band back home and crossed their arms.

"You know those eyes don't lie, boy. I know you're a pretty boy from Imperius. Ol' diamond eyes."

The way Dash spoke made Hal wince. Even the way he said "Imperius" seemed uniformed and brutish. One of the goons walked around to the other side where Kristilin said, a crooked grin on his face as he stood behind her.

"You don't know me," Hal replied.

"The Ash ain't for you." Dash placed his fingers to his chest. "Outcasts like us, it's the only place we can call home since our exile. Some were born here, and others were sent against their will. Doesn't matter how. Rather deal with the others than folk like you."

"I didn't send you here."

"It ain't about you. It's the whole damn system. You're nothing but a name out here, and I intend to show people that, Prince Hal Skyborn. Only failures get sent. Looks like you're one of them."

"I would watch your mouth," Hal said through gritted teeth.

Dash leaned over the table. "Or? You gonna let your blue elf girlfriend here handle me? We ride different here in the Ash."

The comment earned a chuckle from the goons behind him, and one reached for Kristilin. When the goon placed a hand on her, Hal slowly rose with Dash. His lightvolver was cocked with energy, ready to be released as he nestled it under Dash's chin.

Hal glared at the goon. "Take your filthy hand off her."

The goon slowly backed off with his hands raised before Hal lowered his weapon and shoved Dash away.

"That's the fire I remember," Dash said, an imprint of the lightvolver on his skin. "Ol' princey boy still got it."

Hal's fist shot upward. There was a crack as his fist connected with Dash's chin, and the man reeled backward into the goon behind him. Ash puffed up into the air as they fell to the ground. Hal stared at him with stern eyes, lightvolver still ready to fire. His fist ached, but he wouldn't show it. The goon from around the table rushed to help Dash off the ground, grumbling with disbelief as he did.

"Next time I catch you anywhere near us, I won't be so lenient. You don't know who I am." Hal stared directly at him. "Get out of my sight."

"Won't forget this, Outsiders," Dash hissed as he felt around his jaw. "You don't belong out here. And you just made your bed."

As they scurried off with tails between their legs, Kristilin looked back at him with a smile.

"*Alu,*" she said in her native tongue.

"*Aurein,*" he replied in Velran.

Her eyes lit up, and a tug in his chest wanted him to tell her how he felt. It had been a long time, but there was still something there, and the look in her eyes said more than he could have asked for. Just as he cleared the lump in his throat, a siren aired through the city, and Hellan guards rushed the streets and to the wall.

The moment lasers began to fly through the sky and over the wall, Hal knew they had to do something. Whoever was on the other side didn't matter. This was a chance to gain favor with the Hellans, not just for himself, but for Kristilin too.

"Come on," he said as they packed up their belongings.

They made their way to the wall, where a large group of Ashborn guards had collected. Laser bolts ripped through the sky as Asher Zyte barked orders from the front. Explosions boomed outside the walls, and heavy repeater cannons launched a rain of energy bolts down onto the ash. When the gates opened, the Hellans flooded out, Hal and Kristilin among them.

Warriors in worn, tattered armor charged from the dunes. It didn't take long before the two forces collided in hand-to-hand combat, and blood began to spill. Hal fired a few shots before he slashed his kyr at another warrior. The energy blade easily pierced the soft armor and dropped the warrior. Smoke rose from the explosions and clouded the skirmish with the help of ashfall, but it didn't stop Hal. He went from one foe to the next, putting two energy bolts into each like it was routine, and only stopped when his weapon needed to be cooled.

All the months spent at war had cultivated muscle memory, and he easily avoided outdated axe swings and shield bashes. He knew what to do before the enemy even thought about it. It felt like second nature.

Kristilin brought her karver to battle and sliced through armor like it was made of plastic. Every sword swing was followed by a blast from her weapon. She rolled over one warrior's back after they swung their axe and ripped it up across their back before she spun and fired two blasts at another.

Hal was so distracted by her elegant mastery of the karver that he almost didn't see the brute barreling down on him. He ducked and rolled on his back, and the brute sailed over him. When he stood back up, it only took one blast before the brute dropped.

Though the lasers continued to rip overhead, the attacking force seemed defeated and withered. They turned and ran back to wherever they'd come from and disappeared into the ash. Hal found Asher, who bashed a hardlite shield into a brute before he finished the enemy off with a final shot from an energy pistol.

He turned to Hal and said, "Thank you. You didn't have to do this. You weren't part of the town."

"What did they want?" Hal asked.

"Access to gem mines near us. The gems help power our town," Asher said as he cleaned off his energy sword. "Conflict is a part of life out here I'm afraid."

"You mean there's more?"

Asher nodded. "This entire place is littered with pockets of broken civilization and broken souls. We get some who want a chance at a real life that most other clans can't provide. As you can imagine, that rubs some of these warlords the wrong way. Instead of diplomacy they result to this." He placed a hand on Hal's shoulder and leaned in. "A warning: be careful of them. Most people have gone insane in the ash here. Don't end up like them."

"Noted," Hal replied with a nod.

As Asher walked by, he said, "This little skirmish won't be the end of it, and outsiders don't usually lend a hand."

Asher held out his hand as thunder boomed overhead. Hal looked at it for a moment before he took it and shook with the leader of the clan.

"Welcome to Hellas. You earned it."

CHAPTER XXI

The path up the mountain was a rocky mess. Every step they took involved some sort of leap of faith or high step to get over the rocky ledges. One misplaced step could set off a rockslide, which neither of them wanted. When Stravis had given them the location of the Watcher Stones, he'd failed to mention the difficulty of reaching them, though as Hal had come to know, nothing was easy here.

Kristilin climbed in front of him. There was no question that she had grown since he had left. The aristocratic life on Velra had to be one of the best. When the president of Velra granted noble titles, it was not in favoritism or bought by bribes, but for the service provided to the planet. Some called it privilege, but he knew how hard her family had worked to become the barons of their province and build Vaçone into the premier city for Vel medicine. Though when Hal had first met her, she'd been a shadow of who she was now. The reserved girl he had first encountered had turned into a fierce, impressive woman. In their academy days, she'd dressed without the grandeur of fine clothes. A simple dress or outfit was all she needed. He admired her for that. Being grateful for the simplest things was something he was going to have to learn. It was just one of the many reasons he wanted to take her hand.

They finally reached the top, where the path ended in a circular area. The view was breathtaking, overlooking the sheer vastness of the ocean of ash. Three stones stood in the center of the circular area. The two on the ends were half the size of the center one, and as they approached, Hal noted the same intricate designs from the temple. Each one had a ruby in it, and the stone encirclement of a platform lay in ruins all around them. Hal had no idea what to expect. Runes ran down the front of the middle stone, and as he bent to read, he made out the words "Watcher Stones." The satisfaction of being able to read even the slightest of runes made him smile behind his face mask.

"What do we do now?" Kristilin asked.

Hal sat cross-legged in front of the stones and stared at them for a moment. "As far as I know, the way the Empyreans communed was through meditation."

He held his hands out to his sides. With a deep breath, he closed his eyes. In the darkness, Hal waited to see what would happen. If they had identified him, a sign of some sort would be given, according to Stravis. As Kristilin stood behind him, his nerves relaxed.

It felt like ages since he'd meditated; the last time he remembered meditating was with his sister in the forest.

Hal sat patiently and allowed his mind to open and focus. It did not take long before a white fog rolled in and engulfed him. The runes he had studied with Stravis flashed in his mind, and swirls and abstract lines danced everywhere. It felt like someone had lifted him up, and a warmth circled all around. When a flash of white blinded his eyes behind the darkness of his lids, he opened them, and fire encircled him and the stones.

The stones shot a ray from their crystals, and it touched Hal. It felt cool, like a hand dipped in a river. As fast as everything had happened, the fires receded and the ray sucked back into the stones. Hal was lowered to the ground and stared up in awe. Three lights rose from the stones and circled him before intertwining with one another and shooting out over the distance, twinkling in the ash.

Kristilin rushed to his side. "Are you all right? What was that?" she asked, her lavender eyes sparkling with concern and joy.

"I think they decided to guide me."

Warmth rushed across his body as he gazed back out to where the lights had taken off to. The warmth stayed for a moment longer before it faded and succumbed to the dark emptiness of his soul. The sight fascinated him, though, and reminded him that there was hope. He was happy Kristilin was with him, and soon they would know what lay in that temple, the place in which his mother had risked her life to hide something from the high minister.

He looked out to the land beyond, where the lights twinkled again. "What do you say? Ready for another adventure?"

Kristilin helped him back up, an arm around his waist. "I'm with you. To wherever this brings us. I'm with you."

The words fueled his aching heart. She was with him always, whether she knew it or not, and soon he would make sure she knew. He wanted nothing more than to feel her embrace again, but they had to finish this first.

Their dusters sped across the ash like two lone missiles in an open valley. Hal held the throttle at max and rode side by side with Kristilin to where the lights led them. They weaved around giant holes in the ground that made him think back to his first days in the ash. It reminded him how unpredictable this land could be.

But as they moved through the maze of giant holes, something caught his attention. For as long as he could remember, the ash fell constantly. It fell even now as they rode, yet the holes remained uncovered by it. The darkness of the dirt under the ash showed around the edges. Then he thought he saw something move. Hal weaved a little closer to one of the holes, and a giant insect nearly knocked him off his duster.

"What is that?" Hal said through his earpiece, hoping it picked up what he said and not the whine of the duster engines.

Kristilin glanced back, her eyes steady as she looked at the large fly-like insect in the sky. "Ashbuggers. Damn. We are going through a hive."

Hal looked around as the scaly elongated insects crawled from the depths of the holes and spread their wings. Their pincers tapped twice, and they seemed to communicate with one another before they turned the sky into a dark mass.

"We have to leave here at once," Kristilin said as she drew her weapon.

Hal followed suit and pulled out his lightvolver. He fired two bolts that ripped through one of the ashbuggers and sprayed a mist of green behind him. One buzzed him, and Hal ducked as the massive stinger on the end of its tail scraped the front of his duster. Hal could only imagine the pain that would inject into him, and who knew what toxins lay within it. All his survival skills would not be able to save him from something like that. He shot another bolt that ripped apart an insect that was aiming at Kristilin before she swerved around another hole.

Hal weaved the other way as he fired off another shot. The two insects he aimed at avoided his blasts and closed in. Fire was a sure thing against insects, and he wished he could bake them out of the sky right about now.

The ashbuggers moved closer, and their insectoid chatter sent a chill up his spine. Holes lay all around him with no clear way to get by. More insects rose from the ground as Hal neared a hole. He had one chance to make this work, or he would become bug food, and that was not the fitting death he had in mind for a prince.

Hal gunned the duster and hit the lip of the hole. The duster launched into the air as Hal turned and fired two blasts at the insects. Their bodies exploded in a green mist that shot over Hal as the duster landed. Hal spat the sour goo out of his mouth as he sped across the ash. Behind him, the ashbuggers ceased their pursuit.

Clear land lay ahead, and he linked back up with Kristilin, who looked like she'd had a similar time. Despite a few globs of dead insect guts across her evosuit, she had no apparent injuries. She was fine.

They continued across the land, following the lights to the first of many ruins. Ash had reclaimed most of the structures, which were now buried within the ocean of gray. The lights stood atop a walled gate as their dusters gently pulled up.

The gate was cracked open, and Hal drew his lightvolver and peeked inside, unsure of what called this place home now. When he saw nothing, he stepped inside with Kristilin and looked around. Dilapidated buildings sat stoic with years of history to be told. Ash had built high enough to touch the roofs of some and completely engulf others. It looked like a war zone, a city of shattered dreams.

Again he felt a pulse from deep within him as he stepped closer. A flash of warmth coated his body down to the nerve endings in his fingers. The feeling was so great he almost felt like he could cast his flames once more. But as he looked at his hand, where before he could easily spawn a flame, it was empty. Still, the warmth lingered for a time longer.

Hal approached a column and analyzed its structure, the details. "These are Empyrean," he said.

"How can you tell?"

Hal brushed the ash aside. "The etchings." He looked back at Kristilin. "We're in an Empyrean city."

The thought aroused much speculation and wonder. This place could hold everything he needed to know about their secrets. All he had to do was find resources, and this place had to be chock-full of them.

The lights twinkled on and swirled to a tower in the center of the city before disappearing. The tower stood higher than any building in the city. Four small spires lined the corners of the roof, and a large cauldron sat at the center. He didn't know what they did, but it was where the Watcher Stones had guided him.

As he stepped forward, an ungodly roar echoed through the city. Hal froze and tightened his grip on the lightvolver while Kristilin drew her karver. Another roar followed as a creature emerged from around a corner. Its three eyes stared at them, and thick gray fur covered most of its body. It resembled the beasts he'd encountered the first night he was in the Ashlands: a troll. The troll stood a foot taller than him, and drool dripped from the pointed spears for teeth in its mouth. Muscles that rivaled those of the gods themselves popped when it beat its chest and charged at them. It moved fast, faster than Hal had expected, but he was quick to the trigger.

The beast dropped to the ashy ground as another appeared behind them. It raised a huge clawed hand, ready to slice down, but Kristilin brought her karver across it, and it dropped. More roars answered the earlier one as Hal looked at Kristilin.

They moved through the streets toward the tower. The roars of the trolls became more frequent as they pushed farther in. Blocks of stone and marble were thrown from the tops of abandoned buildings at them, but the trolls remained hidden. They continued to call out to the invaders louder and louder, but Hal would not be deterred by them. With Kristilin by his side, he felt they could take on anything. No trolls would stop them.

The tower stood above them, its shadow blanketing the area of the city they were in. Despite the deterioration of the rest of the city, the tower stood proud. As Hal went to the door, heavy breathing sounded behind him. He and Kristilin turned around.

Two trolls, larger than the others, stood behind them. The first one had muscles the others couldn't compete with, massive with veins bulging. Its teeth looked more like tusks and reached below its jaw. The second was smaller, but not by much, and had less fur and a slimmer frame. Still, the muscles and claws would dissuade any opposition. Hal assumed them to be the patriarch and matriarch of the troll band, and their invasion wasn't welcome.

The others gathered on the rooftops to watch like spectators at a sports game. Hal eyed the troll in front of him. Hard armor made from recovered scraps of metal found in the ash covered its head and chest, and eyes as yellow as the setting sun glared back at him. It roared louder than the others before the matriarch joined in. They beat their chests and smashed the ground, throwing ash into the air, no doubt trying to intimidate Hal and Kristilin. But when he looked over, she had a determined look in her eyes. Hal readied himself.

The trolls charged.

Hal evaded the first strike from the patriarchal troll. A bolt left his weapon and bounced off the troll's armor. Stunned, Hal met the furry backhand of the troll and slid across the ash to the wicked chants and hollers of the other trolls. The patriarchal troll reared around and roared before charging Hal again. Hal sidestepped the beast and fired another shot. This time it struck the exposed flesh of the troll's leg, and it roared in pain. Hal knew to avoid its grip. If it grabbed him, it was over. He tried to gain distance as Kristilin rolled away from the matriarch, leaving a nice gash on its legs.

When Hal turned back around, he fired another bolt and struck the troll in the head. The bolt bounced off its skull and ricocheted into one of the other buildings. The troll rushed him and Hal went to dodge the attack, but the troll was too fast. It grabbed him by the collar and yanked him down before it threw him across the makeshift arena, and he bounced off a broken wall into a pile of ash. The troll barreled down on him again, and he had to act fast. Hal pushed himself up and snuck around the corner of the wall, fighting the aches of the battle but keeping his hand firmly on the grip of his lightvolver.

The troll pounced onto the ash pile, waiting to get its massive claws on the human who'd invaded its home. It scanned around, nose sniffing the air for Hal's scent. Hal came around the corner, ash falling from him, and fired bolt after bolt at the troll. A few went straight through the opening of the troll's helmet, and it fell to the ground with a single breath. Looking at the beast, Hal felt for the creature. It was protecting its kind, like he had wanted to do.

As he turned back around, Kristilin sunk her blade through the matriarch's abdomen, and the matriarch dropped to the ground. Hal nodded to her, and when she looked at the buildings, he did as well. The trolls there stood quiet before they left one by one. Their leaders had fallen, and they'd watched it happen. Before a sudden troll uprising could be mounted, Hal hurried to Kristilin and looked her over.

"Are you all right?"

"I am fine," she said.

Silence turned to ominous grunts that echoed through the abandoned city as they stood in front of the tower's door and entered. As the troll grunts grew in numbers, Hal placed his hand on the door seal and watched as a blue glow formed and deteriorated before his eyes. With the sound of a click, Hal pushed the door open and led Kristilin inside.

They were greeted by a long hallway as they entered. Hal lowered his face mask and breathed in the stale musty air. At the end of the hall was another door, and Hal had a sinking feeling. As they walked, orblights glowed blue along the hallway. Hal only focused on the door.

When they reached it, the door stayed shut, and Hal read the runes embedded in the metal. A sigh escaped his mouth.

"What is the Kell's duty?" Hal said as he read the runes.

He thought long and hard about the phrase, the word, trying to remember if he'd heard it before. He remembered how his mother would speak about her journeys in Primordial archeology. Then he thought of the Imperial Archives, but even then the word stumped him and he thought if it was something else purposefully omitted. *But why*, he wondered.

"What does it mean?" Kristilin asked.

"I don't know."

An ominous click sounded inches from Hal's ear. He turned his head slightly. People stood behind him, but dark cloaks and masks covered their faces.

"Lookee here," a male said. "If it ain't the Outsiders."

"Dash, you *putroi*," Kristilin said.

Hal smirked at the insult. But when the butt of a blaster rifle slammed across Kristilin's face, Hal was ready to beat the daylights out of that man. He spun around, ready to bring his fist down across Dash's face, but as he cocked his fist back, a metal plasma pistol came across his own face.

Darkness set in amidst an echoed chuckle.

CHAPTER XXII

H al groaned as he reached for his head. An incredible headache pulsed within as a cold sweat built up on his brow, but the weight of heavy metal chains around his wrists made it a struggle to do anything. Pain was nothing new, but his location certainly was. Torchlight flickered in the air while long shadows danced along the ceiling. He had to get them out of here. But as he sat upright and looked around his cell, he didn't see Kristilin. His heart dropped into the pit of his stomach.

"Kristilin?" he whispered. "Kristi?"

Silence. He had to find her.

If only he had his Wielding. He could've burned through this poor excuse of a cell and wreaked havoc on whoever had imprisoned them here. He would make Dash pay for ever laying a hand on Kristilin. Hal pushed himself up from the ground and walked toward the metal jail door with the weight of the chains dragging behind him. Whoever chained him was generous with the length, though he would had made sure to keep the chains as short as possible.

The room had a small wooden table and nothing else. It felt like some ancient prison cell, and as Hal jerked on the door, the metal clang of the lock and chain reinforced that. Behind him stood a barred window. Hal grabbed the bars and hoisted himself up. An ocean of ash blinded his view.

A door opened, and footsteps echoed along the hallway. Hal dropped from the window and returned to his sitting position. A helmed guard stumbled to his door, grasping the neck of a bottle in one hand, and mumbled something incoherent as he used the door to hold himself up.

Wearing a tattered evosuit and cloth wrappings, the guard mimicked Dash's shaggy appearance. The guard looked him over and smiled before Hal heard a zipper go down and liquid sploshed in the center of his cell. Blood boiled in Hal as the guard dared to do such an act to him, but he should've known to expect something so degenerate from one of Dash's goons.

After the guard finished relieving himself, he took out a set of keys and stuck one into the lock. Hal kept a neutral face, but inside he livened up. This was his way out of here, but he had to do it quietly. Whoever had sent this guard would be waiting for them to return with him. Everything Hal did here had to save time.

When the guard opened the cell door and took a couple of steps in, Hal lunged from his spot and grabbed hold of him like a caged animal. He threw him against the wall repeatedly until the keys dropped. The guard landed where Hal had been sitting while he scooped the keys up. After he found the right key, Hal undid the locks to his chains and slapped them on the guard, but before he left, Hal ripped a piece of cloth from the guard's body and tied it around his mouth. When he did so, he noticed an insignia of two triangles intersecting each other. Though he would had loved to investigate the insignia more, he had no time. Hal grabbed the guard's kyr and shut the door behind him, turning the lock. Light weapons would cause too much noise, and he had to find Kristilin fast. He didn't want to think about what the people here would do to her. She could take care of herself, but they were a team, and she was his priority.

Hal creaked the door open and looked around. No other guards roamed the hall, and the dim torchlight played to his advantage. He stuck to the shadows as he rounded the corner, looking into the other cells. Some were filled and others were not, but he was only looking for one other, the one he trusted.

A beastly roar echoed through the prison ward. Blaster fire and screams followed. As Hal turned to look down a dark hallway, a rogue bolt of energy whizzed by him and crashed into the wall.

The door at the far end of the hallway opened, and guards poured in. Hal used the keys and ducked into the nearest cell. He backed into the shadows as guards passed by, and then something grabbed him. It pulled him down and thrashed about before letting out an ungodly groan. The tussle on the floor threatened to reveal him and struck him with fear. Hal could not play this game. Not now.

With what strength he had, Hal grappled the prisoner in the dark and covered their mouth.

The other prisoners' eyes glared through the dark as the guards ran by. Hal tightened his grip on the prisoner. Light from handheld torches grazed the walls as the guards ran by. Hal remained still, behind what little cover the cell offered. One guard meandered down the hall and stopped in front of where Hal lay. As the prisoner thrashed again, Hal tightened his grip and focused.

The guard turned and peered through the darkness, then reached for their torch. Hal slowed his breathing. He worried his heartbeat was too loud, but then something crashed from farther down the hall. Voices yelled and echoed in the distance, and the guard rushed off.

The footsteps faded down the hall, and when they were gone, Hal threw the prisoner off him. Its hideous body hunched over, unmoving. Lumps covered its sickly flesh. Hal remembered what Asher had said about people going crazy from the ash; perhaps this was what he'd meant.

Hal peeked his head out from the cell and looked down the hall to where the guards rushed to. When he saw nothing, not even the glow of a torch growing brighter, he closed the cell door and locked it before he ran down the hall away from the guards.

Outside, he could only see a few feet ahead. Sheets of ash came down like a monsoon and covered everything as darkness took hold. Still, he clung to the shadows like a thief infiltrating a restricted zone. More guards stormed the compound and entered the cellblock he had just left. Another roar in the ash was followed by an answer. Gunfire erupted, and Hal ducked. Whatever was going on was not his concern.

Hal crept around the first building that came into view from the blizzard of ash. He slowly opened the door. Inside, another guard stood with their back to him and spoke to someone Hal could not see.

"He's here. I'm certain," the guard said. "Yes. Dash has proven valuable. I understand. No loose ends."

The communication came to an end, and Hal came face-to-face with the guard, whose eyes went wide. Hal swatted the guard's gun away and aimed the kyr at his throat.

"Where is she?" Hal said through gritted teeth. "Answer me."

"Eat shit, traitor," the guard replied, reaching for his own kyr.

Hal quickly thrust his blade into the guard and twisted. The guard gasped, and a few breaths escaped him before he dropped.

Hal stood in silence.

Anger. He felt it in many layers. Anger for what he had done. Anger for what had happened. Anger for the life he had to fight for.

Blood pooled around the guard as Hal searched the body for information. He pulled something wrapped in cloth from the guard's pocket. He unfurled it to reveal a piece of plastic, and his eyes narrowed.

Imperial identification. Agent Kaus.

Hal looked at the man's face to see if he recognized him. Unlike the others, he was clean and freshly kept, a foreign object in these lands. But why was an Imperial agent here?

After a brief moment, pieces began to fall into place.

He didn't understand everything, but the Empire and Dash were the bridge to more information. He would have to ask Stravis when he returned, but he would not leave until he found Kristilin.

The door opened again, and cold air rushed across Hal's exposed face. He grabbed the kyr and whirled around.

To his relief, Kristilin lowered her sidearm and rushed over to him, giving him the tightest hug he'd ever received. It felt good, and at any other time he would've wanted to stay there forever, but they could not.

Hal pulled back. "Are you all right?"

She nodded. "I was looking for you, and then something attacked the guards."

That explains the gunfire, he thought. He removed his free hand from her hip, the kyr still gripped in the other.

"I see you did not have an easy time either," she said, still holding his arms.

"I was looking for you," he said, and Kristilin's eyes twinkled.

Gunfire broke through the silence, and an explosion blew the door open. Hal shielded Kristilin before turning back around.

"We need to get out of here."

"Here." Kristilin handed him his lightvolver and smiled. "I found the armory along the way."

Hal took it and placed it in his holster. "Any idea where our dusters are?"

Kristilin nodded. "They keep their vehicles near the back of the camp. I saw them when I snuck into the armory."

Hal motioned toward the door. "Lead the way."

Yells of confusion and frustration sounded through the layer of ash as they moved through the shadows. Hal had wondered what had caused the sudden chaos. Those he had spoken to before had said the ash did strange things to the body if not properly equipped. The more he looked, he saw the prisoners did not have face coverings. He wondered if he would have met the same fate if Kristilin had not come around when she did.

They came to an open barn-shaped building as streaks of red flashed through the ash like a series of fireworks. Inside was an assortment of tethered vehicles, parts of them scrapped and used on the others. Their dusters looked out of place next to the disarranged vehicles, like two show currus in a dump. Hal moved to the monitor that sat between the two dusters and hit the button that said "release." More voices yelled in the distance, followed by energy blasts.

They hopped onto their dusters, and Hal hit the activator switch. The sound of the engine coming alive never got old, and Hal shared a look of determination with Kristilin.

The dusters flew out of the barn like missiles. They swerved through the narrow roads in the camp until they burst out of the gates, laser bolts flying past them.

As Hal looked back, the headlights of a multiperson vehicle resembling a prowler illuminated him. They had to lose them, and fast.

Hal drew his weapon and aimed at the prowler. Two shots raced toward the vehicle and crashed through the windshield. He thought he had them, but the prowler only got closer. They jumped a hill and landed, the headlights of the prowler still coming at them.

They're persistent for crazed souls, he thought. He aimed and fired another bolt with a squeeze of the trigger. This time the headlights veered off and disappeared into the ash.

Hal breathed a sigh of relief, but now he had yet more questions. The presence of an Imperial agent made him wonder if the Empire had other goals here in the Ashlands.

He turned and followed Kristilin, his mind swarming with what the Empire could want out here.

Chapter XXIII

Hal dropped the identification card on the shop's countertop. It sat alone on the polished wood like a symbol to some foreign land. To its core, it was.

Stravis looked at Hal before taking the small piece of plastic. He analyzed it like one of his relics, going over every aspect of the card while Misselie studied it from behind him.

Hal waited, his eyes trained on the old man, his heart racing.

There could only be one explanation: agents and scouts were always the first to observe worlds before an invasion. He'd done it during the war.

Utilizing soft units to feed information to a command center was vital for the invasion preparation. It also meant they didn't have much time until the Imperial forces showed up. But being in the depths of the known Realmverse on Asha, he had no way of knowing or guessing the size of the invasion force. It could've been a thousand soldiers or a hundred thousand. There could be a fleet just out of orbit above the city but without reliable information, scanners, and sensors, it was impossible to figure out. That was why he'd turned to Stravis.

Though he'd only just met the man, the old-timer seemed to have an abundance of knowledge from Primordials to the Ashlands. He would've been a fool not to tap into what the old man knew. He wanted to hear the old man's thoughts. Every detail mattered.

Stravis cleared his throat, his eyes trained on the card. "Where did you find this?"

"At a camp far from here," Hal replied. He looked over to where Kristilin sat with her feet propped up on a table, hands behind her head. "Took us a little longer than expected to lose the goons."

The old man put on his specs and shook his head. "Imperial design, but the markings look different. Did they recognize you?"

Hal tilted his head and raised a brow. "There must've been no more than a couple dozen guards there. But only one was Imperial. The others were something else."

"Many roamers call the Ashlands home. Most are raiders or bandits who prey on travelers from the clans. But there is one faction that is more . . . unkind than the others." The old man sighed. "Last they attacked Hellas, they nearly broke through the walls."

"Who are they?" Hal asked.

"They don't go by a single name, but we Hellans refer to them as the Nameless. Most carry an identifying brand on their skin with two inverted triangles intersecting each other."

"They wore that insignia on tattered evosuits," Hal said. He looked at Kristilin who nodded. "Why did they allow an Imperial agent in with them, then?"

"Perhaps because the Empire is already here," Stravis said as he looked up. "They are all descendants of exiled criminals. A warlord leads the fringe clans, but nobody knows who that is. I'm sure that if Asher knew he would send a force to end their threat once and for all."

Hal's stomach dropped. If the Empire was here, their luck was running out. He leaned in. "You think they're relaying information to someone?"

Stravis nodded. "I'm almost certain of it. And I think you know who."

"The high minister?"

The old man shrugged. "Possibly." He looked into Hal's eyes and smiled. "Welcome to the reality of the Ashlands, Prince Hal."

Hal pulled out a chair from Kristilin's table and leaned back in it as he sat with a sigh. If this warlord or Imperial informant was broadcasting information about him, it was only a matter of time before a squad of executioners paid him a visit in his sleep. It could all just be a ploy to watch him suffer and wither away as a discarded prince, traitor to the people he'd once served. That thought sent a shiver up his spine and raised goose bumps on his forearms. To have his legacy smeared like that would not just be a disservice to him but to the history of the people of the Empire.

"What else?" Stravis asked as he placed the identification card back down.

"Dash is working with them," Kristilin said from her seat. "He's the one who captured us."

"That's unsettling. I think Asher needs to hear that one," Stravis said as he shook his head.

"I think the Empire and the disappearances are intertwined," Hal added. "I don't know all the pieces, but something doesn't seem right with all of it."

"Speculations are for those with curious imaginations," Stravis said. "The information will reveal itself in time, like the long sought-after answer to a riddle."

"What about the Watcher Stones? Were they helpful?" Misselie asked.

Hal took a deep breath. "They led me to an abandoned city with a tower. Trolls surprised us, but when we got into the tower, the door was sealed."

"Were there runes?" Misselie asked.

Hal nodded. "It said, '*What is the Kell's duty?*'"

"You found it? The Altar?" The old man leaned over the counter with wide eyes. It seemed Hal had discovered some missing part of an equation Stravis had been searching years for.

Hal looked at Kristilin, who had shifted in her seat and now leaned forward with her hand under her chin. He turned back to the old man. "Yeah. It didn't look like much. Abandoned with some ruined buildings and a tower in the center."

"No, no, no, boy. Their terranean structures are nothing. You should know by now that things last far longer underground in this hellish landscape. Built by loyal devotees of the Empyreans, that city was an ancient fortress and their center for everything in these parts. The sealed door you came across led to the activation site for the tower, and the tower guided the way to the underground labyrinth."

"What's down there?"

Misselie shook her head and shrugged. "Nobody knows. Non-Wielders can't get past the sealed doors. Rumor says it was a central part of the Wielding religion here, an altar of focused charna, but those stories could have changed a hundred times over the years. Some even say Emperor Atis built it as a shrine."

"But if those rumors are true, and it is connected to the Primordials and Empyreans, can I regain my Wielding?"

"It depends on the Kells themselves. More importantly, one specific Kell," Stravis stated. "Don't get ahead of yourself though, boy. You still need to pass through the sealed door."

"How?"

"Runebreaker," Misselie answered.

The name didn't ring any bells for Hal, but it sounded like a weapon of some sort. It seemed the Primordials had tricks upon tricks, but also keys upon keys to unlock those tricks. They'd taken their security seriously.

"Runebreaker is a tool the Empyreans used to secure structures after the Cataclysm, when Atis banished Primordial influence from the Realmverse," Stravis said. "It contained all their phrases and answers within it. Atis wrote it."

"Where do we find it?" Hal asked.

"Luckily for you, I stumbled across it in an Empyrean ruin years ago, when I was much younger and slimmer." The old man laughed, and Hal exchanged a smirk with Kristilin. Misselie only rolled her eyes. "It should still be there, but the ruins were filled with traps and tricks that have no doubt reseted by now."

"You didn't take it?" Hal asked. He looked around the shop. "Given your vast collection of books, I'm surprised it's not here."

Stravis shook his head. "No. Runebreaker can only be held by an Empyrean. If I touched it, the book would turn to ash in a heartbeat. Or was it I would? That's not important. I just wanted to feast my eyes upon it once and see the silk threads of the cover react to my presence."

"Where's the ruin site? We'll go at first light," Hal said.

The old man held up his hand. "Not so fast. You'll need guidance inside the ruins. I'm coming along."

Hal was taken aback. "Why? You've done so much already."

Stravis took a deep breath. "Your name transcends the systems of the Realm-verse, Hal. Exiles who made it to Hellas spoke of your kindness to the people. You never let the ego that came with royal blood corrupt you. They said you were brave and tough but understanding, and they clung to the hope that you would change the Empire for the better. Though you were much younger then, I believed in their tales. Now I see your determination and courage and your passion for your homeland. That is the leader I want for the Empire, and it would be my honor to help him get there."

"I heard the same stories about the generosity you showed your people," Misselie said. She nodded to Kristilin. "She has told many of those stories."

A long sigh escaped his lungs as he relaxed in the seat. It had been a long time since Hal had heard kind words like that. They were not the flowery ones people said to his face, washing away the moment they turned their backs. These words came from deep within, and it took a small load off his shoulders to know people still thought highly of him. It gave him hope.

"Besides, you need me," the old man added, earning a light slap on the shoulder from Misselie. "Us, I mean."

Hal couldn't help but smile. Kristilin moved from her spot and placed an arm around Hal's. It only added to the warmth he felt. She had been with Hal from the start and had helped him get his feet under him once more. They were all important, but none more so than her. He wished to return the feeling to her and eventually his sister.

"Are you able?" Kristilin asked.

"For an expedition, I'm always ready," the old man said with a wink. He grabbed a few leather rucksacks from under the counter and handed one to Hal. "We'll leave at dawn."

Night soon came, and the residents of Hellas settled in for the evening. Hal watched from the small clearing at the top of the enclave where the rocks flattened and he could see the vastness of the Ashlands. As the lights dimmed and the town disappeared into the ash, it felt almost humbling to watch, knowing that at any point his life could disappear just as the town did. He sat with his back to a rock wall and just took it in. Life here was so simple yet so complicated. Live or die—those were the only options, and living seemed the hardest of all.

He looked at his hands, opening and closing them a few times. Fire had once engulfed them, charged him with a never-ending thrill that no other living being could understand except for his family. The raw power that had come to his fingertips was unparalleled. Yet as he looked at them, they were vacant. Empty. A shell. He sighed as small jolterbugs fluttered in the distance, their dancing colors creating a spectacle in the dreary darkening gray.

Kristilin emerged from behind him, and a door closed. Taking a seat next to him, she brought her knees up to her chest and wrapped her arms around them. She pointed to the sky, where bright stars peeked through the thick ash clouds above. "How many do you think are up there?"

Hal followed her finger. He hadn't counted the stars in quite a while, since the last time he'd spent a night with Kristilin.

"Thousands? Billions? Scholars and instructors never taught us about the cosmos. They said the stars were part of the Maw, the space between the realms of existence. Only our stars in the Realmverse existed in our space," Kristilin said.

"There were a lot of things they failed to teach. Corruption, dishonesty, infusion. They cared about their views more than the truth." He stared at the stars as they twinkled dimly under the veil of ash.

Now was the time.

"Kristilin, I'm sorry."

She turned to look at him.

"I'm sorry for leaving when I did. It wasn't right, and I should have fought to stay a few more days and get word to you."

"Hal, it is not your fault."

"It is my fault for not standing up . . . for us. I should've gone with you to Velra . . ." His voice trailed off, and when he looked back at Kristilin, her gaze was glued to the ground before her.

"I was so excited when you asked for my hand," she said, and the words cut through Hal like a dagger through paper. "I called my *mora* and *para* the next morning on the holo, and they could not have been prouder. But then the war started, and I was recalled to Velra . . ."

Hal fought back the burning in his nose, his hands trembling. When the sniffles came from beside him, he broke, and a tear ran down his cheek. The pain of having hurt her stung him. He couldn't change the fact that he'd left her in turmoil on Velra.

"The only thing that kept me going through hell was the fact that you were still out there somewhere and that I might have the chance to explain myself." Hal wiped the tears from his eyes and reached inside his chest pocket. He pulled out the locket with the photo of him, Miri, and Kristilin and smiled. "That I might be able to earn your love again."

Silence followed, and only the wind spoke. Hal's heart raced as the minutes went by, and all he could do was wipe his stray tears away.

"I never stopped loving you, Hal," Kristilin said. Her lavender eyes sparkled under the starlight and were the most beautiful thing he had ever seen.

"And I never stopped loving you," Hal echoed.

She rested her head on his shoulder, and Hal took a deep breath, his head against the rock wall behind them. Wrapping an arm around her shoulders, he closed his eyes and felt her against him. A piece of the puzzle had been put back into place, and he cherished the closeness, her touch, her warmth, her love.

Hope.

Chapter XXIV

T he tower stretched high into the sky like a long finger trying to touch the sun itself.

The boat rocked in the choppy water as a steady breeze blew. Hal was fixated by the structure, and he admired its ingenuity. So much was still unknown about the Primordials, hidden away behind locked doors so those in favor could relish what they offered. No sane soul would dare hide the treasure trove of information this past civilization held, at least in Hal's mind. There was still so much to learn and capture, reveal and master, and it brought the spark of wonderment back to him. If he wanted to be like Atis or Sarin, he had to embrace everything this world would throw at him.

The boat came to the shore, and Hal jumped out, dragging it up and out of the tidewater. The tower loomed behind him in the center of hills that rose and fell, solemn guardians that dared travelers to traverse them. The thought made him cast a glance at Stravis.

How did he manage to do it alone? It earned the old man some courage points from Hal.

"Impressive, isn't it?" Stravis said as he hopped out of the boat with his staff, shouldering his satchel. "Four hundred floors tall."

"You climbed that?" Kristilin asked as she stood next to Hal. "That is taller than the Velra capital spire in Parsi."

"Much younger days," Stravis said as Misselie stepped onto the shore. Nodding, he pointed with his staff to an area away from the tower. "Our entrance will lead us to the underground temple. I caution you to stay behind me and watch out for traps."

They walked across the openness of the island, saved from the wind by the occasional dip of the hills. Ash ripped across the landscape with such fury that their cloaks flapped and snapped like the crack of a whip.

Hal's boots sank into the gray with each step. More ash rained down upon him, collecting on his shoulders and hood. He focused on Stravis so as not to lose him in the few feet of visibility he had. Kristilin kept close behind him with Misselie at the rear.

In the valley of two hills, they came to a door, its old wood warped and stained. The hills provided some shelter from the wind and gave them time to wipe the loose ash from their faces. Stravis approached the door and pulled a small book from his satchel.

"*Viska*," he said, and the iron chain that held the door shut glowed a faint purple before it fell to the ground and turned to ash. Stravis faced the others and said, "In time the chain will reform, but we should be out of here long before that happens."

Hal turned to him, stunned. "You can speak their language and cast spells?"

The old man smiled. "I can."

"Then why do we need Runebreaker if you can break spells with simple words?" Hal asked, his impatience growing. "Why can't you do it? Teach me?"

"Because there is still much you need to learn." Stravis turned to face him, his once friendly and welcoming look turned serious. "These cosmic beings hold many secrets, secrets the Empyreans learned and used, and you would do yourself a favor by studying them, young prince. I can teach you many things, but you will not learn them. *You* need to experience them." He pointed to the door. "This place is filled with inklings of their past wisdom. Do try to learn."

Stravis entered the tower, Misselie close behind. Hal stood there, anger coursing through his veins. It felt like a waste of time. What Stravis said would be true under any ordinary circumstances, but he was pressured for time. He had no clue what was happening in Imperius, and if Varim discovered what he was up to, it would only be a matter of time before they arrived, ready to silence him. Spies lurked everywhere, and the Lumnis Stone would be the ultimate prize.

Hal stepped through the door and followed Stravis and the girls. Orbs of light illuminated the path, and everyone looked up in awe at the mural above. It snaked around like a stream of water, illuminating the path as they walked. Cold air slapped Hal's face as he pulled his face mask back up, the weight of dampness building on his evosuit. All the while he kept his ears open and listened to every creak and crack.

When they finally rounded a corner, a massive cavern stretched before them. A large blue light illuminated the darkness. It sat on a cylindrical metal structure that rose to the rocky ceiling and sank below the earth. Arched pathways met at the central column, railings along the sides to keep ancient souls from a freefall. Hal felt drawn to the light, and he wanted to discover just how it brightened up such darkness.

A couple dozen spheres of red energy flashed throughout the area and grew in size. Hal froze as Primordial guardians materialized out of them. The large charna creations had long slender arms, and they reached through the red void and pulled themselves out. As they emerged, their armor formed around them like it was part of their being. Dark material covered them until only their glowing red eyes were visible.

Hal wondered how the souls of years past could still reform, but his momentary wonderment was cut short when a blast of red energy shot their way.

Hal ducked, and the bolt crashed into the rocks behind him. He pulled out his lightvolver and fired a few quick shots, each one striking a guardian. They exploded in a flash of red and dematerialized, sent back to the void they'd come from. Kristilin cut through them, keeping Stravis and Misselie behind her. The two pushed up, following the land bridge and sending the guardians back. More materialized toward the column and set up a defensive line. The group took cover behind crumbled structures and caught their breath as streaks of red flew overhead.

"Was this part of the trap?" Hal asked as he fired a few shots before ducking for cover, a bolt ricocheting where he had just been.

"No! I don't know where these guardians came from," Stravis said as he clutched his satchel, Misselie taking shots from beside him.

Kristilin absorbed a bolt with her karver and fired it back. The explosion rocked three guardians and instantly dematerialized them. When she ducked back into cover, she said, "Why now, then?"

Stravis looked at Hal. "They sense a Kell . . ."

"What are you talking about?" Hal said, firing more shots before red bolts struck and shattered part of his cover. The stone sprayed and cut through the first layer of his evosuit. "They think I'm a Kell?"

"In lore, Primordial guardians would test a new Kell in different ways. I've read some of Atis's notes on them. Depending on the class, it could vary. Fire is considered to be destruction and rebirth. A cleanse." Another explosion sent dirt flying over them. "I believe they are testing you."

Hal narrowed his eyes. He had never heard of such a thing, but he wouldn't put it past the Imperial court to withhold such information. Still, he had no idea what it meant.

Stravis seemed surprised, and when Hal turned to look at Kristilin and Misselie, their eyes contained the same puzzlement. This could be his chance to prove he was worthy.

With a deep breath, he leapt out of cover amid protests.

The firestorm of red energy bolts turned to him, but the call to battle did not faze him. It was like the switch of battle had been flipped again, and his military mind took hold.

Hal landed two shots at a couple guardians before ducking behind a column, then dematerialized two more before jumping into their position. The guardians morphed their arms almost poetically. Their cannon arms turned to glowing red swords and the guardians shrieked at Hal as loud as they could. When one swung,

Hal rolled and fired a shot. Dematerialized. Another attacked, and Hal ducked under the arm before firing at another behind it. The guardian tried to catch him off guard, but Hal avoided the attack and slid between its legs, firing a shot right under its face. The guardian dematerialized, and Hal stood as leftover red energy wafted through the air.

"You are crazy," Kristilin said to him, her accent thickening with anger. "They could have killed you."

"I couldn't let them hurt you," he said. As her glare softened, he turned to Stravis and said, "Why are they doing this now? Nobody mentioned any of this."

The old man approached him and sighed. "I haven't been completely honest."

Hal gripped his lightvolver even tighter, rage at a tipping point. He should have known better than to trust a hermit he barely knew.

Stravis raised a hand. "Forgive me, dear prince, but I had to make sure you were ready."

"Why?"

"You saw only part of the recording and then Empress Irina's message in Starlight Temple, yes?" Stravis removed a small puck from his bag and placed it on the ground. "I found this during one of my expeditions nearly two years ago. Watch."

A hologram of Hal's mother sprang up. She wore simple clothes to combat the cold, a scarf wrapped around her neck. Behind her stood an open chamber with columns all around.

"I have done years of research in these temples, have activated rituals and solved puzzles. And now I fear the answer." She sighed heavily and rubbed her temples. "Grace of Empyrea guide us."

Hal stepped closer and looked into her eyes. They were different from his in every way: normal pupils within blue irises that stood in stark contrast to his and Miri's white. Even their father's brown eyes were different, but Hal had never thought anything of it. They all shared the same diamond pupils except for his mother.

"The blood and DNA tests came back positive. The charna nodes within Hal and Miri are the same in strength as Atis's and Sarin's. We thought over the centuries that the DNA strain would have fallen to the wayside. That's not the case, I guess. This means they have the potential to be Kells of their own. They, by their own accord, are the second coming of Empyreans, which is why they must find the Lumnis Stones before it is too late. Of course, they will have to go through their trials like the Empyreans before them." She shook her head. "The Imperial Council would not like this, not with High Minister Varim urging for the abolition of magic wielding research. He's peculiar about this, but I don't know why. What they don't understand about our world . . . But there's—"

Irina Skyborn looked behind her as people scrambled in the back, and energy bolts flew through the air. The recording ended, and Hal stood there in disbelief.

Stravis picked up the puck and brushed it off before looking at Hal. "That's why you were exiled. Varim knew the truth and knew you would be an obstacle to whatever his plan was." He placed the puck back into his satchel. "The guardians sense it too."

"Why not Miri?" Hal asked. "Why was she not exiled with me if Varim fears us?"

"I don't know, but I can only assume things happened during your conflict with the Polarians. Maybe he saw something he wasn't quite sure of before. Or maybe it's part of something grander." He placed a hand on Hal's shoulder and offered a smile. "You two are Empyreans, but what is even more interesting is that, by your mother's word, you share almost an exact replica of Atis's and Sarin's charna node structure."

"How? Like a reincarnation?" Hal asked.

"No, not to that extent. Take genes, for example. They can skip generations, and a great-grandchild can have the same abnormal uniqueness as the great-grandparent. Yours, however, skipped hundreds of years to be reawakened in you and Miri."

"How is that possible?"

Stravis shrugged. "Charna and Wielders are strange. You're an example I cannot explain, but perhaps your mother could. Or perhaps Atis and Sarin are watching over you." He nodded to the holopuck. "If I found this in an abandoned ruin, I'm sure there could be more."

"Sounds like wishful thinking," Misselie said.

"It's plausible," Stravis answered.

"I just want to save my sister and help my people," Hal finally said, a breath of regret escaping him. "I want my people protected and not lied to by these false revolutionaries."

"Then let's find Runebreaker and get you back to being a Wielder. That's a good step."

Hal looked at Stravis and Misselie as Kristilin's arm wrapped around his. So many things he wanted to know and do kept slipping away. But as he looked into Kristilin's eyes, there was trust and loyalty within. That was one thing he'd never questioned. They all wanted what he wanted: a stable and prosperous Empire. If that was to happen, he needed to accept help where it presented itself. Hal nodded to the old man, who returned it with a smile.

They walked down the spiral staircase that had presented itself in the column of stone. Stravis guided them down. Occasionally he would stop and throw some powder on the ground. Sometimes it lay there unremarkably, but other times it revealed hidden traps. Spoken words of Primordial runes deactivated the traps and allowed them to proceed with Stravis at the forefront.

Hal listened carefully to the words the old man spoke. Each trap had a different word, like it was a collection of one giant phrase. To him it sounded like a jumbled mess in a crossword puzzle like the ones his grandfather used to try to solve. Then again, it could've been a secret hidden in plain sight.

When they finally came to the bottom of the stairs, more guardians waited for them.

Hal jumped in front of the old man and fired two shots. Each one dematerialized the guardians and left behind the same red energy waves that faded through the air. Hal spun the gun and slipped it into his holster as Stravis walked farther, sprinkling his powder. Kristilin brushed a hand across Hal's back, a smile on her lips as she pressed on. The gesture did more for Hal's mood than anything. It showed the love of his life still cared for him, that he was not alone. That by itself was monumental. The playful wink from Misselie after made him blush just a bit.

Stravis stood before a light bridge. Flickering in the dark, sparks flew into the air on the opposite side, the strong blue fading in and out. The hardlight bridge spanned the abyss, leading to the gates of a temple-like structure buried in the mountain. As Hal looked around, no other way to cross made itself present, and he sighed.

"This is our only way across," Stravis said.

"Was it this bad when you came here before?" Kristilin asked.

Stravis nodded. "The trick is to be slow and steady. Too much pressure and the bridge will give out." He turned back to the other two. "Unless one of you two knows how to calibrate hardlight technology, I'll go first."

"Actually," Kristilin began, "back home I worked with Vel engineers who toyed with something similar. I can attempt to strengthen the hardlite connectivity of the bridge."

"I'll go with her and help. We're the lightest of the bunch, so the bridge should still stay intact," Misselie said as she pulled a small grapple hook from her satchel. "And if anything happens, I have this."

"Is that a bag of tricks where you just have everything?" Hal joked.

"Would you prefer I not be prepared?"

Hal nodded. "Point taken."

Stravis moved away from the bridge as Kristilin and Misselie stepped up to it. Hal wanted to protest, but he knew they had to get across.

"Hey, be careful," he said, and Kristilin's lavender eyes twinkled as she turned back and smiled.

They took their first steps, and the bridge fluctuated. Hal looked down, and the darkness consumed all. Anything could be down there. That was one thing he'd learned about the Ashlands: anything could be anywhere.

"She's a good girl, Hal," Stravis said.

Hal only looked away for a moment before his eyes returned to Kristilin. "We've been through a lot together, but we've spent so long apart."

"So I've heard. She reminds me of a girl I used to know in Imperius. Do listen to an old man and don't allow pettiness to grow between you."

Hal nodded before looking at Stravis. "Can you tell me anything more about Varim? What does he want this Lumnis Stone for?"

"I'm afraid that knowledge is limited to your own family and that of Imperius, Prince Hal."

Misselie called from the other side while Kristilin began to work on the electrical components there. Stravis patted Hal's back before shuffling forward. The sight almost made Hal laugh, but he knew that would be uncalled for, especially in a tense situation like this. Still, watching a weary man shuffle across an unstable hardlight bridge was something he'd never thought he would see.

By the time Stravis made his way to the other side and waved at Hal to follow, Hal had already sunk into his own thoughts of what to do next. One look below made his stomach queasy. It wasn't the height that bothered him but the unknown of what lay below. He remembered his first hours here when he fell through the crevasse and heard the sinister hissing from the darkness below. If he could just see what waited for him down there, he would be fine, but the unknown terrified him.

With a deep breath, he took the first step.

He paused and listened with each step like he was walking on ice. The bridge continued to flicker, more so when he placed a foot down. Lines of energy ran up and down it, stopped by a step from his boot.

When he got to the halfway point, the bridge fizzled out, and the support slipped out from under him. His eyes went wide as he reached for a nonexistent rail to grab. As he fell toward the darkness, his name was called after him.

CHAPTER XXV

Hal landed with a thud, and ash flew into the air. Struggling for breath, he pushed himself up and gasped for air. The fall had knocked everything out, and it felt like his lungs had deflated. As the air slowly returned to his lungs, Hal looked around the darkness. Only faint blue orblights brought light to the shroud of darkness, and as he looked up, the bridge flickered before becoming solid again. He dusted off the ash and stood with a groan. It felt like he'd landed on a pile of rocks. Still, the fall had left him relatively unscathed.

When he turned around, bright flashes of red met him, and Hal drew his weapon. Guardians spawned right on him, and he didn't waste any time sending them back where they'd come from. The bright red lights lit up the darkness like bombs flashing in the night. It reminded him all too much of his past battles, and he never stopped firing his lightvolver.

The guardians met a swift end by a bolt from his weapon before they could fully emerge from their materialization portals. The hardlite energy lingered for a moment and looked like strands of light against the ashy backdrop, before they disappeared like a shadow. Silence fell, the crackling energy of materialization portals stopped, and he took a much-needed deep breath.

After the confrontation, he spotted an exit path off to the side of the pit he'd fallen into. How he wished he had his abilities back and could navigate this darkness, but it would be worth it in the end. He only had to wait a little longer.

As he felt around in the darkness, his hands found an opening in the wall, and he stepped through.

Orblight lit the way, twinkling along the walls in the darkness. Hal followed the path without a choice. Consumed by darkness with only the orblight to lead him made him remember where he was and how far he'd fallen. Hal straightened up and vowed to rise from the ashes they'd buried him under. They could bend him if they wanted, but he would never break.

When he came to an opening, he stopped and looked around. The hall widened before it narrowed again on the far side. He waited for more guardians to spawn, but when they didn't, he decided the area was safe enough.

He took a step, and electricity ran up his leg and through his body, shocking him to his core. A pained scream broke through the darkness as the electricity touched every nerve. Flashes of blue and white blinded his eyes before the jolt sent him flying back against the wall. Smoke rose from his suit while he trembled with the aftershocks of electricity still in him. His body felt like it was on fire, pins and needles poking at every nerve. It hurt to move, and every flex of a muscle took strength. He managed to push himself up, still tender from the shock, and look at the area before him again.

He picked up a handful of dust and threw it to reveal the magical trap.

Pesky devils, he thought, trying to remember the words Stravis had used to navigate the traps. As he looked across the trap field, a rocky ash covered incline led to a central room. He had to get there, but as he looked around the area, he saw darkness. He thought hard, recounting every word the old man had said for each trap set by the Primordials. *What was it?* There would be consequences if he got the word wrong. As he looked at the orblight on the other side of the incline for answers, he remembered.

"*Yartu.*"

The trap glowed bright blue before disappearing. Hal took the first step with extra caution and braced for the shock. When it did not come, he smiled and threw dust before him again to reveal the next trap.

"*Yartu.*"

The trap disappeared. A newfound pride encapsulated Hal; he'd finally used the ancient language for himself. Utterance of words forgotten by man brought him a sense of clarity and passion. A dead language could be resurrected one speaker at a time.

When the last trap vanished, Hal hurried up the incline.

At the top, Hal was awed by the might of the great hall. A rocky ceiling with chandeliers of orblight lit the way to where rocks were etched with runic symbols and scenes from ancient history, though still stained by ash that had crept in over the years. It looked as though this place was built into the cavern hundreds of years ago, but still retained its beauty from its creation. Hal marveled at the sight and wondered what stories these scenes told.

As he walked to the center along the circular floor of marble, the rings on the ground shifted like gears. He had to stop as his section of floor turned to step onto the next. To his fortune, no traps lay in wait for him. Instead, more guardians spawned.

These appeared different; they were larger and wore bulkier armor. Hal drew his weapon and fired a shot that bounced off the otherworldly material. The guardians whipped out their sword arms and displayed hardlight shields that absorbed his other shots. Hal backed up, trying to search for a way to take on these foes.

Stravis and the girls barged in through the other side of the room, where the walls of the hall parted for a dark tunnel. As Hal fired a few more shots to slow the guardians' advance, another set of five materialization portals formed, and guardians emerged, firing bolts of energy that screamed by. The bolts put off heat and smelled of chemical reactions, and Hal spun behind a column for cover.

"The exposed parts!" Stravis yelled from across the room. "Hit them!"

Another guardian flanked and swung its sword at Hal. He ducked under the glowing weapon as it sliced through the pillar like it was soft wood. The heat from the hardlight reflected off his face. He looked the guardian in its glowing eyes, and it was almost humanlike. It roared at him before Hal fired a round into the unprotected neck area. It instantly dematerialized and was sucked into the void it had come from.

Kristilin drew her karver and caught the blade of a guardian who'd tried to swipe at Stravis. The guardian shoved her away with its shield and refocused its effort on her. It spoke in an unknown language, the sound hostile and angry. With a mighty swing, the guardian struck, but Kristilin slipped under its arm and sliced her karver against the exposed arm joint of the armor. The guardian roared as its arm disappeared and charged her with its shield. At the right moment, she sidestepped the guardian and slashed its back before following up with a strike to the head. The guardian dematerialized, and Kristilin rushed back over to protect Stravis and Misselie.

As bolts of energy left Hal's weapon and struck the exposed faces of the guardians, another approached him from behind. Hal saw it too late, and when he went to fire, the sting of hardlight met his face. Dazed, he staggered back. The guardian grabbed him by the collar and raised him into the air to look him in the eye. It was taller and bigger than the others and spoke in Primordial runes, and Hal understood.

"False Kells have no purpose here."

It threw Hal across the room. Old marble splintered as he crashed through a column. The guardian marched to where he lay. Hal pushed himself up and looked at the towering figure of pure charna. Their eyes met like two soldiers on a battlefield with an understanding of what had to be done. Only one would walk away from this. The guardian wasn't angry at him, but it had a job to do, just like he did.

When the guardian started its swing, Hal spun to face it and fired a single shot. Heat passed over him as the shot ripped through the guardian. It dematerialized with a flash and left its energy waves in its wake.

Kristilin rushed over to him while Misselie fired a last shot that ended a guardian who'd been crawling across the floor toward a weapon. Hal turned, and his body burned with a controlled fire like someone had stabbed him. Kristilin looked him over as he fought the aches in his body. He raised a hand to brush a stray strand of white hair from her eyes and wiped away the ashy smudges that covered her ice-blue cheek. She cupped his hand and smiled.

All around, the remnants of red heat waves tarnished the pristine chamber before they faded away. Stravis had taken a seat in the middle of the room and faced a wall that had a circular door. Hal stood next to him with the girls and looked at the carvings and etchings that told hidden stories.

"A Story Wall," Stravis said. "This one tells the story of two Kells during the Dawning, the beginning of time."

"The first Fire Wielders," Hal said.

"War starved and divided them for years. Warlords used the arcane art to gain power by destruction and fear until a pair of Kells defeated the warlords and developed the Empyrean Kingdom in Athos. Archkell Atis and Kell Sarin used Runebreaker to seal their treasures and knowledge and buried it here afterward so others would not be tempted to wage war again."

"This is all starting to make sense, whether I want it to or not," Hal said with a deep breath. "He's the founder of everything the Empire holds near."

Stravis nodded with a smile. "And where you get your Empyrean blood."

Hal looked at the circular door, his heart fluttering with anticipation. "It's in there, isn't it?"

The old man stood with a groan and rubbed his aged knees. "I feel as old as it is."

He approached the door and spoke a series of words Hal had not heard before. The segments of the door spun opposite one another: one clockwise, the other counterclockwise, and the third clockwise again. When they aligned with the same rune, the door groaned and split apart, dust falling from the top.

Inside, lit by a single orblight, was a pedestal holding a small book with faded leather bindings and a leather strap that looked ready to split in two. One rune rested in the center of the cover, and smaller runes ran up and down either side of the larger rune. Hal cast a glance at Stravis, who nodded for him to go on.

Hal slowly raised his hand, his breath short and rapid, and touched the smooth leather. A sigh of relief escaped his mouth as he gripped it. There was energy within it, like the book was alive and communicating with him. It felt surreal and alien, and he wanted to know more.

"Runebreaker," Hal said as he read the runes, and the book glowed a soft purple in response. "Knowledge is power."

Hal returned to the others with the book in hand, and Stravis's eyes said all that needed to be said.

"It's so beautiful. To think thousands of years ago Atis and Sarin used this very artifact." Stravis went to touch the leather but stopped himself and smiled. "So much rich history."

"This contains the phrases to all of their safeguards?" Hal asked.

Stravis nodded. "Each and every one. In the wrong hands it can unlock ancient weapons and vehicles of immense power. But it reacted to you, which means it trusts you."

"How can a book react?" Misselie asked.

"It can feel the presence of a possible Kell. The charna within the person is the same as what is in the book. They communicate with each other. This was created by Empyreans to be used by other Empyreans in a way that passed the security responsibility to later generations. A blood oath, if you will. Someone with false or artificial blood would not be able to see the words inside, but he can."

"Fascinating," Hal said as the words became visible to him.

"Indeed, it is."

Hal froze. Everyone peeled their eyes away from the book and turned around.

Miri stopped in the center of the room, her arms crossed and a glare in her eyes.

"What's wrong? You look like you've seen a ghost," she said as she shifted in her silver armor, a cape of gold behind her and her silver circlet shining in the orblight.

As he took a step forward, he kept a hand close to his weapon and the other with a firm grip on Runebreaker. "What are you doing here?"

"Simple really. You have something I want," she said. "Hand it over, and the sisterly part of me will let you live in this decrepit hellhole."

"Why would I do that after what you've done?"

Miri smirked. "Oh, I don't expect you to, which makes this little reunion that much more exciting."

Without breaking his gaze, Hal spoke to the others. "Get to the exit."

"Are you crazy? She can still Wield, Hal, and you—"

The panic in Kristilin's voice hurt, but this was something he could not involve her in. She was right—Miri could still Wield—and the skills Kristilin had were no match for someone who could lob fireballs at her. He had to make sure she and the others were safe first.

"Kristi. Go."

Hal looked at her with stern eyes. After a second or two, she nodded and moved to stand by Stravis.

"Oh, look at dear Kristilin Äcroix. Another traitor to her nation. Someone I called a sister. How does it feel?"

"Miri, you're here for me, aren't you? How about you stay focused for once," Hal said, and Miri whipped around to face him. Her anger was raw, animalistic. Something had changed her. "What do you want?"

"I know where the Stone is. Give me Runebreaker." She charged her hands with fire energy.

"I can't do that, Meer."

"Typical. Always hiding something, like how you killed Father," she said, then let loose a volley of flames.

Hal dove to one side while the others ducked for cover on the other. Miri laughed as he hid behind a marble column.

"Oh, Hal. Can't fight back? How sad."

He peeked out of cover for a second to fire two shots. Miri rose a flame wall, and the bolts smacked into it. When the flame wall came down, her wicked smile gave him goose bumps. She slung a fireball that sailed right by him and exploded against the wall, sending bits of stone flying. Hal shielded himself as Kristilin led the others to the tunnel. His momentary distraction had worked, but now he had to find a way out.

"I remember the relentless Halcion Skyborn from the war stories soldiers told with pride. Hal the Backbreaker. Hal the Fire Spirit. Hal the Honorable, they called you. This place changed you. It's made you weak."

More lightbolts flew from his weapon and caught Miri off guard. She side-stepped the bolts and raised her arms as streams of flames shot out. Hal slid to more cover and rotated. The exit was near, but he had to get closer. As he sank behind the cover, he knew what he had to do.

"Weaker? Someone has been drinking palm sap. Look how slow you are, Meer. You need to catch up. Can't get the job done like that. What would they say if Princess Miriam Skyborn failed at finding a little book? They would find you in contempt of court like your brother. But at least I tried to discover the truth about our parents. You're just going along with the lie."

"Shut up," she said, her words echoing through the chamber.

A fireball flew over his head and exploded with a heat so intense he thought his eyebrows had been singed right off. Hal popped over for an instant and fired two more shots before moving again. He didn't want to hit her, but he trusted his aim with a weapon. Miri caught the bolts with her fire wall as Hal kept up his blasts. As she sent another fireball at him, Hal ducked through the tunnel.

"Run, Hal. Run as far as you want, but I know you. Hear me? I know your every move."

His sister's voice echoed through the confines of the tunnel. He would've been lying to himself if he said he didn't feel the urge to look over his shoulder every second. It felt like she was right there, and as he turned to look back, firelight flickered from the tunnel behind him. Hal ran as fast as he could, his body crying for him to stop. If he did, it would all be over, and now that he'd found the key, he had to continue. The heat began to caress his back, and he dared not look behind him. Every step mattered, and one stumble meant the end. The scent of burnt fungi filled his nose as he ran, the embrace of fire so close. The opening appeared in front of him, and he used every last ounce of strength he had.

Hal dove through the opening and rolled along the ashy ground of the cavern as his sister's flames reached out for him. The flames roared out of the tunnel with fury as Hal scrambled to his feet just out of reach. The heat from the flames caused sweat to build on his forehead, and he took a step back.

The flames subsided, and Kristilin ran to check him while Stravis stood with hands on knees and caught his breath with Misselie beside him.

"Are you all right?" Kristilin asked.

"I'm fine." He looked around as rock pillars in the cavern supported the weight of the ceiling. Small holes in it trickled ash down. *They were near the surface,* he thought.

"Through here," Stravis said with bated breath as he pointed to a path that had scorch marks on the side and smoke rising from dried out creeper vines. "Princess Miriam must've come through here. It should lead us back out to the Ashlands."

"Those vines covered the opening when we came through here using the tunnel Stravis brought us through," Misselie said.

"Imperials could be waiting for us on the other side," Hal said as he brushed the ash off only to duck when a screaming fireball streaked by them. It slammed into the rocky wall near the door and exploded with a fiery fury, incinerating every mushroom in its vicinity.

"Would you rather face the flames of the princess?" Stravis asked as he stood up.

"Oh Hal, we have unfinished business to discuss," Miri called from the other side of the tunnel, her voice echoing off the walls.

Hal turned back to Stravis and nodded.

Stravis led them through the tunnel, and the glowing mushrooms on the walls put off a soft light. As they came to the end, a spiral stone staircase stood alone in a small room. They followed it up, and Hal couldn't help but look over his shoulder every couple seconds. He waited to hear his sister's footsteps racing up the stairs after them. It was a bad spot to be in. They didn't know what was on the other side, but they couldn't stay where they were. It was a lose-lose situation all around.

It felt like the steps would never end, and Hal's thighs burned with exhaustion. The glowing mushrooms became scarce as they ascended, and the first sign of light illuminated the top of the stairwell.

Stravis peeked his head out of the opening first, and the cold air of the Ashlands slapped Hal's face. As they filed out, Hal scanned the area for any signs of Imperials. He saw no vehicles and no soldiers waited for them outside. All he saw was an empty wasteland and as he looked back to the hole they crawled out of, he wondered how his sister knew about it. In the distance, covered by a haze of ash, stood the tower from where they had entered.

"Ha. See? Told you there was nothing to worry about," Stravis said.

"I don't like this at all," Hal said. "Miri would never come here alone. This doesn't feel right."

"Bah. Fine, fine, young one. There are caves a few miles south from here where we can take refuge for the day and wait out the princess."

"We should leave now," Hal said.

"Aw, so soon, Hal?" Miri cooed. "We just reacquainted, and I'm dying to know what my brother has learned here."

Hal turned, frozen, as his sister marched toward them. Two Praetorians spawned next to her as the warp effect of personal teleportation technology engulfed their bodies. He was about to step up to her when Stravis jumped in front of him with staff held outright.

He turned to Hal. "Protect Runebreaker."

"But you can't face her alone," Hal said.

"I will buy you time. Go."

Before he could protest more, Kristilin pulled on his arm, and the first fireball was launched. Stravis spun his staff, and the crystal on top forged a blue wall that the fireball slammed into. Miri spewed a river of flames from her hands as she pressed closer to Stravis. Stravis held on as the weight and force of the flames pushed against him and turned the center of the shield bright orange.

Hal could only watch as they took the boat they'd used to cross back to the other side of the bank. Stravis gripped his staff before the charna wall exploded and the flames sent him backward.

Two corsair starfighters buzzed overhead and banked toward them. Misselie slid down the large ash dune followed by Kristilin as Hal turned to look back. A small squad of Imperial soldiers escorted Stravis away while Miri stared and locked eyes with him. His sister's gaze was intense, her eyes like daggers. He wished he could have a minute to try to convince her he wasn't the enemy, but the thud of energy bolts impacting the ground near him snapped him out of his distracted trance.

He met the girls at the bottom of the ash dune as the two Praetorians crested the top. Energy bolts rained down on them as they weaved through the open sea of dunes with little cover. Ash kicked into the sky each time a bolt struck the ground. Hal drew his lightvolver and returned fire, but it wasn't enough. All he could do was run. Air became the only thing he needed as he focused on the next dune in sight. It was their only choice for a reprieve and to regroup. The rain of energy bolts kept coming, impacting left and right, until the Praetorians had to reload their weapons. The trio came to the next dune and jumped behind it.

"What do we do? She has Stravis. We have to go back," Misselie said between breaths.

"Not with the Praetorians raining energy bolts on us," Kristilin said.

Hal peeked around the dune as the Praetorians slid down, weapons reloaded, and then more Imperial light soldiers crested the top. Officers shouted orders to their troops as more came into view.

He pulled back in and looked at Kristilin. "We need to split."

"What?"

"They're after me. I can't let you two get hurt."

"We can handle ourselves," Kristilin said.

"I know that, but you need to hear me when I say this. Miri is not the same. She will use you to hurt me," Hal said. "We need to split up for now. Just to lose her."

"And Stravis?" Misselie asked.

"When we regroup, we'll form a plan," Hal said as a fireball screamed over the dune, turning the top to glass.

Kristilin looked him in the eyes and grabbed the front of his evosuit. "You better promise me you will not do anything stupid. Contact me when you are safe."

"I promise," Hal said.

"The caves are due south of us, and another is southwest," Misselie said.

"I'll go southwest and lead them away from you," Hal said. "Go."

Hal turned back around and fired from his lightvolver. Two soldiers went down, and the hailstorm of energy bolts resumed. He looked back as the girls ran for the valley between two dunes and disappeared from sight. Hal fired a few more shots before he swapped sides. He just had to buy them a few more seconds. Hal raced across the open to the adjacent dune, firing off as many rounds as he could before he slid to safety behind the dune just as a bolt impacted the ground beside him. There were way too many of them to fend off alone, and he'd bought them enough time. Now he needed to leave.

He looked behind him, where the terrain dipped down over a small ledge and led to a rocky area. After a few more quick shots, he slid down and bolted for the rocks, disappearing into the haze of ash.

Chapter XXVI

Darkness. Though he'd escaped its clutches before, Hal found himself alone in a cave once more. Miri was a tenacious one, he knew, and their rush away from her had only separated him from the girls. It could've been part of her plan from the start, and what came next was a mystery. All he knew was his sister was here, in the Ashlands, and that would worry anyone now.

Hal sighed as he shifted in the darkness, looking out to the Ashlands. Miri had to have found the recording from their mother, though too late now. Hal looked at his lap, where Runebreaker sat and glowed soft purple. It pained him to not read it now, but it was for the best. He had to meet back up with the girls.

A seeker drone whizzed by, the rumble of its engine a reminder of what Miri had brought with her. Its buzz faded into the distance as it searched for any hints of activity. No doubt they were searching for him and the others. He only hoped Kristilin and Misselie had found the other caves and were lying low. The thought of them in danger worried him. It would be a perfect chance to lure him out if Miri managed to capture them, though he knew Kristilin would give his sister a fight. Poor Misselie was probably worried sick about Stravis. The old man had proven himself kind and an influential teacher of the ancient beings.

He reminded Hal of his grandfather on his mother's side. Though married to the Duchess of Valkara, no blood of gods flowed through him. He'd been a simple man with a passion like a normal person, and it reminded Hal what being normal felt like.

After he regrouped with the girls, they'd have to form a plan to figure out where Miri was, and Stravis too. He owed that much to the old man and Misselie after all they'd helped him and Kristilin with.

But he couldn't do anything against Miri just yet. She had the power here, and the torture she was capable of added to his worry. Too much time had been wasted searching for answers, and now his sister was here. He had to regain his Wielding if he was to stop Miri from whatever she was doing here. Though if the Lumnis Stone fell into her grasp, he feared what she would do with it. Like his mother said in the hologram, they had a choice of what to do with it and it had to be the correct one.

He placed Runebreaker into his bag, then stood up and looked out into the ash. The sunlight had faded from the canopy of clouds and had given way to a glow of blues. It was the first time he had seen something like this in the sky. It looked like the northern lights of Velra, which he had seen many times before. Bits and pieces of familiarity weaved their way through the alien landscape, like a place that wanted to have its stories told but couldn't find out how. The lights glowed through the clouds of ash and pulsed like lightning was trapped within.

Spotlights roamed the ash. The seeker bots had one priority, and that was to find them and Runebreaker. Hal didn't know how many now scoured the Ashlands, but Miri would use every resource available to her to find them. If she was working for Varim, protecting Runebreaker was that much more important.

As Hal watched them in the distance, a noise came from deeper in the cave. The hum of the seeker bot echoed in the dark, and Hal grabbed his bag before he took cover behind the stalagmites. He cursed to himself; he'd checked all the possible entrances he could find, but that didn't mean one hadn't been lying hidden or the seeker bot hadn't made its own entrance.

Wind picked up and swept more ash into the cave as the once-blue glow turned into charged electricity that struck the ground outside. He could not run even if he tried; he'd be swallowed by the ash in seconds.

As the hum grew, Hal slowed his breathing until it was barely audible. He reached over to where ash had piled up beside him and rubbed it across his forehead and under his eyes to avoid the bot's infrared. After spending so long in war and infiltration operations, he'd mastered his own body. To be stealthy without the tools of cloaking devices meant to have true control, and he used it to his advantage.

Time froze when he saw the first glare of the bot's spotlight. The hum grew louder until the red eye of the seeker bot showed itself. Red light shunned the darkness into shadows. The seeker bot roamed into the area, its eye oscillating. Hal ducked just in time as the bot sat in the center, feet away from where he had just been. The sounds it made, collecting data and communicating with the others, filled him with horror stories of the war, when Polarian bots had hunted down survivors. Now he knew how it felt to be hunted.

A rock fell from a nearby ledge and crashed into the ground with a thunderous echo. Hal froze. His heartbeat drummed in his chest, and he worried the seeker bot would pick up on it. He took a deep silent breath in an attempt to quiet his heart.

The seeker bot turned in his direction, and the shadows along the wall grew larger. It came his way, but to fight it would be suicide. The bot stopped right on the other side of the rock formations, exhaust flowing from its bowels.

He did not breathe. He did not blink. All he could do was keep his eyes trained on the wall.

It scanned again and beeped before backing off. The bot roamed toward the exit, and the shadows on the wall changed. When it finally left and the pulse engines fired up, Hal breathed in.

He stood from his hiding spot and brushed away the ash that had accumulated on him. The bot was nowhere to be seen, hidden in the veil of ash, but at least Runebreaker was safe. He had to find Kristilin and get back on track if this was to end.

Static filled his earpiece, and at first he thought it was Kristilin, but the voice was too masculine. Perhaps it was someone else stuck in the ash or a soldier of the Empire.

"Sky . . . Skyborn . . . Ashen . . . Meet at Ash Sea Bluff . . . Repeat . . ."

The static took hold of the voice again before it fizzled out. Hearing his name gave him hope, but he was cautious. He had never heard of anything or anyone by the name of Ashen, and it sounded like a trap. Either way, he needed to find the others sooner rather than later.

The other caves Misselie had mentioned weren't far from here, but it was easy to get lost in the fury of an ashstorm. As he looked back out, he decided the reward outweighed the risk.

Hal grabbed his bag before marching into the ash, the wind pelting his back. Ash flew in every direction, and knee-high mounds tried to stop his advance. Hal pushed on in the direction of the caves the girls had headed toward. Every step was a fight to reclaim his foot from the hungry ash. It was also a gamble. A misplaced step could land him stuck in a hole like his first day here.

The sea of ash was only one obstacle; he looked back to where he had come from and saw a swarm of seeker bots. Their spotlights lit up the cave he'd been in only moments ago. Then one spotlight turned toward him, and Hal stopped. Maybe their sensors had picked him up.

Hal squatted in the ash as the light grew larger, only his head above the mounds of ash. The seeker bot zipped by overhead and banked to the right before disappearing into the ash. As he looked back, the other bots followed suit and raced through the sky to be consumed by the veil of ash. He put a hand on his bag, where Runebreaker rested, and took a deep breath. He had to cross these ash plains before they claimed him.

It took time, but as Hal looked up, he could make out another ridgeline up ahead. The glow of green and blue resembled the bioluminescent fungi he'd seen earlier and foretold of shelter and the hopes of finding the others. Already battered, he changed direction and headed for it.

It felt good to be inside and out of the elements. He threw his hood down, and ash fell from him like snow. Even through the sturdiness of his evosuit, the wind had tired him out. Hal wiped the ash and sweat from his eyes, and arms wrapped around him. He tensed, then relaxed when he saw who the arms belonged to.

As Kristilin pulled back, he rubbed away the ash that plagued her pale blue face, and she smiled.

Misselie emerged from the shadows with a smile. "We thought you were ash fodder."

"I thought I was too," Hal said with a smile. "Had a close encounter with a seeker bot."

"We hid from several," Kristilin said. "And someone almost gave away our position."

Misselie crossed her arms. "I had to sneeze."

Kristilin rolled her eyes before she looked back at Hal. "What now?"

He moved across the cave and took a seat on one of the ledges. As he pulled Runebreaker out, it glowed to his touch. He wanted to open it, but he had to wait for the right time. Seeker bots still roamed the ash, and now that he had something Miri needed, he could rest for a bit. She needed this just as much as he did, and now he dictated the rules.

Hal looked up at Kristilin and Misselie. "I received some sort of distorted communication. Bits and pieces got through, but all I could make out was Ashen, Skyborn, and Ash Sea Bluff, and whoever it was wanted to meet." His eyes fell on Misselie for any sort of information.

"They're not in any books at the library back in Hellas that I can remember, nor are they something the ash manifested."

Hal thumbed the cover of the book, and the colors reacted to his touch. "Whoever it was sounded grizzled."

"Do you think we can trust them?" Kristilin asked, taking a seat next to him.

Hal looked back to Misselie, who only shrugged.

Hal sighed. "I don't know. How they found me is another question. But what if they have more information about Primordials and Runebreaker? It's strange they contacted me after we retrieved it."

"That's a valid point. Maybe they're more scholars than warriors, though the former doesn't last long out in the ash," Misselie said. "A double-edged sword. Do you think it's a risk we should take?"

Before Hal could answer, the ground vibrated, and rocks and dust shook loose of their holdings. Hal grabbed Kristilin and pulled her away before a stalactite broke loose and crashed down, shattering against the ground. The vibration grew more violent as Hal stood and steadied himself. Then engines roared overhead.

Hal made his way to the cave entrance and looked up to see a large cruiser part the ashen clouds. The front hull of the ship tapered down into two parts that sat disconnected from each other; a gap between them housed a large opening farther back where the bulk of the ship was. Plasma turrets lined the ship, ready to put up a wall of protective destruction, but Hal eyed the opening and saw the circular pattern of a hardlight cannon. He knew what that weapon could do, and it made it more important for him to confront his sister. Orange streams of residue from the twin engines left a trail in the ship's wake as it sailed overhead. The unmistakable golden eagle emblem painted on the side made Hal's stomach drop and his heart twist.

It was the cruiser his mother had used, and now his sister had claimed it. She had to have found it, for no ship would reach the Ashlands so fast without a Gate. She would not stop until she found what she needed, and now the whole of the Ashlands was in jeopardy.

"Imperial Advanced Cruiser. Light with firepower," Hal said as the small dots of the seeker bots raced back up to the ship. He turned around to face the others. "She won't stop."

"She wants Runebreaker," Misselie said. "Should you not use it before she does?"

"Is it safe to do it here? Now?" Kristilin asked.

Hal picked up the book and stared at the cover. "If she gets to us before I've read it, then that means she's a step ahead of us and we have to play catch-up. You should always be one step ahead of your adversary."

Kristilin placed a hand on his arm. "Are you sure?"

"It'll protect us," Hal said, and the concern in her eyes gradually faded. She nodded.

Misselie led Hal back to the ledge and sat down. Hal presented Runebreaker and laid it down on the ash-covered rock.

"Runebreaker will react and connect with you. When you look at the pages, the magic within will test your fortitude limits, and if you pass its test, it will grant you access to its knowledge." Misselie placed a hand on his shoulder. "Are you ready? We can wait until we find Stravis to do this."

"I trust you," Hal said.

With a smile and nod, Misselie motioned for him to begin.

Hal opened the cover slowly and feasted his eyes on the words within. Some were understandable, but others seemed different, more advanced. They glowed bright purple, blue, orange, and green. The colors entered his eyes, popping out of the page and into his mind. Then everything went blank.

The room around him disappeared and was replaced by a chamber of darkness. The echoes of his footsteps bounced off the walls and traveled forever as he searched around. Emptiness engulfed him and dragged him down, and he found himself standing upside down.

Every step felt like he was underwater, slowed at every turn. Then the first color hit him from the darkness. Hal fell to a knee as the energy entered him. It ripped through his insides like a hot stake that had been plunged through his body. But as he clutched where the energy had entered, there was no wound or burn through his suit. He stood back up, and another wave of energy hit him from behind and knocked him to the ground. The air was knocked out of his lungs, and he gasped for breath. The burning pain of another stake plunging through his body shot across his nerves and into his head.

When he caught his breath and got to his feet, a third wave brought him back down to his knees. Fire coursed through his veins and burned his insides. Sweat poured from his face and dripped into a never-ending puddle. Hal forced himself to push farther, closing in on the light beyond.

Another energy blast rocked him and sent a jolt of electricity through his body. The blow sent him backward a few feet to the ground, and his muscles spasmed and shook. He had never felt such pain before, even during the war, and it taxed his mental fortitude. He didn't know whether he could withstand another shot.

Fire raced at him like an inferno. Flames as high as he could see stared him down. His eyes grew wide as the heat reached his face and the glow of orange shined into his eyes. He tried to turn and run, but something forced him to face the danger. Above the raging fire was the purple glow of Runebreaker's symbol. All the fear and panic left him, and he looked back to the flames. Hal raised his hands, and a wall of white-hot fire emerged from his fingertips.

The inferno clashed with his, and his skin turned red from the heat. It took everything for him to keep the ward up. His feet slid back as the immense power of the inferno raged. Hal gritted his teeth and raised his arms higher until the inferno passed over him. A thud echoed as he dropped to the ground, his ward gone. The inferno crackled in the distance behind him. His shoulders burned, but the light stood right in front of him. He pushed himself up one final time and stepped through it.

When his eyes shot back open, he gasped for air and shook. Kristilin's arms held him down as he regained himself, and the vision in his eyes returned. Misselie watched him intently, her eyes wide with wonder. When he caught himself, he sat up with a deep breath.

"You fought through what Runebreaker was created for: fear."

Hal looked at her, aftershocks still rocking his body. But when he looked down to the pages below, the once-strange Primordial scripture had turned into the normal words he knew.

Encoded words no more, he thought. Though he'd bested the trial, Hal looked for the rune that had broken his code. He flipped through the pages until he found the answer he was searching for: "To Follow the Knowledge."

Chapter XXVII

The ash storm lifted its veil of darkness over the land only to return it to a sea of dreary gray. The sun glared through the ash-filled clouds as Hal and his companions made the trek across the ocean of ash. Despite protests from Kristilin, they headed toward Ash Sea Bluff. Misselie seemed to be the only one optimistic about meeting this phantom of the ash.

Hal would've been lying to himself if he said he wasn't worried. To break bread with strangers was akin to walking over hot coals. Everything in him pulled at his sense of caution. They had no rides to get back to the Hellas region, and with the emergence of the cruiser, Hal felt the weight on his shoulders become a bit heavier.

As they trudged through ankle-high mounds of ash, nothing could beat the exhaustion that came with the journey. All around him lay nothing but slopes and hills of gray. If the weather did not make lost souls go insane, the mundane color certainly would.

As he breathed through his mask, his cracked lips savored the sweat that built beneath his nose. The sun stood over them like peering eyes, waiting for them to drop. Every step felt like a marathon. Sweat radiated from his body, yet the unwanted shivers of cold kissed the exposed skin on his face. He prayed for anyone caught out here, because he knew the chances of making it out alive were slim.

Minutes turned to hours as they marched, and he would've loved nothing more than to lie down in the soft ash and rest. But where he rested, others lurked. Wolves, trolls, and who knew what else would crave the chance to tear into him. To rest here would mean death, and death wasn't an option no matter how many times it crossed his mind.

As he walked, he stopped thinking. Thinking would drain what little energy he had left. He still kept a wary eye out, but he shut his own thoughts down for the time. Step after step, he led the way for Kristilin and Misselie. It looked as though the ash sea stretched on forever with nothing to break the horizon.

Hal caught himself just before walking off the edge of a drop-off. He peered over the ledge, and it was a sheer drop to the ashy ground below. Windswept ashen dunes stretched to the low mountains beyond, the first resemblance of actual land in a while. Kristilin and Misselie stood on either side of him and looked down at the sheer drop.

"Ash Sea Bluff," Misselie said.

Hal looked at her before scouring the ash behind them for any signs of the Ashen. There was nothing but the ghostly moan of the wind. If they'd been led astray, this would be a perfect ambush for his sister. He reached for his lightvolver as the thought sank in.

Like monsters awakened from a deep slumber, figures rose from the ash mounds all around. Hal counted at least two dozen, and all wore the same gray suits. Their face masks hid their identities except for the bright red eyes that stared back at them.

Hal tightened his grip on the lightvolver, but before he could react, his body clenched with intense contractions. His muscles spasmed, the cramps forcing him to contort without any sense of direction. The end of a dart stuck out from his chest, having pierced through the fabric of his suit. He fell to the ash, body numb, along with his companions.

When Hal awoke, he found himself chained to a rocky wall. The girls sat beside him with their arms bound above them. As he shifted his position, a jolt of pain rocked his chest, like someone had stabbed him with a kyr a dozen times and forced him back down with a groan.

"Are you okay?" Kristilin said, her eyes glowing through the darkness.

"I've been better," he said as he looked at where the dart had pierced through his suit. "You?"

"Sore, nothing more. What did they hit us with?"

"Poison darts from the horned ash viper," Misselie said. "It's the only poison here strong enough to paralyze large prey without killing it. In a sense, they spared us."

"I should have known better than to trust some static-filled communication," Hal said as he shook his head.

"We had to take a chance," Kristilin said. "They could have been allies."

"Or know where Stravis is," Misselie added.

"Let's figure out if they're friend or foe before we go asking for information," Hal said, then sat back and let his thoughts wander.

He hadn't been captured during the war, but others had, and those who'd survived told horror stories of what had been done to them by the Polarians. Now he was imprisoned. If these Ashen were foes, he wouldn't let anything happen to Kristilin and Misselie.

The door to their cell opened, and in walked a man with armor over his evosuit. Two others flanked him with their weapons at a low ready.

"Halcion Skyborn, it is an honor to finally meet you."

Hal scanned the others, watched their movements and the way they positioned themselves, before looking back to the man in front of him.

"Who are you?"

"I am Jorrin Feidrin, leader of my clan," the man said.

Hal eyed him. Light-colored hair and a matching bushy beard covered the man's weathered face. Heavy metal armor sat on top of a black evosuit while gray fabric draped around his waist and skirted the ground. A gray cloak with fur at the neck dangled behind him.

"You are in our domain," Jorrin said.

"We received a communication from the Ashen. You contacted us."

"The Crown Princess of Athos contacted us."

Hal tensed as the man spoke words he didn't want to hear. The perversion of the Code has gone to the extremes under what Varim has done. But now Miri played the game they were all competing in. He knew the true word of the Code and when his abilities were restored, he would see it followed.

"In exchange for your head, we would be granted governorship of all of Asha instead of those exiles in Hellas under this grand empire the Crown Princess speaks about. We are the true children of this planet." The Commander looked at Misselie. "Cowards and traitors would be dealt with, and true Ashborn would have full control over our planet."

"So, you have come to collect?" Hal asked.

The Commander smiled and shook his head. "No. Imperials who wander our lands are intruders, and we do not take orders from those who intrude. We are honorable, like our ancestors who called this world home for thousands of years."

The two Ashen beside the Commander walked toward Hal. Expecting to look down the barrel of a gun, he braced for the fire. But when the tension on his wrists lifted, he looked up and stared at the Commander in question.

"You are not our enemy, so you can be of use. Follow us."

"We have questions first," Hal said as he stood with the others.

"Do you want to live past tomorrow? If you do, then you will save your questions and follow."

The Commander turned to exit the room and said something in a foreign language to the guards. They motioned for Hal and the others to follow. With a weary look to his companions, Hal led them.

Cave life seemed to be the only way of living for those hiding out in the ash. Hal sat at a large holotable and looked out to the entrance. Towers of stone stood on either side of a gated wall, and Ashen patrolled the tops. Inside, Ashen stared at him and the others as they came and went. Some soldiers trained outside with energy swords, and others manned communication stations. He assumed there were still others who thrived in the ash, which would explain how they'd found him.

Torchlight flickered along the walls. Conventional electricity seemed to be used only for the most valuable gear, like the holotable—a mixture of old and new, primitive and advanced. Still, he wondered how the Ashen managed to live out here without Imperial interference. If what the Commander had said was true, this planet was inhabited long before the Empire used it for its dumping grounds which meant these Ashen were its native inhabitants. He shook his head as he realized how much information was hidden from the archives in Imperius.

Hal cast a glance down at Runebreaker, which sat in his bag. The information, lessons, and history he'd been taught from when he was just a boy were only the tip of the Primordial and Empyrean knowledge iceberg. He'd been too blind to see it when he was younger. But now that same knowledge was buried so only a bite of it could be understood. That was what his mother had been searching for, to show the way of the Wielders to everyone and allow the true insight of the Primordials to be seen by all, not just those of the Empyrean bloodline. Varim was afraid of that.

Varim's misguided ways had paved lanes of deception in the minds of Imperials, who followed a code of ethics. The Code was a guiding hand through life, and one that he found useful. Outsiders couldn't understand what the Code meant, but true Imperials did, and that rat Varim had perverted it.

The memory of how his fellow countrymen had cheered his exile only solidified his truth. Those in Imperius were not in control of their own minds. In war tried times, people desired a strong ruler capable of leading them to victory. But when the war was over, all of it was supposed to return to normal. They fell for it, the desire of security over personal liberties. They'd granted that to Varim through the council, and he'd emboldened himself. They'd fallen for the lie. His sister had fallen for it too, and now here he was taking refuge in a cave for his blindness.

Jorrin approached the holotable and leaned over it. The scar over his right eye told countless stories that would need to be recorded for the history books. He tapped a few buttons on the holotable before he spoke.

"What do you know about the Ashlands?"

Hal sat upright. "Land of the Exiles."

The commander chuckled. He tapped a few more buttons, and a map appeared over the table. Hal analyzed the image in front of him. Unlike most of the maps he had seen, this was in the shape of a sphere. A globe.

"The Ashlands is the Land of the Exiles to the other realms. To us it is our home and a nexus for your fancy magic wielding. To us it's Asha."

Jorrin zoomed out until the entire system was shown and then further out to reveal the Realmverse. Out of all the star systems, five had special markers that read "Charna Nexus." Hal rose from his seat to see everything more clearly. Asha stood alone with no moons to orbit it, but it held the tag of a charna nexus.

"What is this? Where did you get this information?"

"This is a Primordial star map from an Empyrean temple located here," Jorrin said. "Each nexus here is a hub with a Gate in connection with the Primordial Gateway System."

"How?" Hal asked as he studied the map with narrowed eyes.

"The Empire and other worlds have secrets, Prince Halcion, secrets they dare not tell you, secrets of the Realmverse. They feared you and thus denied you knowledge."

Jorrin brought up more information panels.

"The systems are all connected by the Gateway system. Take Athos for example. You can easily travel to the moons of Valkara, Jurrium, and Eastrite from the teleportals. But to travel from Athos to Velra, you would need to take a hyperspace route. It would shorten months or years of travel time to only a few hours. The Gateway system will turn those hours into seconds."

Jorrin panned and zoomed across the maps to show the connection lines through empty space. Hyperspace routes connected the major systems, which Hal was familiar with. But he also saw the different Gate markers on the worlds where travel time would be significantly reduced to a fraction. When the hyper-lanes had been charted, everyone had thought they'd found the key to space travel, but with the Gates, space travel was almost unnecessary.

"Once all are connected, it would be only a matter of time before they are used to move armies and ships, and Asha is the last remaining Great Gate unconnected. The only way to reach Asha is to connect the Polarian and Asha Gates, but the codes were sealed away. Teleportals constructed have made minimal travel between the two realms easier, which is how you entered."

Hal leaned over the table. He feared the perversion of Primordial relics, feared them being used by power hungry individuals, but then he remembered his own use of the Athonian and Polarian Gates. It pained him to know this had all started after he'd discovered those codes. As he looked down at the table, he regretted even touching those codes. They should've stayed in that decrepit cave where he'd found them.

He'd been manipulated, and he wondered if his father had known about it. Perhaps it was another test to see if he would let power get the better of him. Though he'd thought he did the right thing, Varim had seen a thirst for power in him and reacted. Hal had enabled Varim's dirty deeds. He was the catalyst for everything that was going on.

"Where were the codes sealed away?" Misselie asked.

"We don't know, but an individual named Fable contacted us from within Imperius and warned us of an impending invasion," Jorrin continued. "I have no reason to trust an Imperial, but you know him, Prince Halcion, according to what he says, and he wanted us to find you for this."

As far as he knew, only Imperius was compromised, but he had no way of knowing what had befallen the rest of the Empire. It was risky to trust anyone in the city but if this person sought him out by name, there had to be something they needed to tell him. Perhaps it was a friend, but he didn't know if they could be trusted.

The commander closed the data files and map. He opened a new file, and several holograms appeared on the table, High Minister Varim seated amongst them. They all gathered around a circular table before the high minister spoke.

"In a few short months, this war will come to an end. Activation codes have been acquired, and the start of internal conflict has begun. When Prince Halcion conquers Rahallo and returns home, Princess Miriam will have already been exposed to our way. Her devotion to the Code will easily help sway her, and whether she conforms or not will not matter. It will show the entirety of the Realmverse how disillusioned the past was. Then the seeds of reimagination will flower, and we will have our dominion of peace, a one-Realmverse government not reliant on the petty faith of outdated gods. You all will be remembered as disciples for this great undertaking."

One member of the secret council at the far end of the table stood. Her elegant robes and violet colors suggested she was someone important from Velra, but Hal didn't recognize her. "And if the prince doesn't conform?"

"Exile," the high minister said without missing a beat. "There will not be any other choice. Together we will have built a union of this system, and we will have what we want most: peace."

The recording ended, and Hal stood there in fury. All of this was a plan formed long ago. This was not about being an Empyrean or strengthening the Empire or even his mother's death. This was a change in society, a lack of thought. This was a perverted utopia.

Hal grabbed the holotable's rim, the blue lights fluctuating under his grip.

Piece by piece, he saw the plan as it unfolded. From the assassination, to the war, to his finding of the activation codes, and everything after. This had been the plan all along: to overthrow a world of liberty. He'd been too blind at the time.

Hal looked at his hands, the hands of an accomplice.

When he looked over at Kristilin, she had the same confused, worried look he'd once had. Misselie stared wide-eyed at him and fumbled with her long black hair. And when he looked at the Commander, the man had sincerity in his eyes.

"This needs to be stopped," Hal said, seething with anger. "To preserve individuality and simple liberties, this cannot be allowed to come to fruition."

The commander sighed and nodded. "We will protect our home at all costs, Halcion Skyborn. This is our fight, but this is your fight too. Stand with us, and we will stand with you. The Great Gate must not be activated here."

Hal nodded to the commander and felt the warmth of Kristilin's arm on his shoulder. This had become so much more than a personal grudge. It was a war within a war, and they had to stop it before it was too late.

A chime went off on one of the communication monitors. Jorrin went to see what it was, and a hologram of Miri appeared on the holotable. Everyone stared in shocked silence except Hal. The poor girl thought she was doing the right thing.

"This is Crown Princess Miriam Skyborn of the Empire of Athos contacting the Ashen. We know you harbor an outlaw of the Empire, Halcion Skyborn, and aided him before the brutality of your petty planet could swallow him whole. Do not be swayed by his silver tongue. He is an enemy and traitor to the Empire. If you release him to me, I will not have you executed for—"

The recording fizzled to a halt when Jorrin kicked the table. He looked at Hal. "My people and I are loyal only to Asha."

Alarms went off. Soldiers ran from the bowels of the cave and into the courtyard. Hal followed the commander out as two Imperial corsairs streaked through the ash. Anti-air guns fired from the tops of the Ashen towers while emplaced rotary turrets lit up the sky. The corsairs launched photon bombs, which exploded with green fire upon impacting the walls. A tower crashed down, sending the stones tumbling into the ash. Another set of photon missiles streaked through the air and left craters in the earth around the courtyard and the mountainside. One struck the wall and blew a hole wide open.

Ash kicked up everywhere like a manifested smokescreen. The anti-air guns kept their fire up as smoke rose from their heated barrels, the smell of burnt energy residue filling the air. The commander pushed Hal out of the way before a bomb exploded nearby and sent ash into the air only for it to come crashing down with dirt seconds later. The explosion left Hal's ears ringing as he searched the air for the aircraft responsible.

One corsair caught fire, its wing ripped apart by energy blasts from the anti-air guns. The stream of smoke disappeared over the mountain, and the explosion echoed with the roar of the rotary guns. The other corsair turned tail and disappeared into the ash, the hum of the engine vanishing with it. Soldiers rushed over to the wall and aided wounded trapped under. Jorrin gave orders to scout the wreckage before he turned back to Hal and helped him up.

"She won't stop until the Gate is active. Then she will have full movement and control over Asha," Jorrin said.

"By Empyrea, guide us," Hal said under his breath as the flames from the wreckage grew over the ash dune. "We will stop her."

Jorrin nodded and extended his hand to Hal. With a firm shake, they forged a fragile new alliance. Now he had to worry about how Asher and the Hellans would take it. Jorrin had been clear when he'd called them out earlier, but Hal was unfamiliar with the politics between the two sides. He would have to learn and broker a possible pact between the two. They all needed to work together to stop Miri.

"I will supply two dusters for you to return to Hellas. We want to help," Jorrin said. "But Asher is against outsiders. He needs to be convinced and allow us to use his gem mines."

"What for?"

"The gems are precious to us Ashen. They allow us to see through the ash on the most violent of days. They're not to be worn like jewelry," Jorrin said. "Convince him to give access. That is all we ask for a partnership."

"I'll see what I can do. Thank you," Hal said.

The two shook hands once more before going their separate ways.

Chapter XXVIII

I t only took a couple days to get back to the enclave, but every hour was spent looking over their shoulders. Seeker bots roamed the ash, though the cruiser stayed out of sight. Hal knew Miri was up there, searching through every cave and turning over every rock to find him. The Ashen had wanted him to leave as soon as he could, and he hadn't argued. He was a target that would bring too much attention to them. More had to be learned if he was to prepare himself for the inevitable fight that brewed.

Their dusters ascended the mountainous path and came to a stop in the enclave's courtyard. Hal activated the remote door signaler he found when they first encountered the structure before the door opened and they entered the enclave. As the large door closed behind them, Misselie hopped off the duster with Kristilin and approached Hal.

"Much to take in, no?"

"Too much," Hal replied, shaking the ash off before turning to brush the loose ash from Kristilin. "We still have much to figure out. Stravis is top of our priorities right now. We have to figure out where he is."

"The old man is a hardy one. He can withstand your sister, but for how long, I don't know," Misselie replied, her eyes downcast. "You have the blood of the Empyreans, Hal. Everyone wants a piece of you, for only you and your sister can revive the ancient secrets of millenniums gone by. It's exciting but also terrifying."

"And now our time is cut short thanks to Miri," Kristilin said. She turned to Hal. "You need to get your Wielding back now."

"Then we need to get back to the door seal where Dash ambushed us. But even then, there's no guarantee of what lies beyond that door," Hal said.

"You have grown from when I first met you," Misselie said with a smile. "Your thirst for power has been replaced by a thirst for knowledge. It suits you well. But you must use that knowledge to seek out the answers. At least that's what Stravis used to tell me."

Knowledge built power, and power would allow him to claim what he wanted. Knowledge was the tool, and power was the force, like the weapon that hung on his hip. He glanced down at it. It took knowledge to design the shape, craft the materials, and build the final product. The result was the power it produced.

At first he'd wanted the power of his ancestors to seek revenge against a traitor in the midst, but the seed of knowledge had proven more valuable. He knew that now, though too late. Power created hunger. Knowledge granted fulfillment.

Misselie placed a hand on his shoulder. "I think you're ready for the final piece of knowledge you need."

"What?"

Misselie smiled and beckoned him to follow with Kristilin close behind. They marched through the room where they'd encountered the artificial intelligence before they came to the room where Misselie had been trapped. She felt along the stone walls until her hand stopped and pushed inward. Hal jumped back as the floor under his feet shook and began to slide open. As he took a spot beside Kristilin, the floor revealed a hidden room lit by blue orblight.

"Follow me," Misselie said.

They descended the stairs, and there were etchings on the walls. At first they showed a barren landscape with dunes of ash, but as they descended, an etched structure appeared and gradually grew larger. The etchings showed people build it and defend it from troll attacks. Then it was on fire, and the giant ash snake loomed over it. As they neared the end, the people rejoiced over the completion of the enclave building. The final rune etched in the wall said "Completion." It wasn't a large building, but it had been important to its builders.

As they entered the hidden room, its walls curved with the etchings of a larger wall of stories. Misselie placed a hand on it and spoke archaic language, and part of the wall disappeared. Behind stood a single orblight that brightened the circular room. Three pillars stretched up to support the ceiling, and in the middle was a vacant space.

Misselie turned around. "I have been here before. Wielders used this room for meditation many years ago. It's useless to me, for I don't have the same connection as you."

"What do I need to do?" Hal asked.

"To regain your Wielding, you must commune with the past Kells. It's not as easy as walking in and relearning. You must prove to them that you know every aspect of Fire Wielding." She held a finger up to stop any protest from Hal before she continued. "You must show *them*—not me, not Kristilin, not Stravis. Wielding is a gift, and to achieve the gift, you must pass their trials. One of those trials is for the past Kells, masters of charna wielding, to see you."

"And if he succeeds?" Kristilin asked.

"This will begin the baptism process, or in your case, reclamation," Misselie said.

"How do I start?"

Misselie waved her hand around the room. "This was for meditation. Meditate. If the past Kells deem you ready, they will answer your call. I can't tell you anything else, for you must do it alone. Only then will the clues be presented to you."

She walked past him and stopped in the doorway to flash him a small smile. As she left, Hal turned to face Kristilin, who stared back at him. Her eyes glowed in the darkness, and a smile crossed her face before she backed away, and the wall sealed itself.

Left alone in the room, Hal walked to the center and sat down. He sat with his hands outstretched and palms upward. It felt empty without the warmth of his fire around his hands. His eyes closed, and he took a deep breath. He cleared his thoughts with an exhale, and the weight of all his burdens lifted.

Light flashed, and he found himself in an empty chamber burning with wildfire. When he tried to take a step away, the fire lunged and encircled him, striking like vipers. Smoke hovered overhead and made his eyes water. He used an arm to keep it from entering his lungs.

He looked through the smoke and flames, searching for a way out. Then a rune formed in the hazy air. It glowed before vanishing. The fire shrunk, its flames enlarging his circle, and he realized the runes had something to do with the pillars.

He took another step, too close to the flames, and they lashed out at him. The flames bit into his skin and burned his flesh. As he jumped back to look at his wound, another rune appeared. Again, it glowed before the flames receded. Two runes down and only one to go. The bright flames blinded his eyes, but he forced past the discomfort and peered through, searching for it. A bright rune formed, and the flames dissipated with a flash.

He opened his eyes. Before him stood the pillars, and on each one were the runes he'd seen. They glowed a bright orange as Hal fought to remember how to pronounce them. It took a few more times than he would have liked, but he finally managed to get the pronunciation right.

"*Aktosh*. Fire. *Wikir*. Wind. *Vulnar*. Smoke."

The runes disappeared. Hal repeated the runes, but nothing happened, and he looked on with confusion. Then the runes reappeared without their glow, their outlines now etched into the stone pillars. It felt like a game, one Hal loathed to play. Then he heard fire crackling behind him.

When he turned around, he almost jumped out of his boots. A figure hovered before him, glowing light red. It had bright orange eyes and wore robes with intricate flame designs. A belt of pure fire wrapped around the robes and dripped flames that singed the ground as a circle of fire surrounded the area in which they stood. Hal studied the being for a moment before it raised its hand and spoke.

"*Kultir*."

Hal stood frozen. It was the Primordial word for Kell.

As the Kell hovered closer to him, the face under the robes became clear, and Hal's jaw dropped. He couldn't decide whether to stand tall or kneel in respect, for this was not an ordinary Kell. It was the one who'd begun the Empire so many years ago.

Emperor Atis.

He wanted to say so much to the man, but before he could react properly, the spirit faded away and left him alone with the orblight.

Behind him, the wall opened. Still in shock, Hal turned around to see his two companions. Kristilin was the first to him, and Misselie looked around the room. A satisfied smile crossed her face as she turned from the runes on the pillars and looked at Hal.

"So, you saw the first Kell of Inferno. Archkell Atis."

"What does it mean? There're statues of him in the Imperial throne room," Hal said. "He was the first emperor."

Misselie nodded. "It means he saw you from beyond the mortal planes of existence. That is a very good start. There has only been one Archkell to ever grace the Realmverse, and had you not been worthy, you would have seen nothing. I assume his coven is watching too, for they see greatness in you. Now that you have Runebreaker and the ritual words, the time has come for you to gain what you have lost." Misselie stood in front of him, her youthful eyes full of wonderment. "This must be done alone. Only then can the ritual work. I cannot guide you through this part, and neither can she." She glanced at Kristilin. "You must return to where the Watcher Stones led you—back to the Altar."

Hal locked eyes with Misselie as Kristilin wrapped her hands around his arm. He placed a hand over hers and took a deep breath, then nodded. This was what he'd been waiting for.

He turned to Kristilin and wrapped his arms around her, pulling her in tight, grateful for her softness against him. There was no telling how long this ritual would take, and the thought of being separated from her again after they'd fought so hard to get back to each other sent daggers through him. Hal held his beloved for what seemed like an eternity, but he had to go. This time, though, it wouldn't be without a goodbye.

As he pulled away, tears ran down her cheek. He wiped them away softly and stared deep into her eyes. He leaned in slowly, and when their lips touched, fireworks went off in Hal's mind. Kristilin squeezed him tighter, and he reciprocated. They stayed like that for a few seconds before pulling away.

"Be safe," Kristilin said softly.

She buried her head into his chest, and Hal stroked the ends of her hair as he fought back the same tears that welled in her eyes.

"I'll be safe. And before you know it, we'll be right back in each other's arms."

Chapter XXIX

To travel alone in an inhospitable land was suicidal to many, but he had no other option. He could not risk the lives of the others in a quest he had to fulfill on his own. This was his journey to take alone.

Ash blew by him as the duster carved a path through the thick layer of ash. The clouds above rumbled with thunder, and the wind met him with inklings of acid rain, but it made no difference. Come rain or storm, he would make it to the city at any cost.

His duster sped around the bug mounds from the previous journey. They waited by their openings, wings twitching with anticipation, but he traversed their holes and sped away without looking back. The taste of reclamation was so close, and he felt the fibers of his muscles tingle with anticipation. Hal focused on the way forward and gunned his duster, the whine of the engine echoing in his ears.

Hours passed, and the silhouette of the city shined through the veil of ash. As he approached, it looked as though it stood frozen in time. The gate hung open like before, and more ash covered the tops of the buildings. Hal parked his duster behind a mound of ash and scanned the city. Empty.

As he reentered the city, he took a long and thoughtful look around. To think this used to be the capital of the planet made him wonder what had happened. In a different time, he imagined this place as a hub like Imperius, where hundreds of mortals had perused the streets and markets under the eyes of Primordial masters. They'd come from all over the land, but now it was a shadow of its former self, much like how he felt. Asha must have been different back then. Perhaps it had looked like Athos or Velra or a combination of the two, but anything would be better than the gray veil that now covered it.

Hal drew his weapon, knowing the ancient city still held dangers. Wind moaned through the streets and buildings as he walked. He double-checked every corner. Those trolls were skilled, more so than he would have liked, and what remained of their little band would surely be angry to see him again. Hal kept looking over his shoulder, waiting for one to show itself.

When he arrived at an intersection of old streets, he stopped. The tower was his destination, but as he looked for it, the wind brought in the storm. The first drops of rain fell on his boots and then his hood. Hal tugged his hood forward as the sky opened up. Sulfur filled his nose before he secured his face mask. Steam rose from unprotected metals, which aged with every drop. Hal stood still as the rain burned the ash away, and sulfur filled the air. He narrowed his eyes, focusing, struggling to see through the rain and ash.

Movement.

A troll emerged from the ash, its long arms dragging along the ground. It stared back at him, acid rain separating them by a few feet. It didn't affect the troll, which stood in it as if it were a normal rainstorm. Hal bladed his stance, wary of the beast.

The wind blew Hal's cloak to the side and rustled the troll's fur. Instinct told Hal to raise his weapon and take out the threat, for he knew of the beast's power. But as he continued to look at the troll, he noted its stance and body language. Its muscles stayed relaxed, and its clawed hands hung at its sides. It bared no teeth at him and only watched him with a fixed gaze.

More trolls appeared all around them, stepping like ghosts from the dark veil of ash. Hal cast them a sideways glare before looking back at the troll who stood before him.

The troll took a step forward and looked down at Hal, its size daunting. As best he could, Hal stayed still and refused to show any sign of fright, though every bone in his body told him to stay cautious of the beast.

It knelt to eye level with him and bowed its head. One by one, the others did the same.

Hal looked around, stunned.

The troll raised its head and, to Hal's surprise, spoke in a broken Imperial language, its voice deep and strong. "I Yatar. Tribe. Free. Roam. No enemy. Friend."

Hal had no idea what to say. He hadn't realized he and Kristilin had liberated the trolls from their rulers. As he looked closer at the troll who knelt before him, he noticed Yatar had deep scar tissue and strips of missing fur.

"Were your tribe leaders responsible for this?" Hal asked as he pointed to the wounds.

Yatar looked at them. "Many. Other trolls. Hurt. Abused. Leaders gone now. Thanks. Free."

"We're all the same," Hal said softly as rain dripped from the hood of his evosuit.

Yatar stood back up, his three eyes staring into Hal's. Another troll came up from behind Yatar and presented a necklace to Hal.

"Claws of rulers. Gift to you," Yatar said.

Hal took the trophy offering and held it in his hands. Simple string went through the large and kyr-sharp claws. As Hal looked at them, a faded gray polished to show his reflection, he saw the tiredness of his own eyes.

"Trolls. Meant for peace. Not war."

The trolls beat their chests, and the thunderous sound carried on the wind as the trolls celebrated.

Yatar pointed behind him to a path between the buildings. It looked to lead somewhere near the tower without the openness of the main roads.

"Danger ahead. Beware fire ruler," Yatar said.

With a snort, Yatar waved to his fellow troopmates, and they disappeared into the ash.

As Hal turned, he faced the path into the city. There could only be one fire ruler, and if she was here, he would have to be ready for whatever she presented. Nothing would stop him while he was this close to regaining his power. Hal looked at the claw necklace again before he placed it into his bag and pressed on.

The standing structures protected him from most of the rain and wind. Shadows grew long, and ash lay packed hard on the ground to where his footprints left almost no impression. Hal walked with his lightvolver drawn. The trolls might have let him go, but something else could still lurk in the unexplored city. Imperial soldiers were at the top of his list if Miri was here.

When the path ended and opened into the wide-open courtyard of the tower grounds, Hal stayed in the shadows and peered through the ash. His stomach dropped.

Imperials were guarding the tower doors.

The trolls were right.

A small squad patrolled the area, and guards stood on either side of the doors. One passed right in front of Hal, and he shrunk further back into the comfort of the shadows. Miri must have found out about this place just like he had.

After the guard passed, Hal searched for his way in. The door was the only way through.

One of the guards came back around and stopped near him, murmuring something under their breath. Before they could move, Hal leapt from the shadows and pulled them back into the ash. The Imperial soldier yelled and thrashed, and Hal quickly knocked them out. The wind silenced all, and an unconscious soldier could not relay information over their radio. Hal grabbed their rifle and flipped the switch to the stun setting. He had no intention of killing these soldiers. After all, they were still Imperials—misguided Imperials who served a dictator, but still Imperials.

Hal took a position beside some rubble and aimed through the scope. A lone soldier caught the first stun round and dropped to the ground. Next was the soldier warming their hands over a burning barrel. They dropped like a bag of rocks. Hal took aim at the two guarding the door. Two quick trigger pulls, and they slid down the wall behind them. Hal threw the weapon down and bolted for the door. The stun effects would only last a few moments, and he had to be inside and gone before they woke up.

Hal tried to slide the door open, but it was locked. When the first groan from the soldiers broke through the wind, Hal pulled out his kyr and went to work on the metal chains. The kyr cut through the metal like a saw would through a tree. The rusty chains dropped to the ash, and Hal opened the door. After he stepped inside and closed the metal door, Hal ran his kyr around the locking mechanism, fusing the metal together to create a bond that would take the soldiers a while to cut through. *Bless hardlite technology*, he thought before he ran down the hallway to the far door and shouted the phrase he had learned.

"To Follow the Knowledge."

The door didn't budge.

Confusion struck him as he repeated the phrase, but nothing happened. The soldiers were shouting outside. Bangs came from the tower door as the soldiers tried to figure out how to open it. Time was running thin. Then Hal remembered.

"*Aisu Varik hu Sheinchol*," Hal said.

The same phrase he shouted in Realmverse Standard he said in Primordial and runes faded, and the door opened. Hal stepped in and spun around.

The Imperials opened the tower entrance, and behind them stood Miri, her gaze intense as a hundred suns. The door closed, and the swiftlift lowered him down. It seemed like an eternity before it came to a stop.

When the door opened, Hal stepped into an untouched world that almost blew him away. Block-shaped buildings stretched for as far as he could see, and parts of mountains had been carved out to form even more rooms. The twinkling fungi made the ceiling look like the starry night sky. Pure charna that looked like lava flowed down from cracks in the walls, collecting in pools under bridges that connected the city to where he stood. A spire stood in the center of the underground city with the glow of an orange rune on its side.

Hal crossed the lightbridge and looked down. The charna-lava bubbled and flowed like a river in search of an ocean. Above, orblights glowed along the bridge and led him to the subterranean city. As he walked through the streets, it looked as though time had forgotten about this place. The marble columns and stone buildings looked as clean as any Hal had ever seen. Stained glass windows with etchings of past habitants were displayed on most buildings, but what caught his attention the most were the buildings themselves. The metal sparkled in the orblight and twisted upward in perfect geometry to create diamonds that reached for the starry ceiling. Hal stared in awe at the architectural achievements these past beings had made and the similarities they shared with Imperius.

He could have spent hours exploring the city, but time was not his friend. Hal made it to the spire in the center of the city, and a circular courtyard greeted him. The doors slid open as he approached, an invitation for him to enter the main chamber, and he did so. Inside stood one altar with a smoldering ember on top. Glass walls stretched all around the room while the glow of orblight from the ceiling reflected a red-orange glow onto the metal floor. Across the chamber, and on the other side of a charna river, large stairs rose to grand temple doors nestled into the rock. But as Hal went to take a step farther in, the doors closed behind him.

Hal tried to force them open, but they wouldn't budge. When he turned back around, he nearly froze.

Emperor Tiberius stood on the opposite side of the room, his hood lowered and the sleeves of his robes covering his hands. Hal lowered his face mask and hood and met the ghostly gaze of his father as he dropped to a knee.

"Father?" he said as he fought back the wave of tears building behind his eyes.

"Stand," the echoey voice of the emperor said. As Hal stood up, Tiberius added, "There are no royal customs here, son."

"What are you doing here?"

Tiberius stared with his ghostly eyes. "I am but a spirit in the Lands of Rophera deep within the grace of Empyrea. My burden has been shed, and I walk peaceful-ly in the gardens of salvation with your mother." Tiberius's spectral eyes looked down. "I only regret my blindness to the snakes within our own city. That burden has shifted to you and Miri, and for that I am sorry. Varim seeks to erase the art of Wielding from history. With only two Wielders left, he's nearly succeeded. But there is always a way."

Tiberius approached the altar, and flames erupted from it. Hal was awed by the power his father held even in a ghostly apparition of his former self. It made him wonder even more how Varim had managed to sneak right under their noses.

"You're here because a born gift has been stolen by someone who is afraid of what Wielders are and what can become of it. You must earn that right back. And if you succeed, you must enlighten the people of the Realmverse."

Tiberius waved a hand over the flames and extinguished them until only the ember remained. "You have sought the knowledge of Communion and followed the path of ancient Archkell Atis. It is a testament to your will and thus the beginning of a new chapter of Wielding history. The path of the Archkell is unlike most."

A chill ran up Hal's spine. The man before him had died, yet here he stood talking. The weight of a thousand moons was lifted from his shoulders, and he took a deep breath as the experience consumed him.

As he looked through the glass windows all around him, superheated charna crackled and popped, flowing through the subterranean caverns like a river. But even with all the movement, time felt still. Tiberius motioned for him to step up to the altar. When he did, the late emperor spoke.

"Take this ember to the Temple of the Fire Wielders farther within and follow Atis's trials of enlightenment. To pass his test, you must keep the ember alight. Only then will you gain what you have lost."

Hal's eyes went wide. He was about to set foot into a piece of not only Empyrean history, but also Realmverse history.

Hal carefully grasped the ember cup, the heat radiating through his gloves. It was warm and soothing, and its red heat pulsed and crackled softly. When Hal looked back up, Emperor Tiberius stared at him and spoke.

"Once you start this journey, you cannot stop. You will either succeed or succumb to the fates of thousands who dared attempt the Archkell's trials. If you have questions, now is the time to ask."

Hal looked back at the ember in the cup as his mind raced. Everything from his past played in flashes, and he fought the urge to release his rage. Instead, he asked a single question.

"Why am I here?"

The otherworldly hand of his father reached out and touched his shoulder. Ghostly eyes stared at him. Even though they were empty, Hal could feel the warmth of a father's gaze radiate from them before the emperor spoke.

"Because you are a Kell."

Hal looked back down to the small glow of the ember. He was clear on what he needed to do now, but one thought still gnawed at the back of his mind.

"Did you know about the Gate, Father?"

Tiberius stayed silent for a moment.

"I knew they were of Primordial origin. I knew they could teleport on the grandest of scales."

"Why didn't you tell me when I found the keycodes? I could've avoided all of this," Hal said.

"I cannot tell you what your actions should or shouldn't be. To do something, you must understand the ramifications," Tiberius said. "You must learn."

"I still have much to learn, it seems," Hal said, his gaze once again dropping to the ember in his hands.

Emperor Tiberius Skyborn stepped aside from the altar and the doors that were once locked now slid open.

"Follow Atis and his Coven's path to unravel the secrets your mother explored. Become what you were destined to be, save Wielding, and make sure the legacy of the Skyborns is not tainted with lies."

Hal narrowed his eyes in thought, but shouts from outside kept him from further questions. The door to the swiftlift opened, and Imperials raced over the lightbridge. When he turned back around, the ghostly form of his father disappeared, and all he had was the warmth of the ember. He wanted to ask so many questions and speak to his father like had before, but time had not allowed it. He'd come too far to be taken now. He had to get to the temple, and fast.

As Imperials flooded the underground cavern, Hal took off in a full sprint out through the altar chamber doors and towards the lightbridge that led to the temple. Energy bolts zipped by him and left their mark on the pristine buildings. As he crossed the lightbridge, one ricocheted off the rocks and nearly hit Hal. He ascended the large steps steadily, shielding the ember cup in his hands. More energy bolts flew by him, their heat nipping at his feet.

When Hal was nearly at the top, an energy bolt slammed into his arm. It almost threw the ember from his hands as he stumbled on the steps. But he got up despite the pain, channeling it like he always had. Another bolt ripped through his leg, and he let out a cry of pain as he dropped to the ground. The burn tore through his evosuit and singed his skin beneath it. Hal looked back; Miri and her soldiers were closing in. The anger on her face, the snarl, only proved Varim's manipulation of her.

She sent a fireball screaming toward him as Hal pushed himself back up and leapt to the top steps of the temple. Though as he landed, a stun round sent a jolt of electricity through his body and locked his muscles up. He fought through the spasms it caused and forced his muscles to work as the fireball grew closer. Hal crawled on his back and cupped the ember as tight as he could without smothering it. The fireball crested the top steps and slammed into an invisible wall, exploding on impact inches before him. Hal looked around to see what contraption had just saved his skin, but nothing appeared. As he staggered up, Miri breached the top steps with a flock of soldiers, her eyes like daggers. Mere inches separated them.

Hal shook his head. "Miri, this isn't you."

"Don't try to turn me. You betrayed your people, the Code. You betrayed me! Why would I listen to anything you say?"

"Miri, Varim isn't—"

She sent a wall of flames that crashed into the invisible forcefield and covered the entirety of it like veins made of fire. When the flames died down, Miri stood there out of breath. This was not the way to get through to her.

He took a step back, and her glare hardened before he turned and entered the temple.

Chapter XXX

Hal finished the tie on his bandages—made from torn parts of his evo-suit—before continuing. His footsteps echoed through the dark halls. The only light available was the soft glow of the ember held tightly in his hands. For a fire temple, he expected monuments of flames like the Imperial palace had. So far that was not the case here.

His father had failed to explain what exactly the trial entailed. Hal looked at the ember glowing in his hands. This was part of the trial, to see if he could keep the most benign form of fire alive. If he could not even do that, then the title of Fire Wielder and possibly Kell was not for him. He would show the highest of gods that he was a true Fire Wielder.

Smoke began to tickle his nose. The darkness receded, and lights flickered in the distance. Crackles and snaps of wicked flames filled his ears, and as he came to steps that led down, he saw walls of fire. The flames reached the ceiling, covering it in a blazing blanket. As he descended the steps and entered the chamber, the heat hit him like a brick wall and forced him to raise his face mask. The flames danced a bright orange for him. Lines within the wall made frames similar to a door, two in total. Between them was a runic phrase that read '*How Does Fire Spread?*'

Each doorframe outline contained an answer. One read '*By Force*' while the other read '*By Hand.*'

Hal thought back to his studies. A Fire Wielder used his body force to cast the spells needed. That force manifested into the hand and was used as a tool. The flames left the hand and ignited what the caster targeted.

Hal reached for the second rune door and placed a hand on the metallic surface. Warmth seeped from the other side as he pushed on it. Flames leapt out in a spit of violent rage and singed the fibers of his evosuit. Smoke rose from it as Hal recoiled and looked on in shock. The door stayed closed.

Beside him, the other door faded away, and the runic phrase changed. '*Ignorance Trial of Fire*,' it read, and the flames turned transparent. He had to walk through as punishment for his ignorance. As much as he wanted to protest his understanding of Fire Wielding knowledge, he wanted to finish the trials more than anything, and that involved swallowing his pride. But now he had to find out how he was to pass through a wall of flames without burning himself. One thing he did know was that speed beat heat.

Hal stepped back and raised his hood as he eyed the flames. He nestled the ember cup into the elbow of one arm while the other covered the top. Hal charged the fire and dove through the wall. Flames kissed his evosuit as his body speared through to the other side. Though smoke rose from his body like a well-cooked meal, he was unscathed, and the ember still glowed.

Thank the gods for a hardy evosuit, he thought. As he stood, the first wall disappeared, and Hal faced the second, which had a new runic phrase.

'*Fire Lives With*?'

The two doors read '*Oxygen*' and '*Charna.*' Hal studied the question this time, not wanting to risk the ember again.

For fire to burn, it needs both ingredients: charna to throw and oxygen to build. But as Hal continued to think, he questioned the purpose of the phrase. Both answers read true if it only talked about the fire he produced, but if it referred to natural fire, then oxygen would be the correct answer. The whole journey here taught the natural way to become a Fire Wielder, and knowledge of how to wield it did not matter; all that did was the natural way.

Hal looked at the door marked *"Oxygen"* and placed his hand against it. Unlike the first one, this door was cool to the touch, and no heat transferred. When the flame wall began to disappear, he smiled behind his mask.

Smoke clouded the floor as he stepped up to the next wall. Though he could breathe, the smoke burned his eyes as he tried to read the next phrase. When his vision cleared, he read, '*Though Embers Burn and Fires Churn . . .*'

Hal paused. It was not a question like the others but an actual phrase.

A Runebreaker phrase, he thought. Hal reached into his bag and pulled out the book. Smoke clouded the room now and seeped past his mask. He coughed and blinked to alleviate the sting that clouded his eyes and filled his nose. The smoke grew and filled the entire room, threatening to snuff out all the oxygen he needed to breathe. Hal flipped through the pages quickly until he found the phrase.

He looked up with watering eyes and said, "*Seeds of Rebirth are Learned.*"

The runes glowed and faded away while the flame wall receded. The smoke dispersed, and the flames that tickled the ceiling shrunk back down into barrels of light along the columns. At the steps that led out of the pit, a gate of hardlight unlocked and beckoned Hal to follow with its cool glow. When the last of the smoke faded, he breathed a breath of fresh air before continuing.

His achy muscles pushed him up the steps while he kept his eyes on the small ember in the cup, which still glowed softly at him. Still blinking away the sting of smoke, Hal ascended the steps and stood in the center of a glowing platform. Flames streaked into the air and domed over him in an accepting embrace. The heat was not aggressive, but warmly comforting. It was like the flames accepted him and invited him in further. Understanding the principles of fire had earned him this. The platform rose and brought him to the next test.

The temperature dropped, and a cool breeze pushed against him. When he reached the top and the platform stopped, a gust of wind nearly knocked him back. The ember cup bounced in his hands before he tightened his grip and turned away from the gusts. The wind howled through the dark halls, where only dim orblight shined. The lights swung in their holds whenever a wind gust blew by. Hal shielded the ember as he stood at the opening of the hallway and stared down it. One of young fire's formidable enemies stood in his way, and he had no choice but to push through it.

Wind slapped his face from all angles. There was no rhyme or reason; the wind bounced off the walls and zigzagged through the hall. Hal leaned forward and fought the wind head-on as he covered the young ember. Every step took effort, and he struggled to find the strength to push on.

One step was off-balance, and the wind knocked him over. Hal slid across the floor and tumbled into an alcove. With a groan, he sat against the wall and checked the ember. Glowing softly in its cup, it still radiated energy, but he could tell the life it had was near the end. He blew on it gently to bring some of its light back, and before long the ember glowed a warm orange. Time was running thin. The young ember would not last much longer.

Hal listened to the wind. Unlike the other puzzles, this one was about pure strength and will. High wind sucked the air away from a fire and tossed it elsewhere. Though it would cause a wildfire to spread, the gusts were too much for a single ember. He had to protect it against the wind's harshness at all costs. He took a deep breath and stepped back into the windstorm.

Step after step, Hal planted himself against the wind. His legs became the roots of trees that refused to bow, and every step inched him closer to the end. Every time he lifted his leg, though, he feared being caught in a gust and blown back. Too much of this and the ember would extinguish. He had to be fast.

He hated fear, the mortal enemy of Man. It dictated too much in the world and offered little to no reason. Fear guided mistruths and doubt. He would not let fear guide him like it did his sister.

Hal fixed his gaze forward and trudged on through what he feared.

The steps up were just in reach, but so too were the strongest winds. It took everything for Hal to shield the ember cup from the gusts. His cheeks stung and his eyes watered, their moisture sucked away instantly. Hal leaned as far forward as he could without bending over, lowering his center of gravity, as he fought against the wind's force. Wind loved to abuse mountains, so he made himself as small as possible.

The wind pushed back against his hand as he reached for the first of the steps, a fight between a force of nature and the will of a single person. He dared not look up. The wind felt as strong as any hurricane, and losing his balance would certainly send him back to the beginning. The ember would not survive that.

When he touched the first step, Hal used all his strength to pull himself up. The wind's onslaught gradually reduced until it was nothing more than a breeze in the air. Hal climbed the stairs on his hands and knees before resting against the wall and looking at the tunnel he'd conquered. Not even the most daring mountain climbers would be caught dead in winds that strong. Hal smiled at his feat, but as he looked at the ember protected in his grasp, his smile faded.

The once-orange glow had faded into gray obscurity. His heart sank as he placed the ember cup down on the steps. He had been careless with the wind, and it had sucked the life out of the thing he needed to protect the most.

"Damn it," Hal whispered to the darkness.

To fail now would certainly result in the worst he could think of. He could not compete against his sister without Wielding, for she was knowledgeable. Both he and Varim knew that. That rat didn't care about her. Only power consumed him, and he would use Miri to achieve that before discarding her. Hal couldn't let that happen. He had to make her see that he wasn't the enemy, and to do that, he needed to Wield. Only then could he work to show her the truth. But with the ember in peril, his chances shrunk.

He blew on the ember gently, careful not to smite what little life the small ember had left, and with each breath, it fluttered. Sweat dripped from his brow, and he contorted his head so it wouldn't drip on the ember. Wind was a formidable opponent, but water was the killer. As Hal shielded the cup from one side and blew on the cup the other way, the smallest inkling of an ember glowed inside. It still had life, but for it to survive, Hal had to find a fuel source, and fast.

There were few options in a tunnel of wind. Then his gaze fell on the bandages he had tied. He cut a piece off with his kyr and wrapped it around the small ember inside. He blew gently, and the ember grew. Hal stayed his course, concentrating only on the ember and making it glow.

The first signs of smoke rose into the air as Hal gave a final blow. The ember smoked, and the first glow of a flame appeared inside the cup. Hal cupped the flame as it crawled along the cloth bandage and rose upward. Before long, flame engulfed the bandage and burned without worry. Deep inside its nest, the ember feasted on the fuel, and Hal breathed a sigh of relief. A click sounded behind him, and as he turned, the pathway opened for him.

"So help me, this is the last time I prove myself to anyone," Hal said before standing up, the ember cup in hand.

Hal walked through the gates and down a long hallway. It was absent of wind, and the orblights hung steady and bestowed their bright glow upon the darkness below. One side of the hall was a flat wall where etchings of ancient Wielders told stories of battle and discovery. Hal had to force himself away or risk losing time.

The hallway opened to a circular chamber that looked more like a classroom than anything. Rows of seats encircled a central stage with a holotable. Hal walked down the steps, admiring the sharp architecture like always, before stopping at the stage. A hologram of his mother appeared and walked around to fiddle with the holotable. A projection of a Gate appeared when his mother turned around, and she spoke.

"I have done extensive research in secret. I know when, if, I return back to Imperius, I will undoubtedly be silenced by the skeptics who have infiltrated our political realms. However, these massive structures that our teleporters were based off of were instruments of war, mass teleportation channels that moved fleets of warships and armies of soldiers within seconds." She shook her head. "One code is unique to each one, and once it's activated, it's a portal to anywhere in the system. I fear the Imperial Council will use this ancient technology for their own gain if they find out about it."

The projection fizzled out, and Hal glanced down in shame. Whether he'd known it or not, he had been an accomplice to this grand scheme to overthrow the system. It pained him to think about the countless Imperials who'd died for a phony war, the very people he'd sworn to protect, but no amount of sorrow would bring them back. The council needed to be stopped, and this was the first step.

He left the room, taking one last look back at the stage before continuing.

Past the doors of the stage chamber, smoke hid Hal's feet. The smoke grew in ferocity and distorted his vision. Eyes blurry, he searched for the source of the smoke but could find nothing. It hung just below the ceiling. He waved his hand, and more smoke filled the void. Even through his face mask, the smoke stung his eyes, and he let out a cough and a wheeze. His eyes watered, and it felt like the air had been sucked from his lungs. Hal pushed himself into a light jog as he gasped for air, removing his face mask to get any ounce of it. Coughing burned his lungs more, but he searched through the haze and saw light. Hal ran with the ember cup in hand, fighting through the smokescreen until he emerged.

Hal collapsed on the ground and gasped for air. Smoke left his lungs with every cough as he struggled to regain his sight. The smoke had sucked every bit of oxygen out of the air, and now he knew how it felt to almost suffocate, something he wished never to feel again. Taking a breath, he looked over to where he'd dropped the cup, and the struggling ember glowed faintly.

Like before, Hal comforted the ember. He blew on it softly to fuel the bright orange it had once had, but this time he did not fret. Panic would only feed his fear, and his struggle would be like that in the wind tunnel. Instead, he calmed himself. Before long, the flames of hope returned to both him and the fire source.

Hal sighed a breath of relief and picked up the ember cup. He wiped the lingering burn of smoke from his eyes and stood up, carrying the ember like it was his own child.

"You're not going out on me," he said.

The final door unlocked with a click and slid open for Hal to enter. A long pathway stretched out before him, where flames tickled the sides of it. Below, charna and magma from the planet's core churned together in a mixture of bright reds and oranges. Sweat rolled down his face, the heat like a thousand suns, but as he looked at the ember, it thrived. With each step he took toward the altar at the end, the small flames grew in size, and the reds turned into glowing blue, the heat radiating through the cup and sinking into Hal's gloves.

Toward the end, where flames created a wall, tall marble statues stared at him as he walked. Each one of their jeweled eyes seemed to follow him as he approached. They wore robes like his father used to and had the same trio of lines etched onto their clothes.

Fire Kells, Hal thought as he continued. At the end of the pathway, Hal stood in front of the altar. Streams of flame rose behind it.

He climbed the stairs and placed the ember in the altar's cup before taking a step back. The flames built within the container and flicked blue before they shot up and merged with the flames behind them. Blue flames overrode the orange and sank down. They crept along the floor toward Hal, and when they touched his feet, he expected to jump back in pain. Instead, he felt nothing but a weight.

The flames continued down the stairs and pathways before joining with the flames that tickled the bridge. Hal waited for the explosion and wondered where his sister would emerge from to confront him again. But as quickly as the flames had spread, they were sucked past Hal and back into the cup.

Hal approached the cup, the flames glowing off his body. The warmth beckoned him in, and he reached out and touched the flames. Coolness. The fire did not burn or scorch him. The flames danced on his hands like they were one. They moved up his arm and over his chest. The fire stretched all the way down his legs and over his head. Warmth entered his body and raced through him. The one thing he'd been missing had finally come home. He smiled as the emptiness faded and the warmth reached the farthest parts of his body. As he took a deep breath and embraced the warmth, the fire within him came alive and brewed in his chest, full and complete.

As he looked at his hands, the flames of Inferno entered through one and shot out through the other. Where they left through his hand, the flames formed a swordlike weapon with the power of a hundred suns. Hal's eyes widened at the sight, and his thoughts drifted back to the story wall where Atis stood over a defeated Xirna holding a similar weapon. He realized this was just one of the many secrets true Wielding offered, and it lay guarded by the past. No more.

"Now go forth, my child," his mother and father whispered, their voices rolling together. "Take your first steps as a Kell of Inferno."

Hal fell to one knee as the last of the flames left the altar and entered him. He took a deep breath to settle himself and take everything in. He looked at one hand and charged himself. Heated flames of raw power emitted from his fingertips and danced around his hand. He could not help but smile as tears clouded his eyes.

It felt like it had been so long since he could Wield. A part of him had just been restored, and it was time to grow it. Still, his shaky breaths gave way to more tears that streaked down his cheeks. In terms of personal satisfaction, he was a failure to no one. He'd communed with ancient beings no one had before. He'd fought and journeyed through the pits of a hellish landscape for weeks and had come out on top.

Sitting back on his knees, he took another deep breath. All the weight he'd felt was gone, and only his fire burned in his chest. It felt smaller than before, and he'd have to condition it, but he was just glad it was back and reconnected.

But where his smile grew, it faded just as quickly. Now the real work began.

The Ashlands were under threat from his unintentional aid, and his sister was lost and confused. Both needed to be corrected if anything was to come of this journey. So many people had helped him get here. Now it was time to return the favor.

CHAPTER XXXI

Hal crawled through the collapsed tunnel and inched his way toward the surface. A final test of the Kells, the way he had come had been blocked by unseen force fields. The temple allowed for no quitters, and the force fields proved it. He had only discovered this place when he'd returned to the altar, where a secret path to escape the underground confines of the temple had revealed itself.

His muscles felt ready to pop as he climbed, a testament to the physicality of the journey. Dust fell on him while rocks tugged and frayed the hardy suit he wore. Athonians back home wouldn't recognize him with disheveled hair and cuts across his battered body. The soldiers might, for they'd formed a bond in the crucible of battle, but with the brainwashing in recent weeks, Hal feared that bond might have been broken. It was his fault for not having been able to stop it. Each foot he ascended through the tunnel got him closer to reversing that mistake.

Daylight showed itself as Hal squeezed through a narrow crevice in the mountain wall. Groaning in discomfort, he stretched an arm through the hole, but he could only fit his shoulder through. Pausing to catch his breath, Hal shifted his position so his legs bent and stored his power. With a strong push, he breached the hole, rocks exploding as he climbed from the depths of the underground. If any had seen him, they would've assumed he was a demon from below come to claim poor souls. As he stood upright, he thought that claim could be true.

Ash blew all around him as he got his bearings. He was in a part of the city he had never explored. More deteriorated buildings plagued the area, their smaller walls and foundations reminiscent of a residential district. Hal stepped into one and looked around. The walls still had their original designs, though the color had faded due to years of elemental exposure. A family had once called this home, but it had been torn from them through war. With a sigh, Hal traced his fingers along the etchings that had stood the test of time.

He felt a renewed sense of purpose. The natural world was within reach. The wind danced across the piles of ash, and the ash itself scattered in the ghostly song. Hal held out his hand and charged a ball of fire in it. The energy crackled, the heat kissed his cheeks, and the charna formed a unique scent he had never smelled before. He felt awakened, like the part of him that had been locked behind the lies and mistruths had finally broken out. The world seemed clearer, and as Hal stared at his fire, he felt whole.

In the distance, boots stomped the ground, and Hal hid in the shadows. Imperial soldiers showed themselves and began to search the area. Miri was still hunting him, but he'd expected that. His sister was nothing if not determined, but to see her in this state was just another reminder of his failure.

The soldiers continued their search as Hal moved through the shadows. They were not his enemy, but if he had to, he would not hesitate to defend himself. He drew his kyr, readying himself against anything. Hal stopped and listened for a moment, and a smile crossed his face.

The soldiers talked about home and how they missed it. Brainwashed or not, home was their center. They still cared for Imperius. One day he would love to be able to call Imperius home again, and if the people wanted it, he'd be their crowned prince. But those were thoughts for another day.

He snaked his way through the shadows, dodging soldier after soldier.

These must be the rear guard, he thought. Common military doctrine said to leave an element behind while the main force moved ahead. That was standard for offensive operations and conquering enemy-held areas, though this was not a war.

Now the same techniques he'd utilized were being used against him. A strange sense of irony washed over him as he sank back into the shadows.

Hal came to a crossroads where a soldier stood guard. The streets narrowed, and shadows succumbed to the light. Dare he test his bond now? If it would save this soldier's life, the answer was simple.

Like a phantom, Hal emerged from the shadows. The soldier's look of pure terror and surprise answered most of Hal's questions, but he still tried. With an outstretched hand of peace, Hal pulled his face mask down.

"Easy, soldier."

"Stop right there," the soldier said, a tremble in his voice.

Hal did as the soldier wished. "Do you know who I am?"

"A traitor."

Those words still stung, although he knew they were not true. "I am Prince Halcion Skyborn, true heir to the throne."

"The council says you're a traitor." The soldier raised his weapon and aimed it at Hal.

It was not the first time he'd looked down the end of a barrel. He noted the soldier's trigger discipline, finger off the trigger. The soldier did not want to shoot, not yet. He still had time.

"The council? Or Varim?" Hal asked.

The soldier reached to the side of his helmet, ready to call in backup, but Hal knew how to get to the heart of an Imperial soldier.

"Good soldiers follow orders. That's why the Imperial Army was so feared by our foes and respected by our allies," Hal said as he looked into the clear visor of the soldier's helmet. The soldier's hand slowly lowered back to his rifle. "Do you ever question them? Question where they come from? Question who gave them? Question the outcomes?"

When the soldier did not respond, he continued. "I served my nation like you are now. I've seen things no one should see and done things most wouldn't have the courage for. I questioned each order. I even questioned the origins of the war, and I can tell you Varim is not innocent. Where was our sense of freedom to agree and disagree? We lost that freedom when Varim took the throne illegitimately. Even I, a prince, cannot question the politicians who sent me there or who sent me here. And now look at the broken empire we have inherited."

The soldier stayed silent. For a moment, he lowered the barrel of his weapon and looked away. Hal thought he'd gotten through to him, reasoned with him, but then the rifle came back up, and the soldier took a firing stance.

"Halcion Skyborn, you are under arrest by order of the Imperial Council," the soldier said. "Comply."

Hal shook his head. "I can't do that."

Energy charged up his hands, and Hal sent a whip of flames crashing into the soldier. Stone shattered as the soldier slammed through old walls, and the ceiling collapsed. Rubble buried the soldier in ash and ancient stone as Hal disappeared back into the shadows.

As he walked, he had to stop for a moment. Using a hand to brace himself against a wall, Hal took a deep breath. Hal's heart beat fast, and it felt like he had just run a marathon. Sweat built on his brow as he looked back to where the soldier had fallen.

Conditioning, he thought. His conditioning level of controlling charna had decreased. Many hours of meditation were in his future when he returned to the enclave.

Moving through the streets, he avoided more soldiers and stayed in the shadows. The brainwash effect was too strong right now, and it was foolish to think one man, no matter his rank, could override what twisted science the high minister had subjected this platoon to. He would have to bide his time.

When the soldiers who patrolled the town circle parted ways, Hal bolted from the shadows and headed toward the gate. Hopefully the duster would still be there.

The gate was only yards in front of him when a fireball whizzed by him and crashed into the gate. It exploded and shattered wood and metal alike in a fiery rain of debris. The force of its energy sent him backward onto the ash-covered ground. Ringing filled his ears as he stared up into the sky, the ash falling over him like snow. It felt like he'd gotten kicked by a horse, but he couldn't stay where he was.

As Hal pushed himself up and looked back, Miri strutted toward him, donned in golden plate armor. She was flanked by two Praetorians, who ignited their golden hardlight xiphirs and shields, and more soldiers rushed to where they stood with their weapons aimed at him.

Hal looked all around before his eyes finally rested on Miri, who just stared back.

It took only a few seconds before the first Praetorian charged him with the shield. Hal avoided it before he fired a round at a soldier. Hal danced around the Praetorians, using them as cover so the soldiers had to work around them, though he dared not get too close. Hal looked into the Praetorians' helmets, their golden visors reflecting his image. The horsehair crests wiggled atop their helms with every movement. When one swung, Hal avoided it and took out the nearest soldier with a well-placed hardlight shard. Miri stood like a spectator watching a lackluster sporting event.

One Praetorian managed to sweep Hal's legs out from under him. Exhausted, Hal fell to the ashy ground with the Praetorian on top. The elite guard drew a kyr and forced it down, braced only by Hal's arms. Hal gritted his teeth as the strength of three men pushed down on him. He almost expected his sister to call it off in mercy, but that was not the case.

Hal reached for his kyr while struggling to hold the Praetorian off. One wrong move or one twitch of his body would send the kyr plunging into his throat. Death wasn't an option.

As the Praetorian reared back to make a final shove of force, Hal grabbed the handle of his kyr. In a moment of life or death, Hal thrust the kyr under the Praetorian's helm and into their throat. Dead weight fell on him before he pushed the fallen guard off and jumped up with his weapon drawn.

"Stop," Miri said.

All the soldiers obeyed the command. Even the Praetorian lowered their shield and returned to the princess.

She cocked her head to the side and looked at him. "Why risk the lives of countrymen? This is between you and me."

"It's not like you to make deals, Meer."

"For the sake of royal blood and familial bond, I will." She stepped in front of the Praetorian, her ivory cloak blowing in the wind. "Allow us to battle. I win, and you hand over Runebreaker."

"And if I win?"

Miri smirked. "You're alive for a little while longer."

Hal eyed his sister. It was a risk to take her on, but if it bought him time to find the Lumnis Stone, then so be it. They were after the same thing, and it was a race to get it, and she knew the advantage he held over her. When she assumed her stance, it was clear what had to be done.

Hal attacked first. His fireballs streaked through the air toward his sister. Miri redirected the balls of fire, and Hal dove out of the way before they crashed into the wall behind him. A sinister chuckle escaped Miri as she pressed forward with streams of flames.

Fire shields emitted from his hands and deflected the stream whips, but as he continued to fight, his strength faded. Sweat poured down his face from the heat, and he didn't know how much longer he could hold out.

Miri kept up her onslaught and replaced her streams with fire daggers, which she launched through the air like a dozen arrows. Hal blocked the majority, but one struck his leg and another hit his shoulder. Exhausted and out of breath, Hal dropped to a knee as the fire seared the strike points.

Miri smiled. "How fitting of you to kneel before me, the Crown Princess."

Anger. Frustration. Rage. Every emotion built within Hal as his fingers gripped the earth. Soldiers began to move in to apprehend him as the fire within brewed and stewed. It was ready to erupt like a volcano after being dormant for so long. Hal looked into Miri's diamond eyes, his heart full of pain and anger. Fire ignited from his hands and built up his arms toward his shoulders. If he could produce a large enough shock wave, it could buy him time to get away.

Beastly roars filled the air as trolls emerged from the ash. They raced past Hal and crashed into the confused soldiers with such power that it sent them sliding across the ground. Blaster bolts shot through the air, and some met their mark, but the trolls outnumbered them.

Hal jumped to his feet, sending a ball of fire toward his sister. Miri recoiled and protected herself with a ward while barking orders like an officer on a battlefield.

More flames left his hands and engulfed the surrounding buildings like dry tinder. He used every ounce of energy he had left before his body slumped. Hal could only stand, his body shouting in pain, as he looked at Miri's shocked expression. The surprise in her eyes only lasted a second before she had to dodge an overzealous troll attack with a bladed hand of fire. The troll's claws dropped to the ashy ground, and it wailed in pain before Miri sent a firebolt through its heart.

She had grown in power. This was a battle he could not win, not now. Too exhausted to carry on, Hal backed away through the gate and into the ash as the inferno raged.

ACT III

CHAPTER XXXII

The duster carried Hal through the wild darkness and hovered through the narrow passageway in the mountainside. As he roamed closer to the enclave, the main door opened, and he drove the duster inside. When he came to a stop, he nearly collapsed from exhaustion, his body pleading for him to stop. As he removed the soaked bandages he'd tied on his wounds, the relief from the pressure sent newfound jolts of pain through his body. Scorch wounds and burn marks were nothing when he had a healing tank to rest in, but without it, they proved to be stingers.

Hal pushed himself to the medical lab in the enclave and found some things to clean his wounds. He had come too far to be slowed by simple infections that could grow into festering wounds. Stripping the top part of his evosuit off, he looked in the mirror at his battered body. Black and blue bruises clashed with his fair skin, and the irritated red wounds left his body open to infection. Hal took the bottle of the cleaning solution and gritted his teeth.

The cleaning solution flowed into the open wounds, bubbling white as it fought the infection and bacteria. Hal gritted his teeth as the solution cleaned and sterilized the wounds, then took a roll of bandages and tied them around himself.

When he'd finished bandaging the plasma wound on his leg, he sat silent for a moment. The cost of finding his Wielding had taken a toll on his body and mind. The journey had been difficult, but there was much more still to be done. Miri knew where the Lumnis Stone was, but he had to get to it before she did. Their mother had feared it would be used for all the wrong reasons, and he worried that the vileness harbored in his sister's mind would spread across the Realmverse. Power in the hands of the corrupt would only certify the fall of a free world. This was more than just his fight within. This new war he had stumbled into held the balance of life in its grasp before an evil empire. His thoughts turned to Varim. He had to stop what was happening—he had to stop *him*—but he could not do it alone.

Despite the pain, he stood and shrugged the evosuit back on, then went to find his companions. They should have surrounded him upon his return, and Kristilin would have tended to his wounds had she seen him. Curious, he headed for the main hall.

Inside were empty seats and a blank holotable. Perhaps they'd visited the town again or met with the Ashen. They'd likely be back before long, and Hal decided this would be a perfect time to meditate.

He found a couch and sat down. Legs crossed, he held both hands out to his sides and closed his eyes. Fire ignited from his hands and burned low as the thoughts left his mind. Deep breaths calmed his aching body. He channeled those breaths into something more. Each breath fueled his fire, his ember, and the flames on his hands reacted. They grew and shrunk with each breath, and warmth spread throughout his body. A Wielder had to be in control of their flames, and it had been a long while since Hal had sat with them.

His pain was replaced with an embrace like a warm blanket on a cold night. He grew his fire, the warmth kissing his face as the flames rose higher with each breath. With a final breath, he opened his eyes and held the flames still. He concentrated on them and held them for as long as he could. Seconds passed before they turned into minutes and then hours. By the second hour, he had sweated enough.

The flames shrunk back into his hands as he took deep breaths. It was a good start for not having meditated in a while. To build his stamina back to where it had once been, he would have to meditate twice a day. Still, it felt good to finally feel the burning warmth inside, and his body thanked him with puffed up veins coursing across his muscles.

As he stood and stretched his limbs, he took note of the room. Empty. Suspicion brewed in Hal, and he walked to the holotable. Perhaps they'd left a message for him.

When he activated it, he expected something, anything, but all he saw was the terrain map of the barren ash. His heart skipped a beat. Kristilin wouldn't have left without an explanation. He took a deep breath to quell the panic rising in him. Just as he was about to go for his duster, a message came over the holotable's communications tab. The symbol flickered, and he wondered if it was her. Too excited to reason, he accepted the call.

A hologram of a cloaked person formed on the table, and Hal clenched his jaw. If this was Miri's attempt to find his location, she could triangulate his position in a matter of seconds. He wouldn't jeopardize himself or the others, and his hand hovered over the button to end the call.

"Wait," the figure said. Their voice was distorted by a voice modulator, which added to his growing suspicion.

Hal stopped and obliged. "Who are you?"

"My name is Fable," the figure said.

The messenger from the Ashen, Hal thought.

If the Ashen were to be believed, Fable was an insider amongst Imperius. Hal looked at the holographic clothes and noted the fine cloth and style that resembled something his cousin would wear. But why someone inside a broken city wanted to help him remained a mystery. Varim could have easily instructed them to do this, though that would hinder his plan. Varim needed him alive because Miri needed him alive. With that in mind, Hal eyed the messenger before him.

"Please, Prince Halcion, I have urgent news for you."

"Why should I trust you?" Hal asked as he leaned on the holotable, his eyes narrowed. "You take me for a fool?"

"Forgive me, Your Highness, but we both have a common adversary in the high minister. My friends, the Ashen, have kept me updated on your progress in the Ashlands." The connection fizzled, and the hologram distorted for a second before it found itself again. "There is tension in the world unlike we have ever seen, and you were the first to expose it."

"What are you talking about?"

"The hologram video you saw in the archives. It was brought to my attention, and now we see the high minister's ugly nature." Fable clasped their hands together. "The Realmverse is in danger. Zeramor, Polaris, Eifa, Velra, all the major systems have seen swift coups just like the one in Imperius."

"How do I know you're telling the truth? I saw my people brainwashed before my eyes. I was publicly disgraced," Hal said.

"A wrong that needs to be righted. You are the heir to the throne to my people, to all Imperials of the Empire, and you are a beacon of hope for countless others." Fable paused for a moment as Hal stared on in confusion. "I can say no more for now, but know that we are loyal to someone who stands for the Code, for our way of life, and for our history. I look forward to meeting you. But I contacted you—"

The communication fizzled again. The color faded from the holotable, and Hal tried to restart it, but the lights flickered, and the whole room went dark. Silence followed, and Hal drew his lightvolver while flames danced along his other hand. The main door moaned open, and he thought of Kristilin, then quickly refocused. The power would not go out upon their return. This had to be something else—someone else.

Hal patrolled the halls toward the main door, careful to make the slightest sound. Light shined through, and he scanned the entry port. Silhouetted like ghosts in a misty field, figures appeared from behind the boxes stacked outside. Energy bolts ripped through the air, and Hal jumped behind cover. The energy bolts slammed into the wall he was using to shield himself, tearing away the concrete. It was clear these people were not a part of Miri's entourage, for they would have shown might instead of stealth upon breaching.

Hal charged his hand and sent a fireball screaming through the air. It crashed into a few crates, and some of the intruders dove for cover. There was a momentary lapse in energy bolts, and Hal peeked from his cover, sending hardlight shards through the open door. They ripped into one intruder, riddling their body with holes.

As he was about to send another fireball, one of the intruders tossed a grenade that rolled right in front of Hal's feet. With little time to react, he dove through the doorway of a nearby room before the grenade exploded. Dust rose into the air, and a smell he knew from the war filled his nose. His fire leached out to it like it wanted to absorb as much as it could.

Toxic gas. Without a second thought, Hal snuffed his fire and focused on the enemies while raising his face mask.

An intruder rushed through the room, their steps growing louder. It only took one shot, a momentary flash of light, to drop the intruder to the cold ground. And in that flash of light, he saw the same insignia on the assailant's evosuit as before, the twin triangles.

Energy bolts peppered the corner of the hallway where he'd once stood, faster than before and with more vigor than anything he had seen in a long time. Another shadow emerged and tossed a smoke grenade. The blast blinded Hal for a moment, and the smoke filled the room. Hal rushed to the door and closed it, throwing the lock and heading to the back. These intruders wanted him dead, and they would go through hell to get it.

Two more shadows ran by on the opposite side as Hal looked through the hard glass window in the room. Golden flashes streaked through the smoke before the red bolts turned their way. It was like a light show of death that illuminated the dark halls of the enclave, and one Hal had a front seat too.

A final golden light sailed through the smoky air, and silence grasped the room. Hal gripped his weapon and sniffed the air once more. The smell was gone. His other hand was kept at the ready to charge with energy as the lock turned. He expected more of the cloaked figures to barge in, but the door opened slowly.

"Hal, it's me. Don't shoot."

Two figures emerged from the smoke wearing fitted armor and enclosed helmets. They stood in front of him and holstered their weapons. When they removed their helmets, shock and confusion crossed Hal's face.

"Misselie?"

She nodded and smiled at him. "I know you have questions, but now is not the time." She nudged the man beside her. "This is Jaeger from the Ashen."

Hal holstered his weapon and took a deep breath. "You have to forgive me if I find this odd timing, but I won't turn down unlikely help. Where did you learn to fight like that?"

"I'm Ashborn. You either fight or die. You know that."

"Let's just say I'm a little shocked."

Misselie nodded again. "Jaeger is the Ashen agent for Hellas. He helped me back to an Ashen outpost. When Dash's gang came, I was scared." Her gaze flicked to the ground. "Kristilin went to try and talk with Asher, but then Dash showed up with a lot of people. They took her and Asher into the town hall and ransacked the town. I didn't know when you would be back, so I went . . . I . . . I can't lose her too . . ."

"It's okay," Hal said as he tried to put on a calm face, but the news sent a shock through his body. He shouldn't have left them, not when Miri was on their tail. Dash was only a roadblock, but one they had to deal with before Miri could exploit it. "We're going to get them back."

"We have our disagreements with the Hellans, but they are not our enemy. We value our home and have greater threats," Jaeger said, his voice strong and hardy. "We are all Ashborn."

Hal knew what it was like to fight for his homeland. He was still fighting for it. He looked past them to the fallen figures in the hallway.

"Dash's gang?" Hal asked.

Misselie nodded as she looked back to the bodies.

Hal clenched his jaw. Jaeger stepped up to him and offered his hand. Hal looked at the man, who was no older than him, and there was determination in his eyes. He trusted Misselie, who trusted Stravis.

Hal clasped Jaeger's hand. "Let's get them."

Chapter XXXIII

Hellas stood silent under the veil of ash. Little light shone in the streets, but the main gate had a couple spotlights to watch the empty wasteland that stretched as far as the eye could see. Hal snuck behind a dune that overlooked the city, and Misselie and Jaeger followed him. He noted the same soft armor and swagger the goons of Dash's gang had. These were no different. Dash had had it out for him ever since the public embarrassment at the saloon, but this was a level of pettiness new to him. He could only imagine what the madman had planned for Kristilin and the others.

He shook the thought away and focused on the mission.

Goons roamed the walls and searched the ash with spotlights to catch anyone that approached the town, but Hal had a thought that it was meant to catch him out in the open. He wasn't that stupid, though entering straight on through the main entrance would start a firefight that he didn't want to start.

Hal followed the walls to where a break in the stone caught his gaze. It was a stealthier entrance, but they'd have to navigate the roaming spotlights. He slid back down the dune with the others to formulate a plan.

"There's an entrance down the walls. Best spot to enter," he said.

"Spotlights aren't the only thing we need to worry about," Jaeger said. "Look there. Automated turrets. We'll be dead if they spot us."

"We need to rescue our friends first," Misselie added. "We can't fight a whole gang with just the three of us."

"That's what you Hellans think. We Ashen are everywhere," Jaeger said.

"Meaning what?" Misselie said.

"They're standing by waiting for my signal," Jaeger said. "After we rescue them, they will come."

Hal stayed silent for a moment as the glow from a spotlight traveled over their dune. "Okay, new plan. Jaeger, you take down the power to their defenses. Misselie and I will head for the town hall and search for the others."

"Agreed."

Hal nodded. "First we need to get across this stretch of ash."

He took the lead and climbed back to the top of the ash dune. The spotlight roamed just in front of them, illuminating everything in its path. Hal waited for the moment, and as it passed, he hurdled over the crest of the dune and slid down the other side. They sprinted across the open field of ash toward the walls of the city. Memories of the war kicked in, and Hal remembered sprinting across open fields as blaster bolts ripped by him and his fellow soldiers fell. The soft ash was like the mud of Athonian forests or the clay of Polarian deserts. All it would take was one goon who had their eyes in the right place at the right time.

They came to the crack and hugged the wall. Hal peeked through to see nothing but crates and discarded supplies. Under the veil of shadow, they slipped in and crouched behind the wooden cover, and Hal searched the town before he spoke.

"All right. This is where we split."

"I'll take care of the defenses. Free the others," Jaeger said before disappearing into the darkness.

Hal watched him go before looking toward the town hall. Somewhere in there Dash had his friends, had *her*. If a single hair had been harmed, he would make Dash regret ever meeting him. He'd dealt with failures for too long. This would not be another one.

When he was about to move, Misselie placed an arm along his chest with a finger to her lips. A few of Dash's goons strolled around, speaking drunken vulgarities as they passed by. Hal sat and listened, sure one of them might slip something, but drunken banter and emotional jabs were the only thing these lowlifes were capable of. They stepped into the saloon and left Hal and Misselie alone.

Best for them to stay in there, Hal thought.

Stone buildings blocked their path to the town hall. Little natural light shined down through the ash clouds above, and goons meandered along the wooden walkways between the buildings. Their thudding boots were so close that any other sound would be sure to alert them.

As Hal and Misselie crept closer, emplaced turrets became visible at the town hall's entrance. Hal pulled Misselie into the shadows.

"There's got to be another way in," he whispered. "We can't get past those until Jaeger deactivates them."

"Come. I know a way around," she said.

Misselie led him back around the buildings as light shined out from inside. Music blasted, and beer mugs clunked on wooden surfaces. They must have raided the saloon earlier and spread the wealth around, which made him wonder what the saloon was being used for now. A few yips and high-pitched screams from its direction made his skin crawl. Cigar smoke and the foul odor of drying vomit filled his nose, and he lifted his face mask to rid it of the putrid scent.

As they crept under a window, beer was thrown out into the ash beside them before another mug spilled and drenched him. He could've easily reached up through the window and fired streams of flames at those goons, but he resisted the urge. Fists balled up, he kept moving despite his new stains and the stale smell of old booze.

Behind them, the doors flew open, and one of the goons landed in the ash. Hal and Misselie froze in the shadows as another one leapt on top of the man. Fists landed against flesh with sinister smacks as more goons swarmed the brawl. Hal tapped Misselie's shoulder, and they carried on.

Misselie led him around the town hall's foundation and to a place with two wooden doors sunken in the ground. Carefully, she stuck a lockpick inside and twisted it with a small screwdriver-like item. The lock clicked, and Misselie ripped the lock and chain off. She opened one of the doors and motioned for Hal to go first. Fire ignited in his hand as he stepped down the stairs and entered the cellar.

Inside, Hal used the light from his fire to find a switch on the wall. Flipping it, he hoped to find Kristilin and Asher; most deviants would hide their captures underground. But as light filled the room, there was nothing but boxes and different household items. He should have guessed Dash was no ordinary man.

"They're not here," he said as he turned to Misselie.

"Asher's office? That would be the only other place," Misselie said. "It's on the second floor."

A door creaked open, and they drew their weapons. Hal turned the light off as the first step squeaked. A man stumbled down the steps, mumbling to himself. Hal backed away from the light switch as the goon stumbled toward him, no doubt in search of more beer. When the man reached for the switch and flipped it on, Hal aimed his blaster right between his eyes. Startled, the goon backed up.

"Please don't kill me," he pleaded as he tripped over a crate.

"Where is she?"

"I don't know who you mean."

"The ones Dash captured. Where. Are. They?" Hal thrust the barrel of his lightvolver against the man's head.

"They're up in the tower room with the books! Please don't—"

The butt of his lightvolver came crashing down against the goon's head, knocking him out in one swing. Hal looked at him on the ground, disgusted by what he was and who he affiliated himself with.

"You care about her," Misselie said. "A lot."

He turned to her and nodded. "I do. She wouldn't be here if I had seen the signs early enough. Neither would you."

Misselie smiled.

"Do you know how to get there?"

She nodded. "It's the library room, where Asher keeps all the books he collected over the years. I even brought him a few during my expeditions. Come." She stepped by and led him upstairs.

It took every evasion tactic he knew to move through the town hall undetected. The goons were not on high alert, but in their drunken state they stumbled in unpredictable paths that made navigation nearly impossible.

They snaked through the halls and avoided the men who were not as drunk as the others. They came to a hallway and discovered the stairwell entrance to the tower blocked by two guards that leaned against the walls with their weapons sitting beside them. Hal drew his blaster, but Misselie stopped him.

"Too much noise."

Hal slid his blaster back into its holster. Fire would be a lot quieter, but much of the building was made of wood. One stray flame and the whole place would ignite. But if he could concentrate his flame into a smaller projectile, it might be enough to take out the goons without causing a mess.

Hal took a deep breath. Charging himself would give away their position, so he would have to act fast. Fire engulfed his hands, and the goons quickly reached for their weapons at the sound of energy crackling. Hal used two fingers and directed two quick pulses of energy. The flames took the shape of his fingertips, and two fire spikes flew through the air. They pierced through the goons' leather armor and through the stone wall they stood by. They dropped to the ground as smoke rose from their wounds.

Misselie looked over at him and nodded, then moved toward the stairwell.

The climb was exhausting. Hal guessed there were easily over two hundred steps. His legs burned, already weakened by the journey thus far. When they came to the top, Misselie paused and surveyed the area. One door stood at the end of the hall where rows of books lined the walls, and there were no guards.

They closed the distance to the door in seconds and stood on either side of the frame. With a nod from Hal, Misselie started picking the lock. When the lock clicked, Misselie threw the door open.

Hal rushed in and took a deep breath of relief. Blindfolded and gagged, Kristilin and Asher sat tied against metal stakes bolted into the floor. Hal hurried over to her, and she jumped at his touch.

"It's me," he said softly, and she relaxed.

He removed the gag, then the blindfold. He looked her in the eyes, a sense of relief in them, and held her tight for a moment. She appeared unharmed, but he still had to get her out of here.

Hal ignited his hand and reached for the metal shackles binding her arms. Her eyes went wide as the flames worked their magic and melted the shackles away. She threw her arms around him the moment she could.

"It's okay," Hal said softly in her ear.

"That bastard," Kristilin said. "He knew you would come for us. He wants you dead."

Hal pulled back and smiled. "I'm not so easy to kill." He looked back to Misselie, who'd freed Asher. "She helped too. Long story."

Hal helped Kristilin stand up and melted the leg shackles, careful not to hurt her with his flames. They gathered with Misselie while Asher paced around the room feverishly.

"The town is lost, under control by a half-wit madman. I should've tossed him aside long ago," Asher said as he punched his open hand. "This is my fault."

"Where are the guards?" Hal asked.

Asher threw his hands up. "I have no idea."

"I do," Misselie said as she looked at her data receiver. "And you have no need to worry. The Ashen have located and freed the guards from Dash's custody in an isolated bunker away from here. They should be here momentarily to help retake Hellas."

"How do you know that?" asked Asher.

"Jaeger just contacted me," she replied. "The Ashen are helpful."

Asher only growled as he continued to pace back and forth.

"But that means we can expect company right about now," Hal said as he looked down the hall.

No sooner did he say that then the first goon bolted up the stairwell. Hal fired a shot and downed the man before more came and opened fire. What stealth they'd had was gone, and the hallway erupted into a full firefight. Energy bolts zipped through the air as Hal and Misselie returned fire, and the others gathered their weapons from the lockers.

More men swarmed the hallway like ants. Sparks flew from metal struck with energy bolts as Misselie returned fire, but the sheer firepower the goons brought forced her back into cover. Kristilin tried to absorb as much as she could with her karver as Asher dove across the floor for cover when a stray bolt ricocheted in the room. When they were safe, Kristilin turned to follow, but an energy bolt struck her leg. She let out a sharp cry of pain as Asher dragged her from the doorway. She clutched her leg where the bolt had hit her, and fury built within Hal.

Fire charged up his arms as he stepped into the open. Energy bolts raced toward him, and he raised a ward to burn them away. Hal threw a fireball at the closest goons before burning away more energy bolts. The fireball exploded within inches of them, their clothes and armor going up in flame. They screamed as fire engulfed them, but Hal paid no attention to dead men. The flames built high, scorching the carpets and drapery along the windows. They raged up the pillars and arches of the ceilings as Hal continued his rampage.

He launched his flame wall at the next group of goons before streams of fire left his fingertips and burned through the men like they were made of dried wood. As the flames left his body, he began to feel light-headed and out of breath. Still, he continued sending fire down the stairwell in a tunnel of intense flames that burned anyone caught in it. When the last of his flames left, he collapsed onto the floor, gasping for breath, sweat pouring from his body.

The fires burned and crackled all around as they sought out the driest of the wood. Beside him lay a fallen goon, flames dancing along his smoldering body. Smoke clouded the room as Asher and Misselie helped him back to his feet. They assisted him down the stairs, stepping over bodies of goons all the way down.

When he finally regained strength to walk on his own, Hal emerged from the stairwell to find one goon crawling on his hands and knees. Burns covered most of his body, skin melted from muscle, hair but a memory. He reached out to Hal with a groan, and Hal fired a lightshard. The goon fell silent as Hal walked by with the others in tow.

Outside the town hall, blaster bolts raged. The night air flashed red and blue as Dash's men raced to the walls, but they were too late.

The gates blew open, and dozens of Ashen and Hellans poured through. They picked through the first wave of men as more goons took cover and fired back.

Hal did not care for them. He wanted Dash.

They took cover behind a stone wall when a few goons noticed them. Misselie and Asher returned fire, shooting as much as they could before they were forced back down by enemy energy bolts.

"There's too many of them," Asher said as an energy bolt bounced off the top of the stone wall.

Hal scanned the area; there was a secluded building that could provide perfect cover. A flurry of energy bolts ripped overhead as he ducked back down. Asher let out a curse-filled groan as an energy bolt pierced his arm. They needed to move to someplace with more cover.

"That building over there. I'll distract them. Just get to cover," Hal said.

A grenade landed near them, and Hal hurried to raise his ward before the grenade exploded. The initial concussion rocked his brain against the side of his skull, and he blinked rapidly to try and stay conscious. Blood trailed from his nose, but he kept his flame ward up as another grenade exploded. His muscles trembled, and the blast rode up the side of the ward as the others took cover behind him. Despite his focus, he couldn't sustain the ward for long. With burning muscles, he collapsed against the stone wall, breathing rapidly as the ward disappeared.

"You're hurt," Kristilin said, wrapping a piece of cloth around a gash in his arm.

"And so are you. We can't stay here," Hal said as another energy bolt ripped through the stone wall and almost hit him. He looked at the others before his eyes met Kristilin's again. "Go."

Hal leapt over the wall without another word. He raised a fire wall and blocked a hail of energy bolts. His vision blurred, but he forced himself to concentrate. They were depending on him, and he would not fail.

His friends darted for cover, and he held the ward up as long as he could. His muscles screamed at him, and his head throbbed like a steady drumbeat, but he held the ward firm, planting his feet and taking everything they could throw at him. Gritting his teeth, Hal took a step forward, the heat from his flames making sweat drip from his nose. Energy bolts hit in rapid succession as the goons inched forward and forced him back, but his resolve never faltered. He roared as loud as he could before throwing a fireball. It exploded in a fiery ball of light, and Hal collapsed to his knees. He struggled for breath, his body spasming.

The Ashen and Hellans battled the gang. Explosions from grenades sent ash raining down on Hal as he sat on his knees.

A hand clasped his shoulder and spun him around. Before he could react, a fist rocked his jaw and sent him to the ashy ground. He turned to face who had struck him, and all he could see was red. He wanted nothing more than to rip apart the man who stood in front of him.

Dash shook his hand and pulled out his pistol with a chuckle, aiming it at Hal.

"Aw, don't look so down. Look how much fun we're having," Dash said, waving the gun at the firefight in front of them. "If only you could see the new order before you. You could have been a part of it."

"Go to hell," Hal said.

He leapt up and tackled Dash to the ground. A stray shot went off from the blaster, but Hal rained punch after punch onto the madman. Dash blocked some before he threw Hal off, but like a persistent wolf hunting its prey, Hal took the fight back to Dash. All it would take was one stream of flames to melt Dash away, but that wouldn't be as rewarding. It would be too easy.

They tussled in the ash, vying for the upper hand. Dash pinned Hal down, but not before Hal landed a square punch across Dash's jaw. Hal threw the man off and drew his kyr. He sliced Dash's arm, and blood oozed out. The madman only chuckled before leaping at Hal, who plunged the kyr into Dash's abdomen. Dash groaned through smiling lips as he eyed Hal. Gone was any sense of reason as Hal stared at the face of a man who cared not for his own well-being. Hal reached for the blaster, but Dash got to it first.

Dash smirked. "I'll see you there."

A flash of light and the boom of a blaster bolt rang his ears, and Dash slumped onto him. Smoke rose from his chest, and sparks shot through the man's back. Hal threw Dash's body off and sat up. Wiring and mangled metal parts made up Dash's insides and Hal let out a long sigh.

Dash had never been human, just another pawn.

Jaeger ran up beside Hal and holstered his weapon before helping him up.

"Are you all right?" Jaeger asked.

"I've been better," Hal groaned. "Thanks."

The Ashen were finishing the remaining goons while Hellans shielded the citizens of their town. Some of Dash's men were taken prisoner while those who refused met their end right there. A couple Ashen soldiers ran up to them and saluted.

"Sir, the town is secure."

"Aid the Hellans. Make sure none of them are injured," Jaeger said, and the soldiers ran off.

The others emerged from the building and joined Hal. Kristilin stood beside him, and Hal threw an arm around her shoulders.

Asher stood over Dash and shook his head.

"I believe we have some things to address," he said. He looked past Hal and Jaeger to where Commander Jorrin stood. "We're all in this now, whether we like it or not."

Chapter XXXIV

H al's eyes shot open. He sat up, breathing rapidly, his head and body aching. He threw off the blankets, and bandages had been wrapped around his shoulder and legs. Black and blue covered his body, and he throbbed as he moved, his body still tender. He took a deep breath and swung his legs over the side of the bed. It felt like everything was on fire. Most days that would be a good thing, but not like this.

Looking around the room at the stone arches and simple glass windows, he figured he was in one of the buildings in Hellas.

His eyes fell to a note sitting on the wooden nightstand beside his bed. Taking it, he read what was written: '*Meet us at the town hall.*' He could tell by the way the letters swooped that it was Kristilin's handwriting, and a relieved sigh escaped him.

It felt like ages since he'd sat down to just talk, but with everything that had occurred, it seemed outrageous. Hal placed a hand on his head. Now was not the time to dawdle in self-pity. He had done enough of that for now.

His evosuit sat on an armor stand that looked like something out of the old stories wise men used to tell when he was younger. The hardy material, which had once been smooth to the touch, now felt frayed and uncared for. The cloak had tears and holes in it from countless struggles, making the ends look jagged. Life in the ash had proven hard and had knocked him down at every possible corner, but the frays only served to remind him of what had come before and what was to be done later.

He put his evosuit and cloak on, careful of the new bandages all over his body, and embraced their warmth. As light shined through the windows, he threw his hood up and left the room.

Destruction still stained the area. Smoke from smoldering fires rose into the air, and the banging of hammers on nails echoed through the town. It brought a smile to his face to see people helping one another despite what had happened a night ago. Behind him, parts of the walls lay in piles, and the inside of a rampart looked more like a slide of rubble. Ashborn were all around it, trying to rebuild what they could. It wasn't like they could purchase more material. Every bit of it was precious.

He walked down the ashy road as his eyes set on the town hall. Smoke rose from it too, no doubt from the fires he'd set. If there'd been any other way, he would have preferred that.

During the Polarian war, he'd had to make sacrifices and decisions he would not want to make again, but they'd all had a purpose. The goal was clear, and everything brought it one step closer. But here, his purpose felt twisted. He wanted to stop Varim, but he didn't want to hurt his sister, and then there were the Lumnis Stones.

Hal shook his head. Every action had a reaction, and he saw the effects of his own.

When he reached the doors of the town hall, he hesitated. He would've figured Asher would want him in a cell for the damage he'd caused. The least of the punishments would be to exile him again. That he could live with, but if it meant endangering Kristilin, then he could not. Hal shook the thoughts from his mind.

He took a deep breath and went to push the doors, but they opened by themselves. Kristilin's arms wrapped around him, her touch soft. And even though the new pressure tweaked at his sides, he didn't care. Her touch was enough to melt his pain away, and he placed his hands on her hips, pulling her close. It felt like time froze for a second, and the burdens of yesterday lifted from his shoulders.

Kristilin pulled back and gave him a once-over. "How do you feel?"

"Better," Hal said with a small smile, which Kristilin returned.

Behind her, the others stirred in the gathering hall. Jaeger twirled a knife in his hands, and Misselie went over an array of books scattered across a table away from the others. Other Ashborn soldiers hauled out broken pieces of the town hall. As a pair carried an old beam past them, Hal could not help but eye the piece. Scorch marks carried black stains up the once-polished metal, a reminder of his untamed actions.

Kristilin squeezed his arm, and he looked into her beautiful violet eyes. Sometimes that was enough to shake him out of his thoughts.

As he stepped in with the others, they came to greet him. Hal gave them each a smile, and he gave Jaeger a firm handshake. Though he'd expected the worst from the people who called this place home after he brought so much turmoil into their lives, their spirits were far from what he had anticipated. Their gratitude and friendliness washed away any lingering apprehension he had.

The doors to the mayor's hall opened, and two Ashborn motioned for them to enter.

Hal limped into the room behind the others. Commander Jorrin and Asher were gathered around a holotable, the blue glow shining off their faces. Asher looked up and gave him a smile and a nod.

"You're awake. Good," he said.

"I don't remember falling asleep," Hal confessed as he placed his hands on the table.

"You took a beating. Luckily for you, she's very skilled in medicine." Asher nodded toward Kristilin. "She rarely left your side."

Hal looked at her and smiled. "I guess I should have expected that."

Commander Jorrin opened the holomap and scanned the land. The map settled on an area Hal did not recognize, but that could've just been the headache talking. The commander zoomed in and pointed at a mountain in the center of a large crater. Hills stretched in two rows on either side, but what caught Hal's eye was the buildup around the mountain.

"This is why we called you here. Years of gathering information have led to this. The Imperials have built up the Great Mountain in the last two years. On the outside it looks like another military fortification, the only one for miles in any direction. But look at the peak."

Commander Jorrin swapped viewpoints, and the visual zoomed up the mountain to the broken top. Hal's eyes went wide.

The unmistakable metal legs of a Primordial Gate were revealed. The mountain was so tall that the clouds covered most of the peak, but now Hal remembered. This was the mountain he'd seen from a distance when he'd first arrived.

"That is a Primordial Gate, which you know all too well," Commander Jorrin said as he looked at Hal. "One of our spies got a close look at its operation."

Asher cleared his throat. "I don't like this one bit, Prince Halcion. From the research Stravis accumulated, which Misselie graciously provided, these structures were used as mass teleportation devices meant to connect the star system with other systems in the Realmverse. That means anything from cargo to a full warship could come through."

"Or an invasion force," Hal said.

Commander Jorrin nodded.

"Activation codes," Hal said to himself. He looked at the others. "Correct me if I'm wrong, but Asha is situated at the far reaches of this system."

"Correct. It's the last world in line before the Maw begins," Asher stated.

"Even with high speed engines, starships have a limited pulse drive range, about five hundred thousand miles or so. After that, their energy cells need to be recharged, and the starship can only travel at impulse. Even at hyperspace, they are limited to the jump point. From what I understand now, the journey here would take them over two years without the Gate from the hyperspace jump point."

"Are you certain?" Commander Jorrin asked.

"Positive. Miri is here to get the stone and scout for an invasion party. When she's gone, you can expect more." He looked at the map. "Asha is a prime location for a base to expand the Empire's borders."

"Then we destroy the Gate," Commander Jorrin said. "Let them spend months traveling here and weaken themselves."

"There is only one hyperspace route from Athos to Asha," Hal said. "If we destroy the Gate, Miri could blockade the route. Nothing in or out."

"We're self-sufficient," Asher said. "If we work together, our peoples can overcome this."

"Easier said than done," Jorrin said with a huff.

"There has to be a compromise," Hal said.

"We can't destroy the Gate," Misselie said from the other side of the room. "These are Primordial artifacts worth studying. Imagine the history we would be erasing if we destroyed them."

"Those Gates are weapons," Jorrin said. "Every second they're up they threaten Asha."

"I agree with Misselie," Kristilin said. "Primordial infrastructure, whether good or bad, is worth studying, and erasing their history because we don't understand it is wrong in every accord." She crossed her arms and stared at the hulking commander. "Imagine if the Ashen were wiped from the history books. No one would know who you were or how you'd lived here. I am no historian, but those insights to how cultures lived and worked prove valuable to others after them."

"Preservation is the key to furthering our understanding of them. Maybe the Gateway system wasn't always a tool of war. Maybe they were created for something else, but we don't know. To know for sure, we must study them," Misselie said. Her gaze shifted downward. "Stravis would want that."

The table erupted into a debate as everyone tried to make their point. No one took the time to listen to and understand one another's reasons.

Hal stayed silent. An open ear did more than an open mouth.

Asher raised his hand, and the arguing stopped. He looked at Hal.

"Well, Prince Halcion, it's up to you to decide our course of action."

Hal took a deep breath. "We're not destroying the Gate. It can offer much insight into how Primordials operated with charna. Their history is the Realmverse's history. But we can't have them active, not now. We have to shut them down."

"How?"

"Inverted activation codes," Hal said, louder this time. "The keycodes work both ways, but not everyone knows that. Only the royal family does. Type the codes in at the base terminal on one of the pylons from left to right, and they activate the Gate. Reverse them, and it shuts it down. Simple but effective."

Asher rubbed his bearded chin and looked at Jorrin. "We must plan and act before it's too late."

"We are spies. We can't show ourselves."

"I think your time of secrecy here is over, Commander. Everyone knows who you are. Your people live in pockets around the planet, waiting for a fight. This could be it. If we want to be able to live in peace, we need to work together," Asher said. "Like Prince Halcion said, there must be a compromise."

Hal stood upright and crossed his arms. "He's right, Jorrin. An alliance is best for both of you."

Jorrin leaned over the holotable. Hal watched him, hoping he would make the right decision.

"We will bridge an alliance with Hellas under one condition. We want unrestricted access to the gem mines," Jorrin said.

After a moment, Asher nodded in agreement.

"We may be Ashen, but this is your home now too, and the guidance of Prince Halcion is insightful. Ashen or Hellan, we are all Ashborn," Jorrin said.

"Good choice," Hal said with a nod, and for a second he felt like a ruler. He was no ruler yet, but it felt good to gain experience.

"We'll form a battle plan and course of action if Hellas can provide the resources."

Asher nodded. "Let this be the start of a new partnership."

"Agreed."

Hal looked at the two leaders of the two factions and nodded. Building a bright future would start right here.

"There is one other matter I think the prince would like to be aware of," Asher said. An aide brought a datacard to the table and handed it to Asher. After he plugged it into the holotable, a string of encoded information emerged, "This is Dash's memory cortex. I had my specialists decode it."

As Asher worked the table controls, the encoded symbols decoded to standard language and Hal followed what Asher highlighted. A string of code held orders from none other than High Minister Varim.

"Terminate Halcion Skyborn," Hal said under his breath.

"I thought you should know," Asher said. "Maybe it could be useful once all of this is over and he stands trial."

"Thank you, Asher," Hal said.

The rest of the meeting dealt with the little things such as who would repair the walls and bury the dead, so Hal took his leave and roamed the town. He found himself standing on one of the ramparts that overlooked the sea of ash. Wind carried the gray material through the air, shifting it like the ocean tide. Softly glowing ghost trees lit up the dark land, defying the ash.

The calmness of the wind mixed with the soft chatter of patrons in the saloon, making it a good time to be alone and collect his thoughts.

He opened and closed his hand, and fire lit and extinguished in his palm, flashing like a quick firefly. Though it was a simple exercise, it built up his speed, and he went faster and faster until his hand began to cramp. Every bit of conditioning mattered, and it helped ease the worry from returning to his thoughts. As he stretched his hand and looked back to the ashy sea and mountains beyond, he realized someone standing behind him.

Kristilin settled next to him, leaning against the stone wall with two cups in her hands. She offered one to him with a smile. "It is tea."

Hal took the mug and brought it up to take a sip. When the cold liquid hit, his eyes closed in bliss, the minty flavor making his mouth dance with joy. It was the best thing he'd drank in a long while.

He opened his eyes. "It's wonderful. Thank you."

Kristilin smiled and placed her mug on the wall. "What happens now?"

Hal had a hundred different answers to that single question. He knew what she meant, but there was still so much he wanted to say.

He sighed. "Go back to Starlite Temple. Unlock the seal. Find the stone."

"I mean after."

"That's up to Jorrin and Asher. I don't know how strong their alliance is as of now. It could all boil over once this conflict is settled. Or it could last, and they could turn Asha from a decrepit barren world into something more fruitful. United."

"No, Hal," she said, looking into his eyes with a smile. "I mean you and me. Where do we stand?"

Hal held his mug in his hands and thought hard before he spoke. "When you hugged me earlier today, it felt just like our Academy days. I felt happy." He traced random patterns on the condensation that had formed on the mug. "When the war broke out and I was called away, I felt so angry. Angry because I couldn't talk to you face-to-face. I couldn't feel you. It sounds selfish now, but it hurt." He looked at her. "If I'm being honest, I never stopped caring for you. But you probably hated me for how things went."

"Hal, I have never hated you since we first met in my family's château," she said with a sigh. "But it was your duty."

"My duty should have been to you first," Hal said. "I was the prince, for Empyrea's sake. I should've found a way."

"Whenever I returned to Velra, my parents would ask me about you. Not because you were a prince but because I think they saw how happy you made me. I was just a daughter of two parents who worked to be where they were, but being an only child, I did not have many friends, however, it means everything when your best friend is the one you love the most." She wiped a stray tear from her eye and looked back out to the landscape beyond. "The war caused such uncertainty, and when my home world plunged into chaos . . ."

She reached inside the collar of her suit and pulled out a necklace Hal remembered all too well. His nose stung as tears welled up in his eyes. The double lily stem intertwined, and the two flower heads arched into the shape of a heart. They were her favorite flowers.

"You gave me this for my eighteenth birthday. We had been dating for four years then. I never take it off. It gives me hope."

"You mean the world to me," was all Hal could say.

Kristilin stepped toward him. Though she only came up to his chin, she reached a hand to cup his cheek. Hal's eyes searched hers as his hands went to her hips. She stood on her tiptoes, and Hal leaned down to catch her lips in the softest touch he had ever felt. He could've stayed there for hours, lips locked and hands roaming.

When she pulled back and smiled, Hal brushed a stray lock of hair from her face, then went for another kiss that tasted just as sweet.

"Let's go somewhere private," Kristilin whispered in his ear. "I would like to be close with my Halcie."

Hal was happy to indulge.

❧❧❧ ❧❧❧

Minutes melted into hours, and Hal wiped a bead of sweat from his brow as a coolness kissed his skin. His beloved was resting peacefully on his chest, her arm stretched around him. It felt good to take a breath and pause. It would only last for a bit, but they all needed it.

Hal looked out the windows in the room they'd made their own, and lightning danced along the ashy clouds as rain fell outside. They couldn't move in this weather, and the thought of not doing anything gnawed at him.

He gazed back down at Kristilin and rubbed her smooth shoulder. She moaned softly in delight, her eyes fluttering open. He placed a soft kiss on the top of her head.

"Halcie," she said softly.

The pet name sent goosebumps all over his body. Kristilin shifted and pushed up so she sat on top of him, the fur blanket barely covering them. Hal ran his hand up her thigh as she leaned down and kissed him. It seemed like ages before they parted for oxygen, smiles forming on their lips.

"I could stay here all day with you by my side," Hal said.

"So could I," Kristilin said.

She placed her head on Hal's chest. Hal wrapped his arms around her and held her close. Their breathing was in sync, and for a moment it felt like old times.

"I love you," he said.

Kristilin picked her head up from his chest and stared deep into his eyes. He searched hers, and she placed a hand along his cheek.

"I love you too."

Hal leaned up for another kiss, and it felt like magic when their lips met, like their bond had been sealed for good. It felt right.

As they parted, the door to their room opened, and Misselie walked in. Kristilin quickly pulled the covers over her, leaving Hal to scramble for the little he could before Misselie looked up from her data receiver and quickly spun around.

"Oh goodness. I didn't see anything. I mean, I did . . . but I didn't . . . and, I mean, you're both pretty . . . but . . ."

"What is it, Misselie?" Hal said as he tried to wrestle a few more inches of the blanket from Kristilin.

"Nothing. I was just wondering if we were going to head out after this storm and if I should pack some supplies."

"That's a good idea," Hal said. "And yes, we'll be heading out in the morning when the storm clears a bit."

"Okay. Sorry to disturb your . . . um . . . I'll just go," Misselie said. "Make sure you lock the door next time."

The door closed, and Kristilin peeked over the covers at him. They both nestled back into the bed, and Hal took her in his arms with a smile.

"What?" Hal said. "She said we were both pretty."

Kristilin giggled and slapped his shoulder lightly. She stood from the bed and walked to the large windows that overlooked the ash, the light highlighting her beautiful silhouette. Every time she allowed him to see her like this, his heart fluttered.

Hal threw the covers off and made his way to join her. He stood behind her and wrapped his arms around her, placing kisses along her neck.

By Empyrea was he lucky.

Chapter XXXV

It was a beautiful night Hal would not soon forget, but as a new day dawned, he had to refocus on what came next.

Orblight glowed across the ceiling of Starlite Temple's rocky cavern as Hal led Kristilin and Misselie toward the stairwell. He had expected more guardians to manifest and confront them, but the only thing that met them were small insects and creatures that scurried across the rocky earth in search of a hiding spot.

Hal stepped up to the podium and activated the stairwell. The floor moved, and the stairwell revealed itself, dropping down below them.

"Fascinating," Misselie said. "I wish Stravis were here to see this."

Hal smiled. Like Stravis, Misselie was a scholar, and these ancient beings were as important to her as they were to him.

"We'll find him, Misselie. I promise," Hal said as he led them down the stairwell.

She gave a small nod with a smile. Hal knew time mattered, but he was not ready to face his sister yet. She was far stronger and more conditioned than he was. If he charged in there, she would wipe the floor with him. Stravis was a strong old dog. He just had to hold on for a while longer. Miri was intense, but she wasn't evil, and that gave him hope for Stravis.

Hal and the girls crossed the lightbridge and came to the sealed door from before. What had once been another obstacle was now only a bump in the road. He launched four fireballs from his hands and lit the chandeliers hanging from the ceiling. When the fires burned high, the runes on the door glowed a deep red, and it opened. Dust and small rocks shook from the top, and the low rumble vibrated within his body.

The doors opened fully, and more orblight glowed down the dark hallway. A breeze of stale air greeted them. Hal took a deep breath and entered the Temple of the Fire Wielders.

On either side of the hall stood holographic portraits of past Kells of Inferno, their names written in Primordial runes below them. Hal stared at them in awe. After the time of the Primordials, it seemed there'd been dozens of beings who'd claimed the title of Kell, all immortalized here in an ancient chamber.

At the end of the hall was a circular room that connected the other halls. Hal approached the pedestal. Before he could do anything, a hologram shot up in the image of his mother. Hal froze, the comfort of Kristilin's hand easing the emotions swelling within.

"Amazing, isn't it? For thousands of years, we have tried to reforge what Atis and Sarin created for us. They ascended the ladder of mortality and rivaled the celestial Primordials," Empress Irina said, her voice clear and joyful. "Inside you will find the Lumnis Stone of Inferno. Only a capable Wielder can handle its burn and learn the knowledge contained within it."

The hologram ended just as fast as it had started. Doors opposite the pedestal opened, and torches of fire hung low. As Hal and the girls followed the path, the flames sent shadows dancing along the walls. Warmth trickled in and seeped through his clothes. Light shone from the end of the hall, and as they reached the end, a raging inferno encapsulated the chamber before them. Wicked flames snapped and danced in the air. The path headed directly into the inferno.

Hal looked at Misselie. "Any other way around?"

Misselie scanned the area with her tablet and shook her head. "No. This is the only way."

"That fire does not seem happy to see us," Kristilin said.

The walls circled around to the other side. Hal considered shuffling across the lip, but as he placed a foot out to test it, the stone under his foot crumbled. He caught himself before a tendril of fire shot up and almost seared his foot.

How fitting, he thought, looking back to the waves of flames. As another whip of flame shot out at them, an idea struck.

Hal inhaled deeply and calmed his nerves. Fire charged up his arms, and as he raised them, two streams shot out and formed an umbrella of fire energy. They ripped through the wild flames and tore a hole through to the other side.

Hal looked back to the girls. "Go."

They wasted no time and hurried around him. Walls of fire on either side, Kristilin and Misselie ran toward the end of the pathway.

Hal fought to keep his will up, knowing they would be nothing but burnt corpses if he failed. The image frightened him, and he channeled all his focus into his charna. His muscles ached, and the pressure caused his fingertips to go numb.

The girls made it to the other side, and Kristilin waved to signal they were out of the fire's wrath. Now all he had to do was get himself across. The technique he'd used was easier stationary; movement added a whole new element to it. He took a step forward, and his strength buckled. The left stream of flames faltered and caused the wild flames on that side to push across until he found his balance again.

If he failed, Kristilin and Misselie would be stuck here for as long as it took Miri to tear this place apart—another issue he was not all too thrilled about.

He took another deep breath. The flame streams shrunk to just before him, and the walls of fire closed, merging back into each other. The girls disappeared on the other side.

Hal turned one of his hands upright and shot a stream of fire just above him. The umbrella sank all around him, the flames licking the floor. Less output meant more endurance, and he had to make sure he made it to the other side.

He took one step, then another. The flames flicked furiously at the shell he had made. Cracks and snaps boomed from the outside of his protective flame shield. He could not see anything in front of him, just the ground right below him. The flames crashed in front of him, sending waves of energy flowing over his bubble. Raw power was testing his fortitude, and he'd found a way to counter it. Walking through the fury of flames, he smiled.

He emerged from the other side as the flames tried to grab him one last time. The fire parted around him, and he stepped out to meet the girls, awe in their eyes. It was not every day someone walked through walls of fire. It sure felt like he did often though.

"Singe anything off that head of yours?" Misselie asked as she worked on the door.

"Not yet," Hal replied as he stepped up to Kristilin, who looked him over despite his attempts to ward her off. "How's it coming?"

With a single rotation of the circular keyway, the door clicked open, and Misselie smiled up at him. "What would you two do without me?" She slid her lockpick back along her belt and pushed the door open.

Hal smiled and walked into the room. Spheres of orblight revolved around a glowing pillar like planets around the sun. His footsteps echoed as Hal walked down the few steps and took in the gravity-defying sight. Before he reached the pillar in the center of the room, another hologram projected itself, and his mother returned as if she were following them.

"Fascinating, isn't it? There is so much long forgotten history we have yet to learn." She turned back to the pillar and the orblights that encircled it. "While this is an Inferno Temple, the Wielders under Atis often used other charna branches, like Void for instance. This is just one of the five forms of charna Wielding, along with what they referred to as Inferno, linked together in a web of possibilities. There is so much more to learn." Irina touched the pillar before she looked back and said, "Imagine a world where all the forms were used in tandem. Such was the way of the Archkell, the way of Atis. I've hidden a Primordial artifact in the Lumnis Stone chamber. Continue forth, my children."

The doors on the far side slid open. As the girls pressed forth, Hal stayed put. Nobody had seen a Lumnis Stone for over a millennium, and he was about to walk into one of their resting chambers. Some would call this historical, and perhaps it would be later on, but all he could think about was how desperately the stones were needed. Whichever side held them would control the Realmverse and the knowledge of Kells before him. Hal looked back to the console.

Everyone saw balance as black and white, but it was so much more complicated than that. To achieve balance, one had to teeter in the middle of order and liberty. To step too far over one side or the other would shift the balance, and the two sides would run rampant. He saw that here, in the Ashlands, where order was but a faint concept championed by those in Hellas and the Ashen clans. The Lumnis Stone and the Gates all shifted the balance of the Realmverse, yet they were needed.

He had to find a way to achieve that balance before the fate of the Realmverse was sealed. He pondered for a moment more before following the others.

Walls of old marble stretched high to the domed ceilings. The carved stone floors gave way to a polish as Hal set his eyes on what lay at the top of the stairs. Old runes in every shape stood in front of the hardlight vault they protected, radiating a cool green.

This had to be it.

As he took a step forward, materialization portals appeared, and guardians spawned in a cloud of red light. Misselie drew her pistol while Kristilin activated her karver. Hal, however, stayed still. The guardians marched like conscripted souls, their hands spasming uncontrollably.

Moans of their past souls called out to him, sending a chill up his spine. A solid red skull with energy pouring from its eyes faced Hal and let out a deep moan. These guardians seemed different than the others they'd dealt with, almost begging for an ending. As the guardian nearest Hal reached out, heat radiated off its crimson arms, charna dripping like melted flesh. Hal took a step back, and all three of them stood back-to-back, encircled by the tortured souls.

"They are not attacking. Why?" Kristilin asked.

"They're hurting," Hal said as the guardians limped toward them.

"But why?" Kristilin asked.

"Maybe a question for another time. They're getting a little too close for my comfort," Misselie said.

Flames charged up Hal's hands, and he sent a fistful of flames into the nearest guardian. The force from the flame incinerated the guardian into nothing but waves of energy that fluttered in the air, before fading into cool nothingness. Echoes of blasters dulled in comparison to the knowledge of power he felt. It was like everything became clearer, and he saw the truth.

Knowledge is power, he thought.

The guardians continued their meandering march toward them. He punched a guardian with a fist full of fire, and it turned to embers that faded into energy waves. Hal swept out the legs of the other, and as it fell, he brought his foot down as hard as he could, incinerating the guardian.

When the dust settled and the ashes dissolved back to their otherworldly realm, Hal focused on the flames still crackling in his hands. To be destroyed by fire meant to be reborn into something else. Much like in nature, when wildfires burned swaths of forests, under the charred remains grew the seeds of life that would replenish what had been lost. Like a fire hawk, the true nature of his Wielding prowess revealed itself to him as an aspect of the Realmverse.

This was what it meant to be a Wielder, to wield nature as a tool but to not underestimate its brutality.

"Hal?" Kristilin had lowered her karver sword and stood next to Misselie. "Are you all right?" Her soft eyes were concerned, and Hal shook away his thoughts.

"I'm fine. Just getting used to this again." He smiled at her, and she returned it.

Another hologram of his mother sprang up from the center of the chamber. Her silver clothes had holes and tears in them, and she faced the vault that contained the Lumnis Stone.

"I fear I know Varim's plot. To end the Empyrean legacy in the Realmverse, he wishes to bring the spirit of Xirna back. The Lumnis Stones are his key. They're what Atis and Sarin used to send the Primordial queen to the Kaleidosphere." She turned around and looked at Hal as if she'd known he would be standing right there. "But to do so, he needs a medium, or rather *she* needs one."

"Miri," Hal said as the reality hit him.

"The Lumnis Stones cannot be allowed to fall into Varim's hands. If they do, the Realmverse will never be the same."

The hologram, and Hal stood there. He knew Varim was arrogant and cunning, but for him to use his own sister to harbor the spirit of the dreaded Primordial queen meant there was no saving grace about that man. Miri had fallen victim to Madness, and now he needed to figure out how Varim could even use such a vile form of charna. The worry he felt for his sister only grew, and time was running thin.

With a deep breath, Hal ascended the steps to the vault. At the top, the runes danced different colors of fire. Greens and blues danced with reds and oranges, welcoming the return of a Fire Wielder. Hal looked down at where a pedestal stood. It was made of smooth stone, and a perfectly shaped hand cutout lay in the center, and in the center of that was a small circle opening. He took a deep breath, feeling eyes on his back. They'd come this far, sacrificed more than he could ever ask for, and now it all depended on him.

Butterflies fluttered in his stomach as uncertainty kicked in. *To hell with being scared now*, he thought as he placed his hand on the pedestal.

A quick jolt of pain stabbed his palm before he pulled it back to find a drop of blood on the stone surface. When he didn't drop dead, he exhaled.

A small price to pay to prove my blood and gain entry. All he could think of was the box that lay within.

The hardlight shields dropped, and he stepped in. Heart racing, he stood over the chest, his hand resting on the elegant exterior, which looked like intertwined flames. The lock had the rune for Inferno, and Hal wasted no time opening it.

When it opened, bright white light shot from the chest. Hal let his eyes adjust before picking up the precious stone to gaze upon it. Gentle flames flowed within its shell, their warmth radiating to his fingertips. For the first time in over a thousand years, a Wielder held a Lumnis Stone.

Kristilin stood near him at the top of the steps, her eyes sparkling as she looked upon the stone. "It is beautiful. What now?"

Hal placed it gently back into its nest and closed the lid to the chest. "It's supposed to commune with a Wielder and grant knowledge of spectacular power. Like my mother said, only the strongest can see what it holds." He looked at her and shrugged. "Study it? Miri will be hot on our heels once she finds the temple open."

"We cannot take it back to Hellas," Kristilin said. "Not while they plan. It will be too much of a risk."

"And the enclave is too close."

Misselie pulled her data receiver from her bag and joined them at the top of the steps. "I have a suggestion. There's an old settlement a couple miles from here. Most of it is in ruins, but there's a stone keep still intact." She flipped the screen back to them. "There's also an ashstorm heading this way. I suggest we seek shelter soon."

Hal nodded. He picked up the delicate chest and held it like he had never held anything more precious before. The door behind them opened to a passage long forgotten, and it led them back outside. The quicker they vacated, the better.

CHAPTER XXXVI

Wind whipped across the dunes, and tunnels of ash formed in the wake of the dusters as they sped through the storm. Keeping close to the wake of the jetdrive, Hal followed Kristilin across the grayed-out landscape. Only the whine of the jetdrive and the howl of the wind broke the haunting stillness of the land. It was such a stark difference from Athos, where green was a common sight over the drab gray. Still, this land housed many secrets and knowledge known to Atis and Sarin and their coven of followers.

Hal followed the trail Kristilin carved through the ash as the first flash of lighting struck the ground and thunder rumbled. Hal kept his eyes trained on the blue glow of the duster's drive trail, making sure it was not lost in the ash. It was easy to get turned around in such a hostile land.

The blue glow swooped over a hill before coming to a stop. Ruins of age-old buildings lay scattered off to the sides as Hal pulled his duster up to where Kristilin's was and parked it in what appeared to have been an enclosed room of some sort, now open to the elements.

In the distance, the night sky looked like it was in a war. Flashes of lighting painted pictures of abstract designs over the tallest hills, eclipsing the mountains behind them.

Hal took the Lumnis Stone chest in his hands, the sporadic flashes lighting him up like flares overhead. The sight brought back memories of the war, when bombs dropped and flashed the same. As the thunder rumbled, Kristilin joined him, and they entered the stone building.

Much like everything else, the stone refuge was worse for wear. Abandoned to time, ash had intruded on the cobblestone ground and coated the walls with its sickly gray. It looked like time had forgotten about this place.

"I'll see if I can predict when the storm will end," Misselie said. "I'll need your help, Kristilin."

The girls disappeared down a hall, and Hal found himself in the central room with halls extending in several ways. The old structure had so much to tell, having stood against the harshness of Father Time. Wind howled through holes in the ceiling as he entered a room to the rear. He sat on the ground and placed the chest in front of him. Only the wind called out to him, singing a song that made him ask if he should be considering what he was about to do.

The more Hal thought about it, the warier he grew. Personal sacrifice could only go so far, and if he died in the process, all of this would be for nothing. He shook his head and opened the chest. That was if he died. If he didn't do this, the outcome remained the same, and his sister and Varim would have the final say. But if he did, he would be a step ahead of Miri and, more importantly, that snake Varim. Miri was not his true adversary. Varim was the rat, and he was making Imperius his den. He'd used his sister as a pawn in the game he was playing.

As Hal's eyes landed back on the Lumnis Stone, he knew what he needed to do.

A soft knock came from the doorway, and Kristilin leaned against the frame, a concerned pout on her face.

"What are you thinking?" she asked.

"Communing with this thing," Hal replied as his eyes drifted to the stone again.

"Is it safe?" Kristilin asked as she stepped into the room. "I mean, you have just regained your Wielding. Is this the right time?"

"My whole life I've been swayed by what other people thought of me, expected of me, because of my ancestry," Hal said as he looked away. "As a Skyborn and descendent of Emperor Atis and Empress Sarin, our sworn duty was to protect Imperius, protect Athos and her people, and uphold the Code." He sighed and looked back at her. "I'm not perfect. Hell, my family has crumbled in a way that would cause our forefathers to wince in pain, and all because of a fellow countryman. We lost control." Hal pointed at the small stone in front of him. "But if I can commune with this, learn what it holds, then maybe I can stop another world from descending into madness. Athos is hurting, but that doesn't mean Asha has to hurt too."

Smiling, Kristilin knelt beside him and took his hand. "My only worry is if it is safe."

"I won't lie to you. I don't know, Kristi," he said. "I've heard tales from thousands of years ago where the souls of those who tried were sucked away and their bodies turned to ghoulish heathens."

"Are you sure about this, Hal?"

"It could help everyone here if I did," he replied.

She wrapped her arms around him, and Hal returned the embrace. Hal buried his face in the crease of her neck and allowed himself to worry about what was to come. The unknown had always frightened him. But before he could second-guess himself, Kristilin pulled back and placed a kiss on his cheek. Her eyes met his before she leaned forward and pressed her forehead to his.

"If I hear anything, I will barge back in here. Do you understand me?"

"I do."

"Be safe. I love you." She stood back up and closed the door behind her.

As the door latched, his eyes fell back to the stone. The glow of the Lumnis Stone outshined the dark dreariness of the room, and Hal could not tear his eyes away from it.

The light was warm as he took the stone in his hands and placed it on the floor before him. Hal sat tall, his hands outstretched to either side, and took a deep breath. He closed his eyes, and flames grew from his palms like they always did. But in the presence of the Lumnis Stone, his flames were answered by it. Thunderous rattles boomed as if the sound came from right out of his ear. Hal felt his flames shift one way and then to the other, dancing to the sound of the booms.

White light glowed on the inside of his eyes and his eyes danced back and forth to the rhythm of the booms. His face contorted with the pressure the Lumnis Stone exerted upon him. It felt like someone was pressing against his skull with all their might, threatening to burst it, but it was too late to back down. He had to get this done.

With a controlled breath, he relaxed and allowed the Lumnis Stone to access his mind. The pressure turned into a hot dagger that seemed to thrust into the very matter of his brain, probing it until he felt numb.

He saw himself standing in darkness. Thunder crashed overhead, and lightning revealed the stoic branches of tall trees. Then the trees wilted and withered away, replaced by sickly gray ash.

Fire bellowed from deep under the ground and shot high into the air. Smoke hazed the landscape like it had during the war, making it impossible to see even a few feet.

As he stood there, thunderous beats shook the ground. They were like rhythms a bass drummer would use. They grew louder with every second.

He tried to back up, but no matter where he went, the smoke stayed the same around him. He charged his hand, ready to fight, but nothing happened.

Through the haze of smoke, an orange glow approached. It stepped through the veil and revealed itself. Hal looked on with wide eyes. The figure looked both familiar and different at the same time. Only legends had mentioned what he saw, and he wondered if it was real.

Before him stood the ghostly apparition of a Kell, but not the same as before. Flames draped off it like a majestic coat and burned as regal as anything the Empire could have made. Concealed by a hood covered in flames, the Kell stood unwavering. Hal couldn't move, but even if he'd been able to, he didn't want to upset such a noble and revered figure with a sudden movement. He felt small in the presence of the godlike being. He gravitated toward this spirit, and he didn't know why.

The Kell didn't move, but its flames rose high and surrounded Hal. They tightened around him like a constrictor before entering his body. Runes of every sort lined the flame tendrils like codes on computers. Hal could see their meanings, teachings, and the techniques the Wielders had used long ago. Their knowledge became a part of him. Warmth touched his soul, and as he exhaled, flames came from his mouth.

The Kell had blessed him.

This was what his family wanted, to know the true power of charna, and what the high minister wanted to erase: knowledge.

The flames parted, and both he and the Kell looked up. Spatial gasses collided with each other, and rocks flew in every direction, crashing into one another in fiery explosions. Light flashed, and massive rocks collided again while the gasses glowed an array of interstellar colors. Dust sailed by, and Hal saw the whole Athonian star system. He saw every planet and moon, every asteroid and comet, and the twin suns. It changed from one star system into a small interconnecting star community where the Realmverse systems coalesced in the void of space while the Maw encircled it.

He was in awe.

The Realmverse was expansive, but seeing it like this, with Athos as a dot on a map and the Maw's energy field encircling everything like a barrier, showed just how small yet massive the Realmverse was.

The flames went back to the Kell spirit, which gave Hal one last long look with its white-hot eyes before lowering its hood. Hal sank to his knees.

Without a single utterance, his father smiled and nodded. But before he could say anything, the veil of smoke took hold, and everything turned back to darkness.

The beam of energy from the Lumnis Stone stopped its pulses and withdrew back to its core. It slowly lowered back to the ground, the turbulence continuing inside. But unlike before, when the flames inside the stone danced one way, Hal's stayed perfectly still. He commanded them. His eyes darted back and forth under his lids until they calmed down and stayed still like everything else.

When his eyes opened, though, they struggled to remain open. Rapid blinking cleared some of the blur, but an intense pain rocked his head like someone had punched him with all their might. He fought to control his body as the effects of the Lumnis Stone communion rippled through him. After a few moments, his body calmed down, and he took a deep breath. His flames stood proud in his palms like sturdy pillars ready to support the weight to come.

But as he stood, his vision blurred. He braced himself against the wall as light-headedness engulfed his mind. Even trying to lift his arm to rub his head proved impossible. It hurt to blink and think as the Lumnis Stone magic lingered in his body. At least he was still here and not a perished soul like countless others. A small consolation prize, to say the least.

Kristilin entered the room, and her eyes went wide with concern. Like any good nurse, she rushed over to him, draping his arm over her shoulders.

"What is wrong?" Her eyes fell on the Lumnis Stone nearby.

"It has so much . . . knowledge," he said through heavy breaths. "I communed . . . I saw . . ."

"Enough. Let me get you something to keep you upright," she said, leading him across the room.

"Wait . . . The stone . . . We can't leave it here . . ."

"Your health is more important than any stone right now, Halcion Skyborn," Kristilin snapped. "Misselie, get a chair ready!"

With a groan, Hal limped out of the room with a headache to rival any earth-quake.

Old wooden chairs sufficed for a cot as Hal sat with a hand on his forehead, a cup of water beside him. Kristilin watched over him with a hawkish gaze, but the only thing he felt was a drumline booming in his mind. He could see all the runes, the knowledge, flowing into him, enough to fill archives the size of Imperius itself, and he struggled to catalog it all. A sip of water helped more than nothing for a short while.

Misselie entered the central room and placed the chest on the stone table. Ash flew up into the air as she removed her gloves and took a seat. Hal lifted his head up to see what commotion required to be so loud, but the thunderous booms within him forced him to bury his head back down.

"He actually communed with it?" Misselie asked.

"I do not know whether to be proud of or angry at him," Kristilin said.

"Both," Hal groaned.

"Only legends or fools attempt a communion with a godlike stone without any knowledge on how to do so," Misselie said as she picked up her data receiver. "While you two were gawking at the stone back at the temple, look what I found."

She slid the tablet to the center of the table, where a holomap projected into the air. Mapped much like the known world, five beacons glowed. Hal stirred and looked at the map, the yellow markers gaining his attention.

"A map?" Hal said as he turned to face the projection.

"The Lumnis Stones," Misselie replied. "There are five stones in total, created by the ancient Wielders of Atis's coven. They might have Primordial connections too, but I'm not sure yet. Each stone is marred by a different sect of charna, containing the secrets and teachings of thousands of years in each Wielding art form."

"Sounds like something Miri would want," Kristilin said as she looked at Hal and gently rubbed his back.

"Her goal lies with the stone we have," Hal replied, looking back at her. "We beat her to it. But if she knows there are others, she won't stop."

A boom of thunder crashed above them and rocked the small structure as the lights cut out. The room fell silent. Hal reached for his lightvolver, keeping an ear out for anything that sounded strange, but silence filled that void. When nothing happened, he figured lightning had struck what little remaining power supply they had, but the creak of a door made him turn his head.

Energy bolts flew through the air.

Despite his better judgment, Hal cast a ward of fire in front of him while the girls sought cover. The energy bolts slammed into the energy ward, hitting with such impact that he felt the vibrations in the palm of his hands. When the girls were safe behind cover and returned fire, Hal set his eyes on the dark armored Praetorians and turned the protective ward into two whips of fire. The soldiers turned to him, but it was too late.

Hal leapt in and threw his fire whips at those who'd tried to harm him, striking their armor with a hiss from his flames. More soldiers fired at him, but each evasion or absorption of their blaster bolts was followed by another downed body. Bright flames lit up the darkness, and Hal shot his whip at the final Imperial, sending them back through the tunnel they'd crawled out of.

Though sweat poured down his nose and the drums in his mind had not stopped, he focused and listened. When nothing else happened, he doubled over and gasped for breath. It was clear that the knowledge the Lumnis Stone had gifted came with a price, and he had to pay it. He only wished it could come later.

Kristilin bolted to him, and she stood him upright to inhale more oxygen. Misselie peeked around the corner the assailants had come through in case more returned, but when none did, she regrouped with Hal.

"Praetorians . . ." Hal said. "They tracked us here."

"Then we need to go," Misselie said as she went to secure the Lumnis Stone chest.

Another boom echoed through the ghostly halls, and as Hal looked up, the holes in the ceiling grew larger. He barely had enough time to alert the others before dust and ash filled the room and the first rays of morning light shined through.

Chunks of concrete pinned his body to the ground. The haze of ash made it hard to see the girls, but as he looked up, the sight both frightened and angered him. Praetorians rappelled from the hole in the ceiling and touched down, but one stood out in particular. Engraved in one of the soldier's armor was the fire hawk symbol. As the soldier moved closer to him, the soldier's metal arm aimed a plasma rifle at him. Miri's loyal guard, Neeux, had tracked them, and he was after one thing: the chest.

Hal tried to move, but the concrete debris pinned his arms down, and all he could do was watch Neeux grab the chest and ascend back through the ceiling, the roar of a transport ship fading through the distance.

Pain and exhaustion rocked his body as ash rained down from above, and his vision faded to darkness.

Chapter XXXVII

When Hal's eyes opened, he leaned up from the cot and went to touch his aching head. As he looked around, ash fluttered through the stale air. Out the window, an ashstorm brewed, and wind swept across the wooden walkways.

The bandages wrapped tightly around his shoulder pulled on his skin as he tried to push himself up to stand. His body screamed at him to stop, and it didn't take long for his curtains to be thrown aside. Kristilin wrapped her arms around him with a sigh of relief, and he returned her embrace.

She pulled back. "How are you feeling?" she asked, her accent sweet to his ear.

"Sore. Like always," he said with a smirk, earning a smile from her. "How about you?"

Kristilin stood up and shrugged. "Scratches, but that is all. Misselie barely had a mark on her."

Hal stood and looked past her to where Ashborn agents worked on monitors, others using headphones to listen for communications. Dust fluttered from the rocky ceiling while the clang of picks hitting rocks echoed from further within the cave system. They were not in Hellas.

He looked back to Kristilin. "Ashen pulled us out?"

She nodded. "Misselie said this is one of their home cities. Torval Keep. Its cave passages run throughout the mountain."

An Ashen agent donned in worn armor and a red cloak approached them, and Hal stood tall despite the bandages.

The Ashen agent removed their helmet, and Hal stared into his one good eye while the other was protected by a leather patch.

An old war injury, Hal thought.

"Prince Halcion," the agent said with a salute to the chest. "I am Elder Mixa, Ashen captain. We have much to discuss. If you are able, please follow me."

The Ashen spun on his heel and headed down the cave path he had come from. Hal went to follow, but the pain in his body from the communion made him brace himself against the wall. Kristilin helped, and he placed an arm around her again and walked down the tunnel with her support.

Under orblight, Hal approached the holotable where the Ashen leader stood. Misselie stood beside him and offered a small smile before the holomap came to life at the captain's touch.

"Commander Jorrin and our forces have intercepted messages from the Imperial encampments within the base," Elder Mixa said. "The weather across the Ashlands leaves us all in a state of darkness, which means the Imperials can't work on the Gate either."

Hal looked at the map, and the ashstorm stretched from one side of the land to the other. His gaze shifted to the captain. "Which means we can't move?"

Elder Mixa nodded. "Storms like these come occasionally, and they are nothing to be toyed with. The wind speeds will melt the skin from your bones. If you have an evosuit, you'll last a while longer. You'll stay here until it passes."

Before Hal could protest, Kristilin placed an arm around him. He collected himself before speaking again.

"We can't stay here."

The Ashen elder looked at him with a wary eye. "There is no other way. You're injured, and the ferocity of the storm is building. I cannot let you leave in these conditions. Jorrin would have my head."

"We need to get back to Hellas, Elder Mixa. She has it."

"The Lumnis Stone," Elder Mixa said. "I know of it."

"Then you know why we need to return to Hellas and formulate a plan."

"There is nothing I can do to control the forces of nature, Prince Halcion. I am sorry."

The Ashen leader saluted and moved on through the encampment, leaving Hal at the holotable.

Hal felt useless, stuck in a state of inaction, and the itch to do something grew with every passing moment.

"Hal?" Kristilin placed a hand on his shoulder.

"I'm fine, Kristi. I just feel stagnant here. By now the stone will be in my sister's hands."

"And she can't go anywhere," Misselie said from the other side of the holotable. "The Gate is inoperative, and she would be a fool to try to fly out of here while the storm ravages the land."

What she'd said made sense, but that did not make it any easier to accept. A twinge of pain jolted through his head, and placed a hand on his temple. Kristilin stepped forward, but Hal waved her off.

"It's nothing. I just need to meditate."

The pout on her face told him he had not convinced her. "Are you sure? After the communion?"

"As sure as my feelings for you are," Hal said, hoping the compliment would make for an easy escape. Misselie smirked and rolled her eyes.

Kristilin shook her head with a smile. "You really did hit your head. If you need me, I will be with Misselie."

He kissed her forehead before retreating into the caverns of the keep. Little light guided his way as he walked. He charged his hand and pressed forward. Dripping water echoed through the cave system, and shadows flickered along the walls. He followed the tunnel, and it widened until he came to a large cavern. Mounds of ash were built up along the rim, and brackets of rotted torch handles sat alone higher up. But that was not what caught his attention.

Hal stood in front of an old starship. The semicircle design with the protruding bridge was something he hadn't seen before. It was smaller than a standard transport ship but larger than a starfighter, and he reasoned it to be some sort of freighter class vessel.

Ash coated its oxidized hull, but Hal felt drawn to it. He walked closer and used a hand to wipe a line of loose ash away, revealing the silver metal underneath. He gave it the walk around like any enterprising young captain would when they were about to purchase a ship. A small button lay on the side where the cargo hold would be, and with a push, the loading ramp hissed open, stale air flowing out.

Inside, the ship had seen better days. Damaged floor panels exposed piping, and the local spider population seemed to call this place home. Empty containers and bags stood in the corners of the cargo hold while a few hung from shelves.

Hal mounted the ladder and pulled himself up to the main deck, which had fared a bit better. He turned around and ran into a spiderweb the size of his head. After a brief panic, he ignited his hand and burned the sticky trap away.

Based on the holomap in the central room, he could tell this was a Mark VII Starrunner jumpship. He remembered his grandfather owning one when he was just a child and the trips they would go on across the Empire. It had made him want to see everything the Realmverse had to offer, and as he placed a hand on the old holotable, he realized he was doing that now. He shook his head with a smile and took a deep breath as he looked at what the ship had to offer.

As he walked by, a door slid open, and Hal was almost too quick on his draw. But no stowed-away droid lay in wait to attack him. Inside the small room was a set of royal Imperial robes. Smuggled or hidden away, the means of how they'd ended up here mattered not. Hal eyed the old robes, which were the same as those he'd worn over his armor for nearly two years while at war. Dated and tattered, they reminded him of days past. As he ran a hand across the robes, the soft silk reached out to grab him in a familiar embrace. Until the world was righted, he would forever don the burden of hope that came with those robes.

Hal slid back down the ladder to the cargo bay. Very few seemed to come here, which made it a perfect place to meditate in solace.

He remembered when he and his sister would meditate together. The sensation had been outstanding. As Hal found a seat on the ground, the thought struck a chord with him. He wished to have those days back, to find joy in the comfort of his sister. In the current state of things, that seemed more like a dream.

Fire energy charged in his palms as he took a deep breath. He cleared his thoughts, focusing on the fire within. Another deep breath followed. His stress and pain were channeled into strength from the deepest parts of his body to the outermost extremities. The fire grew, wrapping him with its warmth. The runes and teachings he'd absorbed brewed within. He said them in Primordial, seeing their imprints on his eyelids. Their teachings spoke back to him and entered deeper into his mind. The pain reemerged in his mind, but it was quickly stomped out by the power he now understood, the knowledge that the Primordials hid from others but had gifted to him. It all became clear. When his eyes opened, he saw the new power he wielded.

He focused on a box in front of him. The rest of the room faded from his vision until only the box remained. His eyes narrowed in concentration. Warmth built in him, caressed him, until he felt a connection with the box. Smoke started to rise, and the first flame sparked and ignited the dry wood.

Fire shot out of his hands, lighting up the cargo bay with flashes of superheated flames. But instead of crashing into the box, the flames stood frozen. The force from the energy extinguished the flames and circulated the little smoke in the air. Unified in strength, the wild flames formed a cylindrical stream. No stray lick of fire flicked out.

With his other hand, Hal formed his fire charna into a swordlike weapon sculpted to his will. Hal eyed the light of fire he'd created and held. Flames flowed behind it as he swung it through the air, power and control all rolled into a single spell. Hal moved through the cargo bay, swinging the sword at imaginary targets with grace and fury.

Swordsmanship was a skill he was accustomed to, although he had no reason to use it in the palace, but his skills were nothing compared to what Kristilin could do. He used his other hand to cast a ward behind him before he threw the sword out of the cargo bay, where it struck the rock wall outside. The sword plunged into it like the rocks were made of hay, and as he reached his hand out to it, the energy from the sword returned to him.

Hal walked over to where a hanging bag stood, his fists charged with energy. He touched it, the energy from his fist making the bag sway while the frayed ends burned away. A harder tap and the bag swung with the force of a punch without his fist ever touching it. Hal smiled and got into a fighting stance. As he cocked back and brought his fist forth, the bag exploded into embers that sparked through the cargo bay like fireworks.

Hal looked around at his handiwork. Charna was a destructive force. But where destruction reigned, rebirth followed. That was the key principle to understanding his gift: destruction and rebirth went hand in hand.

As he stepped back, a ball of fire formed in his hand, and he threw it. It hovered out to the center of the room and stopped where he commanded, illuminating the darkness.

Kristilin entered the cargo bay, her arms crossed in front of her, while Hal stood with flames dancing in his hands. He looked at her, and his smile slowly faded. He was a bit embarrassed she'd caught him, but he should have known better than to try to trick a Vel.

"I should have suspected this," Kristilin said.

Misselie popped her head in too. "Look at this ship!" she exclaimed, then went straight for the ladder.

Kristilin shook her head with a half-smile. "You said you needed to lie down."

"Actually, I said I needed to meditate, which I did," Hal replied.

"Right," she said with a roll of her eyes. She looked around the cargo bay. "A new transmission came through from Jorrin. Elder Mixa wants you there."

Hal pointed behind him. "Did I tell you about the ship I found?"

Kristilin smacked him in the arm, then called for Misselie. The fire diminished from his hand as Hal looked back around the cargo bay. Meditation had never felt so good. He slung an arm around Kristilin and headed for the holotable, Misselie close behind them.

A holographic form of Commander Jorrin stood to the side of the table and watched as they entered.

"Welcome, Lord Hal," Jorrin said as Hal stepped up to the holotable. "I see you have found refuge in one of our settlements."

"Commander. It's much appreciated."

"Elder Mixa has no doubt told you about the weather situation. First ash-storm?"

He shook his head. "Not quite. I've been in a few since I arrived."

"None like this."

Hal leaned over the table. "With all due respect, Commander, I know you didn't call for me to ask about the weather."

Commander Jorrin fixed his gaze on Hal. "Perceptive. No, I didn't." He rubbed his thick beard. "Battle preparations were underway when some of my scouts picked up Imperial transmissions."

"What kind?"

Jorrin nodded to the captain, who pressed a few buttons on the holotable. An image of a seeker bot appeared on screen with full diagnostics.

"Code words back and forth mentioned a 'Bridge.' My scouts have linked it to this seeker bot, but the reason is unknown."

Hal eyed the image of the bot. "I can tell you why. Seeker bots are smart—pro-grammed, but smart. The Gate needs an activation code before it'll be opera-tional, but the code is in Primordial. I bet any amount of luck that the seeker bot has the code and is transporting it to a safe location. It's what I did during the war. That raises concern though."

"Elaborate, Prince Halcion," Jorrin said.

"Though I found the codes for the Athonian Gate, it was Miri who deciphered them. She has more insight as to how they work. Those under her know what they're doing."

Jorrin nodded as he stroked his beard. "That would explain the buildup of Imperial forces along the Jaded Ridge." The screen returned to the map and zoomed in on a ridgeline of massive rocks spiking up from the ground. The Imperial structures that had been built upon the rocky ledges seemed to withstand the storm, protected by the ridge. "Abandoned years ago, these structures have become alive again with Imperials."

"Where's the seeker bot?"

"Our scouts have tracked it," Elder Mixa added. He moved the map to an area where the storm was light. "It's moving southwest at a steady pace."

"Right to the camp," Hal said.

He took control of the map and calculated the reasonable path the bot would take. No other Imperial camps were present this far north, which made the ridge even more apparent. Hal looked back at the commander.

"We can't let that bot reach the camp. If it does, Miri will have the codes and escape with the stone or invite a larger force into the Ashlands."

"I can't risk my soldiers. We are already too few," Jorrin said. "In time we will have enough from supporting clans."

"That's right," another voice said as a hologram formed next to the commander. Asher appeared and crossed his arms. "We can't spread our forces too thin if we are to strike the fortress near the Gate."

"The seeker bot has what we need to stop the Imperial garrison there, Asher," Jorrin replied.

While the leaders squabbled, the beacon that represented the bot moved toward the ridge map marker at a snail's pace. The storm could last for days, even weeks, and they did not have that time to spare. His sister could've already been learning the secrets of the Primordials, and that was reason enough to go.

"I'll go," he said.

"That's suicide," Elder Mixa said. "Nobody in their right mind would venture out into a storm like this."

"Doing nothing is suicide. Those codes can't get to my sister until the battle plans are finished," Hal said in a stern tone. "If nobody will take the risk, then I will."

"You will not be alone," Kristilin said.

Hal nodded. He looked at Misselie. "I need you to secure transport and get back to Hellas. Monitor the situation and keep eyes on that seeker bot's signal."

Elder Mixa scoffed. "You can't give orders here."

Commander Jorrin cleared his throat. "Prince Halcion has free rein in this matter, Captain. Our concern is the inevitable conflict that will arise. I need you to raise awareness with your surrounding clans. The prince is right. If we do nothing, we will all die here."

Despite a disgruntled growl, the wary elder stepped back. Misselie nodded at Hal before she tended to her data receiver.

"That old ship should work," Misselie said. "If there is enough power, I can triangulate the seeker bot's signal from the holotable onboard. I wouldn't have to fly until the storm clears."

"Do it," Hal said.

"Be safe, Misselie," Kristilin said before the two exchanged a hug and Misselie disappeared through the halls.

Hal looked at Kristilin. "Ready?"

"Always."

He smirked. "Let's go hunt."

CHAPTER XXXVIII

Powerful winds whipped across the landscape. Light faded from the faintly lit ground, and in crept the cold grip of darkness as ash rained down on the whirlwind of hostility below. On the ground, the ashstorm hazed the land.

The vehicle they traveled in was anything but subtle, but one Hal found interesting: a landship. It was the size of two currus put together but lacked the propulsion to hover, and he felt every bump, incline, and decline over the nasty terrain. It was a metal machine made only for the violent nature of Asha. Its tracks mowed through the ash with relative ease, the grinding of gears muffled by the howl of the wind. Debris whipped against the steel shell of the landship like gunshots, nature's way of testing their resolve or their wit, but Hal sat unfazed, used to the similar sound war brought. He looked out the window only to see a sickly screen of gray.

"Beautiful, is it not?" Kristilin said from the driver's seat. "Most people would be scared to travel in such a storm."

"We're not most people," Hal said as he swung the chair back around.

"True." Kristilin smiled and shifted the gears inside the cockpit, and the landship replied with a gentle thrust of power. "Athos has its wildfires and hurricanes, and Velra has its blizzards. We are accustomed to nature and its ferocity."

Hal nodded. Nature could be a beautiful scene or a devastating witch. He had seen both.

He remembered the great fire that had burned much of the forests near Imperius. Windstorms engulfed with fire had rocked the very center of the nation and had taken many things with them. The heartland struggled with food shortages for years after, but with destruction came rebirth. He made sure to remind his people about that, the Code. It had been tough those few years, but they'd come through it stronger than ever. All it took was dedication and sheer willpower. Everyone had fought for what they needed and learned the hard work it took, though some had refused such a notion. *Dishonorable Codebreakers*, he thought.

The ashstorm was a different kind of beast. Wicked and uncaring, it brought its touch to everything and served no purpose but to aggravate. It held all the power of a hurricane and all the bitter cold of a blizzard. It was a literal hell.

"What do you think has become of the other star nations?" Hal asked as he shifted in his seat.

Kristilin glanced over at him. "I do not know. If what we have seen is true, that Varim plotted with the world leaders, then I can only hope our people rise up to challenge them. Misguided democracies are no better than dictatorships."

Hal looked at the metal floor of the landship. He'd always seen himself as a warrior and a patriot of the Imperial Code. His morals were his guiding principles, and he hoped Kristilin was right. Issues had been apparent before the war—anyone with a glass eye could see them—but he favored the path not many politicians walked, that of common sense, perhaps because he was no politician. If that was going to change, more prudent minds would have to rise.

He closed his eyes and took a deep breath. Atis and Sarin had revolted against the tyrannical rule of the celestial Primordials for similar reasons.

The fate of the Realmverse was in their hands.

"We are nearing the camp," Kristilin said.

Under concealment of the wind, the landship rolled to a stop just out of view of the watchtowers' lights. Hal moved to the front of the vehicle with a set of binocs and surveyed the area, taking in as much as he could. A door was silhouetted by the glow of the watchtower light. No soldiers were in sight, which made it the perfect entry point.

"Single door," he said as he put the binocs away. "The ash will give us cover to move."

"We will not have to worry about thermal optics either," Kristilin said as she grabbed her pack. "Nothing gets through a storm this dense."

Hal raised his hood and mask before looking at Kristilin. When she nodded, Hal hit the rear hatch button. The rear door of the vehicle lowered, and the wind instantly swept in. Ash coated the seats and floor, bringing the bitter cold with it. Hal peered into the void for a second more before jumping out and into the storm.

Trudging through the knee-high ash, Hal and Kristilin rushed to the door without detection by the spotlights. It required a passcode key. By now his personal code would have been wiped from Imperial databases, and so would his mother's. If he used his father's, that would draw too much suspicion from the commanders of this installation.

Only one would be reasonable.

As he leaned over the keypad, cold began to creep through his suit, sending a shiver up his spine. Kristilin's jaw was beginning to chatter as the effect of the storm set in.

All it took was a few taps on the keypad to punch Miri's code in, and the red bar above the lock turned green. Hal gently pulled on the handle and peeked inside to see a room of cargo and limited supplies. They stepped in and closed the door, then dusted the ash off their clothes. Hal lowered his face mask, analyzing the scene. Limited supplies meant the camp had few soldiers, which played in their favor.

Kristilin stepped forward and held out a small scanner. "I count over three dozen Imperials. Looks more like a skeleton crew, no?"

"By design," Hal said as he moved to the doorway and looked up and down the hall. "During the war, I used diversionary tactics to trick the Polarians. Miri is likely doing the same. False security. Something else is probably here."

Imperial soldiers rounded the corner of the hallway, and Hal ducked back into the shadows of the room with Kristilin. The soldiers passed by, muttering about different topics. When a door opened and the soldiers disappeared, Hal turned back to Kristilin.

"We need to find the layout of this facility."

Kristilin pointed to where the soldiers had come from. "If we are to believe this map, beyond those doors is a security room."

Hal looked down the hall, and his gaze fell upon a security camera in the corner of the ceiling, red light blinking. Once they took a step out, whoever was on that camera would spot them in an instant. It had to be neutralized. Hal followed the conduit on the ceiling down the hall and over them. Inside the room, it continued across the top of the doorway and into a wall just beside them. Hal reached for the panel and pulled it open to see the conduit enter a junction.

Kristilin looked at him like he was mad. "What are you doing?"

"The conduit from that camera leads into this junction," Hal said as he searched the room for something made of suitable insulation. When he found an old tire, he slid it next to the junction and stood on it. "We can't let anyone know we're here. Not yet."

"So, what are you planning?"

Hal looked at the conduit line mixing with the other circuitry components, then back at Kristilin. "You might want to take a step back."

A buzz went through his body as his hand latched on to the conduit. Flames charged from his hand, heating up the wires, and sparks flew. When a bright flash and smoke came from inside the junction, he knew it had been done. Hal looked back to the camera, and the red light was gone. It had worked. But Kristilin had a less-than-amused face that begged for an explanation.

"Electricity hates heat. Heat causes failures. If I overloaded the circuitry, then we wouldn't have to worry about the camera or anything it was connected to."

"You could have said that," she said with a light smack to his arm. "Now let us go before someone comes to repair this."

Hal smirked. "After you, madam."

They hurried to the door. The silence in the halls was enough to cause that devilish chill to return, and Hal's heart raced. If they were discovered, there was no telling what would happen.

Kristilin peeked through as the door slid open, then stepped inside, and Hal followed. They hurried to the terminal, where another keypad lay in wait. But before he typed anything in, Hal looked through the windows, and inside one of the containment cells was Stravis. His heart sank at the sight, a numbness filling his body.

"Oh my," Kristilin whispered beside him.

Time became even more precious. Now they had to transition into a rescue, because by the gods, he was not going to leave the old man behind in this forsaken base. Hal entered his sister's code again, but the red bar remained the same color. He tried again to no avail.

"What is wrong?"

"It's not taking the code," Hal said as he tried again, hoping he'd entered a wrong digit. If someone was onto them, it was only a matter of time before the whole base was on lockdown. Stravis needed them.

As he worked, an Imperial soldier rounded the corner, then froze when Hal looked up to see him. Hal raised a hand to calm the officer.

"Easy," Hal said as he stood up and showed himself to the officer, too late to hide. "You don't want to do this."

"It's you. The traitorous prince," the officer said with a tremble, fumbling for the communications device on his belt. "She was right. You did come."

Hal acted fast. He sprinted to the officer, who had just grabbed his communications device, and tackled him to the ground. They tossed and turned on the floor until Hal wrapped his arms around the officer's neck and pinned him down. Seconds went by as the officer kicked and tried to scream, muffled by Hal's hand. Hal stared at the gray wall, thinking about what he was doing and what he had done. He hated every moment of it. But it was necessary. When the officer lost consciousness, Hal pushed the officer off him and took the credentials stuffed inside the officer's uniform.

He returned to Kristilin, a little sweatier than before, and swiped the card through the slot. The red bar turned green, and the door opened. Hal looked up, and the cameras in the halls were still off. Kristilin entered first and quickly went to Stravis. With the push of a button, the energy fields around the containment cell disappeared, and she placed her fingers on the old man's neck. Hal stepped closer, and Stravis's face was covered in bruises.

"He still has a pulse," she said. "Stravis, can you hear me?"

The old man opened his eyes slowly and groaned. "Beware the lies of the mad queen . . . for she seeks—" Stravis coughed. "Retribution."

"Hey, Stravis. Don't you give up on me. Wake up," Hal said as he began to pump the old man's chest. "Get up. Misselie is waiting for you. Come on."

"Hal . . ."

"I'm not losing you."

"Hal," Kristilin said with a stern tone.

He looked over to her. Her eyes pleaded with him, but he could not give up on the old man. He used every ounce of strength he had to continue compressions on Stravis's chest.

He wouldn't die here in a cold cell. He didn't deserve that.

With muscles beginning to burn, Hal gave the old man's chest a final punch and brought his ear down to listen. One beat. Two beats. And after a few seconds, the heartbeats grew stronger, although weak.

Kristilin grabbed Stravis's limp wrist. "He has a pulse, but it is very weak. We have to get him to the landship," she said. She pulled a small syringe from one of the pouches on her belt and injected it into Stravis's neck. "This will buy us time to get him back. What did he mean by 'Beware the mad queen for she seeks retribution'?"

"Primordial Queen Xirna. Old legends say that although Atis defeated her and locked her away in the Kaleidosphere, she's still influencing the Realmverse to this day." Hal shook his head. "Lord Carnn spoke of this, and I didn't believe it then, but Stravis would not say something like that out of nowhere. He saw something, heard something, to make him believe. By Empyrea, what are we going to do?"

"Continue what we set out for. We owe it to Stravis, Misselie, and the rest of the Ashborn," Kristilin said as she handed the datapad to him.

Hal nodded. As Kristilin tended to Stravis, Hal approached one of the security terminals and plugged the datapad in. He navigated the installation's interface and brought up the schematics. A ping of the bot's signature appeared, and he followed the maze of routes from the security center until he found the rear storage bay where it sat. It felt like all the air vanished from his lungs.

"Anything?" Kristilin asked.

He unplugged the datapad and handed it back to her. "We need to go now. Whoever is in charge of the download is probably already there. We don't have time. Let's grab Stravis and move."

Alarms sounded off through the halls. Hal and Kristilin moved to the windows to see red lights flashing, and the lights in the halls dimmed. The doors they'd come through opened to reveal a squad of Imperial soldiers. Hal ducked under the glass and locked the door from the inside. He heard them enter codes on the other side and the buzz of denial soon after. Lockdown.

He looked over at Kristilin. "We've got to find a way out of here and to that bot."

Kristilin looked at her datapad, which was now filled with new information. She pointed to a spot in the room. "Crawlspace. It leads up to the service tubes and toward the storage bay."

"Work on it," Hal said as the security door opened.

Before the first soldier could enter, Hal launched a ball of fire into them. Blaster fire erupted and slammed into his ward, the impacts vibrating in his palms. He stood guard in the doorway as more soldiers flooded in, some trying to rush through him. They were met with the force of fire and thrown back as Hal stood grounded.

The clang of a metal panel hitting the ground caught his attention. As he looked back, Kristilin heaved Stravis up and motioned for him to follow. Backing up, he threw more fireballs followed by streams of flames, keeping the Imperials at bay. Blaster bolts came from behind him and downed a few of the soldiers so

Hal could duck into the crawlspace. He attacked the soldiers with another volley of flames, then grabbed the panel and pulled it closed. He held it in place, and flames from his opposite hand welded the panel shut just before the first dent in the metal followed. He sighed a deep breath before turning and joining Kristilin at the ladder.

Hal hoisted himself up to the crawlspace above as more bangs came from the welded panel below. It would only be a matter of time until the Imperials found out what they were after, but he had a feeling his sister already knew. They had to work fast.

He followed Kristilin through the space, the metal walls seemingly closing in on them as they crawled on their hands and knees, taking turns pulling Stravis along. At any point the ceiling could give out and they could fall right into a detachment of soldiers.

Kristilin led him through the tunnels as silently as two mice trying to evade an ever-looming cat. When the sheet metal buckled, Hal froze and listened. Soldiers ran under him as the walls continued to flash red. After they passed, he continued to crawl along.

Kristilin sat in front of another access ladder and waited for him before she slid down. Hal lowered the old man down before descending the ladder.

At the bottom, Kristilin gently pushed on the access panel and peeked through. The seeker bot sat in a stall alone at the back of the room. Its one eye rotated, signaling it was still powered up. As Kristilin was about to emerge from the access tubes, the door to the room opened. Kristilin recoiled and looked at Hal.

"It is a soldier."

Hal peeked through the panel as the Imperial rushed to the seeker bot and plugged something into it.

Transfer of the codes, he thought. Hal emerged from the hiding spot and drew his weapon.

"Don't move," he said in a commanding tone, aiming his lightvolver at the soldier.

The Imperial tensed and slowly turned, putting his hands up.

"This is far beyond you, soldier," Hal said. "Walk away."

For a second, Hal thought the term '*soldier*' had gotten through to him, like he had heard it before. His face changed, but when he reached for his sidearm, Hal had no choice.

Hal pulled the trigger, and the soldier dropped to the ground. Beside the body lay a small datacard with an upload signal on it. Hal scooped it up and looked at the seeker bot, whose eye oscillated in return. He raised his weapon and fired a single shot through the bot's metal husk. It dropped to the ground with the soldier, blood and oil mixing.

"Fastest way back to the landship?" Hal asked as he turned to Kristilin.

"Through that door. It leads to a maintenance tunnel that goes toward where we parked."

Hal hurried to the door and swiped the keycard. When it opened, he jumped down the small ledge, helping Kristilin down after him. Rock and dust stretched all the way up and down the tunnel with only the dim flicker of overused lights to illuminate the way. As the door closed behind them, Hal charged his hand with firelight. They pressed forward with the muffled shouts of soldiers in the distance, dragging an unconscious Stravis.

Chapter XXXIX

A fter nearly a day traveling through the storm, the landship rolled up to the gates of Hellas where Ashborn soldiers met it with an old wooden cart. Hal flung the back hatch open and ordered the soldiers to carry the unconscious Stravis to the town hospital. But before he and Kristilin could follow, Jorrin stopped them.

"Come, we have things to discuss."

"We have to make sure Stravis is all right," Hal said.

"The doctors will bring him back to health," Jorrin said. "Right now, we have more pressing matters."

Hal watched the cart carrying Stravis disappear around the street corner before he looked back at Kristilin and followed the commander.

Hal found himself in Asher's Hall. A deafening silence fell over the roundtable. Each member stood stiff, expressions uncertain. The air was thicker than a humid summer's night. The news did not make him happy either. He of all people knew the cost of being a second late. But to these people, many of whom had not seen battle like he had, it was worse than defeat itself. He should've known his sister had a trick up her sleeve. All he could do was stare at the gray whirlwind before him as it took up most of the holotable projection.

Asher adjusted his leather coat and cleared his throat. "How late?"

The communication officer who'd delivered the news shifted his stance. "It wasn't an account of being late. The seeker bot constructed duplicate codes."

"But Hal shot the bot," Kristilin said.

"Its memory cortex still holds data," Hal said. "All you need to do is upload it to a secure terminal and download its data."

The commander leaned over the holotable and sighed.

The news only made their fight that much more important, and the next action they took as a new alliance would decide their fate.

"They have the codes," Asher said as he rubbed the side of his head. "Once the portal is activated, they'll send an invasion fleet, and we'll be subject to Imperial rule yet again. Our ancestors were sentenced here, escaped here, and now we will feel their wrath again."

"Not if we head there now," Commander Jorrin said. "We take the fight to the Imperials before they get the chance to use those codes."

"In this storm?" Asher asked. "Kristilin and Prince Halcion barely made it back in one piece with Stravis."

"The storm is the largest this land has seen in a century, and you want to launch an attack, sir?" Elder Mixa asked, drawing the commander's gaze.

"What choice do we have? If we don't, then our home is dead, destined to live in servitude." He pounded his fists on the table, shaking the communicators and datacards to the ground. After a moment of silence and a heavy breath, the commander collected himself. "We've spent too long proving this is our home too. We fought for it. Bled for it in our own name. We are Ashborn."

"And it is our home," Asher stated. "But we need you around to help protect it." He looked at Hal. "What do you think, Prince Halcion?"

All eyes turned to him, seeming to ask for guidance and advice. He leaned over the table, his fingers leaving behind imprints on the screen.

During the war he would always plan out the course of action, but that was before the action started. The unexpected was what he couldn't plan for. Adapting was just as important as a plan, and that was exactly what they faced now. They were right in the middle of it, and their only option was to adapt. That was the nature of warfare, to attack and counterattack and always be a step ahead of the enemy. As he looked into Kristilin's eyes, and then Misselie's, he knew they saw him as a sign of hope, someone who had gone through it before and had come out on top.

He took a deep breath. "We have no other choice but to assault the fortress at the foot of the Gate."

Jacger and Commander Jorrin stood a little straighter, but Hal was quick to raise a hand and stave off any protests from the others.

"But we have to be calculated." He looked at the map as it zoomed in on the fort. "The key is to get inside, open it up, and deactivate the Gate."

"So, what's the plan?" Asher asked.

Hal leaned forward on the table and eyed the mighty base. "We need a diversion along the forward-facing edge so a small team can penetrate the fortress. Under the cover of ash, they won't see us coming until we're too close. These rock formations can be used to conceal the majority of our forces until we're ready." Hal panned the map around the base and pointed at a cave along its side. Highlighted, it showed a path through the rocks and into the facility. "That small team would enter here through a service port and gain access to the facility. We open the doors and neutralize the Gate."

"What about the Lumnis Stone?" Kristilin asked.

Hal stared at the hologram. "I'll deal with that."

Asher and Commander Jorrin exchanged a look.

"Your thoughts, Commander?"

Commander Jorrin cracked his knuckles and smiled. "I trust in the commander who won the Polarian War."

Hal nodded at the commander. Though this was not the place to outwardly show his appreciation, that little statement went a long way in reinforcing his resolve.

"We need something to rally behind," Elder Mixa said. "We are a mixture of clans with banners of different meanings. If we are to show unity against the invaders, then we need something we all can cherish."

While the other men debated what was best to use, Hal looked at Misselie across the table.

"Misselie, do you have an idea?" Hal said.

The leaders stopped their debate for a moment, and all eyes turned to Misselie. She looked at Hal like a surprised deer before she spoke.

"Oh. Um. I mean . . ."

"As a child of the ash, this is as much your decision as anyone's," Hal said.

She hugged her body as she looked down. After a short ponderance, she spoke.

"Stravis spoke of a symbol found all over the Ashlands. It wasn't Primordial in nature, but he thought it was the first sigil of these lands that was used by the first inhabitants that came to the planet. It had a wolf head with several glowing yellow eyes etched onto the backdrop of the great mountain. He said it roamed the ashlands as a guardian of the lands."

Asher moved from the table and went to a row of books along the back wall. After scouring their contents, he pulled a book from the shelf and returned to the table, placing it down. On the cover was the same wolf Misselie had described.

"The Rigorbite, used by the first Ashen," he said as he looked at Jorrin and Mixa.

"Able to roam the ash whenever it wants," Jorrin said. "Mythical, but it describes what we all want."

"Freedom," Mixa said.

"Then it's settled. Thank you, Misselie."

Asher nodded, and Misselie nodded back. She looked at Hal, and he winked.

"We'll strike the day after tomorrow, when the storm clears a bit. There is still much to prepare for," Asher said. "I suggest we not take these next days for granted. There's no telling what the future will hold, but if we fight in the footsteps of the future Crown Prince, then we should know nothing but victory."

The short but roaring speech was enough to arouse an applause from most of those around the roundtable. Hal could not help but smile at the show of unity these new allies displayed, and it gave him some desperate hope. They'd even gone so far as to name him the future Crown Prince. It sent warmth cascading through his body.

Kristilin did not join the applause, and before he could do anything, she disappeared in the shuffle after the meeting. He went to follow, but a short beep from the holotable caught his attention. It beeped again while his eyes lingered on the doors Kristilin had gone through. Fists balling up, he turned and approached the table, tapping the button that had sent the first beep.

A hologram of the cloaked figure from the enclave, Fable, appeared. Hal stood with his arms crossed and patience at a low. Static took hold of the communication before Fable spoke.

"Greetings, Prince Halcion."

"I don't have the time. We have more pressing matters to attend to," Hal stated, not wanting to give away more detailed information. "What do you want?"

"To share a sliver of information we have discovered," Fable said. "Do you remember the unrest the Empire felt a year ago?"

"I was at war then," Hal said with a raised brow.

Fable nodded. "Which is why you were spared. Tell me, Prince Halcion, does this seem familiar to you?"

An image of a purple crystal appeared beside Fable. Hal studied it for a moment and noted the stress cracks lining it from top to bottom. The center shined brighter compared to the dim points of the crystal. The translucent swirl mark in the core revealed exactly what it was.

"That's Queen Xirna's stone necklace."

"You know what it is, but do you know what it does?"

"It was the necklace Atis severed from the queen when he sealed her away in the Kaleidosphere, after she used Madness on Sarin," Hal said. "Why are you showing me this now?"

But as soon as he said that, pieces of the puzzle began to click in his mind. A short video clip appeared on the opposite side of Fable's figure, and Hal furrowed his brow. Varim stood over a podium with a fist in the air, appearing to give a speech. The elegant robes the high minister wore parted for a brief second, and underneath hung a stone necklace. Hal amplified the projection with the holotable controls and brought up a clearer snapshot of the stone. His throat tightened, and his breath became short and choppy.

Hanging from a golden chain was the same stone necklace with the swirl mark of the Primordial queen.

"How did he come into possession of it?" Hal asked.

Fable looked at the clip of Varim. "What did Atis do with the necklace after he severed it from Xirna?"

"He locked it away deep in the northern pole of Athos. Though nobody knew exactly where," Hal said. "It was thought to be in an impenetrable bunker hidden by Empyrean magic."

"Did you know the high minister was an apprentice archeologist before he entered politics?"

"No," Hal said as he looked back at Fable.

"One of my spies managed to capture his journal. I'll let you read this snippet."

A third image appeared under Fable, the words crystal clear, and Hal read.

'Today, I mark the beginning of my new life. In precious time, I will come to overthrow the Throne and usher in a new era of mortal control over our rightful land. Empyreans are a distant memory of a history wrought with destruction and cataclysmic violence. The world needs no more. I have you to thank, my teacher, for encouraging me to do the undoable. Though I am sorry your blood is on my hands, I spare thee with life in a world of gray. Now I know what must be done. And with this crystal necklace, I will hunt the stones. Primordials are the true rulers of the Realmverse. And the Queen needs her Throne.'

Hal didn't know whether to be sick to his stomach or angry at his blindness. It made sense now, what Stravis had said; he'd been the mentor to the hidden madman. Varim had used the necklace to instill Madness in the population. Now all he needed were the Lumnis Stones, and the ritual could commence. But there was still so much more he needed to understand. It seemed Varim had learned much of it right under their noses.

Hal gripped the edge of the table tighter and let out a frustrated growl. "Why couldn't I see this?" he said under his breath.

"He fooled us all," Fable answered. "And now all of the star nations in the Realmverse are at risk."

"Why are you telling me this?" Hal asked. "Why is someone inside Imperius, which has fallen victim to Madness, concerned for me? Who are you, and why the hell should I trust you?"

"You are the rightful Crown Prince of Athos. You have a right to know. I see you, Prince Halcion, as an Athonian that wants the best for the Empire and not solely a prince that cares only about the fruits of labor from the Empire," Fable said. "Varim is not yet adept enough to understand the intricacies of charna and his use of Madness is unrefined. Those not affected by the spell whisper your name in the towns and villages in the wilds of planets and moons hardly touched by Madness. They know who you truly are and wait eagerly for your return in hope of repulsing these hideous lies. They are loyal to the old ways, as am I. Empyreans freed the Realmverse from the Primordial makers. We do not want to go back."

"They'll have to wait," Hal said. "I can't let Miri activate the Gate of Asha."

"A price they're willing to pay. A few others and I have formed an underground network of loyalists to the Code. We can do what we must, but we need your help too. The Empire has an ever-watchful eye."

Hal tilted his head up. "Ask."

"Varim has reorganized the Empire to become the new Realmverse Republic, though republic in name only. It threads itself in the other star systems' affairs to coerce them to join this monstrosity. It's no longer a planetary government like the Empire. The planet has taken direct control of everything. Former Imperial assets govern the worlds under their jurisdiction for Varim. It's a way to form this new Realmverse-wide order in preparation for what Varim has planned. That chain needs to be broken if the Realmverse is to survive. Neutralize the puppet governors and break the chain."

"You're asking me to attack the other systems?" Hal asked. "That's no better than terrorists."

"I'm asking nothing. I'm merely suggesting you liberate them from the grip of Varim and his phony leaders," Fable stated. "Once the web is broken and more people see, we can rise and take back Athos and rid ourselves of this stain on our history. If we don't, I fear what is to come."

Hal brought a hand up and covered his mouth as he thought long and hard. The idea made sense—cripple the puppet governments and expose Varim—but that was nothing short of a mission itself, and none of it would matter if the Gate in the Ashlands became operational. Though whatever Varim called his new regime, this was still the Empire of Athos to Hal.

He met Fable's eyes. "I've got a job to do here first."

Fable only gave a respectful nod before the hologram faded away.

What weight had been lifted when he'd regained his powers now returned to sit upon his shoulders with a pressure equal to the twin suns of Athos. They had to stop this wicked idea from coming to fruition, and it started here. He took a deep breath before leaving the room.

Outside, the storm raged on, blowing heaps of ash onto the walkways and into some buildings. He braved the onslaught for a moment and ran across the open air to where the ship from Torval Keep sat and raised the lift.

Kristilin sat near one of the windows, gazing outside. Hal took a spot next to her, eyes out to the display of nature before them. He looked over to her, and her eyes were full of questions. He was the first to speak, unable to deal with the strange tension that had fallen over them.

"Something wrong?"

She looked at him like she always did when she was annoyed. "Hal, you ended a war not even a month ago, and now you want to battle against the Empire of Athos?"

"What choice do we have?" Hal asked. "Besides, it's only an expeditionary force."

"It is your sister." She shook her head. "I do not know, but so much conflict for one person cannot be good, no?"

A wave of feelings washed over him. He searched for words but didn't know what to say or how to say it, so he spoke his mind.

"Kristi, I fought a war night and day for two years. What happened there haunts me. That's a burden I carry as the Prince of the Empire. I can't change that." He took her hand in his. "But it brings me peace knowing these people are safe from any incursions by an illegitimate regime, even if it's to buy them a little more time. I . . . We can't let them down."

A heavy sigh escaped her mouth. "I know, Hal. And I should think the same for calling this place my home for over a year. But something does not seem right." She shook her head as she looked at their hands together. "I am afraid I will lose you again."

Hal cupped his other hand over both of theirs and took a deep breath. His eyes searched hers and held her lavender gaze.

"I will never leave you. Never again."

Kristilin smiled as they both leaned in, and their lips touched. Hal savored the softness of her lips, wishing never to part ways.

They turned and faced the window, watching the chaos nature created outside, and held on to each other.

⇁⇉⇉⁊ ⇇⇇⇇↼

As the hours went on, the wind's ferocity was unrelenting. Hal walked through the streets of Hellas with the walls of the town as the only protection from the wind's high speeds. Most patrons of the city knew better and hid inside as the ash built up on the wooden walkways and railings, but he couldn't stay cooped up. Lights from inside the buildings cast shadows of the people who lived in them. Once ransacked by Dash and his crew, the town started to heal. Now innocent people had to pick up the pieces of what hadn't been destroyed by those goons.

A wave of guilt washed over Hal as he stopped at the crossroads and saw the side of a building separated and collapsed. Because of him, these people had known conflict and had their homes stolen from them. Though they'd won it back, it should've never been taken from them in the first place. Dash had worked for Varim. Varim's influence seemed to be everywhere now, and Hal cursed himself for how it had slipped right under their noses. It seemed his mother was the only one who'd caught wind of it, but she'd been silenced before anything could be said. And now he lived the life of so many here as outcasts.

As the ash blew against his evosuit, he looked up to the gray skies, where dim light turned it a hazy color. He knew what needed to be done to repay his debts to these people, who had helped him for so long.

Hal walked in silence along the back streets that ran around the wall. The battle that was to come would be nothing like the war he'd fought; there would be no massive artillery strikes or aerial bombardments, no crashing ships or stealth suit ambushes, just a skeleton crew and a single fort. But what hid behind that made him sick to his stomach. He couldn't fathom what would happen if he had to fight his sister. He'd never faced his own blood on the battlefield before, but now he might have to.

Continuing down the streets, Hal stopped when he rounded a bend. Separated from any buildings by a couple hundred yards was an ash-covered field. Headstones of remembrance rose up to defy the ash's dominance while a larger statue stood in the center of the field. But what caught his attention was who stood alone in the field of graves.

As he walked closer, stifled cries floated on the wind to him. He didn't say anything as he walked up. Misselie turned as he stopped beside her, and her eyes were red with tears. He glanced down at the names on the two headstones she stood in front of: Eison Ragniheim and Sava Ragniheim.

"My father and mother, or so Stravis tells me. I don't remember them much, but Stravis told me they were good friends. He said they were from a region of the Empire called Valkara. I have no idea what it looks like there or where it's even at . . . I was only a child before they . . . before . . ." She paused and wiped the tears from her eyes. "I wish I knew my parents better. Stravis was like a grandfather to me. He took me in when my parents died and raised me like his own."

"He's a good man."

Misselie wiped a stray tear from her cheek and turned to face Hal. "Now I might be alone again."

When Hal had first entered this land, he'd felt the same way: alone, abandoned, discarded. But all it took was one person he cared about to change his mind. It took time, but he'd overcome his dejection because of Kristilin's compassion. Now he saw the look he'd once had on Misselie's face, and it was one he wished no one to have.

He placed a hand on her shoulder. "No, you're not. Stravis will live. You're a bright, kind young woman. Your passion and drive to study the Primordial arts is commendable, and Stravis would be proud to see how much you've done for Asha, for us, for everyone. Your insight is irreplaceable."

Misselie's lips quivered, her wide eyes still stained with rogue tears. She placed a hand on top of his as a small smile formed.

"Thank you, Hal. Kristilin has been the closest thing to a sister I have known. She showed me compassion and understanding. Stravis showed me knowledge and the wonder of the arcane world. And you . . ." She patted his hand. "Call me naïve, but you're like the brother I never had. You've shown me determination and power but also grace and respect. These are things I could never have learned on my own."

"Don't sell yourself short. Without you, where would we be in trying to understand all these ancient scriptures? You're invaluable, not just for your knowledge, but for your friendship too."

Her smile grew.

"We're a team," Misselie said. She wrapped an arm around Hal and pulled him in for a hug. "Let's finish this as a team."

Hal nodded and hugged her back.

"But be truthful to me, Hal," Misselie said. "Do you think Stravis will survive?"

"He has Kristilin looking after him," Hal said with a smile. "He'll be just fine."

"Good." She let out a deep breath. "And your sister? From what Kristilin told me of her, she sounded like a good person, one I would've liked to be friends with. But now I see only the fear she imposes. Do you think she will get better?"

"I believe so, Misselie. She is just twisted by things not in our control, at least not now. In time she will return to her normal self. I'm certain of it."

"I hope so," Misselie said. "If she does, I would like to try and befriend her."

"And I'll tell you what, when this is all over, I would be happy to show you where your parents hailed from."

"I would like that." As the wind blew stronger bands of ash around, Misselie turned to him and said, "Shall we get out of this weather now?"

"How about we drop by the town hospital?"

Misselie smiled and nodded.

⤜⤜⤜ ⤛⤛⤛

Back at the hospital, Hal and Misselie walked through the large and open room. A few crude medical machines beeped rhythmically beside a bed. The old man lay on his back, a tube going into his nose and another sending much-needed medicine into his body through his arm.

Misselie knelt beside the bed and looked at the old man's still face as he took slow steady breaths. Hal stood behind her with his arms crossed.

At least he's alive, he thought.

"He's doing better," Kristilin said as she entered through the curtains holding bandages in her arms. "The doctor has been here around the clock."

She rolled up one of Stravis's sleeves to reveal a burn mark that covered most of his bicep. Hal tensed when he saw it.

As Kristilin went to work on the burn, the old man opened his eyes.

"Stravis," Misselie said, reaching for his hand. "You old dog. You had us worried."

"Where is the prince?" Stravis said, his voice dry and hoarse.

"Right here," Hal said.

"Xirna . . ."

"Is it true?" Hal asked.

"I've seen the mark . . . in . . . in the princess's eyes."

Stravis passed out again. Kristilin put a hand to his neck while Misselie gripped the old man's hand.

"He is fine," Kristilin said. "He is just exhausted. In time he will recuperate."

"Get better, Stravis. Please," Misselie said as she stood up from the bed.

Hal placed a hand on her shoulder as she fought back tears. It was even clearer now as to who was to blame, but he still needed to confirm what the old man had said.

CHAPTER XXXX

Hal peeked over the hill of ash, scanners raised to his eyes. Donned in the old Imperial robes, he felt as proud as ever, like a beacon of hope for the true path of Imperials. He wore it with honor and patriotism and would die in it if the forces that be demanded it. He was an Athonian first.

As the ash built on his shoulders, his gaze fell upon the location where the main assault force had gathered under the cover of darkness. Tucked inside the intertwined natural tunnels of the earth, the force of Ashborn warriors waited for the time to strike, ready to give their lives for the place they had been exiled to and the place they called home. The ash aided them in concealment; the spotlights atop the fortress passed harmlessly over them.

Hal smiled at the fact that these two weary neighbors had joined forces to protect their home. Differences aside, they knew they were stronger united rather than divided.

Ash covered the mountaintop in the near distance, and drones patrolled like bees around a hive. A sea of hills stood all around the fortress where the foot of the Gate stood atop the mountain.

After putting the scanners away, Hal slid back down the hill to where the others from his fireteam sat. He took a seat near Kristilin, and she handed him a canteen that smelled of minty water. He took it from her, downing a sip of tea that warmed his insides. After taking another sip, he handed it back to Kristilin.

"How many do you think are in there?" she asked.

Like a flood breaking through a dam, his memories of the invasion came back in force. He remembered the aerial battle and the destruction of both fleets and the soldiers who had fallen in the line of duty. He remembered the ascent to the palace and the confrontation with the Polarian royals.

A heavy sigh escaped him as he buried his head in his hands, fighting the pain that came with war. He remembered the similar words spoken to him by his sister.

Kristilin looked at him and then to Misselie before she placed a hand on his shoulder. It was not her fault but something he had to live with, the pain and torture of the war within the war. He reached up and touched her hand to soothe the worried thoughts she no doubt had.

He cleared his thoughts and lifted his head. "I'm sorry. My sister said those same words right before we invaded Polaris."

"Oh, Hal," Kristilin said, shaking her head. "I did not know."

"It's not your fault," he said as his stare drifted to the small fire crackling before them. "I've kept my demons away for so long."

"I've only heard a little about the war from what Stravis and new exiles have shared," Misselie said, catching Hal's attention. "They said the Polarians tried to invade a region of space claimed by Athos and began arresting Imperial settlers for 'trespassing.' Is that true?"

"It is . . . partially. The attacks were used to encourage the Imperial Council on a proper retaliation. Polaris claimed it as holy ground because their goddess-ruler, Kymra, passed through there many years ago in search of refuge before the founding of Polaris. For a time, both Imperials and Polarians lived on a divided Yasu that was jointly governed. But the war started with the death of the empress, though I'm not sure of anything right now," Hal said. "All I know is that I fought for my planet, and I lost countless soldiers. To see what the Empire has become is revolting and a slap in the face to all those who died in its name."

Hal had to quell his rage and channel it through his body to his extremities, taking what wanted to be kinetic energy and transforming it to potential. After a deep breath and a moment to collect himself, he sat upright. Kristilin's touch brought a new vision to him, one that clutched at the fabric of hope. It was reaffirmed when Misselie smiled. Whatever the next hours brought, at least he would be in the company of friends.

"Right," Hal said with a breath. "How're your thrusterpacks? Do they fit properly?"

"They are fine, Hal," Kristilin said.

"I'm surprised we even found any in the town's armory," Misselie said.

"I just want to make sure you two will be all right." He looked back to where the assault force had taken position. "We have some time to kill."

Hours passed as the storm lingered on its last legs, the winds still too strong for the base to open. Kristilin crawled up next to Hal as he looked through the scanners once more. The Imperial base was nothing short of imposing. Built into the mountain, its angled walls made it easier for blaster bolts and cannons to ricochet, and laser mounted emplacements were trained on the wasteland in front of it, though it paled in comparison to the scale of the Gate atop of the mountain. Hal shook off his anticipation and looked back down. Hal panned to where the troops sat, some covered in cloth to mimic ash and others braced for a battle to come. He just had to wait. It all depended on the troops below.

"Guys," Misselie said from below them, hand against her ear as she listened to whatever came over the other end. She looked back at them. "It's happening."

Hal looked back to the forces as the first of many cannons streaked through the hazed air, turning it an alien green. They whistled over the allied troops and smashed into the walls of the fort with an impact so hard that the ash under him shook down the hill. Another volley followed when the rotary blasters and lasers returned fire from the fortress. Smaller blue bolts raced through the air and passed golden bolts on the way. The time was now. Hal raised his mask and slid down the hill with Kristilin.

"Load up. Let's go."

They sped across the ash on their dusters, careful to avoid the main fight at the front and to not fall into one of the many crevices. Falling into one like he had done before would doom the plan before it started. But as the flood of energy bolts raced through the air in both directions, his instincts kicked in. A spotlight crossed their path in search of the ghostly attackers, and Hal gunned the throttle before it made its pass back. As he looked back, Misselie and Kristilin followed suit, and he breathed a sigh of relief. To be caught so early would risk everything.

They weaved through the valley as drones raced overhead, bringing the fight to the Ashborn attackers farther back. Their red lasers lit up the dark ravine they followed, casting long shadows that threatened to reveal their position. He worried, but he had to have faith in the Ashborn and in himself. They were the masters of this land, and no invading army would ever be as eager to defend their home as they were.

Hal reached the cave entrance first and jumped off the duster. The great mountain loomed before him, taller than anything he could have imagined. The girls made it just behind him and took positions around the opening. Hal sent a small fireball through the tunnel, and as its light touched the walls, it illuminated and cleared the way of any hidden obstacles. No Imperials. Kristilin nodded at him, and he charged his hand with flames before pushing in.

The echoes of battle shook the ground beneath the fortress as Hal led them through the tunnel. Ash and dirt rained down from the rocky ceiling each time an explosion boomed nearby. Misselie and Kristilin ducked whenever one went off. The sounds were nothing more than background noise to him, something he'd heard a thousand times before. Another explosion rumbled through the ground as Hal came upon a back door sealed from the inside. As they took position near it, Misselie stepped up and placed a device where the lock would have been on the opposite side. With the click of a button, the device fried the electrical components of the lock, and Hal slid the door open, holding it as the girls snuck in.

Inside, alarms blared. Hal looked over the railing and down to where soldiers frantically ran to take firing positions. He analyzed his surroundings, and a few floors above them was the entrance to the Primordial Gate controls.

Before he could give orders, a squad of soldiers rounded the corner, and Hal sank into the shadows like the girls. As the soldiers passed by and took the lift, static came through their earpieces, and Hal froze at the message.

"Imperial cruiser! Repeat. Imperial cruiser . . . entered the airspace!"

Hal tensed up. There was only one person with a cruiser. He'd expected it, but not so soon. It seemed his sister was like him in more ways than one. More soldiers flooded the halls and toward the base defenses. They had to do this now.

He turned to Misselie. "Which way to the security room?"

"Down the hall to the lift and up a few floors to level thirteen," she replied.

"We have to get the entrance open or the Ashborn outside are done for," Kristilin said.

"Agreed."

Hal raced down the hall with the girls, making sure to watch out for roaming soldiers. When they came to the lift, they funneled inside, and Hal hit the button to go up. But just as the lift started to move, an artillery burst cracked through the walls, the explosion rocking the entire base. The wave of energy knocked them to the floor and sent the lift into a freefall before another blast jackknifed the lift and stuck it two floors down. Smoke filled the cabin as Hal staggered up and pried the door open. Misselie helped Kristilin back to her feet while metal pieces of the lift clanged against its jagged edges of twisted metal.

As Hal stepped out, blaster bolts streaked through the air toward him. He was quick to return fire and downed the soldiers. Communications came over their radios, and the voice on the other side sounded desperate.

"Prince Halcion, that cruiser is tearing us apart."

"Hold on for a little longer," Hal replied calmly as the girls crawled out. Misselie quickly got to work locating where they were at. "We're working on getting the entrance open. Use the caves as natural protection." When the transmission ended, he said, "Misselie, where are we?"

"A few floors farther down but still near the security room."

He cursed under his breath. "Is there anything we can use to deal with the cruiser?"

Misselie shook her head. "Nothing we have. But the proton cannons on the roof of the fort could work."

"Better than nothing," Hal replied. "Kristi, go with Misselie and get that entrance open. I'll head to the roof."

Misselie headed for the stairwell, but Kristilin hung back. Explosions shook sparks from the ceilings while fires raged from fallen debris. Soldiers shouted, and blaster fire pierced through the air. Kristilin hurried to Hal, pulling his mask away and placing a quick kiss on his lips. As she stepped back, Hal met her eyes and smiled.

"Do not do anything stupid," she said, then ran to join Misselie.

With her out of sight, he turned and bolted for the other stairwell.

Blaster shots and shouts from soldiers filled the stairwell with such deafening booms that Hal was thankful he had something in his ears. No doubt they would be ringing if he were going through this unprotected. Hal leapt up the stairs faster than he should have, wasting as little time as possible. It was a challenge, but his conditioning over the last month helped him prevail and soon reach the top.

He opened the door carefully. As he looked over the edge, the fortress's wall led to a steep drop that no one would survive, but as he looked toward the other side, a gap in the fortress's roof opened and led down a shaft toward the interior of the structure. Either way, it was a long way down.

The boom of a cannon shook him from his mental analysis of the fort. Massive cannons were aimed at the battlefield below, where droves of Ashborn confronted Imperial soldiers and drones, using everything at their disposal to defeat the enemy. Grenades were lobbed back and forth, and rockets from launchers smacked into the ground and kicked up clouds of dirt. Some shot upward, not from misfire but from fear of the beast above.

His eyes drifted up and followed those stray rockets to the looming presence of an Imperial Pathfinder class cruiser. Shorter than his flagship starcarrier during the war, the cruiser tapered down at the nose. The rockets exploded well away from the hull of the ship, doing nothing more than tickling its shields. Its laser cannons fired retaliatory streams of energy that incinerated the ground below, breaking apart rock like it was nothing. It only lasted for a couple seconds, but the destructive nature of the weapons was all too familiar to him.

A dozen starfighters emerged from the crevice at the tapered nose and focused on the Ashborn below. Hal looked back to the cannons and knew what needed to be done. Arms charged with charna flames, he took off.

Soldiers saw him and aimed their weapons. When the first bolts of blaster fire boomed, Hal rolled to avoid them and sent a ball of fire at the first cannon. Fire exploded everywhere and sent the soldiers off their feet, some toppling over the wall to fall down the height of the base. Hal absorbed the next blaster fire with a ward and launched a stream of flames before he met the final group of Imperial soldiers with a charged ball of fire. Their screams lasted for only a second until they fell to the floor. Each lifeless soldier was a burden on his shoulders, but it was too late to change their minds.

As he turned to the seat of one of the cannons, he was launched from his feet and hit the ground with a thud. It took a few seconds to catch his breath, and he gasped for oxygen to refill his lungs. The sound of a metal spike hitting concrete caught his attention, and he looked up at the Praetorian warrior standing before him. The blades of the twin hardlite xiphirs glowed as the soldier raised them.

Hal reached his right hand out, and the fire charna formed the flame sword. Power left his body and culminated into the weapon like it was a part of him.

The Praetorian wasted no time and pounced on Hal. The flame sword caught the first attack, hardlight energy and charna clashing in a fiery display, but the second xiphir sliced his arm. Blood dripped to the ground as Hal groaned at the slash and took a step back to regain himself. The Praetorian laughed under their helmet and slid the two blades across each other, creating a golden shower of hot sparks.

Hal's arm burned, and he looked down to see the singed fabric of his leather and cloth. Instead of waiting, Hal attacked first. He swung his flame sword at the Praetorian, who caught it with their twin blades, the heat from all three creating a spark in the middle bright enough to rival the sun.

With a kick to the abdomen, the Praetorian sent Hal backward and charged. Hal avoided the attack and spun, slicing his flame sword up the Praetorian's back. The armored warrior roared, then murmured something in old Athonian that Hal knew was not a compliment. Hal charged his other hand and launched a fireball at the warrior, who sidestepped it and lunged at him. This time Hal was ready and caught the one blade in a trap. The momentum sent the Praetorian into a stumble, and Hal would not waste such an opportunity. He recalled his flame sword and charged both hands with flames.

The Praetorian regathered themselves before Hal launched a combined stream of fire. The force lifted the warrior off their feet and threw them over the wall with a scream. Hal stood there and gathered his breath as the last of the flames lingered. A blast from the cruiser caught his attention and brought him back to reality.

Hal moved the fallen Imperial gunner from the cannon seat and took the controls. As he raised the viewfinder to the cruiser, it highlighted vulnerable areas, namely the engines, gun batteries, and bridge. The indicator on the cannon controls showed only four shots left. Each one had to count. He weighed his targets carefully and finally chose where to strike. Lining up the reticle, he aimed for the engines. With a deep breath and a steady hand, he fired the first shot.

It felt like time stood still as the blue orb of energy sailed through the sky. He wondered if he'd aimed right and calculated the correct angle; this shot would tell if he had or not. The blast streaked through the air and under the belly of the cruiser before striking one of the engines. A massive explosion ruptured the rear of the ship, and the aft separated from the main hull. A stream of blue propulsion fuel wafted through the air. Another explosion followed, igniting the fuel and turning the sky to fire. Debris fell, and metal grinded on metal as the ship listed in the air, smoke billowing from the rear.

Below him, the combined forces pushed through the Imperial defenders and toward the base. The entrance had been opened, which meant he had to get to the Gate. As he was about to leave, a small shuttlecraft emerged from the cruiser's nose and zipped overhead before landing on a concealed air pad at the rear of the fortress. He had a feeling who it was, but his speculation was cut short when two Imperial soldiers aimed their weapons at him.

"Hands up," one of them ordered.

Hal did what was ordered just as two shots pierced the soldiers' armor and downed them instantly. He sighed a breath of relief. Kristilin holstered her blaster and hurried to him.

"Always saving you," she said with a smirk. "Misselie opened the entrance."

"Good," he said. "Once the Ashborn make their way inside, it'll only be a matter of time before the Gate gets activated and they call for reinforcements. We need to overload the lava temperature regulators."

He turned to look at the massive structure above them. It sat silently, guarding the destruction and battle under it. Then static filled his ear.

"Hal, I don't know how, but someone initiated the activation codes for the Gate," Misselie said through the radio.

A frustrated growl escaped him as he balled his hands into fists. Any second wasted pouting about a foiled plan gave the Gate that much more precious time to initiate. He wouldn't let that happen.

"How long?" he asked.

"Twenty minutes, judging by this schematic."

He unclenched his fists before turning to Kristilin.

"I need you to guide the Ashborn to the central complex. Clear out the Imperials as you advance, and overload those controls. We need to neutralize this place. I'll deal with the Gate."

An explosion boomed overhead when another engine ruptured. Metal debris fell and crashed into the side of the fort. The Imperial cruiser loomed closer. Small starfighters and transports fled the ship like bees escaping a hive. Metal fragments ripped by them like miniature meteorites. Larger parts were headed right for them, growing bigger with every passing second.

"Run!" he shouted.

They ran across the roof as pieces of superheated metal flew by them and bounced off the concrete. The heat the debris generated built in intensity on their backs as they leapt into the open shaft of the fort, and the disabled ship sailed overhead. Metal scrap and ship parts rammed into the fort and shattered everything they touched. They fell through the gauntlet of the interior as a piece of the ship slammed into the mountainside and sealed off the shaft above them. Chunks of concrete and dust fell and raced them to the bottom.

Hal ignited his hands and used the energy the flames produced to slow his descent as the interior levels grew closer. He hit the metal crosswalk a level above the ground harder than he would have liked but managed to roll out of the way before a chunk of concrete crashed through where he just was and into the ground. Kristilin landed beside him, her thrusterpack giving her a gentler landing. As the dust settled, Kristilin helped him up.

The ground shook, and Hal looked up as a blue portal began to form. What had been so beautiful to him before was now hated. The ocean of blue would take some time to build, but he had to act fast. He turned to Kristilin.

"Go. Help them fight. We all know what needs to be done."

Kristilin looked toward the Gate before nodding and running down the hall. Hal waited until she was gone before he hopped over the railing of the crosswalk. He landed, his feet sending up a plume of ash, and hurried down a corridor.

The door opened as he approached, and he ran down the long hallway toward the swiftlift at the end as charna energy bubbled below him. Everything looked clean. Pristine white walls with glowing orange designs encircled him. Explosions were replaced with silence and the soft gurgle of liquid charna as the door closed. The charna flowed upward in tubes and disappeared through the walls.

Hal approached the lift at the end and stepped in, and it took him back above the Imperial complex and higher into the mountain. Soon, the fortress looked insignificant as little blue and golden laser bolts ripped back and forth.

When he stepped out, smoke and blowing ash greeted him, but he fixed his gaze upon the massive structure before him. The ring of the Gate stretched down to just above him and covered the entirety of the mountaintop. Its hum sang to him, but he would not be swayed by the sounds of discovery now. Looking to the control panel along one of the support pillars, he wasted no more time.

He hurried across the mountaintop like his life depended on it, kicking up ash and dirt with every step. The Gate's hum grew louder, and time slowed down. Data chip in hand, he was about to plug it into the console when he heard that familiar laugh. His fists balled once more as he placed the data chip down on the controls and slowly turned around.

"Impressive aim, dear brother, but I should have known," Miri said with a wicked grin. "Oh, this little skirmish is quite impressive as well. A disgraced prince managed to round up the rats. Easier extermination that way."

Hal stood upright. "Only rat in here is you."

Miri smirked. "I know you saw the stone, communed with it. I followed Mother's steps too, you know. Something Father thought we weren't ready for. He didn't want us to find the true power of our ancestors. Mother saw the possibilities."

"Then you know why the high minister wants the stone and why he can't have it."

She crossed her arms and pouted as if to tease him like they were children again.

"Oh, Hal. This was never about him. This was about our lineage, our mother's and father's ideas for our people. You failed to see our parents' plan."

"I know Varim killed our mother in cold blood, plunged us into war, and dragged the Realmverse into chaos. Father was too sick, but even he could see Varim's unhinged nature. It's your corruption talking now, Meer. Varim is rewriting our history. You're just the hand." Hal raised his hands and pointed toward the valley beneath them. "Look at what chaos he's created."

Miri stifled an amused chuckle. "Mother wanted a world full of Wielders, a school to teach them. So did Father. But they undermined what made us special, strong, revered. We're the only Empyreans left. And with new phony Wielders, our legacy would be for naught." She shook her head. "I don't care what Varim preaches; he's just another pawn I'll cast away when this is all said and done. I only want our—my—legacy to be remembered as it was supposed to be."

"You can't be serious. Empyrean or not, if Varim gets his way, there won't be anything to fight over. He exiled me and murdered our parents, Meer. Mother was onto something, and Varim cut her down out of fear. He wants to eradicate us and bring back the days of the Primordials, and we're the only Empyreans left right now. His plan is working."

Miri paced in front of him. "Varim is a vassal. The people believe in him though they are easily swayed. Look at what happened to you." Miri smirked. "It will be my right of passage to secure the Empire from him and, Code or not, I will become empress. Let him believe he is something other than a pawn. When I have the stones and I find the source of the Primordial charna, I will rival Atis himself and claim an empire made up of the entire Realmverse. Our Empyrean bloodline will rule as it should, and I'll do it with or without you, Hal."

Hal narrowed his eyes at her. Disbelief and anger burned through him. The words she spoke went against everything the Code preached and taught, and it made his heart ache.

"You've fallen victim to Madness. Miri, you need to snap out of it."

Miri softened her gaze. "Hal, it's not too late to repent. You can be forgiven; I'll be lenient. I know that we'll be stronger together." She folded her arms across her chest. "I saw what you did to Father. I know it wasn't you in control. It was Varim and Madness. We can expose him together."

Hal froze and looked at her, dumbfounded. She knew about the Madness Varim inflicted. Why in Empyrea's name did she not believe him, then? She wasn't completely gone, just misled or confused. He did not know the full extent of what Madness did to one's mind, but this had to be an effect of it.

"Renounce your devotion to the old ways and join me in ruling the Empire, and I will forgive what Varim made you do. We can forge our own Code, one that isn't limited by the ways of centuries past. That's what they wanted. What our parents wanted."

She reached out for him with a smile. He stared at her hand and thought of everything that could change if he took it. It would give him a clear chance to explain what he'd learned and found out about Varim and his tricks. She promised him compassion, and it was tempting, but it wasn't the right course of action. He saw through the lies.

"Miri, you're living in the shackles of tricks and lies and fantasies. Varim tore us apart, and he's going to do the same exact thing he did to me and our parents to you," Hal said. "Look me in the eyes and tell me that is what you want."

Her eyes burned into him before they darted to the ground. She stayed silent for a moment as if to consider what Hal had said.

"I . . . I want strength," she said. "I want unity. I want power to drive the Empire in the direction our bloodline demands."

He saw it, her momentary hesitancy. His little sister was in there somewhere, and he wanted to bring her back, but as the ground shook and the hum of the Gate vibrated through the air, there was no time left to reason. Madness's influence was too great to break through right now.

Miri reached into her robes and produced a small chest, one that Hal recognized. "I have the stone, Hal. This is my last offer."

"I won't let you activate that Gate, Meer."

"Then you leave me no choice."

She sprayed a tunnel of flames at him. Hal raised his hands. Charging them with charna energy, he blocked her flames with his ward. Fire erupted when they met, radiating a scolding heat that rivaled any wildfire. The power behind Miri's flames pushed Hal back a step, but he held strong, using his entire body to withstand the onslaught of the inferno. Hal threw her flames aside, and they crashed into the ground with a destructive force that turned the ash and dirt into hardened glass.

Before he could gather himself, Miri was on him, hands charged with flames. She threw punch after punch, and Hal blocked each one with his ward. He knew her fighting style, what moves she liked. They'd trained together for years, and this felt like another sparring match. But this had greater consequences than bragging rights.

He fell for a fake, and a flaming punch landed squarely near his ribs. Though most of the blow was absorbed through his leather armor and robes, he still stumbled back a few feet and fell to one knee. He groaned in pain. Breathing hurt, but he could not stop. Adrenaline replaced his frustration as he dusted the live embers away from his singed armor.

"How fitting for you to kneel before the Crown Princess," Miri said as she walked toward him, ready to land the knockout blow. As she got closer, the swirl mark in the whites of her eyes became visible. The old man was right.

"You could've been there for my coronation," Miri said as she brought a hand back and charged it with flames.

Those words woke something up in him. The Inferno raged inside as he focused on his sister and charged his hands. The pain channeled through him, intensifying the fire that resonated through his body. As he looked up at the Gate, the blue ocean of energy reached the center, and the violent hum of the activator engaged.

Hal lunged and sent a fireball toward Miri, but she redirected it. He fired a volley of three more vengeance-filled fireballs, but she dodged them too. Hal followed the attack up with a spray of flames that nearly met their mark. Miri cast her own fire ward and deflected the stream, but Hal kept up the pressure, generating more heat and power behind his fire before he focused the charna in his hand and formed a sword of fire energy.

Caught off guard, Miri reeled back as she avoided his swings and the flames that trailed off them. Hal sprayed a stream of flames again and followed it up with another swing of his flame sword. Miri raised her ward just in time to catch half of the sword in it and absorb it into her own energy. Hal changed up, keeping the pressure of fire against her ward, and went to sweep out her feet. She knew to avoid his favorite move and used her larger flames to force him back while he deflected.

Each punch was met with another block that sent flames lashing out violently. The entirety of the mountaintop was engulfed in flames, and nothing was spared from their mark. Only destruction would be left in their wake, but with destruction came rebirth.

In unison, both launched powerful streams that met in the middle. The explosion shook loose ash from hidden rocks and broke them into dust. Charna leaked through the facets of the mountaintop and flowed over lower bits of land like lava consuming rock. Charged rocks popped under the heat.

Sweat dripped from Hal's face as he stared into Miri's eyes. Somewhere deep down was the little sister he knew and loved. He would do anything to bring her back, but it would take time, something he did not have right now.

The Gate hummed to life as the blue ocean of energy rippled inward to signify the completion. Both Hal and Miri saw the glow of ancient technology but for different uses: he saw it for study while she saw it for power.

"It's over, Hal. This petty squabble will die here," Miri said with the same smirk as before. "When my invasion fleet arrives, you will spend the rest of your days locked in a prison cell with Varim for defying the future empress."

Hal ignored her, focusing on the tension between them. The flames grew hotter than ever, lashing out where they met to show whose fire was strongest. His feet slid a little, and then he smiled. He recalled everything he'd learned here. He studied the Primordial teachings, explored the Empyrean legacies hidden in the land, and he felt the heartaches of lessons learned to understand the true nature of what it meant to harness this power. He understood that knowledge was the true power of a Kell.

"You're wrong," he said as he looked back at his sister. "I'm a Kell."

The reply was enough to catch her off guard, and the power between them slipped in his favor. He summoned everything within him to force as much energy through his flames and then hers. With a single move, Hal threw his sister's flames to the side. A focused charge engulfed his free hand and ignited the air as it traveled toward Miri. The heated force in the focused channel of flames sent her flying backward and into the Gate's gravity well, and she was absorbed by the ocean of blue.

Exhausted, Hal collapsed to the ground as the flames receded. Bright orange charna came through and encircled part of the mountaintop in a moat. The soft wavelike sounds from the Gate echoed across the mountain, the glow brightening with every passing second. It was only a matter of time before whatever was on the other side came through. He could not let that happen.

His body screamed with shock as he moved. He limped across the bubbling ground and reached for the data chip on the Gate's terminal. After the connection was made, he typed the activation codes backward and pressed the holo button. The hum of the Gate ceased, and the blue aura of energy fizzled back to the outer ring as he collapsed against the console. The liquid charna crept ever so slightly through the cracks in the mountain before it slowly stopped, settling into the calmness of a pond with an occasional flare of energy.

Slumped against the console, too tired to move, Hal let out a deep breath as blaster fire echoed below him. The noise of battle faded into the background when he cast his gaze upward. A soft harmony followed the reds and oranges that came from the setting sun through the haze of sky, and Hal sat back and took another breath.

He'd just sent his sister through a Primordial Gate without a ship, without protection, without anything. He knew not what would become of her, but he only hoped she would end up safe. She was not the enemy, merely an adversary in this game Varim had created.

Voices crept up the mountain as armored Ashborn rushed toward him. Though he did not understand what they said, their quick look over told him they were concerned. Light-headedness swelled within him, for his conditioning level was nowhere near where it needed to be for what he'd done. He fought to stay awake, but the call of darkness was too great.

CHAPTER XXXXI

Hal's eyes slowly opened, and he found himself in an empty room.

He sat up in bed and threw his blanket off. He rubbed his eyes awake and went to pull at his arm, expecting medical tubes to have been sunk into his skin, but there was nothing. Taking a deep breath, he wondered what had happened after he passed out. The last thing he could remember was the bubbling sound of the charna on the mountaintop.

Light came through the window across the room, and as he walked closer to it, an open gray sky could be seen. Guards walked the walls of Hellas, which stood against the backdrop of gray.

Behind him, the creak of a door caught his attention. He turned to see who it was, and a wave of relief washed over him.

Kristilin stepped in, a tattered cloak trailing just above the floor behind her. Her eyes were as radiant as ever. She wrapped her arms around his neck, and he did the same, allowing the last of the weight he carried on his shoulders to finally disappear. After a few minutes of unspoken softness, she pulled back.

"How are you feeling?"

He stared at the ground between them. For so long he had worried about what to do next and how others would see him. Constant battles of self-doubt had driven him to think of nothing but what was at stake and the burden he carried upon his shoulders. With the last of the weight gone, he took a deep, shaky breath.

"Fine. I'm fine," was all he could muster.

"And Miri?"

Hal looked at the gray mountains beyond the walls of the city, where rays of sunlight peeked through the haze of ashy cover. He did not know what had happened to her, but he hoped for the best.

He looked into Kristilin's eyes. "I don't know. All I hope is that she returned safely back to where the Gate led. I could not bear to strike her down in combat."

Kristilin nodded. "It is over now, love." She pulled from the embrace and stood in front of the window. "Imperial forces have either been captured or are in hiding. The other Ashborn clans have joined the cause for a united Asha."

"Stravis?" he asked.

"Better. Conscious. He was injected with a truth serum; however, they either did not inject enough or did not have enough on hand to make him talk. All it really did was weaken him."

"Miri wanted to pry his mind the easy way. I'm glad he's okay," Hal said. "And what of the new leaders?"

She turned back to him and smiled. "They wish to see you."

Kristilin wrapped her hand around his arm, and the gentle path her fingers stroked helped soothe his racing mind as they headed for the door.

As they entered the streets of Hellas, Hal instinctively went to raise his hood, but as he looked through the air around him, the ash stopped falling. He could not remember the last time he'd seen the air without that horrible gray screen. As he looked across the sky, his gaze fell on the great mountain in the distance, where the plume of ash was nothing more than a trickle.

"Where's the ash?" he asked.

"After the battle, while the Ashborn secured the fort and I returned here with you and Misselie, the great mountain quaked. After that, the ash stopped falling."

"Did it have something to do with the Gate?"

She shrugged. "No one knows. But they will have time to understand it, thanks to you."

They continued down the street, and Ashborn people greeted them in kind. Some even went so far as to kiss their hands and give them snacks of salted meat or bread. Hal smiled and took the salted meat strips and handed them to a little boy nearby. The glow on the boy's face said it all, and Hal smirked. These people had so little out here, yet they were endlessly generous.

Hal opened the doors to the Town Hall and allowed Kristilin to enter first. Acknowledging the salutes of the Ashen guards, they walked the halls toward the meeting room. Scars of the past battle still stood where light poured through the walls. The banners had scorch marks, a reminder of the pain before. It felt strange to not worry about the oncoming threat of what loomed beyond, but the threat never fully left his mind. There would always be a new danger to watch out for and overcome, but for now his angst would have to sit with the leaders of this freed land.

In the meeting room, Asher and Jorrin stood around the holotable. Misselie sat off to the side with a tablet in hand and her boots kicked up, the soft blue glow of the holotable reflecting off the soles. Hal and Kristilin took their places.

"Well, I don't know how we did it, but we did," Asher said with a smirk of disbelief. "The Imperial base at the Gate is under our control, and Imperial communications have gone silent."

"Our forces are searching the entire planet for holdouts," Jorrin stated as he crossed his arms. "Those found will have a choice: leave or be imprisoned."

Asher turned his attention to Hal, Kristilin, and Misselie. "Asha owes a lot to you all. What we thought were disappearances was something far greater. I'm ashamed to not have said it earlier, but thank you from all of us."

"Asha is as much your home as it is ours," Jorrin said with a salute to them. "We honor your courage."

Hal took a deep breath. "As honored as I would be to take credit, this could not have been achieved without your courage and sacrifice. New alliances have been bridged and friends made. It took you, as leaders of your respective clans, to accomplish this. I was nothing more than a mediator between you two at most."

"You warded off the Imperial invasion and sent the Huntress back," Jorrin stated.

"Which could not have been done without the spilling of Ashborn blood."

"In any case, we appreciate your help, Prince Halcion Skyborn, Kristilin Äcroix, and Misselie Ragniheim. Tonight we will celebrate your accomplishments and those who were lost," Asher said with a smile. "Let us celebrate."

As the day turned to night, the festivities began to mount. Outdoor vendors filled the city square with food and spirits while others danced to the music of the Ashborn band. Hal sat at one of the tables, a roll of fresh baked bread in his hand, and watched as the Ashen clans and Hellans danced arm in arm. Different factions that had once felt animosity toward each other now danced together like one. It made him smile and helped recapture the one thing he held on to the most: hope.

The scent of spiced tea wafted through the air, and Hal turned to see Kristilin. Taking a seat next to him, she offered him a cup of the sweet-scented liquid. Moments passed, and they said nothing. In a way, he appreciated the jocularity before them, the sounds of happy people freed from war, a welcome change from the anguished cries of pain. They all danced with one another, younger boys and girls chasing each other through the sea of adults. It reminded Hal of simpler times.

Hal placed his bread and cup of tea on the table and stood in front of Kristilin. Butterflies filled his stomach, and he smiled. "Care to dance, m'lady?"

Kristilin raised a brow as she lowered the cup of tea from her lips. "Halcion Skyborn wants to dance? Are you sure the stone didn't do more to your head than we thought?"

Hal brushed off the tease and offered his hand. "Come on. We earned it."

After a few seconds of suspicion, she took his hand. He led her into the crowd, where others moved to the celebratory beat of victory. Hal twirled her, catching her in an embrace when she spun back around. Clapping and happy chants echoed the melody of the band, and Hal smiled with her.

The music slowly changed into a softer, more elegant tune. Those around grabbed their partners and held them close. Hal and Kristilin did the same, wrapping their arms around each other. Hal could not help but enjoy the closeness, her body pressed up against his. They swayed to the music a step at a time, eyes never wavering from each other.

"I have to say, Hal, your dancing skills are impressive," Kristilin said, running her fingers through the hair on the back of his head.

"I have many hidden talents," Hal said with a smirk. "Just wait until you hear my singing."

Kristilin laughed and shook her head. "Please, no. I would rather keep my hearing."

They exchanged a chuckle, and Hal rested his chin atop her head as she buried it against his chest. The music continued its soft trance, and the others kept glancing toward them. Hal would have preferred to share this tender moment in solitude, but he could make an exception. He needed time to unwind and enjoy the moment, something he intended to do now.

Rumbles filled the air, and a thunderous noise sounded over the land. Hal searched the skies, and three flights of Imperial starfighters flew overhead. Hal relaxed when he saw the new Ashborn Republic insignia, the Rigorbite, painted over the Imperial crest on their wings.

A celebration would be nothing without a flyover, he thought.

As much as he wished to stay in the moment, he remembered what Fable had said to him before the attack. Time would not wait for him, and the threat of the Empire still loomed over all it touched. Even here, this scene of happiness would only be temporary if they did nothing. The Empire would regroup, and Miri would come back with a vengeance against him. As long as she had the power she wielded, no place was safe for long.

The music slowed further before the band decided to take a break.

Hal pulled back from the embrace. "Do me a favor? Where's Misselie?"

"In the hospital with Stravis. Why?"

"Grab her and meet me on our ship."

She looked at him with a raised brow but did not protest. Instead, she nodded and left, but not before placing a quick peck on his cheek. Hal squeezed her hand before they separated.

In the central room where he'd once stood before, Hal leaned over the table and looked at the name on the indicator tab. Fable. He had an answer to give, but it would only be right if the two he trusted the most stood by his side. Through the window, the ash settled, and the waning hours of sunlight bathed the land in a soft orange glow like the minutes after an evening storm had passed. He looked around the decaying ship interior. This ship, with some touching up, would carry them where no soul had been in ages. As soon as he thought that, the girls and a hobbling Stravis emerged from the doors, a bit of confusion etched on their faces.

"So, what is this about?" Kristilin said.

Hal took a deep breath. "When I first arrived here, I only cared about the power I'd lost. I vowed to stop at nothing until I recovered that, and the high minister paid." He looked out the window, where the haze of evening transcended to night and ghost trees began to illuminate the distant dunes with bright blues and reds. "I saw the struggles the Empire brought to this place, a land of exiles, and I saw the brotherhood those exiles had." He looked back at the girls. "I fear the Empire's sphere of influence under Varim has extended past its bounds for the sake of power in the Lumnis Stones. Those that lead it now want to destroy the past. What I'm asking you both is if you would undertake that journey with me and stop them."

The two exchanged a look before Kristilin said, "Who else is going to save your butt? Of course I am coming with you."

Hal smirked, his gaze falling to Misselie. "What do you say, Misselie? You've been instrumental to our success, and I would be lying if I said I did not consider you a close friend now."

After a brief pause, Misselie spoke. "If this oldie wants to go, then so will I."

"Since when do you listen to my objections?" the old man said. He sighed deeply. "Misselie, you cannot leave your decisions up to me."

"But who will look after you?" she asked.

Stravis smiled and placed a hand on her shoulder. "Thanks to the help of these two, Asha is looking mighty promising now. Asher needs me here to learn more about the ruins scattered everywhere. He just doesn't know it yet."

"But—"

"Misselie, this isn't goodbye, but it wouldn't be right if I kept you from seeing the Realmverse. You deserve it." Stravis nodded to Hal and Kristilin. "And I trust the company you're in."

Misselie looked at the old man and then glanced back at Hal.

He gave her a smirk as he crossed his arms. "It's your decision."

Misselie took a deep breath. "I would love to go."

Stravis smiled and wrapped his arms around her in a hug.

"And I'll collect anything I see that is Wielder or Empyrean or Primordial related and study Hal."

Hal raised a brow and narrowed his eyes.

"For research!"

Hal smiled and stepped up to the old man, holding out his hand. As Stravis took it and the two shook, Hal said, "I'm glad you're okay."

"It'll take a little more than a truth serum to put down this old dog," Stravis said with a smile.

"Though no more trying to be a hero," Misselie said. "That's what they're for."

"We're all family here," Hal said with a nod.

The holotable fizzled, and Hal turned to face it, but nothing appeared. The excitement that had built up in him faded. He did not want to turn back in embarrassment, having called them all the way out here while a celebration was going on for nothing. Just as he was about to call again, he heard a voice.

"Made a decision?"

Hal turned around to see a familiar face standing in the doorway with someone else following close behind. Eyes wide with disbelief, Hal searched for words. Kristilin looked equally surprised, and Misselie just looked between all three of them. Hal cleared his throat and narrowed his eyes.

"Haywell? Vixera? What are you doing here?"

Haywell smiled at the reception. "Does Fable ring a bell?"

"You're Fable?"

Hal stared in disbelief. After so long wondering if all of Imperius forcibly hated him, his cousin was amongst the few who didn't. Thank the gods for that. And though it seemed like little aid considering what had to be done, it was a good start. He knew Haywell had a silver tongue, and if something could be constructed out of a broken planet, he could do it.

Haywell walked through the room and placed a hand on Hal's shoulder.

He'd never expected his cousin to be the one feeding him information—information that had just became more reliable.

"Hal, I did not believe a word the high minister said when you were exiled. I know you, and thousands of others know who you are as a person. They see you as Hal, hero of the Polarian War and true Crown Prince of the Empire of Athos."

"Those in the countryside of the planets and moons of the Empire whisper your name," Vixera said as she shifted her helmet from one hip to the other.

Hal shook his head in disbelief, a breathy chuckle following. "If I had known it was you, I wouldn't have been so dismissive."

Haywell smiled. "Understandable. But I can't stay long. I came to show you can trust the movement that you started in exposing lies." Haywell stood straight. "So, what is your decision, Prince Hal? Will you slice the tendrils of Varim's lies off or leave the Realmverse destined to wither in his toxic worldview?"

Hal nodded. "To bring down the high minister, we'll search for the remaining Lumnis Stones and help mitigate the Imperial presence where they're found."

"Then I guess it's settled," Haywell said.

"But, Hay, there's something much grander at play here," Hal said.

"I know. We'll be in contact," Haywell said. "Vixera and I have seen the effects." Haywell nodded back the way they'd come. "Now I must go before the Imperial scanners pick up on my absence."

"I'll get him back in one piece," Vixera said.

"Wait, Haywell," Hal said. "Was it *him* that killed my father?"

Haywell nodded. "Lethal injection by the same compound in the gas that struck him ill. We have proof, but that will do nothing as long as the effects of Madness run rampant."

"Understood," Hal said as he felt the rage brew within him.

As Haywell turned to leave, he said, "Long live the Empire."

Hal's ears perked up at the rallying call he'd said many times on the battlefields during the war.

"Long live the Empire," Hal repeated.

As Haywell and Vixera left down the corridor toward the cargo hold, Kristilin stepped up to the table, gazing at Hal. He could tell she was a little worried, but he could not blame her. After all, Haywell was a part of the Imperial inner workings. But he also knew the information his cousin fed was legitimate and a view to the heartland of Athos and the Empire. If they were going to compete against Miri and the Empire, having someone on the inside was a blessing. Spies were nothing new to him, but he'd felt the honesty in his kin's voice.

"Who were they?" Misselie asked.

"My cousins," Hal said.

"So, what now?" Kristilin asked. "Does Miri have the stone?"

"She does, but we have the map. We have Runebreaker." Hal looked at the three of them. "We can find the next Lumnis Stone. She can't."

Misselie stepped forward and placed the datacard from the Lumnis Stone chamber on the table. "I think I know where."

The datacard emitted a bright white-and-blue planet.

Kristilin's eyes went wide. Hal placed a hand on her shoulder as he looked at the image before them.

"We're going to Velra."

AFTERWORD

I would like to take this time and humbly thank you for making it to the end of this novel. It was a thrill to write and share it with the world.

This project took three years to complete. It would mean the world to me if you, the awesome reader that you are, left a review and/or rating for the novel. These are the lifeblood of any self-published piece of work and can help others find it. It will also help the brand grow so others can join in on the journey throughout the Realmverse.

Again, thank you from the bottom of my heart for reading '***Wielders of Woe: Inferno***', and I hope to see you, you glorious reader, on the next part of the journey.

ACKNOWLEDGMENTS

I want to take this time to thank my friends and family who pushed me to write this massive book. You know who you are. Your unyielding support means the world to me.

I would also like to thank the folks over at Enchanted Ink Publishing for the thorough, helpful editing tweaks, as well as the beautiful cover design. Without them, this project would be nothing but a jumbled mess of words.

Thank you all.

www.ingramcontent.com/pod-product-compliance
Lightning Source LLC
Chambersburg PA
CBHW061923170626
46813CB00006B/2282